THE WINGS OF THE MORNING

THE WINGS
OF
THE MORNING

BY

LOUIS TRACY

*If I take the wings of the morning, and
dwell in the uttermost parts of the sea;
even there shall Thy hand lead me, and
Thy right hand shall hold me. Psalm
cxxxix. 9, 10*

Skyhorse Publishing

Copyright © 2014 by Skyhorse Publishing

Skyhorse Publishing books may be purchased in bulk at special discounts for sales promotion, corporate gifts, fund-raising, or educational purposes. Special editions can also be created to specifications. For details, contact the Special Sales Department, Skyhorse Publishing, 307 West 36th Street, 11th Floor, New York, NY 10018 or info@skyhorsepublishing.com.

Skyhorse® and Skyhorse Publishing® are registered trademarks of Skyhorse Publishing, Inc.®, a Delaware corporation.

Visit our website at www.skyhorsepublishing.com.

10 9 8 7 6 5 4 3 2 1

Library of Congress Cataloging-in-Publication Data is available on file.

ISBN: 978-1-62873-765-3
Ebook ISBN: 978-1-62914-135-0

Printed in the United States of America

CONTENTS

I   *The Wreck of the* Sirdar   1

II   *The Survivors*   26

III   *Discoveries*   43

IV   *Rainbow Island*   63

V   *Iris to the Rescue*   83

VI   *Some Explanations*   101

VII   *Surprises*   120

VIII   *Preparations*   141

IX   *The Secret of the Cave*   161

X   *Reality v. Romance — The Case for the Plaintiff*   181

XI   *The Fight*   201

XII   *A Truce*   222

Contents

XIII   *Reality v. Romance — The Case for the Defendant*   245

XIV   *The Unexpected Happens*   269

XV   *The Difficulty of Pleasing Everybody*   293

XVI   *Bargains, Great and Small*   312

XVII   *Rainbow Island Again — and Afterward*   333

CHAPTER I

THE WRECK OF THE *SIRDAR*

LADY TOZER adjusted her gold-rimmed eyeglasses with an air of dignified aggressiveness. She had lived too many years in the Far East. In Hong Kong she was known as the "Mandarin." Her powers of merciless inquisition suggested torments long drawn out. The commander of the *Sirdar*, homeward bound from Shanghai, knew that he was about to be stretched on the rack when he took his seat at the saloon table.

"Is it true, captain, that we are running into a typhoon?" demanded her ladyship.

"From whom did you learn that, Lady Tozer?" Captain Ross was wary, though somewhat surprised.

"From Miss Deane. I understood her a moment ago to say that you had told her."

"I?"

"Didn't you? Some one told me this morning. I couldn't have guessed it, could I?" Miss Iris Deane's large blue eyes surveyed him with innocent indifference to strict accuracy. Incidentally, she had obtained the information from her maid, a nose-tilted coquette who extracted ship's secrets from a youthful quartermaster.

[1]

"Well—er—I had forgotten," explained the tactful sailor.

"Is it true?"

Lady Tozer was unusually abrupt today. But she was annoyed by the assumption that the captain took a mere girl into his confidence and passed over the wife of the ex-Chief Justice of Hong Kong.

"Yes, it is," said Captain Ross, equally curt, and silently thanking the fates that her ladyship was going home for the last time.

"How horrible!" she gasped, in unaffected alarm. This return to femininity soothed the sailor's ruffled temper.

Sir John, her husband, frowned judicially. That frown constituted his legal stock-in-trade, yet it passed current for wisdom with the Hong Kong bar.

"What evidence have you?" he asked.

"Do tell us," chimed in Iris, delightfully unconscious of interrupting the court. "Did you find out when you squinted at the sun?"

The captain smiled. "You are nearer the mark than possibly you imagine, Miss Deane," he said. "When we took our observations yesterday there was a very weird-looking halo around the sun. This morning you may have noticed several light squalls and a smooth sea marked occasionally by strong ripples. The barometer is falling rapidly, and I expect that, as the day wears, we will encounter a heavy swell. If the sky looks wild tonight, and especially if we observe a heavy bank of cloud approaching from the north-west, you will see the crockery dancing about the table at dinner.

I am afraid you are not a good sailor, Lady Tozer. Are you, Miss Deane?"

"Capital! I should just love to see a real storm. Now promise me solemnly that you will take me up into the charthouse when this typhoon is simply tearing things to pieces."

"Oh dear! I do hope it will not be very bad. Is there no way in which you can avoid it, captain? Will it last long?"

The politic skipper for once preferred to answer Lady Tozer. "There is no cause for uneasiness," he said. "Of course, typhoons in the China Sea are nasty things while they last, but a ship like the *Sirdar* is not troubled by them. She will drive through the worst gale she is likely to meet here in less than twelve hours. Besides, I alter the course somewhat as soon as I discover our position with regard to its center. You see, Miss Deane——"

And Captain Ross forthwith illustrated on the back of a menu card the spiral shape and progress of a cyclone. He so thoroughly mystified the girl by his technical references to northern and southern hemispheres, polar directions, revolving air-currents, external circumferences, and diminished atmospheric pressures, that she was too bewildered to reiterate a desire to visit the bridge.

Then the commander hurriedly excused himself, and the passengers saw no more of him that day.

But his short scientific lecture achieved a double result. It rescued him from a request which he could not possibly grant, and reassured Lady Tozer. To the non-nautical mind it is the unknown that is fearful. A storm classed as "periodic," whose velocity can be measured, whose duration and direction can be determined beforehand by hours and distances, ceases to be terrifying. It becomes an accepted fact, akin to the steam-engine and the electric telegraph, marvelous yet commonplace.

So her ladyship dismissed the topic as of no present interest, and focused Miss Deane through her eyeglasses.

"Sir Arthur proposes to come home in June, I understand?" she inquired.

Iris was a remarkably healthy young woman. A large banana momentarily engaged her attention. She nodded affably.

"You will stay with relatives until he arrives?" pursued Lady Tozer.

The banana is a fruit of simple characteristics. The girl was able to reply, with a touch of careless hauteur in her voice:

"Relatives! We have none—none whom we specially cultivate, that is. I will stop in town a day or two to interview my dressmaker, and then go straight to Helmdale, our place in Yorkshire."

"Surely you have a chaperon!"

"A chaperon! My dear Lady Tozer, did my father impress you as one who would permit a fussy and stout old person to make my life miserable?"

The acidity of the retort lay in the word "stout." But Iris was not accustomed to cross-examination. During a three months' residence on the island she had learnt how to avoid Lady Tozer. Here it was impossible, and the older woman fastened upon her asp-like. Miss Iris Deane was a toothsome morsel for gossip. Not yet twenty-one, the only daughter of a wealthy baronet who owned a fleet of stately ships—the *Sirdar* amongst them —a girl who had been mistress of her father's house since her return from Dresden three years ago—young, beautiful, rich—here was a combination for which men thanked a judicious Heaven, whilst women sniffed enviously.

Business detained Sir Arthur. A war-cloud over-shadowed the two great divisions of the yellow race. He must wait to see how matters developed, but he would not expose Iris to the insidious treachery of a Chinese spring. So, with tears, they separated. She was con-fided to the personal charge of Captain Ross. At each point of call the company's agents would be solicitous for her welfare. The cable's telegraphic eye would watch her progress as that of some princely maiden sail-ing in royal caravel. This fair, slender, well-formed girl—delightfully English in face and figure—with her fresh, clear complexion, limpid blue eyes, and shining brown hair, was a personage of some importance.

Lady Tozer knew these things and sighed com-placently.

"Ah, well," she resumed. "Parents had different views when I was a girl. But I assume Sir Arthur thinks you should become used to being your own mis-tress in view of your approaching marriage."

"My—approaching—marriage!" cried Iris, now genuinely amazed.

"Yes. Is it not true that you are going to marry Lord Ventnor?"

A passing steward heard the point-blank question.

It had a curious effect upon him. He gazed with fiercely eager eyes at Miss Deane, and so far forgot himself as to permit a dish of water ice to rest against Sir John Tozer's bald head.

Iris could not help noting his strange behavior. A flash of humor chased away her first angry resentment at Lady Tozer's interrogatory.

"That may be my happy fate," she answered gaily, "but Lord Ventnor has not asked me."

"Every one says in Hong Kong——" began her ladyship.

"Confound you, you stupid rascal! what are you doing?" shouted Sir John. His feeble nerves at last conveyed the information that something more pronounced than a sudden draught affected his scalp; the ice was melting.

The incident amused those passengers who sat near enough to observe it. But the chief steward, hovering watchful near the captain's table, darted forward. Pale with anger he hissed—

"Report yourself for duty in the second saloon to-night," and he hustled his subordinate away from the judge's chair.

Miss Deane, mirthfully radiant, rose.

"Please don't punish the man, Mr. Jones," she said sweetly. "It was a sheer accident. He was taken by surprise. In his place I would have emptied the whole dish."

The Wreck of the Sirdar

The chief steward smirked. He did not know exactly what had happened; nevertheless, great though Sir John Tozer might be, the owner's daughter was greater.

"Certainly, miss, certainly," he agreed, adding confidentially:—"It *is* rather hard on a steward to be sent aft, miss. It makes such a difference in the—er—the little gratuities given by the passengers."

The girl was tactful. She smiled comprehension at the official and bent over Sir John, now carefully polishing the back of his skull with a table napkin.

"I am sure you will forgive him," she whispered. "I can't say why, but the poor fellow was looking so intently at me that he did not see what he was doing."

The ex-Chief Justice was instantly mollified. He did not mind the application of ice in that way—rather liked it, in fact—probably ice was susceptible to the fire in Miss Deane's eyes.

Lady Tozer was not so easily appeased. When Iris left the saloon she inquired tartly: "How is it, John, that Government makes a ship-owner a baronet and a Chief Justice only a knight?"

"That question would provide an interesting subject for debate at the Carlton, my dear," he replied with equal asperity.

Suddenly the passengers still seated experienced a prolonged sinking sensation, as if the vessel had been converted into a gigantic lift. They were pressed hard into their chairs, which creaked and tried to swing round on their pivots. As the ship yielded stiffly to the sea a whiff of spray dashed through an open port.

"There," snapped her ladyship, "I knew we should

[7]

run into a storm, yet Captain Ross led us to believe——
John, take me to my cabin at once."

From the promenade deck the listless groups watched
the rapid advance of the gale. There was mournful
speculation upon the *Sirdar's* chances of reaching Singapore before the next evening.

"We had two hundred and ninety-eight miles to do at
noon," said Experience. "If the wind and sea catch us
on the port bow the ship will pitch awfully. Half the
time the screw will be racing. I once made this trip in
the *Sumatra,* and we were struck by a south-east typhoon in this locality. How long do you think it was
before we dropped anchor in Singapore harbor?"

No one hazarded a guess.

"Three days!" Experience was solemnly pompous.
"Three whole days. They were like three years. By
Jove! I never want to see another gale like that."

A timid lady ventured to say—

"Perhaps this may not be a typhoon. It may only
be a little bit of a storm."

Her sex saved her from a jeer. Experience gloomily
shook his head.

"The barometer resists your plea," he said. "I fear
there will be a good many empty saddles in the saloon at
dinner."

The lady smiled weakly. It was a feeble joke at the
best. "You think we are in for a sort of marine steeple-
chase?" she asked.

"Well, thank Heaven, I had a good lunch," sniggered
a rosy-faced subaltern, and a ripple of laughter greeted
his enthusiasm.

[8]

The Wreck of the Sirdar

Iris stood somewhat apart from the speakers. The wind had freshened and her hat was tied closely over her ears. She leaned against the taffrail, enjoying the cool breeze after hours of sultry heat. The sky was cloudless yet, but there was a queer tinge of burnished copper in the all-pervading sunshine. The sea was coldly blue. The life had gone out of it. It was no longer inviting and translucent. That morning, were such a thing practicable, she would have gladly dived into its crystal depths and disported herself like a frolicsome mermaid. Now something akin to repulsion came with the fanciful remembrance.

Long sullen undulations swept noiselessly past the ship. Once, after a steady climb up a rolling hill of water, the *Sirdar* quickly pecked at the succeeding valley, and the propeller gave a couple of angry flaps on the surface, whilst a tremor ran through the stout iron rails on which the girl's arms rested.

The crew were busy too. Squads of Lascars raced about, industriously obedient to the short shrill whistling of jemadars and quartermasters. Boat lashings were tested and tightened, canvas awnings stretched across the deck forward, ventilator cowls twisted to new angles, and hatches clamped down over the wooden gratings that covered the holds. Officers, spotless in white linen, flitted quietly to and fro. When the watch was changed, Iris noted that the "chief" appeared in an old blue suit and carried oilskins over his arm as he climbed to the bridge.

Nature looked disturbed and fitful, and the ship responded to her mood. There was a sense of preparation in the air, of coming ordeal, of restless foreboding. Chains clanked with a noise the girl never noticed before; the tramp of hurrying men on the hurricane deck overhead sounded heavy and hollow. There was a squeaking of chairs that was abominable when people gathered up books and wraps and staggered ungracefully towards the companion-way. Altogether Miss Deane was not wholly pleased with the preliminaries of a typhoon, whatever the realities might be.

And then, why did gales always spring up at the close of day? Could they not start after breakfast, rage with furious grandeur during lunch, and die away peacefully at dinner-time, permitting one to sleep in comfort without that straining and groaning of the ship which seemed to imply a sharp attack of rheumatism in every joint?

Why did that silly old woman allude to her contemplated marriage to Lord Ventnor, retailing the gossip of Hong Kong with such malicious emphasis? For an instant Iris tried to shake the railing in comic anger. She hated Lord Ventnor. She did not want to marry him, or anybody else, just yet. Of course her father had hinted approval of his lordship's obvious intentions. Countess of Ventnor! Yes, it was a nice title. Still, she wanted another couple of years of careless freedom; in any event, why should Lady Tozer pry and probe?

And finally, why did the steward—oh, poor old Sir John! What *would* have happened if the ice had slid down his neck? Thoroughly comforted by this gleeful hypothesis, Miss Deane seized a favorable opportunity to dart across to the starboard side and see if Captain

The Wreck of the Sirdar

Ross's "heavy bank of cloud in the north-west" had put in an appearance.

Ha! there it was, black, ominous, gigantic, rolling up over the horizon like some monstrous football. Around it the sky deepened into purple, fringed with a wide belt of brick red. She had never seen such a beginning of a gale. From what she had read in books she imagined that only in great deserts were clouds of dust generated. There could not be dust in the dense pall now rushing with giant strides across the trembling sea. Then what was it? Why was it so dark and menacing? And where was desert of stone and sand to compare with this awful expanse of water? What a small dot was this great ship on the visible surface! But the ocean itself extended away beyond there, reaching out to the infinite. The dot became a mere speck, undistinguishable beneath a celestial microscope such as the gods might condescend to use.

Iris shivered and aroused herself with a startled laugh.

A nice book in a sheltered corner, and perhaps forty winks until tea-time—surely a much more sensible proceeding than to stand there, idly conjuring up phantoms of affright.

The lively fanfare of the dinner trumpet failed to fill the saloon. By this time the *Sirdar* was fighting resolutely against a stiff gale. But the stress of actual combat was better than the eerie sensation of impending danger during the earlier hours. The strong, hearty pulsations of the engines, the regular thrashing of the screw, the steadfast onward plunging of the good ship

through racing seas and flying scud, were cheery, confident, and inspiring.

Miss Deane justified her boast that she was an excellent sailor. She smiled delightedly at the ship's surgeon when he caught her eye through the many gaps in
the tables. She was alone, so he joined her.

"You are a credit to the company—quite a sea-king's
daughter," he said.

"Doctor, do you talk to all your lady passengers in
that way?"

"Alas, no! Too often I can only be truthful when I
am dumb."

Iris laughed. "If I remain long on this ship I will
certainly have my head turned," she cried. "I receive
nothing but compliments from the captain down to—
to——"

"The doctor!"

"No. You come a good second on the list."

In very truth she was thinking of the ice-carrying
steward and his queer start of surprise at the announcement of her rumored engagement. The man interested
her. He looked like a broken-down gentleman. Her
quick eyes traveled around the saloon to discover his
whereabouts. She could not see him. The chief steward
stood near, balancing himself in apparent defiance of the
laws of gravitation, for the ship was now pitching and
rolling with a mad zeal. For an instant she meant to
inquire what had become of the transgressor, but she
dismissed the thought at its inception. The matter was
too trivial.

With a wild swoop all the plates, glasses, and cutlery

on the saloon tables crashed to starboard. Were it not for the restraint of the fiddles everything must have been swept to the floor. There were one or two minor accidents. A steward, taken unawares, was thrown headlong on top of his laden tray. Others were compelled to clutch the backs of chairs and cling to pillars. One man involuntarily seized the hair of a lady who devoted an hour before each meal to her coiffure. The *Sirdar*, with a frenzied bound, tried to turn a somersault.

"A change of course," observed the doctor. "They generally try to avoid it when people are in the saloon, but a typhoon admits of no labored politeness. As its center is now right ahead we are going on the starboard tack to get behind it."

"I must hurry up and go on deck," said Miss Deane.

"You will not be able to go on deck until the morning."

She turned on him impetuously. "Indeed I will. Captain Ross promised me—that is, I asked him——"

The doctor smiled. She was so charmingly insistent. "It is simply impossible," he said. "The companion doors are bolted. The promenade deck is swept by heavy seas every minute. A boat has been carried away and several stanchions snapped off like carrots. For the first time in your life, Miss Deane, you are battened down."

The girl's face must have paled somewhat. He added hastily, "There is no danger, you know, but these precautions are necessary. You would not like to see several tons of water rushing down the saloon stairs; now, would you?"

"Decidedly not." Then after a pause, "It is not pleasant to be fastened up in a great iron box, doctor. It reminds one of a huge coffin."

"Not a bit. The *Sirdar* is the safest ship afloat. Your father has always pursued a splendid policy in that respect. The London and Hong Kong Company may not possess fast vessels, but they are seaworthy and well found in every respect."

"Are there many people ill on board?"

"No; just the usual number of disturbed livers. We had a nasty accident shortly before dinner."

"Good gracious! What happened?"

"Some Lascars were caught by a sea forward. One man had his leg broken."

"Anything else?"

The doctor hesitated. He became interested in the color of some Burgundy. "I hardly know the exact details yet," he replied. "Tomorrow after breakfast I will tell you all about it."

An English quartermaster and four Lascars had been licked from off the forecastle by the greedy tongue of a huge wave. The succeeding surge flung the five men back against the quarter. One of the black sailors was pitched aboard, with a fractured leg and other injuries. The others were smashed against the iron hull and disappeared.

For one tremulous moment the engines slowed. The ship commenced to veer off into the path of the cyclone. Captain Ross set his teeth, and the telegraph bell jangled "Full speed ahead."

"Poor Jackson!" he murmured. "One of my best

men. I remember seeing his wife, a pretty little woman, and two children coming to meet him last homeward trip. They will be there again. Good God! That Lascar who was saved has some one to await him in a Bombay village, I suppose."

The gale sang a mad requiem to its victims. The very surface was torn from the sea. The ship drove relentlessly through sheets of spray that caused the officers high up on the bridge to gasp for breath. They held on by main force, though protected by strong canvas sheets bound to the rails. The main deck was quite impassable. The promenade deck, even the lofty spar deck, was scourged with the broken crests of waves that tried with demoniac energy to smash in the starboard bow, for the *Sirdar* was cutting into the heart of the cyclone.

The captain fought his way to the charthouse. He wiped the salt water from his eyes and looked anxiously at the barometer.

"Still falling!" he muttered. "I will keep on until seven o'clock and then bear three points to the southward. By midnight we should be behind it."

He struggled back into the outside fury. By comparison the sturdy citadel he quitted was Paradise on the edge of an inferno.

Down in the saloon the hardier passengers were striving to subdue the ennui of an interval before they sought their cabins. Some talked. One hardened reprobate strummed the piano. Others played cards, chess, draughts, anything that would distract attention.

The stately apartment offered strange contrast to the

warring elements without. Bright lights, costly uphol-
stery, soft carpets, carved panels and gilded cornices,
with uniformed attendants passing to and fro carrying
coffee and glasses—these surroundings suggested a
floating palace in which the raging seas were defied. Yet
forty miles away, somewhere in the furious depths, four
corpses swirled about with horrible uncertainty, lurch-
ing through battling currents, and perchance convoyed
by fighting sharks.

The surgeon had been called away. Iris was the only
lady left in the saloon. She watched a set of whist
players for a time and then essayed the perilous passage
to her stateroom. She found her maid and a stewardess
there. Both women were weeping.

"What is the matter?" she inquired.

The stewardess tried to speak. She choked with grief
and hastily went out. The maid blubbered an explanation.

"A friend of hers was married, miss, to the man who
is drowned."

"Drowned! What man?"

"Haven't you heard, miss? I suppose they are keeping it quiet. An English sailor and some natives were
swept off the ship by a sea. One native was saved, but
he is all smashed up. The others were never seen again."

Iris by degrees learnt the sad chronicles of the Jackson family. She was moved to tears. She remembered
the doctor's hesitancy, and her own idle phrase—"a
huge coffin."

Outside the roaring waves pounded upon the iron
walls.

The Wreck of the Sirdar

Were they not satiated? This tragedy had taken all the grandeur out of the storm. It was no longer a majestic phase of nature's power, but an implacable demon, bellowing for a sacrifice. And that poor woman, with her two children, hopefully scanning the shipping lists for news of the great steamer, news which, to her, meant only the safety of her husband. Oh, it was pitiful!

Iris would not be undressed. The maid sniveled a request to be allowed to remain with her mistress. She would lie on a couch until morning.

Two staterooms had been converted into one to provide Miss Deane with ample accommodation. There were no bunks, but a cozy bed was screwed to the deck. She lay down, and strove to read. It was a difficult task. Her eyes wandered from the printed page to mark the absurd antics of her garments swinging on their hooks. At times the ship rolled so far that she felt sure it must topple over. She was not afraid; but subdued, rather astonished, placidly prepared for vague eventualities. Through it all she wondered why she clung to the belief that in another day or two the storm would be forgotten, and people playing quoits on deck, dancing, singing coon songs in the music-room, or grumbling at the heat.

Things were ridiculous. What need was there for all this external fury? Why should poor sailors be cast forth to instant death in such awful manner? If she could only sleep and forget—if kind oblivion would blot out the storm for a few blissful hours! But how could one sleep with the consciousness of that watery giant thundering his summons upon the iron plates a few inches away?

Then came the blurred picture of Captain Ross high up on the bridge, peering into the moving blackness. How strange that there should be hidden in the convolutions of a man's brain an intelligence that laid bare the pretences of that ravenous demon without. Each of the ship's officers, the commander more than the others, understood the why and the wherefore of this blustering combination of wind and sea. Iris knew the language of poker. Nature was putting up a huge bluff.

What was it the captain said in his little lecture? "When a ship meets a cyclone north of the equator on a westerly course she nearly always has the wind at first on the port side, but, owing to the revolution of the gale, when she passes its center the wind is on the starboard side."

Yes, that was right, as far as the first part was concerned. Evidently they had not yet passed the central path. Oh, dear! She was so tired. It demanded a physical effort to constantly shove away an unseen force that tried to push you over. How funny that a big cloud should travel up against the wind! And so, amidst confused wonderment, she lapsed into an uneasy slumber, her last sentient thought being a quiet thankfulness that the screw went thud-thud, thud-thud with such firm determination.

After the course was changed and the *Sirdar* bore away towards the south-west, the commander consulted the barometer each half-hour. The tell-tale mercury had sunk over two inches in twelve hours. The abnormally low pressure quickly created dense clouds which enhanced the melancholy darkness of the gale.

The Wreck of the Sirdar

For many minutes together the bows of the ship were not visible. Masthead and sidelights were obscured by the pelting scud. The engines thrust the vessel forward like a lance into the vitals of the storm. Wind and wave gushed out of the vortex with impotent fury.

At last, soon after midnight, the barometer showed a slight upward movement. At 1.30 a. m. the change became pronounced; simultaneously the wind swung round a point to the westward.

Then Captain Ross smiled wearily. His face brightened. He opened his oilskin coat, glanced at the compass, and nodded approval.

"That's right," he shouted to the quartermaster at the steam-wheel. "Keep her steady there, south 15 west."

"South 15 west it is, sir," yelled the sailor, impassively watching the moving disk, for the wind alteration necessitated a little less help from the rudder to keep the ship's head true to her course.

Captain Ross ate some sandwiches and washed them down with cold tea. He was more hungry than he imagined, having spent eleven hours without food. The tea was insipid. He called through a speaking-tube for a further supply of sandwiches and some coffee.

Then he turned to consult a chart. He was joined by the chief officer. Both men examined the chart in silence.

Captain Ross finally took a pencil. He stabbed its point on the paper in the neighborhood of 14°N. and 112° E.

"We are about there, I think."

The chief agreed. "That was the locality I had in my mind." He bent closer over the sheet.

"Nothing in the way tonight, sir," he added.

"Nothing whatever. It is a bit of good luck to meet such weather here. We can keep as far south as we like until daybreak, and by that time—— How did it look when you came in?"

"A trifle better, I think."

"I have sent for some refreshments. Let us have another *dekko*[1] before we tackle them."

The two officers passed out into the hurricane. Instantly the wind endeavored to tear the charthouse from off the deck. They looked aloft and ahead. The officer on duty saw them and nodded silent comprehension. It was useless to attempt to speak. The weather was perceptibly clearer.

Then all three peered ahead again. They stood, pressing against the wind, seeking to penetrate the murkiness in front. Suddenly they were galvanized into strenuous activity.

A wild howl came from the lookout forward. The eyes of the three men glared at a huge dismasted Chinese junk, wallowing helplessly in the trough of the sea, dead under the bows.

The captain sprang to the charthouse and signaled in fierce pantomime that the wheel should be put hard over.

The officer in charge of the bridge pressed the telegraph lever to "stop" and "full speed astern," whilst

---

[1] Hindustani for "look" — a word much used by sailors in the East.

with his disengaged hand he pulled hard at the siren cord, and a raucous warning sent stewards flying through the ship to close collision bulkhead doors. The "chief" darted to the port rail, for the *Sirdar's* instant response to the helm seemed to clear her nose from the junk as if by magic.

It all happened so quickly that whilst the hoarse signal was still vibrating through the ship, the junk swept past her quarter. The chief officer, joined now by the commander, looked down into the wretched craft. They could see her crew lashed in a bunch around the capstan on her elevated poop. She was laden with timber. Although water-logged, she could not sink if she held together.

A great wave sucked her away from the steamer and then hurled her back with irresistible force. The *Sirdar* was just completing her turning movement, and she heeled over, yielding to the mighty power of the gale. For an appreciable instant her engines stopped. The mass of water that swayed the junk like a cork lifted the great ship high by the stern. The propeller began to revolve in air—for the third officer had corrected his signal to "full speed ahead" again—and the cumbrous Chinese vessel struck the *Sirdar* a terrible blow in the counter, smashing off the screw close to the thrust-block and wrenching the rudder from its bearings.

There was an awful race by the engines before the engineers could shut off steam. The junk vanished into the wilderness of noise and tumbling seas beyond, and the fine steamer of a few seconds ago, replete with magnificent energy, struggled like a wounded leviathan in the grasp of a vengeful foe.

She swung round, as if in wrath, to pursue the puny assailant which had dealt her this mortal stroke. No longer breasting the storm with stubborn persistency, she now drifted aimlessly before wind and wave. She was merely a larger plaything, tossed about by Titantic gambols. The junk was burst asunder by the collision. Her planks and cargo littered the waves, were even tossed in derision on to the decks of the *Sirdar*. Of what avail was strong timber or bolted iron against the spleen of the unchained and formless monster who loudly proclaimed his triumph? The great steamship drifted on through chaos. The typhoon had broken the lance.

But brave men, skilfully directed, wrought hard to avert further disaster. After the first moment of stupor, gallant British sailors risked life and limb to bring the vessel under control.

By their calm courage they shamed the paralyzed Lascars into activity. A sail was rigged on the foremast, and a sea anchor hastily constructed as soon as it was discovered that the helm was useless. Rockets flared up into the sky at regular intervals, in the faint hope that should they attract the attention of another vessel she would follow the disabled *Sirdar* and render help when the weather moderated.

When the captain ascertained that no water was being shipped, the damage being wholly external, the collision doors were opened and the passengers admitted to the saloon, a brilliant palace, superbly indifferent to the wreck and ruin without.

The Wreck of the Sirdar

Captain Ross himself came down and addressed a few comforting words to the quiet men and pallid women gathered there. He told them exactly what had happened.

Sir John Tozer, self-possessed and critical, asked a question.

"The junk is destroyed, I assume?" he said.

"It is."

"Would it not have been better to have struck her end on?"

"Much better, but that is not the view we should take if we encountered a vessel relatively as big as the *Sirdar* was to the unfortunate junk."

"But," persisted the lawyer, "what would have been the result?"

"You would never have known that the incident had happened, Sir John."

"In other words, the poor despairing Chinamen, clinging to their little craft with some chance of escape, would be quietly murdered to suit our convenience."

It was Iris's clear voice that rang out this downright exposition of the facts. Sir John shook his head; he carried the discussion no further.

The hours passed in tedious misery after Captain Ross's visit. Every one was eager to get a glimpse of the unknown terrors without from the deck. This was out of the question, so people sat around the tables to listen eagerly to Experience and his wise saws on drifting ships and their prospects.

Some cautious persons visited their cabins to secure

valuables in case of further disaster. A few hardy spirits returned to bed.

Meanwhile, in the charthouse, the captain and chief officer were gravely pondering over an open chart, and discussing a fresh risk that loomed ominously before them. The ship was a long way out of her usual course when the accident happened. She was drifting now, they estimated, eleven knots an hour, with wind, sea, and current all forcing her in the same direction, drifting into one of the most dangerous places in the known world, the south China Sea, with its numberless reefs, shoals, and isolated rocks, and the great island of Borneo stretching right across the path of the cyclone.

Still, there was nothing to be done save to make a few unobtrusive preparations and trust to idle chance. To attempt to anchor and ride out the gale in their present position was out of the question.

Two, three, four o'clock came, and went. Another half-hour would witness the dawn and a further clearing of the weather. The barometer was rapidly rising. The center of the cyclone had swept far ahead. There was only left the aftermath of heavy seas and furious but steadier wind.

Captain Ross entered the charthouse for the twentieth time.

He had aged many years in appearance. The smiling, confident, debonair officer was changed into a stricken, mournful man. He had altered with his ship. The *Sirdar* and her master could hardly be recognized, so cruel were the blows they had received.

"It is impossible to see a yard ahead," he confided

to his second in command. "I have never been so anxious before in my life. Thank God the night is drawing to a close. Perhaps, when day breaks——"

His last words contained a prayer and a hope. Even as he spoke the ship seemed to lift herself bodily with an unusual effort for a vessel moving before the wind.

The next instant there was a horrible grinding crash forward. Each person who did not chance to be holding fast to an upright was thrown violently down. The deck was tilted to a dangerous angle and remained there, whilst the heavy buffeting of the sea, now raging afresh at this unlooked-for resistance, drowned the despairing yells raised by the Lascars on duty.

The *Sirdar* had completed her last voyage. She was now a battered wreck on a barrier reef. She hung thus for one heart-breaking second. Then another wave, riding triumphantly through its fellows, caught the great steamer in its tremendous grasp, carried her onward for half her length and smashed her down on the rocks. Her back was broken. She parted in two halves. Both sections turned completely over in the utter wantonness of destruction, and everything—masts, funnels, boats, hull, with every living soul on board— was at once engulfed in a maelstrom of rushing water and far-flung spray.

CHAPTER II

THE SURVIVORS

When the *Sirdar* parted amidships, the floor of the saloon heaved up in the center with a mighty crash of rending woodwork and iron. Men and women, too stupefied to sob out a prayer, were pitched headlong into chaos. Iris, torn from the terrified grasp of her maid, fell through a corridor, and would have gone down with the ship had not a sailor, clinging to a companion ladder, caught her as she whirled along the steep slope of the deck.

He did not know what had happened. With the instinct of self-preservation he seized the nearest support when the vessel struck. It was the mere impulse of ready helpfulness that caused him to stretch out his left arm and clasp the girl's waist as she fluttered past. By idle chance they were on the port side, and the ship, after pausing for one awful second, fell over to starboard.

The man was not prepared for this second gyration. Even as the stairway canted he lost his balance; they were both thrown violently through the open hatchway, and swept off into the boiling surf. Under such conditions thought itself was impossible. A series of impressions, a number of fantastic pictures, were received by the benumbed faculties, and afterwards painfully sorted out by the memory. Fear, anguish, amazement—none of these could exist. All he knew was that the lifeless form of a woman—for Iris had happily fainted—must be held until death itself wrenched her from him. Then there came the headlong plunge into the swirling sea, followed by an indefinite period of gasping oblivion. Something that felt like a moving rock rose up beneath his feet. He was driven clear out of the water and seemed to recognize a familiar object rising rigid and bright close at hand. It was the binnacle pillar, screwed to a portion of the deck which came away from the charthouse and was rent from the upper framework by contact with the reef.

He seized this unlooked-for support with his disengaged hand. For one fleet instant he had a confused vision of the destruction of the ship. Both the fore and aft portions were burst asunder by the force of compressed air. Wreckage and human forms were tossing about foolishly. The sea pounded upon the opposing rocks with the noise of ten thousand mighty steam-hammers.

A uniformed figure—he thought it was the captain—stretched out an unavailing arm to clasp the queer raft which supported the sailor and the girl. But a jealous wave rose under the platform with devilish energy and turned it completely over, hurling the man with his inanimate burthen into the depths. He rose, fighting madly for his life. Now surely he was doomed! But again, as if human existence depended on naught more serious than the spinning of a coin, his knees rested on the same few staunch timbers, now the ceiling of the music-room, and he was given a brief respite. His greatest difficulty was to get his breath, so dense was the spray through which he was driven. Even in that terrible moment he kept his senses. The girl, utterly unconscious, showed by the convulsive heaving of her breast that she was choking. With a wild effort he swung her head round to shield her from the flying scud with his own form.

The tiny air-space thus provided gave her some relief, and in that instant the sailor seemed to recognize her. He was not remotely capable of a definite idea. Just as he vaguely realized the identity of the woman in his arms the unsteady support on which he rested toppled over. Again he renewed the unequal contest. A strong resolute man and a typhoon sea wrestled for supremacy.

This time his feet plunged against something gratefully solid. He was dashed forward, still battling with the raging turmoil of water, and a second time he felt the same firm yet smooth surface. His dormant faculties awoke. It was sand. With frenzied desperation, buoyed now by the inspiring hope of safety, he fought his way onwards like a maniac.

Often he fell, three times did the backwash try to drag him to the swirling death behind, but he staggered blindly on, on, until even the tearing gale ceased to be laden with the suffocating foam, and his faltering feet sank in deep soft white sand.

Then he fell, not to rise again. With a last weak

flicker of exhausted strength he drew the girl closely to him, and the two lay, clasped tightly together, heedless now of all things.

How long the man remained prostrate he could only guess subsequently. The *Sirdar* struck soon after daybreak and the sailor awoke to a hazy consciousness of his surroundings to find a shaft of sunshine flickering through the clouds banked up in the east. The gale was already passing away. Although the wind still whistled with shrill violence it was more blustering than threatening. The sea, too, though running very high, had retreated many yards from the spot where he had finally dropped, and its surface was no longer scourged with venomous spray.

Slowly and painfully he raised himself to a sitting posture, for he was bruised and stiff. With his first movement he became violently ill. He had swallowed much salt water, and it was not until the spasm of sickness had passed that he thought of the girl.

She had slipped from his breast as he rose, and was lying, face downwards, in the sand. The memory of much that had happened surged into his brain with horrifying suddenness.

"She cannot be dead," he hoarsely murmured, feebly trying to lift her. "Surely Providence would not desert her after such an escape. What a weak beggar I must be to give in at the last moment. I am sure she was living when we got ashore. What on earth can I do to revive her?"

Forgetful of his own aching limbs in this newborn anxiety, he sank on one knee and gently pillowed Iris's head and shoulders on the other. Her eyes were closed, her lips and teeth firmly set—a fact to which she undoubtedly owed her life, else she would have been suffocated—and the pallor of her skin seemed to be that terrible bloodless hue which indicates death. The stern lines in the man's face relaxed, and something blurred his vision. He was weak from exhaustion and want of food. For the moment his emotions were easily aroused.

"Oh, it is pitiful," he almost whimpered. "It cannot be!"

With a gesture of despair he drew the sleeve of his thick jersey across his eyes to clear them from the gathering mist. Then he tremblingly endeavored to open the neck of her dress and unclasp her corsets. He had a vague notion that ladies in a fainting condition required such treatment, and he was desperately resolved to bring Iris Deane back to conscious existence if it were possible. His task was rendered difficult by the waistband of her dress. He slipped out a clasp-knife and opened the blade.

Not until then did he discover that the nail of the forefinger on his right hand had been torn out by the quick, probably during his endeavors to grasp the unsteady support which contributed so materially to his escape. It still hung by a shred and hindered the free use of his hand. Without any hesitation he seized the offending nail in his teeth and completed the surgical operation by a rapid jerk.

Bending to resume his task he was startled to find the girl's eyes wide open and surveying him with

shadowy alarm. She was quite conscious, absurdly so
in a sense, and had noticed his strange action.

"Thank God!" he cried hoarsely. "You are alive."

Her mind as yet could only work in a single groove.

"Why did you do that?" she whispered.

"Do what?"

"Bite your nail off!"

"It was in my way. I wished to cut open your dress
at the waist. You were collapsed, almost dead, I
thought, and I wanted to unfasten your corsets."

Her color came back with remarkable rapidity.
From all the rich variety of the English tongue few
words could have been selected of such restorative effect.

She tried to assume a sitting posture, and instinctively her hands traveled to her disarranged costume.

"How ridiculous!" she said, with a little note of
annoyance in her voice, which sounded curiously hollow.
But her brave spirit could not yet command her en-
feebled frame. She was perforce compelled to sink back
to the support of his knee and arm.

"Do you think you could lie quiet until I try to find
some water?" he gasped anxiously.

She nodded a childlike acquiescence, and her eyelids
fell. It was only that her eyes smarted dreadfully from
the salt water, but the sailor was sure that this was a
premonition of a lapse to unconsciousness.

"Please try not to faint again," he said. "Don't you
think I had better loosen these things? You can breathe
more easily."

A ghost of a smile flickered on her lips. "No—no,"

she murmured. "My eyes hurt me—that is all. Is there—any—water?"

He laid her tenderly on the sand and rose to his feet. His first glance was towards the sea. He saw something which made him blink with astonishment. A heavy sea was still running over the barrier reef which enclosed a small lagoon. The contrast between the fierce commotion outside and the comparatively smooth surface of the protected pool was very marked. At low tide the lagoon was almost completely isolated. Indeed, he imagined that only a fierce gale blowing from the northwest would enable the waves to leap the reef, save where a strip of broken water, surging far into the small natural harbor, betrayed the position of the tiny entrance.

Yet at this very point a fine cocoanut palm reared its stately column high in air, and its long tremulous fronds were now swinging wildly before the gale. From where he stood it appeared to be growing in the midst of the sea, for huge breakers completely hid the coral embankment. This sentinel of the land had a weirdly impressive effect. It was the only fixed object in the waste of foam-capped waves. Not a vestige of the *Sirdar* remained seaward, but the sand was littered with wreckage, and—mournful spectacle!—a considerable number of inanimate human forms lay huddled up amidst the relics of the steamer.

This discovery stirred him to action. He turned to survey the land on which he was stranded with his helpless companion. To his great relief he discovered that it was lofty and tree-clad. He knew that the ship could not have drifted to Borneo, which still lay far to the south. This must be one of the hundreds of islands which stud the China Sea and provide resorts for Haïnan fishermen. Probably it was inhabited, though he thought it strange that none of the islanders had put in an appearance. In any event, water and food, of some sort, were assured.

But before setting out upon his quest two things demanded attention. The girl must be removed from her present position. It would be too horrible to permit her first conscious gaze to rest upon those crumpled objects on the beach. Common humanity demanded, too, that he should hastily examine each of the bodies in case life was not wholly extinct.

So he bent over the girl, noting with sudden wonder that, weak as she was, she had managed to refasten part of her bodice.

"You must permit me to carry you a little further inland," he explained gently.

Without another word he lifted her in his arms, marveling somewhat at the strength which came of necessity, and bore her some little distance, until a sturdy rock, jutting out of the sand, offered shelter from the wind and protection from the sea and its revelations.

"I am so cold, and tired," murmured Iris. "Is there any water? My throat hurts me."

He pressed back the tangled hair from her forehead as he might soothe a child.

"Try to lie still for a very few minutes," he said.

"You have not long to suffer. I will return immediately."

His own throat and palate were on fire owing to the brine, but he first hurried back to the edge of the lagoon. There were fourteen bodies in all, three women and eleven men, four of the latter being Lascars. The women were saloon passengers whom he did not know. One of the men was the surgeon, another the first officer, a third Sir John Tozer. The rest were passengers and members of the crew. They were all dead; some had been peacefully drowned, others were fearfully mangled by the rocks. Two of the Lascars, bearing signs of dreadful injuries, were lying on a cluster of low rocks overhanging the water. The remainder rested on the sand.

The sailor exhibited no visible emotion whilst he conducted his sad scrutiny. When he was assured that this silent company was beyond mortal help he at once strode away towards the nearest belt of trees. He could not tell how long the search for water might be protracted, and there was pressing need for it.

When he reached the first clump of brushwood he uttered a delighted exclamation. There, growing in prodigal luxuriance, was the beneficent pitcher-plant, whose large curled-up leaf, shaped like a teacup, not only holds a lasting quantity of rain-water, but mixes therewith its own palatable and natural juices.

With his knife he severed two of the leaves, swearing emphatically the while on account of his damaged finger, and hastened to Iris with the precious beverage. She heard him and managed to raise herself on an elbow.

The poor girl's eyes glistened at the prospect of relief. Without a word of question or surprise she swallowed the contents of both leaves.

Then she found utterance. "How odd it tastes! What is it?" she inquired.

But the eagerness with which she quenched her thirst renewed his own momentarily forgotten torture. His tongue seemed to swell. He was absolutely unable to reply.

The water revived Iris like a magic draught. Her quick intuition told her what had happened.

"You have had none yourself," she cried. "Go at once and get some. And please bring me some more."

He required no second bidding. After hastily gulping down the contents of several leaves he returned with a further supply. Iris was now sitting up. The sun had burst royally through the clouds, and her chilled limbs were gaining some degree of warmth and elasticity.

"What is it?" she repeated after another delicious draught.

"The leaf of the pitcher-plant. Nature is not always cruel. In an unusually generous mood she devised this method of storing water."

Miss Deane reached out her hand for more. Her troubled brain refused to wonder at such a reply from an ordinary seaman. The sailor deliberately spilled the contents of a remaining leaf on the sand.

"No, madam," he said, with an odd mixture of deference and firmness. "No more at present. I must first procure you some food."

She looked up at him in momentary silence.

"The ship is lost?" she said after a pause.

"Yes, madam."

"Are we the only people saved?"

"I fear so."

"Is this a desert island?"

"I think not, madam. It may, by chance, be temporarily uninhabited, but fishermen from China come to all these places to collect tortoise-shell and *bêche-de-mer*. I have seen no other living beings except ourselves; nevertheless, the islanders may live on the south side."

Another pause. Amidst the thrilling sensations of the moment Iris found herself idly speculating as to the meaning of *bêche-de-mer*, and why this common sailor pronounced French so well. Her thoughts reverted to the steamer.

"It surely cannot be possible that the *Sirdar* has gone to pieces—a magnificent vessel of her size and strength?"

He answered quietly—"It is too true, madam. I suppose you hardly knew she struck, it happened so suddenly. Afterwards, fortunately for you, you were unconscious."

"How do you know?" she inquired quickly. A flood of vivid recollection was pouring in upon her.

"I—er—well, I happened to be near you, madam, when the ship broke up, and we—er—drifted ashore together."

She rose and faced him. "I remember now," she cried hysterically. "You caught me as I was thrown into the corridor. We fell into the sea when the vessel turned over. You have saved my life. Were it not for you I could not possibly have escaped."

She gazed at him more earnestly, seeing that he blushed beneath the crust of salt and sand that covered his face. "Why," she went on with growing excitement, "you are the steward I noticed in the saloon yesterday. How is it that you are now dressed as a sailor?"

He answered readily enough. "There was an accident on board during the gale, madam. I am a fair sailor but a poor steward, so I applied for a transfer. As the crew were short-handed my offer was accepted."

Iris was now looking at him intently.

"You saved my life," she repeated slowly. It seemed that this obvious fact needed to be indelibly established in her mind. Indeed the girl was overwrought by all that she had gone through. Only by degrees were her thoughts marshaling themselves with lucid coherence. As yet, she recalled so many dramatic incidents that they failed to assume due proportion.

But quickly there came memories of Captain Ross, of Sir John and Lady Tozer, of the doctor, her maid, the hundred and one individualities of her pleasant life aboard ship. Could it be that they were all dead? The notion was monstrous. But its ghastly significance was instantly borne in upon her by the plight in which she stood. Her lips quivered; the tears trembled in her eyes.

"Is it really true that all the ship's company except ourselves are lost?" she brokenly demanded.

The sailor's gravely earnest glance fell before hers. "Unhappily there is no room for doubt," he said.

"Are you quite, quite sure?"

"I am sure—of some." Involuntarily he turned seawards.

She understood him. She sank to her knees, covered her face with her hands, and broke into a passion of weeping. With a look of infinite pity he stooped and would have touched her shoulder, but he suddenly restrained the impulse. Something had hardened this man. It cost him an effort to be callous, but he succeeded. His mouth tightened and his expression lost its tenderness.

"Come, come, my dear lady," he exclaimed, and there was a tinge of studied roughness in his voice, "you must calm yourself. It is the fortune of shipwreck as well as of war, you know. We are alive and must look after ourselves. Those who have gone are beyond our help."

"But not beyond our sympathy," wailed Iris, uncovering her swimming eyes for a fleeting look at him. Even in the utter desolation of the moment she could not help marveling that this queer-mannered sailor, who spoke like a gentleman and tried to pose as her inferior, who had rescued her with the utmost gallantry, who carried his Quixotic zeal to the point of first supplying her needs when he was in far worse case himself, should be so utterly indifferent to the fate of others.

He waited silently until her sobs ceased.

"Now, madam," he said, "it is essential that we should obtain some food. I don't wish to leave you alone until we are better acquainted with our whereabouts. Can you walk a little way towards the trees, or shall I assist you?"

Iris immediately stood up. She pressed her hair back defiantly.

"Certainly I can walk," she answered. "What do you propose to do?"

"Well, madam——"

"What is your name?" she interrupted imperiously.

"Jenks, madam. Robert Jenks."

"Thank you. Now, listen, Mr. Robert Jenks. My name is Miss Iris Deane. On board ship I was a passenger and you were a steward—that is, until you became a seaman. Here we are equals in misfortune, but in all else you are the leader—I am quite useless. I can only help in matters by your direction, so I do not wish to be addressed as 'madam' in every breath. Do you understand me?"

Conscious that her large blue eyes were fixed indignantly upon him Mr. Robert Jenks repressed a smile. She was still hysterical and must be humored in her vagaries. What an odd moment for a discussion on etiquette!

"As you wish, Miss Deane," he said. "The fact remains that I have many things to attend to, and we really must eat something."

"What can we eat?"

"Let us find out," he replied, scanning the nearest trees with keen scrutiny.

They plodded together through the sand in silence. Physically, they were a superb couple, but in raiment they resembled scarecrows. Both, of course, were bareheaded. The sailor's jersey and trousers were old and torn, and the sea-water still soughed loudly in his heavy boots with each step.

But Iris was in a deplorable plight. Her hair fell in

a great wave of golden brown strands over her neck and shoulders. Every hairpin had vanished, but with a few dexterous twists she coiled the flying tresses into a loose knot. Her beautiful muslin dress was rent and draggled. It was drying rapidly under the ever-increasing power of the sun, and she surreptitiously endeavored to complete the fastening of the open portion about her neck. Other details must be left until a more favorable opportunity.

She recalled the strange sight that first met her eyes when she recovered consciousness.

"You hurt your finger," she said abruptly. "Let me see it."

They had reached the shelter of the trees, pleasantly grateful now, so powerful are tropical sunbeams at even an early hour.

He held out his right hand without looking at her. Indeed, his eyes had been studiously averted during the past few minutes. Her womanly feelings were aroused by the condition of the ragged wound.

"Oh, you poor fellow," she said. "How awful it must be! How did it happen? Let me tie it up."

"It is not so bad now," he said. "It has been well soaked in salt water, you know. I think the nail was torn off when we—when a piece of wreckage miraculously turned up beneath us."

Iris shredded a strip from her dress. She bound the finger with deft tenderness.

"Thank you," he said simply. Then he gave a glad shout. "By Jove! Miss Deane, we are in luck's way. There is a fine plantain tree."

The Survivors

The pangs of hunger could not be resisted. Although the fruit was hardly ripe they tore at the great bunches and ate ravenously. Iris made no pretence in the matter, and the sailor was in worse plight, for he had been on duty continuously since four o'clock the previous afternoon.

At last their appetite was somewhat appeased, though plantains might not appeal to a gourmand as the solitary joint.

"Now," decided Jenks, "you must rest here a little while, Miss Deane. I am going back to the beach. You need not be afraid. There are no animals to harm you, and I will not be far away."

"What are you going to do on the beach?" she demanded.

"To rescue stores, for the most part."

"May I not come with you—I can be of some little service, surely?"

He answered slowly: "Please oblige me by remaining here at present. In less than an hour I will return, and then, perhaps, you will find plenty to do."

She read his meaning intuitively and shivered. "I could not do *that*," she murmured. "I would faint. Whilst you are away I will pray for them—my unfortunate friends."

As he passed from her side he heard her sobbing quietly.

When he reached the lagoon he halted suddenly. Something startled him. He was quite certain that he had counted fourteen corpses. Now there were only twelve.   The two Lascars' bodies, which rested on the small group of rocks on the verge of the lagoon, had vanished.

Where had they gone to?

CHAPTER III

DISCOVERIES

THE sailor wasted no time in idle bewilderment. He searched carefully for traces of the missing Lascars. He came to the conclusion that the bodies had been dragged from off the sun-dried rocks into the lagoon by some agency the nature of which he could not even conjecture.

They were lying many feet above the sea-level when he last saw them, little more than half an hour earlier. At that point the beach shelved rapidly. He could look far into the depths of the rapidly clearing water. Nothing was visible there save several varieties of small fish.

The incident puzzled and annoyed him. Still thinking about it, he sat down on the highest rock and pulled off his heavy boots to empty the water out. He also divested himself of his stockings and spread them out to dry.

The action reminded him of Miss Deane's necessities. He hurried to a point whence he could call out to her and recommend her to dry some of her clothing during his absence. He retired even more quickly, fearing lest he should be seen. Iris had already displayed to the sunlight a large portion of her costume.

The Wings of the Morning

Without further delay he set about a disagreeable but necessary task. From the pockets of the first officer and doctor he secured two revolvers and a supply of cartridges, evidently intended to settle any dispute which might have arisen between the ship's officers and the native members of the crew. He hoped the cartridges were uninjured; but he could not test them at the moment for fear of alarming Miss Deane.

Both officers carried pocket-books and pencils. In one of these, containing dry leaves, the sailor made a careful inventory of the money and other valuable effects he found upon the dead, besides noting names and documents where possible. Curiously enough, the capitalist of this island morgue was a Lascar jemadar, who in a belt around his waist hoarded more than one hundred pounds in gold. The sailor tied in a handkerchief all the money he collected, and ranged pocket-books, letters, and jewelry in separate little heaps. Then he stripped the men of their boots and outer clothing. He could not tell how long the girl and he might be detained on the island before help came, and fresh garments were essential. It would be foolish sentimentality to trust to stores thrown ashore from the ship.

Nevertheless, when it became necessary to search and disrobe the women he almost broke down. For an instant he softened. Gulping back his emotions with a savage imprecation he doggedly persevered. At last he paused to consider what should be done with the bodies. His first intent was to scoop a large hole in the sand with a piece of timber; but when he took into consideration the magnitude of the labor involved, requiring many hours of hard work and a waste of precious time which might be of infinite value to his helpless companion and himself, he was forced to abandon the project. It was not only impracticable but dangerous.

Again he had to set his teeth with grim resolution. One by one the bodies were shot into the lagoon from the little quay of rock. He knew they would not be seen again.

He was quite unnerved now. He felt as if he had committed a colossal crime. In the smooth water of the cove a number of black fins were cutting arrow-shaped ripples. The sharks were soon busy. He shuddered. God's Providence had ferried him and the girl across that very place a few hours ago. How wonderful that he and she should be snatched from the sea whilst hundreds perished! Why was it? And those others—why were they denied rescue? For an instant he was nearer to prayer than he had been for years.

Some lurking fiend of recollection sprang from out the vista of bygone years and choked back the impulse. He arose and shook himself like a dog. There was much to be done. He gathered the clothes and other articles into a heap and placed portions of shattered packing-cases near—to mislead Iris. Whilst thus engaged he kicked up out of the sand a rusty kriss, or Malay sword. The presence of this implement startled him. He examined it slowly and thrust it out of sight.

Then he went back to her, after donning his stockings and boots, now thoroughly dry.

"Are you ready now, Miss Deane?" he sang out cheerily.

"Ready? I have been waiting for you."

Jenks chuckled quietly. "I must guard my tongue: it betrays me," he said to himself.

Iris joined him. By some mysterious means she had effected great improvement in her appearance. Yet there were manifest gaps.

"If only I had a needle and thread——" she began.

"If that is all," said the sailor, fumbling in his pockets. He produced a shabby little hussif, containing a thimble, scissors, needles and some skeins of unbleached thread. Case and contents were sodden or rusted with salt water, but the girl fastened upon this treasure with a sigh of deep content.

"Now, please," she cried, "I want a telegraph office and a ship."

It was impossible to resist the infection of her high spirits. This time he laughed without concealment.

"We will look for them, Miss Deane. Meanwhile, will you oblige me by wearing this? The sun is climbing up rapidly."

He handed her a sou'wester which he carried. He had secured another for himself. The merriment died away from her face. She remembered his errand. Being an eminently sensible young woman she made no protest, even forcing herself to tie the strings beneath her chin.

When they reached the sands she caught sight of the pile of clothes and the broken woodwork, with the small heaps of valuables methodically arranged. The harmless subterfuge did not deceive her. She darted a quick look of gratitude at her companion. How thoughtful he was! After a fearful glance around she was re-assured, though she wondered what had become of——them.

"I see you have been busy," she said, nodding towards the clothes and boots.

It was his turn to steal a look of sharp inquiry. 'Twere an easier task to read the records of time in the solid rock than to glean knowledge from the girl's face.

"Yes," he replied simply. "Lucky find, wasn't it?"

"Most fortunate. When they are quite dry I will replenish my wardrobe. What is the first thing to be done?"

"Well, Miss Deane, I think our programme is, in the first place, to examine the articles thrown ashore and see if any of the cases contain food. Secondly, we should haul high and dry everything that may be of use to us, lest the weather should break again and the next tide sweep away the spoil. Thirdly, we should eat and rest, and finally, we must explore the island before the light fails. I am convinced we are alone here. It is a small place at the best, and if any Chinamen were ashore they would have put in an appearance long since."

"Do you think, then, that we may remain here long?"

"It is impossible to form an opinion on that point. Help may come in a day. On the other hand——"

"Yes?"

"It is a wise thing, Miss Deane, to prepare for other contingencies."

She stood still, and swept the horizon with compre-hensive eyes. The storm had vanished. Masses of cloud were passing away to the west, leaving a glorious expanse of blue sky. Already the sea was calming. Huge breakers roared over the reef, but beyond it the waves were subsiding into a heavy unbroken swell.

The sailor watched her closely. In the quaint oilskin hat and her tattered muslin dress she looked bewitchingly pretty. She reminded him of a well-bred and beautiful society lady whom he once saw figuring as Grace Darling at a fashionable bazaar.

But Miss Iris's thoughts were serious.

"Do you mean," she said slowly, without moving her gaze from the distant meeting-place of sky and water, "that we may be imprisoned here for weeks, perhaps months?"

"If you cast your mind back a few hours you will perhaps admit that we are very fortunate to be here at all."

She whisked round upon him. "Do not fence with my question, Mr. Jenks. Answer me!"

He bowed. There was a perceptible return of his stubborn cynicism when he spoke.

"The facts are obvious, Miss Deane. The loss of the *Sirdar* will not be definitely known for many days. It will be assumed that she has broken down. The agents in Singapore will await cabled tidings of her whereabouts. She might have drifted anywhere in that typhoon. Ultimately they will send out a vessel to search, impelled to that course a little earlier by your father's anxiety. Pardon me. I did not intend to pain you. I am speaking my mind."

"Go on," said Iris bravely.

"The relief ship must search the entire China Sea.

Discoveries

The gale might have driven a disabled steamer north, south, east or west. A typhoon travels in a whirling spiral, you see, and the direction of a drifting ship depends wholly upon the locality where she sustained damage. The coasts of China, Java, Borneo, and the Philippines are not equipped with lighthouses on every headland and cordoned with telegraph wires. There are river pirates and savage races to be reckoned with. Casting aside all other possibilities, and assuming that a prompt search is made to the south of our course, this part of the ocean is full of reefs and small islands, some inhabited permanently, others visited occasionally by fishermen." He was about to add something, but checked himself.

"To sum up," he continued hurriedly, "we may have to remain here for many days, even months. There is always a chance of speedy help. We must act, however, on the basis of detention for an indefinite period. I am discussing appearances as they are. A survey of the island may change all these views."

"In what way?"

He turned and pointed to the summit of the tree-covered hill behind them.

"From that point," he said, "we may see other and larger islands. If so, they will certainly be inhabited. I am surprised this one is not."

He ended abruptly. They were losing time. Before Iris could join him he was already hauling a large undamaged case out of the water.

He laughed unmirthfully. "Champagne!" he said. "A good brand, too!"

This man was certainly an enigma. Iris wrinkled her pretty forehead in the effort to place him in a fitting category. His words and accent were those of an educated gentleman, yet his actions and manners were studiously uncouth when he thought she was observing him. The veneer of roughness puzzled her. That he was naturally of refined temperament she knew quite well, not alone by perception but by the plain evidence of his earlier dealings with her. Then why this affectation of coarseness, this borrowed aroma of the steward's mess and the forecastle?

To the best of her ability she silently helped in the work of salvage. They made a queer collection. A case of champagne, and another of brandy. A box of books. A pair of night glasses. A compass. Several boxes of ship's biscuits, coated with salt, but saved by their hardness, having been immersed but a few seconds. Two large cases of hams in equally good condition. Some huge dish-covers. A bit of twisted ironwork, and a great quantity of cordage and timber.

There was one very heavy package which their united strength could not lift. The sailor searched round until he found an iron bar that could be wrenched from its socket. With this he pried open the strong outer cover and revealed the contents—regulation boxes of Lee-Metford ammunition, each containing 500 rounds.

"Ah!" he cried, "now we want some rifles."

"What good would they be?" inquired Iris.

He softly denounced himself as a fool, but he answered at once: "To shoot birds, of course, Miss Deane. There are plenty here, and many of them are edible."

"You have two revolvers and some cartridges."

"Yes. They are useful in a way, but not for pot-hunting."

"How stupid of me! What you really need is a shot-gun."

He smiled grimly. At times his sense of humor forced a way through the outward shield of reserve, of defiance it might be.

"The only persons I ever heard of," he said, "who landed under compulsion on a desert island with a ship-load of requisites, were the Swiss Family Robinson."

"Good gracious!" cried Iris irrelevantly; "I had not even thought of Robinson Crusoe until this moment. Isn't it odd? I—we——"

She pulled herself up short, firmly resolved not to blush. Without flinching she challenged him to complete her sentence. He dared not do it. He could not be mean enough to take advantage of her slip.

Instantly he helped her embarrassment. "I hope the parallel will not hold good," he said. "In any event, you, Miss Deane, fill a part less familiar in fiction."

The phrase was neat. It meant much or little, as fancy dictated. Iris at first felt profoundly grateful for his tact. Thinking the words over at leisure she became hot and very angry.

They worked in silence for another hour. The sun was nearing the zenith. They were distressed with the increasing heat of the day. Jenks secured a ham and some biscuits, some pieces of driftwood and the binoculars, and invited Miss Deane to accompany him to the grove. She obeyed without a word, though she wondered how he proposed to light a fire. To contribute something towards the expected feast she picked up a dish-cover and a bottle of champagne.

The sailor eyed the concluding item with disfavor. "Not whilst the sun is up," he said. "In the evening, yes."

"It was for you," explained Iris, coldly. "I do not drink wine."

"You must break the pledge whilst you are here, Miss Deane. It is often very cold at night in this latitude. A chill would mean fever and perhaps death."

"What a strange man!" murmured the girl.

She covertly watched his preparations. He tore a dry leaf from a notebook and broke the bullet out of a cartridge, damping the powder with water from a pitcher-plant. Smearing the composition on the paper, he placed it in the sun, where it dried at once. He gathered a small bundle of withered spines from the palms, and arranged the driftwood on top, choosing a place for his bonfire just within the shade. Then, inserting the touch-paper among the spines, he unscrewed one of the lenses of the binoculars, converted it into a burning-glass, and had a fine blaze roaring merrily in a few minutes. With the aid of pointed sticks he grilled some slices of ham, cut with his clasp-knife, which he first carefully cleaned in the earth. The biscuits were of the variety that become soft when toasted, and so he balanced a few by stones near the fire.

Iris forgot her annoyance in her interest. A most appetizing smell filled the air. They were having a picnic amidst delightful surroundings. Yesterday at this time—she almost yielded to a rush of sentiment, but forced it back with instant determination. Tears were a poor resource, unmindful of God's goodness to herself and her companion. Without the sailor what would have become of her, even were she thrown ashore while still living? She knew none of the expedients which seemed to be at his command. It was a most ungrateful proceeding to be vexed with him for her own thoughtless suggestion that she occupied a new rôle as Mrs. Crusoe.

"Can I do nothing to help?" she exclaimed. So contrite was her tone that Jenks was astonished.

"Yes," he said, pointing to the dish-cover. "If you polish the top of that with your sleeve it will serve as a plate. Luncheon is ready."

He neatly dished up two slices of ham on a couple of biscuits and handed them to her, with the clasp-knife.

"I can depend on my fingers," he explained. "It will not be the first time."

"Have you led an adventurous life?" she asked, by way of polite conversation.

"No," he growled.

"I only thought so because you appear to know all sorts of dodges for prolonging existence—things I never heard of."

"Broiled ham—and biscuits—for instance?"

At another time Iris would have snapped at him for the retort. Still humbly regretful for her previous attitude she answered meekly—

"Yes, in this manner of cooking them, I mean. But there are other items—methods of lighting fires, finding water, knowing what fruits and other articles may be found on a desert island, such as plantains and cocoa-nuts, certain sorts of birds—and *bêche-de-mer*."

For the life of her she could not tell why she tacked on that weird item to her list.

The sailor inquired, more civilly—"Then you are acquainted with trepang?"

"Who?"

"Trepang—*bêche-de-mer*, you know."

Iris made a desperate guess. "Yes," she said, de-murely. "It makes beautiful backs for hair brushes. And it looks so nice as a frame for platinotype photo-graphs. I have——"

Jenks swallowed a large piece of ham and became very red. At last he managed to say—"I beg your pardon. You are thinking of tortoise-shell. *Bêche-de-mer* is a sort of marine slug."

"How odd!" said Iris.

She had discovered at an early age the tactical value of this remark, and the experience of maturer years con-firmed the success of juvenile efforts to upset the equa-nimity of governesses. Even the sailor was silenced.

Talk ceased until the meal was ended. Jenks sprang lightly to his feet. Rest and food had restored his facul-ties. The girl thought dreamily, as he stood there in his rough attire, that she had never seen a finer man. He was tall, sinewy, and well formed. In repose his face was pleasant, if masterful. Its somewhat sullen, self-contained expression was occasional and acquired. She wondered how he could be so energetic. Personally she was consumed with sleepiness.

He produced a revolver.

Discoveries

"Do you mind if I fire a shot to test these cartridges?" he inquired. "The powder is all right, but the fulminate in the caps may be damaged."

She agreed promptly. He pointed the weapon at a cluster of cocoanuts, and there was a loud report. Two nuts fell to the ground, and the air was filled with shrill screams and the flapping of innumerable wings. Iris was momentarily dismayed, but her senses confirmed the sailor's explanation—"Sea-birds."

He reloaded the empty chamber, and was about to say something, when a queer sound, exactly resembling the gurgling of water poured from a large bottle, fell upon their ears. It came from the interior of the grove, and the two exchanged a quick look of amazed questioning. Jenks took a hasty step in the direction of the noise, but he stopped and laughed at his own expense. Iris liked the sound of his mirth. It was genuine, not forced.

"I remember now," he explained. "The wou-wou monkey cries in that peculiar warble. The presence of the animal here shows that the island has been inhabited at some time."

"You remember?" repeated the girl. "Then you have been in this part of the world before?"

"No. I mean I have read about it."

Twice in half an hour had he curtly declined to indulge in personal reminiscences.

"Can you use a revolver?" he went on.

"My father taught me. He thinks every woman should know how to defend herself if need be."

"Excellent. Well, Miss Deane, you must try to sleep

for a couple of hours. I purpose examining the coast for some distance on each side. Should you want me, a shot will be the best sort of signal."

"I am very tired," she admitted. "But you?"

"Oh, I am all right. I feel restless; that is, I mean I will not be able to sleep until night comes, and before we climb the hill to survey our domain I want to find better quarters than we now possess."

Perhaps, were she less fatigued, she would have caught the vague anxiety, the note of distrust, in his voice. But the carpet of sand and leaves on which she lay was very seductive. Her eyes closed. She nestled into a comfortable position, and slept.

The man looked at her steadily for a little while. Then he moved the revolver out of harm's way to a spot where she must see it instantly, pulled his sou'wester well over his eyes and walked off quietly.

They were flung ashore on the north-west side of the island. Except for the cove formed by the coral reef, with its mysterious palm-tree growing apparently in the midst of the waves, the shape of the coast was roughly that of the concave side of a bow, the two visible extremities being about three-quarters of a mile apart.

He guessed, by the way in which the sea raced past these points, that the land did not extend beyond them. Behind him, it rose steeply to a considerable height, 150 or 200 feet. In the center was the tallest hill, which seemed to end abruptly towards the south-west. On the north-east side it was connected with a rocky promontory by a ridge of easy grade. The sailor turned to the south-west, as offering the most likely direction for rapid survey.

He followed the line of vegetation; there the ground was firm and level. There was no suggestion of the mariner's roll in his steady gait. Alter his clothing, change the heavy boots into spurred Wellingtons, and he would be the *beau idéal* of a cavalry soldier, the order of Melchisedec in the profession of arms.

He was not surprised to find that the hill terminated in a sheer wall of rock, which stood out, ominous and massive, from the wealth of verdure clothing the remainder of the ridge. Facing the precipice, and separated from it by a strip of ground not twenty feet above the sea-level in the highest part, was another rock-built eminence, quite bare of trees, blackened by the weather and scarred in a manner that attested the attacks of lightning.

He whistled softly. "By Jove!" he said. "Volcanic, and highly mineralized."

The intervening belt was sparsely dotted with trees, casuarinas, poon, and other woods he did not know, resembling ebony and cedar. A number of stumps showed that the axe had been at work, but not recently. He passed into the cleft and climbed a tree that offered easy access. As he expected, after rising a few feet from the ground, his eyes encountered the solemn blue line of the sea, not half a mile distant.

He descended and commenced a systematic search. Men had been here. Was there a house? Would he suddenly encounter some hermit Malay or Chinaman?

At the foot of the main cliff was a cluster of fruit-bearing trees, plantains, areca-nuts, and cocoa-palms. A couple of cinchonas caught his eye. In one spot the undergrowth was rank and vividly green. The cassava, or tapioca plant, reared its high, passion-flower leaves above the grass, and some sago-palms thrust aloft their thick-stemmed trunks.

"Here is a change of menu, at any rate," he communed.

Breaking a thick branch off a poon tree he whittled away the minor stems. A strong stick was needful to explore that leafy fastness thoroughly.

A few cautious strides and vigorous whacks with the stick laid bare the cause of such prodigality in a soil covered with drifted sand and lumps of black and white speckled coral. The trees and bushes enclosed a well— safe-guarded it, in fact, from being choked with sand during the first gale that blew.

Delighted with this discovery, more precious than diamonds at the moment, for he doubted the advisability of existing on the water supply of the pitcher-plant, he knelt to peer into the excavation. The well had been properly made. ·Ten feet down he could see the reflection of his face. Expert hands had tapped the secret reservoir of the island. By stretching to the full extent of his arm, he managed to plunge the stick into the water. Tasting the drops, he found that they were quite sweet. The sand and porous rock provided the best of filter-beds.

He rose, well pleased, and noted that on the opposite side the appearance of the shrubs and tufts of long grass indicated the existence of a grown-over path towards the cliff. He followed it, walking carelessly, with eyes seeking the prospect beyond, when something rattled and cracked beneath his feet. Looking down, he was horrified to find he was trampling on a skeleton.

Had a venomous snake coiled its glistening folds around his leg he would not have been more startled. But this man of iron nerve soon recovered. He frowned deeply after the first involuntary heart-throb.

With the stick he cleared away the undergrowth, and revealed the skeleton of a man. The bones were big and strong, but oxidized by the action of the air. Jenks had injured the left tibia by his tread, but three fractured ribs and a smashed shoulder-blade told some terrible unwritten story.

Beneath the mournful relics were fragments of decayed cloth. It was blue serge. Lying about were a few blackened objects—brass buttons marked with an anchor. The dead man's boots were in the best state of preservation, but the leather had shrunk and the nails protruded like fangs.

A rusted pocket-knife lay there, and on the left breast of the skeleton rested a round piece of tin, the top of a canister, which might have reposed in a coat pocket. Jenks picked it up. Some curious marks and figures were punched into its surface. After a hasty glance he put it aside for more leisurely examination.

No weapon was visible. He could form no estimate as to the cause of the death of this poor unknown, nor the time since the tragedy had occurred.

Jenks must have stood many minutes before he perceived that the skeleton was headless. At first he imagined that in rummaging about with the stick he had disturbed the skull. But the most minute search demonstrated that it had gone, had been taken away, in fact, for the plants which so effectually screened the lighter bones would not permit the skull to vanish.

Then the frown on the sailor's face became threatening, thunderous. He recollected the rusty kriss. Indistinct memories of strange tales of the China Sea crowded unbidden to his brain.

"Dyaks!" he growled fiercely. "A ship's officer, an Englishman probably, murdered by head-hunting Dyak pirates!"

If they came once they would come again.

Five hundred yards away Iris Deane was sleeping. He ought not to have left her alone. And then, with the devilish ingenuity of coincidence, a revolver shot awoke the echoes, and sent all manner of wildfowl hurtling through the trees with clamorous outcry.

Panting and wild-eyed, Jenks was at the girl's side in an inconceivably short space of time. She was not beneath the shelter of the grove, but on the sands, gazing, pallid in cheek and lip, at the group of rocks on the edge of the lagoon.

"What is the matter?" he gasped.

"Oh, I don't know," she wailed brokenly. "I had a dream, such a horrible dream. You were struggling with some awful thing down there." She pointed to the rocks.

"I was not near the place," he said laboriously. It cost him an effort to breathe. His broad chest expanded inches with each respiration.

"Yes, yes, I understand. But I awoke and ran to save you. When I got here I saw something, a thing with waving arms, and fired. It vanished, and then you came."

The sailor walked slowly to the rocks. A fresh chip out of the stone showed where the bullet struck. One huge boulder was wet, as if water had been splashed over it. He halted and looked intently into the water. Not a fish was to be seen, but small spirals of sand were eddying up from the bottom, where it shelved steeply from the shore.

Iris followed him. "See," she cried excitedly. "I was not mistaken. There *was* something here."

A creepy sensation ran up the man's spine and passed behind his ears. At this spot the drowned Lascars were lying. Like an inspiration came the knowledge that the cuttlefish, the dreaded octopus, abounds in the China Sea.

His face was livid when he turned to Iris. "You are over-wrought by fatigue, Miss Deane," he said. "What you saw was probably a seal;" he knew the ludicrous substitution would not be questioned. "Please go and lie down again."

"I cannot," she protested. "I am too frightened."

"Frightened! By a dream! In broad daylight!"

"But why are *you* so pale? What has alarmed you?"

"Can you ask? Did you not give the agreed signal?"

"Yes, but——"

Her inquiring glance fell. He was breathless from agitation rather than running. He was perturbed on her account. For an instant she had looked into his soul.

"I will go back," she said quietly, "though I would rather accompany you. What are you doing?"

"Seeking a place to lay our heads," he answered, with gruff carelessness. "You really must rest, Miss Deane. Otherwise you will be broken up by fatigue and become ill."

So Iris again sought her couch of sand, and the sailor returned to the skeleton. They separated unwillingly, each thinking only of the other's safety and comfort. The girl knew she was not wanted because the man wished to spare her some unpleasant experience. She obeyed him with a sigh, and sat down, not to sleep, but to muse, as girls will, round-eyed, wistful, with the angelic fantasy of youth and innocence.

CHAPTER IV

RAINBOW ISLAND

Across the parched bones lay the stick discarded by Jenks in his alarm. He picked it up and resumed his progress along the pathway. So closely did he now examine the ground that he hardly noted his direction. The track led straight towards the wall of rock. The distance was not great—about forty yards. At first the brushwood impeded him, but soon even this hindrance disappeared, and a well-defined passage meandered through a belt of trees, some strong and lofty, others quite immature.

More bushes gathered at the foot of the cliff. Behind them he could see the mouth of a cave; the six months' old growth of vegetation about the entrance gave clear indication as to the time which had elapsed since a human foot last disturbed the solitude.

A few vigorous blows with the stick cleared away obstructing plants and leafy branches. The sailor stooped and looked into the cavern, for the opening was barely five feet high. He perceived instantly that the excavation was man's handiwork, applied to a fault in the hard rock. A sort of natural shaft existed, and this had been extended by manual labor. Beyond the entrance the cave became more lofty. Owing to its position with reference to the sun at that hour Jenks imagined that sufficient light would be obtainable when the tropical luxuriance of foliage outside was dispensed with.

At present the interior was dark. With the stick he tapped the walls and roof. A startled cluck and the rush of wings heralded the flight of two birds, alarmed by the noise. Soon his eyes, more accustomed to the gloom, made out that the place was about thirty feet deep, ten feet wide in the center, and seven or eight feet high.

At the further end was a collection of objects inviting prompt attention. Each moment he could see with greater distinctness. Kneeling on one side of the little pile he discerned that on a large stone, serving as a rude bench, were some tin utensils, some knives, a sextant, and a quantity of empty cartridge cases. Between the stone and what a miner terms the "face" of the rock was a four-foot space. Here, half imbedded in the sand which covered the floor, were two pickaxes, a shovel, a sledge-hammer, a fine timber-felling axe, and three crowbars.

In the darkest corner of the cave's extremity the "wall" appeared to be very smooth. He prodded with the stick, and there was a sharp clang of tin. He discovered six square kerosene-oil cases carefully stacked up. Three were empty, one seemed to be half full, and the contents of two were untouched. With almost feverish haste he ascertained that the half-filled tin did really contain oil.

"What a find!" he ejaculated aloud. Another pair of birds dashed from a ledge near the roof.

"Confound you!" shouted the sailor. He sprang back and whacked the walls viciously, but all the feathered intruders had gone.

So far as he could judge the cave harbored no further surprises. Returning towards the exit his boots dislodged more empty cartridges from the sand. They were shells adapted to a revolver of heavy caliber. At a short distance from the doorway they were present in dozens.

"The remnants of a fight," he thought. "The man was attacked, and defended himself here. Not expecting the arrival of enemies he provided no store of food or water. He was killed whilst trying to reach the well, probably at night."

He vividly pictured the scene—a brave, hardy European keeping at bay a boatload of Dyak savages, enduring manfully the agonies of hunger, thirst, perhaps wounds. Then the siege, followed by a wild effort to gain the life-giving well, the hiss of a Malay parang wielded by a lurking foe, and the last despairing struggle before death came.

He might be mistaken. Perchance there was a less dramatic explanation. But he could not shake off his first impressions. They were garnered from dumb evidence and developed by some occult but overwhelming sense of certainty.

"What was the poor devil doing here?" he asked. "Why did he bury himself in this rock, with mining utensils and a few rough stores? He could not be a castaway. There is the indication of purpose, of preparation, of method combined with ignorance, for none who knew the ways of Dyaks and Chinese pirates would venture to live here alone, if he could help it, and if he really were alone." The thing was a mystery, would probably remain a mystery for ever.

> "Be it steel or be it lead,
> Anyhow the man is dead."

There was relief in hearing his own voice. He could hum, and think, and act. Arming himself with the axe he attacked the bushes and branches of trees in front of the cave. He cut a fresh approach to the well, and threw the litter over the skeleton. At first he was inclined to bury it where it lay, but he disliked the idea of Iris walking unconsciously over the place. No time could be wasted that day. He would seize an early opportunity to act as grave-digger.

After an absence of little more than an hour he rejoined the girl. She saw him from afar, and wondered whence he obtained the axe he shouldered.

"You are a successful explorer," she cried when he drew near.

"Yes, Miss Deane. I have found water, implements, a shelter, even light."

"What sort of light—spiritual, or material?"

"Oil."

"Oh!"

Iris could not remain serious for many consecutive minutes, but she gathered that he was in no mood for frivolity.

"And the shelter—is it a house?" she continued.

"No, a cave. If you are sufficiently rested you might come and take possession."

Her eyes danced with excitement. He told her what he had seen, with reservations, and she ran on before him to witness these marvels.

"Why did you make a new path to the well?" she inquired after a rapid survey.

"A new path!" The pertinent question staggered him.

"Yes, the people who lived here must have had some sort of free passage."

He lied easily. "I have only cleared away recent growth," he said.

"And why did they dig a cave? It surely would be much more simple to build a house from all these trees."

"There you puzzle me," he said frankly.

They had entered the cavern but a little way and now came out.

"These empty cartridges are funny. They suggest a fort, a battle." Woman-like, her words were carelessly chosen, but they were crammed with inductive force.

Embarked on the toboggan slope of untruth the sailor slid smoothly downwards.

"Events have colored your imagination, Miss Deane. Even in England men often preserve such things for future use. They can be reloaded."

"Yes, I have seen keepers do that. This is different. There is an air of——"

"There is a lot to be done," broke in Jenks emphatically. "We must climb the hill and get back here in time to light another fire before the sun goes down. I want to prop a canvas sheet in front of the cave, and try to devise a lamp."

"Must I sleep inside?" demanded Iris.

"Yes. Where else?"

There was a pause, a mere whiff of awkwardness.

"I will mount guard outside," went on Jenks. He was trying to improve the edge of the axe by grinding it on a soft stone.

The girl went into the cave again. She was inquisitive, uneasy.

"That arrangement——" she began, but ended in a sharp cry of terror. The dispossessed birds had returned during the sailor's absence.

"I will kill them," he shouted in anger.

"Please don't. There has been enough of death in this place already."

The words jarred on his ears. Then he felt that she could only allude to the victims of the wreck.

"I was going to say," she explained, "that we must devise a partition. There is no help for it until you construct a sort of house. Candidly, I do not like this hole in the rock. It is a vault, a tomb."

"You told me that I was in command, yet you dispute my orders." He strove hard to appear brusquely good-humored, indifferent, though for one of his mould he was absurdly irritable. The cause was over-strain, but that explanation escaped him.

"Quite true. But if sleeping in the cold, in dew or rain, is bad for me, it must be equally bad for you. And without you I am helpless, you know."

His arms twitched to give her a reassuring hug. In

some respects she was so childlike; her big blue eyes were so ingenuous. He laughed sardonically, and the harsh note clashed with her frank candor. Here, at least, she was utterly deceived. His changeful moods were incomprehensible.

"I will serve you to the best of my ability, Miss Deane," he exclaimed. "We must hope for a speedy rescue, and I am inured to exposure. It is otherwise with you. Are you ready for the climb?"

Mechanically she picked up a stick at her feet. It was the sailor's wand of investigation. He snatched it from her hands and threw it away among the trees.

"That is a dangerous alpenstock," he said. "The wood is unreliable. It might break. I will cut you a better one," and he swung the axe against a tall sapling.

Iris mentally described him as "funny." She followed him in the upward curve of the ascent, for the grade was not difficult and the ground smooth enough, the storms of years having pulverized the rock and driven sand into its clefts. The persistent inroads of the trees had done the rest. Beyond the flight of birds and the scampering of some tiny monkeys overhead, they did not disturb a living creature.

The crest of the hill was tree-covered, and they could see nothing beyond their immediate locality until the sailor found a point higher than the rest, where a rugged collection of hard basalt and the uprooting of some poon trees provided an open space elevated above the ridge.

For a short distance the foothold was precarious. Jenks helped the girl in this part of the climb. His strong, gentle grasp gave her confidence. She was flushed with exertion when they stood together on the summit of this elevated perch. They could look to every point of the compass except a small section on the south-west. Here the trees rose behind them until the brow of the precipice was reached.

The emergence into a sunlit panorama of land and sea, though expected, was profoundly enthralling. They appeared to stand almost exactly in the center of the island, which was crescent-shaped. It was no larger than the sailor had estimated. The new slopes now revealed were covered with verdure down to the very edge of the water, which, for nearly a mile seawards, broke over jagged reefs. The sea looked strangely calm from this height. Irregular blue patches on the horizon to south and east caught the man's first glance. He unslung the binoculars he still carried and focused them eagerly.

"Islands!" he cried, "and big ones, too!"

"How odd!" whispered Iris, more concerned in the scrutiny of her immediate surroundings. Jenks glanced at her sharply. She was not looking at the islands, but at a curious hollow, a quarry-like depression beneath them to the right, distant about three hundred yards and not far removed from the small plateau containing the well, though isolated from it by the south angle of the main cliff.

Here, in a great circle, there was not a vestige of grass, shrub, or tree, nothing save brown rock and sand. At first the sailor deemed it to be the dried-up bed of a small lake. This hypothesis would not serve, else it would be choked with verdure. The pit stared up at them like an ominous eye, though neither paid further attention to it, for the glorious prospect mapped at their feet momentarily swept aside all other considerations.

"What a beautiful place!" murmured Iris. "I wonder what it is called."

"Limbo."

The word came instantly. The sailor's gaze was again fixed on those distant blue outlines. Miss Deane was dissatisfied.

"Nonsense!" she exclaimed. "We are not dead yet. You must find a better name than that."

"Well, suppose we christen it Rainbow Island?"

"Why 'Rainbow'?"

"That is the English meaning of 'Iris,' in Latin, you know."

"So it is. How clever of you to think of it! Tell me, what is the meaning of 'Robert,' in Greek?"

He turned to survey the north-west side of the island. "I do not know," he answered. "It might not be far-fetched to translate it as 'a ship's steward: a menial.'"

Miss Iris had meant her playful retort as a mere light-hearted quibble. It annoyed her, a young person of much consequence, to have her kindly condescension repelled.

"I suppose so," she agreed; "but I have gone through so much in a few hours that I am bewildered, apt to forget these nice distinctions."

Were these two quareling, or flirting? Who can tell?

Jenks was closely examining the reef on which the *Sirdar* struck. Some square objects were visible near the palm tree. The sun, glinting on the waves, rendered it difficult to discern their significance.

"What do you make of those?" he inquired, handing the glasses, and blandly ignoring Miss Deane's petulance. Her brain was busy with other things while she twisted the binoculars to suit her vision. Rainbow Island—Iris—it was a nice conceit. But "menial" struck a discordant note. This man was no menial in appearance or speech. Why was he so deliberately rude?

"I think they are boxes or packing-cases," she announced.

"Ah, that was my own idea. I must visit that locality."

"How? Will you swim?"

"No," he said, his stern lips relaxing in a smile, "I will not swim; and by the way, Miss Deane, be careful when you are near the water. The lagoon is swarming with sharks at present. I feel tolerably assured that at low tide, when the remnants of the gale have vanished, I will be able to walk there along the reef."

"Sharks!" she cried. "In there! What horrible surprises this speck of land contains! I should not have imagined that sharks and seals could live together."

"You are quite right," he explained, with becoming gravity. "As a rule sharks infest only the leeward side of these islands. Just now they are attracted in shoals by the wreck."

"Oh." Iris shivered slightly.

"We had better go back now. The wind is keen here, Miss Deane."

She knew that he purposely misunderstood her gesture. His attitude conveyed a rebuke. There was no further room for sentiment in their present existence; they had to deal with chill necessities. As for the sailor, he was glad that the chance turn of their conversation enabled him to warn her against the lurking dangers of the lagoon. There was no need to mention the devil-fish now; he must spare her all avoidable thrills.

They gathered the stores from the first *al fresco* dining-room and reached the cave without incident. Another fire was lighted, and whilst Iris attended to the kitchen the sailor felled several young trees. He wanted poles, and these were the right size and shape. He soon cleared a considerable space. The timber was soft and so small in girth that three cuts with the axe usually sufficed. He dragged from the beach the smallest tarpaulin he could find, and propped it against the rock in such manner that it effectually screened the mouth of the cave, though admitting light and air.

He was so busy that he paid little heed to Iris. But the odor of fried ham was wafted to him. He was lifting a couple of heavy stones to stay the canvas and keep it from flapping in the wind, when the girl called out—

"Wouldn't you like to have a wash before dinner?"

He straightened himself and looked at her. Her face and hands were shining, spotless. The change was so great that his brow wrinkled with perplexity.

"I am a good pupil," she cried. "You see I am already learning to help myself. I made a bucket out of one of the dish-covers by slinging it in two ropes.

Another dish-cover, some sand and leaves supplied basin, soap, and towel. I have cleaned the tin cups and the knives, and see, here is my greatest treasure."

She held up a small metal lamp.

"Where in the world did you find that?" he exclaimed.

"Buried in the sand inside the cave."

"Anything else?"

His tone was abrupt. She was so disappointed by the seeming want of appreciation of her industry that a gleam of amusement died from her eyes and she shook her head, stooping at once to attend to the toasting of some biscuits.

This time he was genuinely sorry.

"Forgive me, Miss Deane," he said penitently. "My words are dictated by anxiety. I do not wish you to make discoveries on your own account. This is a strange place, you know—an unpleasant one in some respects."

"Surely I can rummage about my own cave?"

"Most certainly. It was careless of me not to have examined its interior more thoroughly."

"Then why do you grumble because I found the lamp?"

"I did not mean any such thing. I am sorry."

"I think you are horrid. If you want to wash you will find the water over there. Don't wait. The ham will be frizzled to a cinder."

Unlucky Jenks! Was ever man fated to incur such unmerited odium? He savagely laved his face and neck. The fresh cool water was delightful at first, but it caused his injured nail to throb dreadfully. When he

drew near to the fire he experienced an unaccountable
sensation of weakness. Could it be possible that he was
going to faint? It was too absurd. He sank to the
ground. Trees, rocks, and sand-strewn earth indulged
in a mad dance. Iris's voice sounded weak and indistinct. It seemed to travel in waves from a great
distance. He tried to brush away from his brain these
dim fancies, but his iron will for once failed, and he
pitched headlong downwards into darkness.

When he recovered the girl's left arm was round his
neck. For one blissful instant he nestled there contentedly. He looked into her eyes and saw that she was
crying. A gust of anger rose within him that he should
be the cause of those tears.

"Damn!" he said, and tried to rise.

"Oh! are you better?" Her lips quivered pitifully.

"Yes. What happened? Did I faint?"

"Drink this."

She held a cup to his mouth and he obediently strove
to swallow the contents. It was champagne. After the
first spasm of terror, and when the application of water
to his face failed to restore consciousness, Iris had
knocked the head off the bottle of champagne.

He quickly revived. Nature had only given him a
warning that he was overdrawing his resources. He
was deeply humiliated. He did not conceive the truth,
that only a strong man could do all that he had done
and live. For thirty-six hours he had not slept. During
part of the time he fought with wilder beasts than they
knew at Ephesus. The long exposure to the sun, the
mental strain of his foreboding that the charming girl

whose life depended upon him might be exposed to even worse dangers than any yet encountered, the physical labor he had undergone, the irksome restraint he strove to place upon his conduct and utterances—all these things culminated in utter relaxation when the water touched his heated skin.

But he was really very much annoyed. A powerful man always is annoyed when forced to yield. The revelation of a limit to human endurance infuriates him. A woman invariably thinks that the man should be scolded, by way of tonic.

"How *could* you frighten me so?" demanded Iris, hysterically. "You must have felt that you were working too hard. You made me rest. Why didn't you rest yourself?"

He looked at her wistfully. This collapse must not happen again, for her sake. These two said more with eyes than lips. She withdrew her arm; her face and neck crimsoned.

"There," she said with compelled cheerfulness. "You are all right now. Finish the wine."

He emptied the tin. It gave him new life.

"I always thought," he answered gravely, "that champagne was worth its weight in gold under certain conditions. These are the conditions."

Iris reflected, with elastic rebound from despair to relief, that men in the lower ranks of life do not usually form theories on the expensive virtues of the wine of France. But her mind was suddenly occupied by a fresh disaster.

"Good gracious!" she cried. "The ham is ruined."

It was burnt black. She prepared a fresh supply. When it was ready, Jenks was himself again. They ate in silence, and shared the remains of the bottle. The man idly wondered what was the *plat du jour* at the Savoy that evening. He remembered that the last time he was there he had called for *Jambon de York aux épinards* and half a pint of Heidseck.

"*Coelum non animum mutant, qui trans mare currunt*," he thought. By a queer trick of memory he could recall the very page in Horace where this philosophical line occurs. It was in the eleventh epistle of the first book. A smile illumined his tired face.

Iris was watchful. She had never in her life cooked even a potato or boiled an egg. The ham was her first attempt.

"My cooking amuses you?" she demanded suspiciously.

"It gratifies every sense," he murmured. "There is but one thing needful to complete my happiness."

"And that is?"

"Permission to smoke."

"Smoke what?"

He produced a steel box, tightly closed, and a pipe. "I will answer you in Byron's words," he said—

"'Sublime tobacco! which from east to west
Cheers the tar's labour or the Turkman's rest.'"

"Your pockets are absolute shops," said the girl, delighted that his temper had improved. "What other stores do you carry about with you?"

He lit his pipe and solemnly gave an inventory of his worldly goods. Beyond the items she had previously seen he could only enumerate a silver dollar, a very soiled and crumpled handkerchief, and a bit of tin. A box of Norwegian matches he threw away as useless, but Iris recovered them.

"You never know what purpose they may serve," she said. In after days a weird significance was attached to this simple phrase.

"Why do you carry about a bit of tin?" she went on.

How the atmosphere of deception clung to him! Here was a man compelled to lie outrageously who, in happier years, had prided himself on scrupulous accuracy even in small things.

"Plague upon it!" he silently protested. "Subterfuge and deceit are as much at home in this deserted island as in Mayfair."

"I found it here, Miss Deane," he answered.

Luckily she interpreted "here" as applying to the cave.

"Let me see it. May I?"

He handed it to her. She could make nothing of it, so together they puzzled over it. The sailor rubbed it with a mixture of kerosene and sand. Then figures and letters and a sort of diagram were revealed. At last they became decipherable. By exercising patient ingenuity some one had indented the metal with a sharp punch until the marks assumed this aspect (see cut, following page).

Iris was quick-witted. "It is a plan of the island," she cried.

"Also the latitude and the longitude."

"What does 'J. S.' mean?"

"Probably the initials of a man's name; let us say John Smith, for instance."

"And the figures on the island, with the 'X' and the dot?"

"I cannot tell you at present," he said. "I take it that the line across the island signifies this gap or cañon, and the small intersecting line the cave. But 32 divided by 1, and an 'X' surmounted by a dot are

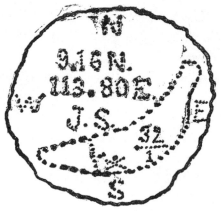

cabalistic. They would cause even Sherlock Holmes to smoke at least two pipes. I have barely started one."

She ran to fetch a glowing stick to enable him to relight his pipe.

"Why do you give me such nasty little digs?" she asked. "You need not have stopped smoking just because I stood close to you."

"Really, Miss Deane——"

"There, don't protest. I like the smell of that tobacco. I thought sailors invariably smoked rank, black stuff which they call thick twist."

"I am a beginner, as a sailor. After a few more years before the mast I may hope to reach perfection."

Their eyes exchanged a quaintly pleasant challenge. Thus the man—"She is determined to learn something of my past, but she will not succeed."

And the woman—"The wretch! He is close as an oyster. But I will make him open his mouth, see if I don't."

She reverted to the piece of tin. "It looks quite mysterious, like the things you read of in stories of pirates and buried treasure."

"Yes," he admitted. "It is unquestionably a plan, a guidance, given to a person not previously acquainted with the island but cognizant of some fact connected with it. Unfortunately none of the buccaneers I can bring to mind frequented these seas. The poor beggar who left it here must have had some other motive than searching for a cache."

"Did he dig the cave and the well, I wonder?"

"Probably the former, but not the well. No man could do it unaided."

"Why do you assume he was alone?"

He strolled towards the fire to kick a stray log. "It is only idle speculation at the best, Miss Deane," he replied. "Would you like to help me to drag some timber up from the beach? If we get a few big planks we can build a fire that will last for hours. We want some extra clothes, too, and it will soon be dark."

The request for co-operation gratified her. She complied eagerly, and without much exertion they hauled a respectable load of firewood to their new camping-ground. They also brought a number of coats to serve as coverings. Then Jenks tackled the lamp. Between the rust and the soreness of his index finger it was a most difficult operation to open it.

Before the sun went down he succeeded, and made a wick by unraveling a few strands of wool from his jersey. When night fell, with the suddenness of the tropics, Iris was able to illuminate her small domain.

They were both utterly tired and ready to drop with fatigue. The girl said "Good night," but instantly reappeared from behind the tarpaulin.

"Am I to keep the lamp alight?" she inquired.

"Please yourself, Miss Deane. Better not, perhaps. It will only burn four or five hours, any way."

Soon the light vanished, and he lay down, his pipe between his teeth, close to the cave's entrance. Weary though he was, he could not sleep forthwith. His mind was occupied with the signs on the canister head.

"32 divided by 1; an 'X' and a dot," he repeated several times. "What do they signify?"

Suddenly he sat up, with every sense alert, and grabbed his revolver. Something impelled him to look towards the spot, a few feet away, where the skeleton was hidden. It was the rustling of a bird among the trees that had caught his ear.

He thought of the white framework of a once power-ful man, lying there among the bushes, abandoned, forgotten, horrific. Then he smothered a cry of surprise.

"By Jove!" he muttered. "There is no 'X' and dot.

That sign is meant for a skull and cross-bones. It lies exactly on the part of the island where we saw that queer-looking bald patch today. First thing tomorrow, before the girl awakes, I must examine that place."

He resolutely stretched himself on his share of the spread-out coats, now thoroughly dried by sun and fire. In a minute he was sound asleep.

CHAPTER V

IRIS TO THE RESCUE

"Before mine eyes in opposition sits
Grim death."   — *Milton.*

HE awoke to find the sun high in the heavens. Iris was preparing breakfast; a fine fire was crackling cheerfully, and the presiding goddess had so altered her appearance that the sailor surveyed her with astonishment.

He noiselessly assumed a sitting posture, tucked his feet beneath him, and blinked. The girl's face was not visible from where he sat, and for a few seconds he thought he must surely be dreaming. She was attired in a neat navy-blue dress and smart blouse. Her white canvas shoes were replaced by strong leather boots. She was quite spick and span, this island Hebe.

So soundly had he slept that his senses returned but slowly. At last he guessed what had happened. She had risen with the dawn, and, conquering her natural feeling of repulsion, selected from the store he accumulated yesterday some more suitable garments than those in which she escaped from the wreck.

He quietly took stock of his own tattered condition, and passed a reflective hand over the stubble on his chin. In a few days his face would resemble a scrubbing-brush. In that mournful moment he would have exchanged even his pipe and tobacco-box—worth untold gold—for shaving tackle. Who can say why his thoughts took such trend? Twenty-four hours can effect great changes in the human mind if controlling influences are active.

Then came a sharp revulsion of feeling. His name was Robert—a menial. He reached for his boots, and Iris heard him.

"Good morning," she cried, smiling sweetly. "I thought you would never awake. I suppose you were very, very tired. You were lying so still that I ventured to peep at you a long time ago."

"Thus might Titania peep at an ogre," he said.

"You didn't look a bit like an ogre. You never do. You only try to talk like one—sometimes."

"I claim a truce until after breakfast. If my rough compliment offends you, let me depend upon a more gentle tongue than my own—

> ' Her Angel's face
> As the great eye of heaven, shyned bright,
> And made a sunshine in the shady place.'

Those lines are surely appropriate. They come from the *Faerie Queene*."

"They are very nice, but please wash quickly. The eggs will be hard."

"Eggs!"

"Yes; I made a collection among the trees. I tasted one of a lot that looked good. It was first-rate."

He had not the moral courage to begin the day with a rebuke. She was irrepressible, but she really must not do these things. He smothered a sigh in the improvised basin which was placed ready for him.

Miss Deane had prepared a capital meal. Of course the ham and biscuits still bulked large in the bill of fare, but there were boiled eggs, fried bananas and an elderly cocoanut. These things, supplemented by clear cold water, were not so bad for a couple of castaways, hundreds of miles from everywhere.

For the life of him the man could not refrain from displaying the conversational art in which he excelled. Their talk dealt with Italy, Egypt, India. He spoke with the ease of culture and enthusiasm. Once he slipped into anecdote *à propos* of the helplessness of British soldiers in any matter outside the scope of the King's Regulations.

"I remember," he said, "seeing a cavalry subaltern and the members of an escort sitting, half starved, on a number of bags piled up in the Suakin desert. And what do you think were in the bags?"

"I don't know," said Iris, keenly alert for deductions.

"Biscuits! They thought the bags contained patent fodder until I enlightened them."

It was on the tip of her tongue to pounce on him with the comment: "Then you have been an officer in the army." But she forbore. She had guessed this earlier. Yet the mischievous light in her eyes defied control. He was warned in time and pulled himself up short.

"You read my face like a book," she cried, with a delightful little *moue*.

"No printed page was ever so—legible."

He was going to say "fascinating," but checked the impulse. He went on with brisk affectation—

"Now, Miss Deane, we have gossiped too long. I am a laggard this morning; but before starting work, I have a few serious remarks to make."

"More digs?" she inquired saucily.

"I repudiate 'digs.' In the first place, you must not make any more experiments in the matter of food. The eggs were a wonderful effort, but, flattered by success, you may poison yourself."

"Secondly?"

"You must never pass out of my sight without carrying a revolver, not so much for defence, but as a signal. Did you take one when you went bird's-nesting?"

"No. Why?"

There was a troubled look in his eyes when he answered—

"It is best to tell you at once that before help reaches us we may be visited by cruel and blood-thirsty savages. I would not even mention this if it were a remote contingency. As matters stand, you ought to know that such a thing may happen. Let us trust in God's goodness that assistance may come soon. The island has seemingly been deserted for many months, and therein lies our best chance of escape. But I am obliged to warn you lest you should be taken unawares."

Iris was serious enough now.

"How do you know that such danger threatens us?" she demanded.

He countered readily. "Because I happen to have read a good deal about the China Sea and its frequenters," he said. "I am the last man in the world to alarm you needlessly. All I mean to convey is that certain precautions should be taken against a risk that is possible, not probable. No more."

She could not repress a shudder. The aspect of nature was so beneficent that evil deeds seemed to be out of place in that fair isle. Birds were singing around them. The sun was mounting into a cloudless sky. The gale had passed away into a pleasant breeze, and the sea was now rippling against the distant reef with peaceful melody.

The sailor wanted to tell her that he would defend her against a host of savages if he were endowed with many lives, but he was perforce tongue-tied. He even reviled himself for having spoken, but she saw the anguish in his face, and her woman's heart acknowledged him as her protector, her shield.

"Mr. Jenks," she said simply, "we are in God's hands. I put my trust in Him, and in you. I am hopeful, nay more, confident. I thank you for what you have done, for all that you will do. If you cannot preserve me from threatening perils no man could, for you are as brave and gallant a gentleman as lives on the earth today."

Now, the strange feature of this extraordinary and unexpected outburst of pent-up emotion was that the girl pronounced his name with the slightly emphasized accentuation of one who knew it to be a mere disguise. The man was so taken aback by her declaration of faith that the minor incident, though it did not escape him, was smothered in a tumult of feeling.

He could not trust himself to speak. He rose hastily and seized the axe to deliver a murderous assault upon a sago palm that stood close at hand.

Iris was the first to recover a degree of self-possession. For a moment she had bared her soul. With reaction came a sensitive shrinking. Her British temperament, no less than her delicate nature, disapproved these sentimental displays. She wanted to box her own ears.

With innate tact she took a keen interest in the felling of the tree.

"What do you want it for?" she inquired, when the sturdy trunk creaked and fell.

Jenks felt better now.

"This is a change of diet," he explained. "No; we don't boil the leaves or nibble the bark. When I split this palm open you will find that the interior is full of pith. I will cut it out for you, and then it will be your task to knead it with water after well washing it, pick out all the fiber, and finally permit the water to evaporate. In a couple of days the residuum will become a white powder, which, when boiled, is sago."

"Good gracious!" said Iris.

"The story sounds unconvincing, but I believe I am correct. It is worth a trial."

"I should have imagined that sago grew on a stalk like rice or wheat."

"Or Topsy!"

She laughed. A difficult situation had passed without undue effort. Unhappily the man reopened it. Whilst using a crowbar as a wedge he endeavored to put matters on a straightforward footing.

Iris to the Rescue

"A little while ago," he said, "you seemed to imply that I had assumed the name of Jenks."

But Miss Deane's confidential mood had gone. "Nothing of the kind," she said, coldly. "I think Jenks is an excellent name."

She regretted the words even as they fell from her lips. The sailor gave a mighty wrench with the bar, splitting the log to its clustering leaves.

"You are right," he said. "It is distinctive, brief, dogmatic. I cling to it passionately."

Soon afterwards, leaving Iris to the manufacture of sago, he went to the leeward side of the island, a search for turtles being his ostensible object. When the trees hid him he quickened his pace and turned to the left, in order to explore the cavity marked on the tin with a skull and cross-bones. To his surprise he hit upon the remnants of a roadway—that is, a line through the wood where there were no well-grown trees, where the ground bore traces of humanity in the shape of a wrinkled and mildewed pair of Chinese boots, a wooden sandal, even the decayed remains of a palki, or litter.

At last he reached the edge of the pit, and the sight that met his eyes held him spellbound.

The labor of many hands had torn a chasm, a quarry, out of the side of the hill. Roughly circular in shape, it had a diameter of perhaps a hundred feet, and at its deepest part, towards the cliff, it ran to a depth of forty feet. On the lower side, where the sailor stood, it descended rapidly for some fifteen feet.

Grasses, shrubs, plants of every variety, grew in profusion down the steep slopes, wherever seeds could find precarious nurture, until a point was reached about ten or eleven feet from the bottom. There all vegetation ceased as if forbidden to cross a magic circle.

Below this belt the place was a charnel-house. The bones of men and animals mingled in weird confusion. Most were mere skeletons. A few bodies—nine the sailor counted—yet preserved some resemblance of humanity. These latter were scattered among the older relics. They wore the clothes of Dyaks. Characteristic hats and weapons denoted their nationality. The others, the first harvest of this modern Golgotha, might have been Chinese coolies. When the sailor's fascinated vision could register details he distinguished yokes, baskets, odd-looking spades and picks strewed amidst the bones. The animals were all of one type, small, lanky, with long pointed skulls. At last he spied a withered hoof. They were pigs.

Over all lay a thick coating of fine sand, deposited from the eddying winds that could never reach the silent depths. The place was gruesome, horribly depressing. Jenks broke out into a clammy perspiration. He seemed to be looking at the secrets of the grave.

At last his superior intelligence asserted itself. His brain became clearer, recovered its power of analysis. He began to criticize, reflect, and this is the theory he evolved—

Some one, long ago, had discovered valuable minerals in the volcanic rock. Mining operations were in full blast when the extinct volcano took its revenge upon the human ants gnawing at its vitals and smothered them by a deadly outpouring of carbonic acid gas, the bottled-up poison of the ages. A horde of pigs, running wild over the island—placed there, no doubt, by Chinese fishers—had met the same fate whilst intent on dreadful orgy.

Then there came a European, who knew how the anhydrate gas, being heavier than the surrounding air, settled like water in that terrible hollow. He, too, had striven to wrest the treasure from the stone by driving a tunnel into the cliff. He had partly succeeded and had gone away, perhaps to obtain help, after crudely registering his knowledge on the lid of a tin canister. This, again, probably fell into the hands of another man, who, curious but unconvinced, caused himself to be set ashore on this desolate spot, with a few inadequate stores. Possibly he had arranged to be taken off within a fixed time.

But a sampan, laden with Dyak pirates, came first, and the intrepid explorer's bones rested near the well, whilst his head had gone to decorate the hut of some fierce village chief. The murderers, after burying their own dead—for the white man fought hard, witness the empty cartridges—searched the island. Some of them, ignorantly inquisitive, descended into the hollow. They remained there. The others, superstitious barbarians, fled for their lives, embarking so hastily that they took from the cave neither tools nor oil, though they would greatly prize these articles.

Such was the tragic web he spun, a compound of fact and fancy. It explained all perplexities save one. What did "$\frac{3 \cdot 2}{1}$" mean? Was there yet another fearsome riddle awaiting solution?

And then his thoughts flew to Iris. Happen what might, her bright picture was seldom absent from his brain. Suppose, egg-hunting, she had stumbled across this Valley of Death! How could he hope to keep it hidden from her? Was not the ghastly knowledge better than the horror of a chance ramble through the wood and the shock of discovery, nay, indeed, the risk of a catastrophe?

He was a man who relieved his surcharged feelings with strong language—a habit of recent acquisition. He indulged in it now and felt better. He rushed back through the trees until he caught sight of Iris industriously kneading the sago pith in one of those most useful dish-covers.

He called to her, led her wondering to the track, and pointed out the fatal quarry, but in such wise that she could not look inside it.

"You remember that round hole we saw from the summit rock?" he said. "Well, it is full of carbonic acid gas, to breathe which means unconsciousness and death. It gives no warning to the inexperienced. It is rather pleasant than otherwise. Promise me you will never come near this place again."

Now, Iris, too, had been thinking deeply. Robert Jenks bulked large in her day-dreams. Her nerves were not yet quite normal. There was a catch in her throat as she answered—

"I don't want to die. Of course I will keep away. What a horrid island this is! Yet it might be a paradise."

She bit her lip to suppress her tears, but, being the Eve in this garden, she continued—

Iris to the Rescue

"How did you find out? Is there anything—nasty—in there?"

"Yes, the remains of animals, and other things. I would not have told you were it not imperative."

"Are you keeping other secrets from me?"

"Oh, quite a number."

He managed to conjure up a smile, and the ruse was effective. She applied the words to his past history.

"I hope they will not be revealed so dramatically," she said.

"You never can tell," he answered. They were in prophetic vein that morning. They returned in silence to the cave.

"I wish to go inside, with a lamp. May I?" he asked.

"Certainly. Why not?"

He had an odd trick of blushing, this bronzed man with a gnarled soul. He could not frame a satisfactory reply, but busied himself in refilling the lamp.

"May I come too?" she demanded.

He flung aside the temptation to answer her in kind, merely assenting, with an explanation of his design. When the lamp was in order he held it close to the wall and conducted a systematic survey. The geological fault which favored the construction of the tunnel seemed to diverge to the left at the further end. The "face" of the rock exhibited the marks of persistent labor. The stone had been hewn away by main force when the dislocation of strata ceased to be helpful.

His knowledge was limited on the subject, yet Jenks believed that the material here was a hard limestone rather than the external basalt. Searching each inch with the feeble light, he paused once, with an exclamation.

"What is it?" cried Iris.

"I cannot be certain," he said, doubtfully. "Would you mind holding the lamp whilst I use a crowbar?"

In the stone was visible a thin vein, bluish white in color. He managed to break off a fair-sized lump containing a well-defined specimen of the foreign metal.

They hurried into the open air and examined the fragment with curious eyes. The sailor picked it with his knife, and the substance in the vein came off in laminated layers, small, brittle scales.

"Is it silver?" Iris was almost excited.

"I do not think so. I am no expert, but I have a vague idea—I have seen——"

He wrinkled his brows and pressed away the furrows with his hand, that physical habit of his when perplexed.

"I have it," he cried. "It is antimony."

Miss Deane pursed her lips in disdain. Antimony! What was antimony?

"So much fuss for nothing," she said.

"It is used in alloys and medicines," he explained. "To us it is useless."

He threw the piece of rock contemptuously among the bushes. But, being thorough in all that he undertook, he returned to the cave and again conducted an inquisition. The silver-hued vein became more strongly marked at the point where it disappeared downwards into a collection of rubble and sand. That was all. Did men give their toil, their lives, for this? So it would appear. Be that as it might, he had a more pressing work. If the cave still held a secret it must remain there.

Iris had gone back to her sago-kneading. Necessity had made the lady a bread-maid.

"Fifteen hundred years of philology bridged by circumstance," mused Jenks. "How Max Müller would have reveled in the incident!"

Shouldering the axe he walked to the beach. The tide was low and the circular sweep of the reef showed up irregularly, its black outlines sticking out of the vividly green water like jagged teeth.

Much débris from the steamer was lying high and dry. It was an easy task for an athletic man to reach the palm tree, yet the sailor hesitated, with almost imperceptible qualms.

"A baited rat-trap," he muttered. Then he quickened his pace. With the first active spring from rock to rock his unacknowledged doubts vanished. He might find stores of priceless utility. The reflection inspired him. Jumping and climbing like a cat, in two minutes he was near the tree.

He could now see the true explanation of its growth in a seemingly impossible place. Here the bed of the sea bulged upwards in a small sand cay, which silted round the base of a limestone rock, so different in color and formation from the coral reef. Nature, whose engineering contrivances can force springs to mountain tops, managed to deliver to this isolated refuge a sufficient supply of water to nourish the palm, and the roots, firmly lodged in deep crevices, were well protected from the waves.

Between the sailor and the tree intervened a small stretch of shallow water. Landward this submerged saddle shelved steeply into the lagoon. Although the water in the cove was twenty fathoms in depth, its crystal clearness was remarkable. The bottom, composed of marvelously white sand and broken coral, rendered other objects conspicuous. He could see plenty of fish, but not a single shark, whilst on the inner slope of the reef was plainly visible the destroyed fore part of the *Sirdar*, which had struck beyond the tree, relatively to his present standpoint. He had wondered why no boats were cast ashore. Now he saw the reason. Three of them were still fastened to the davits and carried down with the hull.

Seaward the water was not so clear. The waves created patches of foam, and long submarine plants swayed gently in the undercurrent.

To reach Palm-tree Rock—anticipating its subsequent name—he must cross a space of some thirty feet and wade up to his waist.

He made the passage with ease.

Pitched against the bole of the tree was a long narrow case, very heavy, iron-clamped, and marked with letters in black triangles and the broad arrow of the British Government.

"Rifles, by all the gods!" shouted the sailor. They were really by the Enfield Small Arms Manufactory, but his glee at this stroke of luck might be held to excuse a verbal inaccuracy.

The *Sirdar* carried a consignment of arms and ammunition from Hong Kong to Singapore. Providence had decreed that a practically inexhaustible store of cartridges should be hurled across the lagoon to the island. And here were Lee-Metfords enough to equip half a company. He would not risk the precious axe in an attempt to open the case. He must go back for a crowbar.

What else was there in this storehouse, thrust by Neptune from the ocean bed? A chest of tea, seemingly undamaged. Three barrels of flour, utterly ruined. A saloon chair, smashed from its pivot. A battered chronometer. For the rest, fragments of timber intermingled with pulverized coral and broken crockery.

A little further on, the deep-water entrance to the lagoon curved between sunken rocks. On one of them rested the *Sirdar's* huge funnel. The north-west section of the reef was bare. Among the wreckage he found a coil of stout rope and a pulley. He instantly conceived the idea of constructing an aërial line to ferry the chest of tea across the channel he had forded.

He threaded the pulley with the rope and climbed the tree, adding a touch of artistic completeness to the ruin of his trousers by the operation. He had fastened the pulley high up the trunk before he realized how much more simple it would be to break open the chest where it lay and transport its contents in small parcels.

He laughed lightly. "I am becoming addleheaded," he said to himself. "Anyhow, now the job is done I may as well make use of it."

Recoiling the rope-ends, he cast them across to the reef. In such small ways do men throw invisible dice with death. With those two lines he would, within a few fleeting seconds, drag himself back from eternity.

Picking up the axe, he carelessly stepped into the water, not knowing that Iris, having welded the incipient sago into a flat pancake, had strolled to the beach and was watching him.

The water was hardly above his knees when there came a swirling rush from the seaweed. A long tentacle shot out like a lasso and gripped his right leg. Another coiled round his waist.

"My God!" he gurgled, as a horrid sucker closed over his mouth and nose. He was in the grip of a devil-fish.

A deadly sensation of nausea almost overpowered him, but the love of life came to his aid, and he tore the suffocating feeler from his face. Then the axe whirled, and one of the eight arms of the octopus lost some of its length. Yet a fourth flung itself around his left ankle. A few feet away, out of range of the axe, and lifting itself bodily out of the water, was the dread form of the cuttle, apparently all head, with distended gills and monstrous eyes.

The sailor's feet were planted wide apart. With frenzied effort he hacked at the murderous tentacles, but the water hindered him, and he was forced to lean back, in superhuman strain, to avoid losing his balance. If once this terrible assailant got him down he knew he was lost. The very need to keep his feet prevented him from attempting to deal a mortal blow.

The cuttle was anchored by three of its tentacles. Its remaining arm darted with sinuous activity to again clutch the man's face or neck. With the axe he smote madly at the curling feeler, diverting its aim time and again, but failing to deliver an effective stroke.

With agonized prescience the sailor knew that he was yielding. Were the devil-fish a giant of its tribe he could not have held out so long. As it was, the creature could afford to wait, strengthening its grasp, tightening its coils, pulling and pumping at its prey with remorseless certainty.

He was nearly spent. In a paroxysm of despair he resolved to give way, and with one mad effort seek to bury the axe in the monster's brain. But ere he could execute this fatal project—for the cuttle would have instantly swept him into the trailing weeds—five revolver shots rang out in quick succession. Iris had reached the nearest rock.

The third bullet gave the octopus cause to reflect. It squirted forth a torrent of dark-colored fluid. Instantly the water became black, opaque. The tentacle flourishing in air thrashed the surface with impotent fury; that around Jenks's waist grew taut and rigid. The axe flashed with the inspiration of hope. Another arm was severed; the huge dismembered coil slackened and fell away.

Yet was he anchored immovably. He turned to look at Iris. She never forgot the fleeting expression of his face. So might Lazarus have looked from the tomb.

"The rope!" she screamed, dropping the revolver and seizing the loose ends lying at her feet.

She drew them tight and leaned back, pulling with all her strength. The sailor flung the axe to the rocks and grasped the two ropes. He raised himself and plunged wildly. He was free. With two convulsive strides he was at the girl's side.

He stumbled to a boulder and dropped in complete collapse. After a time he felt Iris's hand placed timidly on his shoulder. He raised his head and saw her eyes shining.

"Thank you," he said. "We are quits now."

CHAPTER VI

SOME EXPLANATIONS

FIERCE emotions are necessarily transient, but for the hour they exhaust the psychic capacity. The sailor had gone through such mental stress before it was yet noon that he was benumbed, wholly incapable of further sensation. Seneca tells how the island of Theresæa arose in a moment from the sea, thereby astounding ancient mariners, as well it might. Had this manifestation been repeated within a cable's length from the reef, Jenks was in mood to accept it as befitting the new order of things.

Being in good condition, he soon recovered his physical powers. He was outwardly little the worse for the encounter with the devil-fish. The skin around his mouth was sore. His waist and legs were bruised. One sweep of the axe had cut clean through the bulging leather of his left boot without touching the flesh. In a word, he was practically uninjured.

He had the doglike habit of shaking himself at the close of a fray. He did so now when he stood up. Iris showed clearer signs of the ordeal. Her face was drawn and haggard, the pupils of her eyes dilated. She was gazing into depths, illimitable, unexplored. Compassion awoke at sight of her.

"Come," said Jenks, gently. "Let us get back to the island."

He quietly resumed predominance, helping her over the rough pathway of the reef, almost lifting her when the difficulties were great.

He did not ask her how it happened that she came so speedily to his assistance. Enough that she had done it, daring all for his sake. She was weak and trembling. With the acute vision of the soul she saw again, and yet again, the deadly malice of the octopus, the divine despair of the man.

Reaching the firm sand, she could walk alone. She limped. Instantly her companion's blunted emotions quickened into life. He caught her arm and said hoarsely—

"Are you hurt in any way?"

The question brought her back from dreamland. A waking nightmare was happily shattered into dim fragments. She even strove to smile unconcernedly.

"It is nothing," she murmured. "I stumbled on the rocks. There is no sprain. Merely a blow, a bit of skin rubbed off, above my ankle."

"Let me carry you."

"The idea! Carry me! I will race you to the cave."

It was no idle jest. She wanted to run—to get away from that inky blotch in the green water.

"You are sure it is a trifle?"

"Quite sure. My stocking chafes a little; that is all. See, I will show you."

She stooped, and with the quick skill of woman, rolled down the stocking on her right leg. Modestly daring, she stretched out her foot and slightly lifted her dress. On the outer side of the tapering limb was an ugly bruise, scratched deeply by the coral.

He exhibited due surgical interest. His manner, his words, became professional.

"We will soon put that right," he said. "A strip off your muslin dress, soaked in brandy, will——"

"Brandy!" she exclaimed.

"Yes; we have some, you know. Brandy is a great tip for bruised wounds. It can be applied both ways, inside and out."

This was better. They were steadily drifting back to the commonplace. Whilst she stitched together some muslin strips he knocked the head off a bottle of brandy. They each drank a small quantity, and the generous spirit brought color to their wan cheeks. The sailor showed Iris how to fasten a bandage by twisting the muslin round the upper part of his boot. For the first time she saw the cut made by the axe.

"Did—the thing—grip you there?" she nervously inquired.

"There, and elsewhere. All over at once, it felt like. The beast attacked me with five arms."

She shuddered. "I don't know how you could fight it," she said. "How strong, how brave you must be."

This amused him. "The veriest coward will try to save his own life," he answered. "If you use such adjectives to me, what words can I find to do justice to you, who dared to come close to such a vile-looking creature and kill it. I must thank my stars that you carried the revolver."

"Ah!" she said, "that reminds me. You do not practice what you preach. I found your pistol lying on the stone in the cave. That is one reason why I followed you."

It was quite true. He laid the weapon aside when delving at the rock, and forgot to replace it in his belt.

"It was stupid of me," he admitted; "but I am not sorry."

"Why?"

"Because, as it is, I owe you my life."

"You owe me nothing," she snapped. "It is very thoughtless of you to run such risks. What will become of me if anything happens to you? My point of view is purely selfish, you see."

"Quite so. Purely selfish." He smiled sadly. "Selfish people of your type are somewhat rare, Miss Deane."

Not a conversation worth noting, perhaps, save in so far as it is typical of the trite utterances of people striving to recover from some tremendous ordeal. Epigrams delivered at the foot of the scaffold have always been carefully prepared beforehand.

The bandage was ready; one end was well soaked in brandy. She moved towards the cave, but he cried—

"Wait one minute. I want to get a couple of crowbars."

"What for?"

"I must go back there." He jerked his head in the direction of the reef. She uttered a little sob of dismay.

"I will incur no danger this time," he explained. "I

[104]

found rifles there. We must have them; they may mean salvation."

When Iris was determined about anything, her chin dimpled. It puckered delightfully now.

"I will come with you," she announced.

"Very well. I will wait for you. The tide will serve for another hour."

He knew he had decided rightly. She could not bear to be alone—yet. Soon the bandage was adjusted and they returned to the reef. Scrambling now with difficulty over the rough and dangerous track, Iris was secretly amazed by the remembrance of the daring activity she displayed during her earlier passage along the same precarious roadway.

Then she darted from rock to rock with the fearless certainty of a chamois. Her only stumble was caused, she recollected, by an absurd effort to avoid wetting her dress. She laughed nervously when they reached the place. This time Jenks lifted her across the intervening channel.

"Is this the spot where you fell?" he asked, tenderly.

"Yes; how did you guess it?"

"I read it in your eyes."

"Then please do not read my eyes, but look where you are going."

"Perhaps I was doing that too," he said.

They were standing on the landward side of the shallow water in which he fought the octopus.

Already the dark fluid emitted by his assailant in its final discomfiture was passing away, owing to the slight movement of the tide.

Iris was vaguely conscious of a double meaning in his words. She did not trouble to analyze them. All she knew was that the man's voice conveyed a subtle acknowledgment of her feminine divinity. The resultant thrill of happiness startled, even dismayed her. This incipient flirtation must be put a stop to instantly.

"Now that you have brought me here with so much difficulty, what are you going to do?" she said. "It will be madness for you to attempt to ford that passage again. Where there is one of those horrible things there are others, I suppose."

Jenks smiled. Somehow he knew that this strict adherence to business was a cloak for her real thoughts. Already these two were able to dispense with spoken word.

But he sedulously adopted her pretext.

"That is one reason why I brought the crowbars," he explained. "If you will sit down for a little while I will have everything properly fixed."

He delved with one of the bars until it lodged in a crevice of the coral. Then a few powerful blows with the back of the axe wedged it firmly enough to bear any ordinary strain. The rope-ends reeved through the pulley on the tree were lying where they fell from the girl's hand at the close of the struggle. He deftly knotted them to the rigid bar, and a few rapid turns of a piece of wreckage passed between the two lines strung them into a tautness that could not be attained by any amount of pulling.

Iris watched the operation in silence. The sailor always looked at his best when hard at work. The half-sullen, wholly self-contained expression left his face, which lit up with enthusiasm and concentrated intelligence. That which he essayed he did with all his might. Will power and physical force worked harmoniously. She had never before seen such a man. At such moments her admiration of him was unbounded.

He, toiling with steady persistence, felt not the inward spur which sought relief in speech, but Iris was compelled to say something.

"I suppose," she commented with an air of much wisdom, "you are contriving an overhead railway for the safe transit of yourself and the goods?"

"Y—yes."

"Why are you so doubtful about it?"

"Because I personally intended to walk across. The ropes will serve to convey the packages."

She rose imperiously. "I absolutely forbid you to enter the water again. Such a suggestion on your part is quite shameful. You are taking a grave risk for no very great gain that I can see, and if anything happens to you I shall be left all alone in this awful place."

She could think of no better argument. Her only resource was a woman's expedient—a plea for protection against threatening ills.

The sailor seemed to be puzzled how best to act.

"Miss Deane," he said, "there is no such serious danger as you imagine. Last time the cuttle caught me napping. He will not do so again. Those rifles I must have. If it will serve to reassure you, I will go along the line myself."

He made this concession grudgingly. In very truth,

if danger still lurked in the neighboring sea, he would be far less able to avoid it whilst clinging to a rope that sagged with his weight, and thus working a slow progress across the channel, than if he were on his feet and prepared to make a rush backwards or forwards.

Not until Iris watched him swinging along with vigorous overhead clutches did this phase of the undertaking occur to her.

"Stop!" she screamed.

He let go and dropped into the water, turning towards her.

"What is the matter now?" he said.

"Go on; do!"

He stood meekly on the further side to listen to her rating.

"You knew all the time that it would be better to walk, yet to please me you adopted an absurdly difficult method. Why did you do it?"

"You have answered your own question."

"Well, I am very, very angry with you."

"I'll tell you what," he said, "if you will forgive me I will try and jump back. I once did nineteen feet three inches in—er—in a meadow, but it makes such a difference when you look at a stretch of water the same width."

"I wish you would not stand there talking nonsense. The tide will be over the reef in half an hour," she cried.

Without another word he commenced operations. There was plenty of rope, and the plan he adopted was simplicity itself. When each package was securely fastened he attached it to a loop that passed over the line stretched from the tree to the crowbar. To this loop

he tied the lightest rope he could find and threw the other
end to Iris. By pulling slightly she was able to land at
her feet even the cumbrous rifle-chest, for the traveling
angle was so acute that the heavier the article the more
readily it sought the lower level.

They toiled in silence until Jenks could lay hands on
nothing more of value. Then, observing due care, he
quickly passed the channel. For an instant the girl
gazed affrightedly at the sea until the sailor stood at
her side again.

"You see," he said, "you have scared every cuttle
within miles." And he thought that he would give
many years of his life to be able to take her in his arms
and kiss away her anxiety.

But the tide had turned; in a few minutes the reef
would be partly submerged. To carry the case of rifles
to the mainland was a manifestly impossible feat, so
Jenks now did that which, done earlier, would have saved
him some labor—he broke open the chest, and found that
the weapons were apparently in excellent order.

He snapped the locks and squinted down the barrels
of half a dozen to test them. These he laid on one side.
Then he rapidly constructed a small raft from loose timbers, binding them roughly with rope, and to this argosy
he fastened the box of tea, the barrels of flour, the
broken saloon-chair, and other small articles which might
be of use. He avoided any difficulty in launching the
raft by building it close to the water's edge. When all
was ready the rising tide floated it for him; he secured
it to his longest rope, and gave it a vigorous push off
into the lagoon. Then he slung four rifles across his

shoulders, asked Iris to carry the remaining two in like manner, and began to manœuvre the raft landwards.

"Whilst you land the goods I will prepare dinner," announced the girl.

"Please be careful not to slip again on the rocks," he said.

"Indeed I will. My ankle gives me a reminder at each step."

"I was more concerned about the rifles. If you fell you might damage them, and the incoming tide will so hopelessly rust those I leave behind that they will be useless."

She laughed. This assumption at brutality no longer deceived her.

"I will preserve them at any cost, though with six in our possession there is a margin for accidents. However, to reassure you, I will go back quickly. If I fall a second time you will still be able to replace any deficiencies in our armament."

Before he could protest she started off at a run, jumping lightly from rock to rock, though the effort cost her a good deal of pain. Disregarding his shouts, she persevered until she stood safely on the sands. Then saucily waving a farewell, she set off towards the cave.

Had she seen the look of fierce despair that settled down upon Jenks's face as he turned to his task of guiding the raft ashore she might have wondered what it meant. In any case she would certainly have behaved differently.

By the time the sailor had safely landed his cargo Iris had cooked their midday meal. She achieved a fresh culinary triumph. The eggs were fried!

"I am seriously thinking of trying to boil a ham," she stated gravely. "Have you any idea how long it takes to cook one properly?"

"A quarter of an hour for each pound."

"Admirable! But we can measure neither hours nor pounds."

"I think we can do both. I will construct a balance of some kind. Then, with a ham slung to one end, and a rifle and some cartridges to the other, I will tell you the weight of the ham to an ounce. To ascertain the time, I have already determined to fashion a sun-dial. I remember the requisite divisions with reasonable accuracy, and a little observation will enable us to correct any mistakes."

"You are really very clever, Mr. Jenks," said Iris, with childlike candor. "Have you spent several years of your life in preparing for residence on a desert island?"

"Something of the sort. I have led a queer kind of existence, full of useless purposes. Fate has driven me into a corner where my odds and ends of knowledge are actually valuable. Such accidents make men millionaires."

"Useless purposes!" she repeated. "I can hardly credit that. One uses such a phrase to describe fussy people, alive with foolish activity. Your worst enemy would not place you in such a category."

"My worst enemy made the phrase effective at any rate, Miss Deane."

"You mean that he ruined your career?"

"Well—er—yes. I suppose that describes the position with fair accuracy."

"Was he a very great scoundrel?"

"He was, and is."

Jenks spoke with quiet bitterness. The girl's words had evoked a sudden flood of recollection. For the moment he did not notice how he had been trapped into speaking of himself, nor did he see the quiet content on Iris's face when she elicited the information that his chief foe was a man. A certain tremulous hesitancy in her manner when she next spoke might have warned him, but his hungry soul caught only the warm sympathy of her words, which fell like rain on parched soil.

"You are tired," she said. "Won't you smoke for a little while, and talk to me?"

He produced his pipe and tobacco, but he used his right hand awkwardly. It was evident to her alert eyes that the torn quick on his injured finger was hurting him a great deal. The exciting events of the morning had caused him temporarily to forget his wound, and the rapid coursing of the blood through the veins was now causing him agonized throbs.

With a cry of distress she sprang to her feet and insisted upon washing the wound. Then she tenderly dressed it with a strip of linen well soaked in brandy, thinking the while, with a sudden rush of color to her face, that although he could suggest this remedy for her slight hurt, he gave no thought to his own serious injury. Finally she pounced upon his pipe and tobacco-box.

"Don't be alarmed," she laughed. "I have often filled my father's pipe for him. First, you put the tobacco in loosely, taking care not to use any that is too finely powdered. Then you pack the remainder quite tightly. But I was nearly forgetting. I haven't blown through the pipe to see if it is clean."

She suited the action to the word, using much needless breath in the operation.

"That is a first-rate pipe," she declared. "My father always said that a straight stem, with the bowl at a right angle, was the correct shape. You evidently agree with him."

"Absolutely."

"You will like my father when you meet him. He is the very best man alive, I am sure."

"You two are great friends, then?"

"Great friends! He is the only friend I possess in the world."

"What! Is that quite accurate?"

"Oh, quite. Of course, Mr. Jenks, I can never forget how much I owe to you. I like you immensely, too, although you are so—so gruff to me at times. But—but —you see, my father and I have always been together. I have neither brother nor sister, not even a cousin. My dear mother died from some horrid fever when I was quite a little girl. My father is everything to me."

"Dear child!" he murmured, apparently uttering his thoughts aloud rather than addressing her directly. "So you find me gruff, eh?"

"A regular bear, when you lecture me. But that is only occasionally. You can be very nice when you like, when you forget your past troubles. And pray, why do you call me a child?"

"Have I done so?"

"Not a moment ago. How old are you, Mr. Jenks? I am twenty—twenty last December."

"And I," he said, "will be twenty-eight in August."

"Good gracious!" she gasped. "I am very sorry, but I really thought you were forty at least."

"I look it, no doubt. Let me be equally candid and admit that you, too, show your age markedly."

She smiled nervously. "What a lot of trouble you must have had to—to—to give you those little wrinkles in the corners of your mouth and eyes," she said.

"Wrinkles! How terrible!"

"I don't know. I think they rather suit you; besides, it was stupid of me to imagine you were so old. I suppose exposure to the sun creates wrinkles, and you must have lived much in the open air."

"Early rising and late going to bed are bad for the complexion," he declared, solemnly.

"I often wonder how army officers manage to exist," she said. "They never seem to get enough sleep, in the East, at any rate. I have seen them dancing for hours after midnight, and heard of them pig-sticking or schooling hunters at five o'clock next morning."

"So you assume I have been in the army?"

"I am quite sure of it."

"May I ask why?"

"Your manner, your voice, your quiet air of authority, the very way you walk, all betray you."

"Then," he said sadly, "I will not attempt to deny the fact. I held a commission in the Indian Staff Corps for nine years. It was a hobby of mine, Miss Deane, to make myself acquainted with the best means of victualing my men and keeping them in good health under all sorts of fanciful conditions and in every kind of climate, especially under circumstances when ordinary stores were not available. With that object in view I read up every possible country in which my regiment might be engaged, learnt the local names of common articles of food, and ascertained particularly what provision nature made to sustain life. The study interested me. Once, during the Soudan campaign, it was really useful, and procured me promotion."

"Tell me about it."

"During some operations in the desert it was necessary for my troop to follow up a small party of rebels mounted on camels, which, as you probably know, can go without water much longer than horses. We were almost within striking distance, when our horses completely gave out, but I luckily noticed indications which showed that there was water beneath a portion of the plain much below the general level. Half an hour's spade work proved that I was right. We took up the pursuit again, and ran the quarry to earth, and I got my captaincy."

"Was there no fight?"

He paused an appreciable time before replying. Then he evidently made up his mind to perform some disagreeable task. The watching girl could see the change in his face, the sharp transition from eager interest to angry resentment.

"Yes," he went on at last, "there was a fight. It was a rather stiff affair, because a troop of British cavalry which should have supported me had turned back, owing to the want of water already mentioned. But that did not save the officer in charge of the 24th Lancers from being severely reprimanded."

"The 24th Lancers!" cried Iris. "Lord Ventnor's regiment!"

"Lord Ventnor was the officer in question."

Her face crimsoned. "Then you know him?" she said.

"I do."

"Is he your enemy?"

"Yes."

"And that is why you were so agitated that last day on the *Sirdar*, when poor Lady Tozer asked me if I were engaged to him?"

"Yes."

"How could it affect you? You did not even know my name then?"

Poor Iris! She did not stop to ask herself why she framed her question in such manner, but the sailor was now too profoundly moved to heed the slip. She could not tell how he was fighting with himself, fiercely beating down the inner barriers of self-love, sternly determined, once and for all, to reveal himself in such light to this beautiful and bewitching woman that in future she would learn to regard him only as an outcast whose company she must perforce tolerate until relief came.

"It affected me because the sudden mention of his name recalled my own disgrace. I quitted the army six months ago, Miss Deane, under very painful circumstances. A general court-martial found me guilty of conduct unbecoming an officer and a gentleman. I was not even given a chance to resign. I was cashiered."

He pretended to speak with cool truculence. He thought to compel her into shrinking contempt. Yet his face blanched somewhat, and though he steadily kept the pipe between his teeth, and smoked with studied unconcern, his lips twitched a little.

And he dared not look at her, for the girl's wondering eyes were fixed upon him, and the blush had disappeared as quickly as it came.

"I remember something of this," she said slowly, never once averting her gaze. "There was some gossip concerning it when I first came to Hong Kong. You are Captain Robert Anstruther?"

"I am."

"And you publicly thrashed Lord Ventnor as the result of a quarrel about a woman?"

"Your recollection is quite accurate."

"Who was to blame?"

"The lady said that I was."

"Was it true?"

Robert Anstruther, late captain of Bengal Cavalry, rose to his feet. He preferred to take his punishment standing.

"The court-martial agreed with her, Miss Deane, and I am a prejudiced witness," he replied.

"Who was the—lady?"

"The wife of my colonel, Mrs. Costobell."

"Oh!"

Long afterwards he remembered the agony of that moment, and winced even at the remembrance. But he

had decided upon a fixed policy, and he was not a man
to flinch from consequences. Miss Deane must be taught
to despise him, else, God help them both, she might learn
to love him as he now loved her. So, blundering towards
his goal as men always blunder where a woman's heart
is concerned, he blindly persisted in allowing her to make
such false deductions as she chose from his words.

Iris was the first to regain some measure of self-
control.

"I am glad you have been so candid, Captain
Anstruther," she commenced, but he broke in abruptly—

"Jenks, if you please, Miss Deane. Robert Jenks."

There was a curious light in her eyes, but he did not
see it, and her voice was marvelously subdued as she
continued—

"Certainly, Mr. Jenks. Let me be equally explicit
before we quit the subject. I have met Mrs. Costobell.
I do not like her. I consider her a deceitful woman.
Your court-martial might have found a different verdict
had its members been of her sex. As for Lord
Ventnor, he is nothing to me. It is true he asked
my father to be permitted to pay his addresses to me,
but my dear old dad left the matter wholly to my decision, and I certainly never gave Lord Ventnor any
encouragement. I believe now that Mrs. Costobell lied,
and that Lord Ventnor lied, when they attributed any
dishonorable action to you, and I am glad that you beat
him in the Club. I am quite sure he deserved it."

Not one word did this strange man vouchsafe in reply.
He started violently, seized the axe lying at his feet,
and went straight among the trees, keeping his face

turned from Iris so that she might not see the tears in his eyes.

As for the girl, she began to scour her cooking utensils with much energy, and soon commenced a song. Considering that she was compelled to constantly endure the company of a degraded officer, who had been expelled from the service with ignominy, she was absurdly contented. Indeed, with the happy inconsequence of youth, she quickly threw all care to the winds, and devoted her thoughts to planning a surprise for the next day by preparing some tea, provided she could surreptitiously open the chest.

CHAPTER VII

SURPRISES

BEFORE night closed their third day on the island Jenks managed to construct a roomy tent-house, with a framework of sturdy trees selected on account of their location. To these he nailed or tied crossbeams of felled saplings; and the tarpaulins dragged from the beach supplied roof and walls. It required the united strength of Iris and himself to haul into position the heavy sheet that topped the structure, whilst he was compelled to desist from active building operations in order to fashion a rough ladder. Without some such contrivance he could not get the topmost supports adjusted at a sufficient height.

Although the edifice required at least two more days of hard work before it would be fit for habitation Iris wished to take up her quarters there immediately. This the sailor would not hear of.

"In the cave," he said, "you are absolutely sheltered from all the winds that blow or rain that falls. Our villa, however, is painfully leaky and draughty at present. When asleep, the whole body is relaxed, and you are then most open to the attacks of cold or fever, in which case, Miss Deane, I shall be reluctantly obliged to dose you with a concoction of that tree there."

He pointed to a neighboring cinchona, and Iris naturally asked why he selected that particular brand.

"Because it is quinine, not made up in nice little tabloids, but *au naturel*. It will not be a bad plan if we prepare a strong infusion, and take a small quantity every morning on the excellent principle that prevention is better than cure."

The girl laughed.

"Good gracious!" she said; "that reminds me——"

But the words died away on her lips in sudden fright. They were standing on the level plateau in front of the cave, well removed from the trees, and they could see distinctly on all sides, for the sun was sinking in a cloudless sky and the air was preternaturally clear, being free now from the tremulous haze of the hot hours.

Across the smooth expanse of sandy ground came the agonized shrieks of a startled bird—a large bird, it would seem—winging its way towards them with incredible swiftness, and uttering a succession of loud full-voiced notes of alarm.

Yet the strange thing was that not a bird was to be seen. At that hour the ordinary feathered inhabitants of the island were quietly nestling among the branches preparatory to making a final selection of the night's resting-place. None of them would stir unless actually disturbed.

Iris drew near to the sailor. Involuntarily she caught his arm. He stepped a half-pace in front of her to ward off any danger that might be heralded by this new and uncanny phenomenon. Together they strained their eyes in the direction of the approaching sound, but apparently their sight was bewitched, as nothing whatever was visible.

"Oh, what is it?" wailed Iris, who now clung to Jenks in a state of great apprehension.

The clucking noise came nearer, passed them within a yard, and was already some distance away towards the reef when the sailor burst into a hearty laugh, none the less genuine because of the relief it gave to his bewildered senses.

Reassured, but still white with fear, Iris cried: "Do speak, please, Mr. Jenks. What was it?"

"A beetle!" he managed to gasp.

"A beetle?"

"Yes, a small, insignificant-looking fellow, too—so small that I did not see him until he was almost out of range. He has the loudest voice for his size in the whole of creation. A man able to shout on the same scale could easily make himself heard for twenty miles."

"Then I do not like such beetles; I always hated them, but this latest variety is positively detestable. Such nasty things ought to be kept in zoological gardens, and not turned loose. Moreover, my tea will be boiled into spinach."

Nevertheless, the tea, though minus sugar or milk, was grateful enough and particularly acceptable to the sailor, who entertained Iris with a disquisition on the many virtues of that marvelous beverage. Curiously enough, the lifting of the veil upon the man's earlier history made these two much better friends. With more complete acquaintance there was far less tendency towards certain passages which, under ordinary conditions, could be construed as nothing else than downright flirtation.

They made the pleasing discovery that they could both sing. There was hardly an opera in vogue that one or other did not know sufficiently well to be able to recall the chief musical numbers. Iris had a sweet and sympathetic mezzo-soprano voice, Jenks an excellent baritone, and, to the secret amazement of the girl, he rendered one or two well-known Anglo-Indian barrack-room ditties with much humor.

This, then, was the *mise-en-scéne*.

Iris, seated in the broken saloon-chair, which the sailor had firmly wedged into the sand for her accommodation, was attired in a close-fitting costume selected from the small store of garments so wisely preserved by Jenks. She wore a pair of clumsy men's boots several sizes too large for her. Her hair was tied up in a gipsy knot on the back of her head, and the light of a cheerful log fire danced in her blue eyes.

Jenks, unshaven and ragged, squatted tailorwise near her. Close at hand, on two sides, the shaggy walls of rock rose in solemn grandeur. The neighboring trees, decked now in the sable livery of night, were dimly outlined against the deep misty blue of sea and sky or wholly merged in the shadow of the cliffs.

They lost themselves in the peaceful influences of the hour. Shipwrecked, remote from human kind, environed by dangers known or only conjectured, two solitary beings on a tiny island, thrown haphazard from the depths of the China Sea, this young couple, after passing unscathed through perils unknown even to the writers of melodrama, lifted up their voices in the sheer exuberance of good spirits and abounding vitality.

The girl was specially attracted by "The Buffalo Battery," a rollicking lyric known to all Anglo-India from Peshawur to Tuticorin. The air is the familiar one of the "Hen Convention," and the opening verse runs in this wise:

I love to hear the sepoy with his bold and martial tread,
And the thud of the galloping cavalry re-echoes through my head;
But sweeter far than any sound by mortal ever made
Is the tramp of the Buffalo Battery a-going to parade.
   Chorus: For it's "Haiñya! haiñya! haiñya! haiñya!"
          Twist their tails and go.
      With a "Hâthi! hâthi! hâthi!" ele-*phant* and buffa*lo*.
      "Chow-chow, chow-chow, chow-chow, chow-chow,"
         "Tēri ma!" "Chel-lo!"
      Oh, that's the way they shout all day, and drive the buffalo.

Iris would not be satisfied until she understood the meaning of the Hindustani phrases, mastered the nasal pronunciation of "haiñya," and placed the artificial accent on *phant* and *lo* in the second line of the chorus.

Jenks was concluding the last verse when there came, hurtling through the air, the weird cries of the singing beetle, returning, perchance, from successful foray on Palm-tree Rock. This second advent of the insect put an end to the concert. Within a quarter of an hour they were asleep.

Thenceforth, for ten days, they labored unceasingly, starting work at daybreak and stopping only when the light failed, finding the long hours of sunshine all too short for the manifold tasks demanded of them, yet thankful that the night brought rest. The sailor made out a programme to which he rigidly adhered. In the first place, he completed the house, which had two compartments, an inner room in which Iris slept, and an outer, which served as a shelter for their meals and provided a bedroom for the man.

Then he constructed a gigantic sky-sign on Summit Rock, the small cluster of boulders on top of the cliff. His chief difficulty was to hoist into place the tall poles he needed, and for this purpose he had to again visit Palm-tree Rock in order to secure the pulley. By exercising much ingenuity in devising shear-legs, he at last succeeded in lifting the masts into their allotted receptacles, where they were firmly secured. Finally he was able to swing into air, high above the tops of the neighboring trees, the loftiest of which he felled in order to clear the view on all sides, the name of the ship *Sirdar*, fashioned in six-foot letters nailed and spliced together in sections and made from the timbers of that ill-fated vessel.

Meanwhile he taught Iris how to weave a net out of the strands of unraveled cordage. With this, weighted by bullets, he contrived a casting-net and caught a lot of small fish in the lagoon. At first they were unable to decide which varieties were edible, until a happy expedient occurred to the girl.

"The seabirds can tell us," she said. "Let us spread out our haul on the sands and leave them. By observing those specimens seized by the birds and those they reject we should not go far wrong."

Though her reasoning was not infallible it certainly proved to be a reliable guide in this instance. Among the fish selected by the feathered connoisseurs they hit upon two species which most resembled whiting and haddock, and these turned out to be very palatable and wholesome.

Jenks knew a good deal of botany, and enough about birds to differentiate between carnivorous species and those fit for human food, whilst the salt in their most fortunate supply of hams rendered their meals almost epicurean. Think of it, ye dwellers in cities, content with stale buns and leathery sandwiches when ye venture into the wilds of a railway refreshment-room, these two castaways, marooned by queer chance on a desert island, could sit down daily to a banquet of vegetable soup, fish, a roast bird, ham boiled or fried, and a sago pudding, the whole washed down by cool spring water, or, should the need arise, a draught of the best champagne!

From the rusty rifles on the reef Jenks brought away the bayonets and secured all the screws, bolts, and other small odds and ends which might be serviceable. From the barrels he built a handy grate to facilitate Iris's cooking operations, and a careful search each morning amidst the ashes of any burnt wreckage accumulated a store of most useful nails.

The pressing need for a safe yet accessible bathing place led him and the girl to devote one afternoon to a complete survey of the coast-line. By this time they had given names to all the chief localities. The northerly promontory was naturally christened North Cape; the western, Europa Point; the portion of the reef between their habitation and Palm-tree Rock became Filey Brig; the other section North-west Reef. The flat sandy passage across the island, containing the cave, house, and well, was named Prospect Park; and the extensive stretch of sand on the south-east, with its guard of broken reefs, was at once dubbed Turtle Beach when Jenks discovered that an immense number of green turtles were paying their spring visit to the island to bury their eggs in the sand.

The two began their tour of inspection by passing the scene of the first desperate struggle to escape from the clutch of the typhoon. Iris would not be content until the sailor showed her the rock behind which he placed her for shelter whilst he searched for water. For a moment the recollection of their unfortunate companions on board ship brought a lump into her throat and dimmed her eyes.

"I remember them in my prayers every night," she confided to him. "It seems so unutterably sad that they should be lost, whilst we are alive and happy."

The man distracted her attention by pointing out the embers of their first fire. It was the only way to choke back the tumultuous feelings that suddenly stormed his heart. Happy! Yes, he had never before known such happiness. How long would it last? High up on the cliff swung the signal to anxious searchers of the sea that here would be found the survivors of the *Sirdar*. And then, when rescue came, when Miss Deane became once more the daughter of a wealthy baronet, and he a disgraced and a nameless outcast——! He set his teeth and savagely struck at a full cup of the pitcher-plant which had so providentially relieved their killing thirst.

"Oh, why did you do that?" pouted Iris. "Poor

thing! it was a true friend in need. I wish I could do something for it to make it the best and leafiest plant of its kind on the island."

"Very well!" he answered; "you can gratify your wish. A tinful of fresh water from the well, applied daily to its roots, will quickly achieve that end."

The moroseness of his tone and manner surprised her. For once her quick intuition failed to divine the source of his irritation.

"You give your advice ungraciously," she said, "but I will adopt it nevertheless."

A harmless incident, a kindly and quite feminine resolve, yet big with fate for both of them.

Jenks's unwonted ill-humor—for the passage of days had driven from his face all its harshness, and from his tongue all its assumed bitterness—created a passing cloud until the physical exertion of scrambling over the rocks to round the North Cape restored their normal relations.

A strong current raced by this point to the southeast, and tore away the outlying spur of the headland to such an extent that the sailor was almost inclined to choose the easier way through the trees. Yet he persevered, and it may be confessed that the opportunities thus afforded of grasping the girl's arm, of placing a steadying hand on her shoulder, were dominant factors in determining his choice.

At last they reached the south side, and here they at once found themselves in a delightfully secluded and tiny bay, sandy, tree-lined, sheltered on three sides by cliffs and rocks.

Surprises

"Oh," cried Iris, excitedly, "what a lovely spot! a perfect Smugglers' Cove."

"Charming enough to look at," was the answering comment, "but open to the sea. If you look at the smooth riband of water out there, you will perceive a passage through the reef. A great place for sharks, Miss Deane, but no place for bathers."

"Good gracious! I had forgotten the sharks. I suppose they must live, horrid as they are, but I don't want them to dine on me."

The mention of such disagreeable adjuncts to life on the island no longer terrified her. Thus do English newcomers to India pass the first three months' residence in the country in momentary terror of snakes, and the remaining thirty years in complete forgetfulness of them.

They passed on. Whilst traversing the coral-strewn south beach, with its patches of white soft sand baking in the direct rays of the sun, Jenks perceived traces of the turtle which swarmed in the neighboring sea.

"Delicious eggs and turtle soup!" he announced when Iris asked him why he was so intently studying certain marks on the sand, caused by the great sea-tortoise during their nocturnal visits to the breeding-ground.

"If they are green turtle," he continued, "we are in the lap of luxury. They lard the alderman and inspire the poet. When a ship comes to our assistance I will persuade the captain to freight the vessel with them and make my fortune."

"I suppose, under the circumstances, you were not a rich man, Mr. Jenks," said Iris, timidly.

"I possess a wealthy bachelor uncle, who made me his heir and allowed me four hundred a year; so I was a sort of Crœsus among Staff Corps officers. When the smash came he disowned me by cable. By selling my ponies and my other belongings I was able to walk out of my quarters penniless but free from debt."

"And all through a deceitful woman!"

"Yes."

Iris peeped at him from under the brim of her sou'wester. He seemed to be absurdly contented, so different was his tone in discussing a necessarily painful topic to the attitude he adopted during the attack on the pitcher-plant.

She was puzzled, but ventured a further step.

"Was she very bad to you, Mr. Jenks?"

He stopped and laughed—actually roared at the suggestion.

"Bad to me!" he repeated. "I had nothing to do with her. She was humbugging her husband, not me. Fool that I was, I could not mind my own business."

So Mrs. Costobell was not flirting with the man who suffered on her account. It is a regrettable but true statement that Iris would willingly have hugged Mrs. Costobell at that moment. She walked on air during the next half-hour of golden silence, and Jenks did not remind her that they were passing the gruesome Valley of Death.

Rounding Europa Point, the sailor's eyes were fixed on their immediate surroundings, but Iris gazed dreamily ahead. Hence it was that she was the first to cry in amazement—

Surprises

"A boat! See, there! On the rocks!"

There was no mistake. A ship's boat was perched high and dry on the north side of the cape. Even as they scrambled towards it Jenks understood how it had come there.

When the *Sirdar* parted amidships the after section fell back into the depths beyond the reef, and this boat must have broken loose from its davits and been driven ashore here by the force of the western current.

Was it intact? Could they escape? Was this ark stranded on the island for their benefit? If it were seaworthy, whither should they steer—to those islands whose blue outlines were visible on the horizon?

These and a hundred other questions coursed through his brain during the race over the rocks, but all such wild speculations were promptly settled when they reached the craft, for the keel and the whole of the lower timbers were smashed into matchwood.

But there were stores on board. Jenks remembered that Captain Ross's foresight had secured the provisioning of all the ship's boats soon after the first wild rush to steady the vessel after the propeller was lost. Masts, sails, oars, seats—all save two water-casks—had gone; but Jenks, with eager hands, unfastened the lockers, and here he found a good supply of tinned meats and biscuits. They had barely recovered from the excitement of this find when the sailor noticed that behind the rocks on which the craft was firmly lodged lay a small natural basin full of salt water, replenished and freshened by the spray of every gale, and completely shut off from all seaward access.

It was not more than four feet deep, beautifully carpeted with sand, and secluded by rocks on all sides. Not the tiniest crab or fish was to be seen. It provided an ideal bath.

Iris was overjoyed. She pointed towards their habitation.

"Mr. Jenks," she said, "I will be with you at tea-time."

He gathered all the tins he was able to carry and strode off, enjoining her to fire her revolver if for the slightest reason she wanted assistance, and giving a parting warning that if she delayed too long he would come and shout to her.

"I wonder," said the girl to herself, watching his retreating figure, "what he is afraid of. Surely by this time we have exhausted the unpleasant surprises of the island. Anyhow, now for a splash!"

She was hardly in the water before she began to be afraid on account of Jenks. Suppose anything happened to him whilst she was thoughtlessly enjoying herself here. So strongly did the thought possess her that she hurriedly dressed again and ran off to find him.

He was engaged in fastening a number of bayonets transversely to a long piece of timber.

"What are you doing that for?" she asked.

"Why did you return so soon? Did anything alarm you?"

"I thought you might get into mischief," she confessed.

"No. On the other hand, I am trying to make trouble for any unwelcome visitors," he replied. "This is a *cheval de frise,* which I intend to set up in front of our cave in case we are compelled to defend ourselves against an attack by savages. With this barring the way they cannot rush the position."

She sighed. Rainbow Island was a wild spot after all. Did not thorns and briers grow very close to the gates of Eden?

On the nineteenth day of their residence on the island the sailor climbed, as was his invariable habit, to the Summit Rock whilst Iris prepared breakfast. At this early hour the horizon was clearly cut as the rim of a sapphire. He examined the whole arc of the sea with his glasses, but not a sail was in sight. According to his calculations, the growing anxiety as to the fate of the *Sirdar* must long ere this have culminated in the dispatch from Hong Kong or Singapore of a special search vessel, whilst British warships in the China Sea would be warned to keep a close lookout for any traces of the steamer, to visit all islands on their route, and to question fishermen whom they encountered. So help might come any day, or it might be long deferred. He could not pierce the future, and it was useless to vex his soul with questionings as to what might happen next week. The great certainty of the hour was Iris—the blue-eyed, smiling divinity who had come into his life—waiting for him down there beyond the trees, waiting to welcome him with a sweet-voiced greeting; and he knew, with a fierce devouring joy, that her cheek would not pale nor her lip tremble when he announced that at least another sun must set before the expected relief reached them.

He replaced the glasses in their case and dived into the wood, giving a passing thought to the fact that the wind, after blowing steadily from the south for nearly a week, had veered round to the north-east during the night. Did the change portend a storm? Well, they were now prepared for all such eventualities, and he had not forgotten that they possessed, among other treasures, a box of books for rainy days. And a rainy day with Iris for company! What gale that ever blew could offer such compensation for enforced idleness?

The morning sped in uneventful work. Iris did not neglect her cherished pitcher-plant. After luncheon it was her custom now to carry a dishful of water to its apparently arid roots, and she rose to fulfil her self-imposed task.

"Let me help you," said Jenks. "I am not very busy this afternoon."

"No, thank you. I simply won't allow you to touch that shrub. The dear thing looks quite glad to see me. It drinks up the water as greedily as a thirsty animal."

"Even a cabbage has a heart, Miss Deane."

She laughed merrily. "I do believe you are offering me a compliment," she said. "I must indeed have found favor in your eyes."

He had schooled himself to resist the opening given by this class of retort, so he turned to make some corrections in the scale of the sun-dial he had constructed, aided therein by daily observations with the sextant left by the former inhabitant of the cave.

Iris had been gone perhaps five minutes when he heard a distant shriek, twice repeated, and then there came faintly to his ears his own name, not "Jenks," but "Robert," in the girl's voice. Something terrible had happened. It was a cry of supreme distress. Mortal agony or overwhelming terror alone could wring that name from her lips. Precisely in such moments this man acted with the decision, the unerring judgment, the instantaneous acceptance of great risk to accomplish great results, that marked him out as a born soldier.

He rushed into the house and snatched from the rifle-rack one of the six Lee-Metfords reposing there in apple-pie order, each with a filled magazine attached and a cartridge already in position.

Then he ran, with long swift strides, not through the trees, where he could see nothing, but towards the beach, whence, in forty yards, the place where Iris probably was would become visible.

At once he saw her, struggling in the grasp of two ferocious-looking Dyaks, one, by his garments, a person of consequence, the other a half-naked savage, hideous and repulsive in appearance. Around them seven men, armed with guns and parangs, were dancing with excitement.

Iris's captors were endeavoring to tie her arms, but she was a strong and active Englishwoman, with muscles well knit by the constant labor of recent busy days and a frame developed by years of horse-riding and tennis-playing. The pair evidently found her a tough handful, and the inferior Dyak, either to stop her screams—for she was shrieking "Robert, come to me!" with all her might—or to stifle her into submission, roughly placed his huge hand over her mouth.

These things the sailor noticed instantly. Some men, brave to rashness, ready as he to give his life to save her, would have raced madly over the intervening ground, scarce a furlong, and attempted a heroic combat of one against nine.

Not so Jenks.

With the methodical exactness of the parade-ground he settled down on one knee and leveled the rifle. At that range the Lee-Metford bullet travels practically point-blank. Usually it is deficient in "stopping" power, but he had provided against this little drawback by notching all the cartridges in the six rifles after the effective manner devised by an expert named Thomas Atkins during the Tirah campaign.

None of the Dyaks saw him. All were intent on the sensational prize they had secured, a young and beautiful white woman so contentedly roaming about the shores of this Fetish island. With the slow speed advised by the Roman philosopher, the backsight and foresight of the Lee-Metford came into line with the breast of the coarse brute clutching the girl's face.

Then something bit him above the heart and simultaneously tore half of his back into fragments. He fell, with a queer sob, and the others turned to face this unexpected danger.

Iris, knowing only that she was free from that hateful grasp, wrenched herself free from the chief's hold, and ran with all her might along the beach, to Jenks and safety.

Again, and yet again, the rifle gave its short, sharp snarl, and two more Dyaks collapsed on the sand. Six were left, their leader being still unconsciously preserved from death by the figure of the flying girl.

A fourth Dyak dropped.

The survivors, cruel savages but not cowards, unslung their guns. The sailor, white-faced, grim, with an unpleasant gleam in his deep-set eyes and a lower jaw protruding, noticed their preparations.

"To the left!" he shouted. "Run towards the trees!"

Iris heard him and strove to obey. But her strength was failing her, and she staggered blindly. After a few despairing efforts she lurched feebly to her knees, and tumbled face downwards on the broken coral that had tripped her faltering footsteps.

Jenks was watching her, watching the remaining Dyaks, from whom a spluttering volley came, picking out his quarry with the murderous ease of a terrier in a rat-pit. Something like a bee in a violent hurry hummed past his ear, and a rock near his right foot was struck a tremendous blow by an unseen agency. He liked this. It would be a battle, not a battue.

The fifth Dyak crumpled into the distortion of death, and then their leader took deliberate aim at the kneeling marksman who threatened to wipe him and his band out of existence. But his deliberation, though skilful, was too profound. The sailor fired first, and was professionally astonished to see the gaudily attired individual tossed violently backward for many yards, finally pitching headlong to the earth. Had he been charged by a bull in full career he could not have been more utterly discomfited. The incident was sensational but inexplicable.

Yet another member of the band was prostrated ere the two as yet unscathed thought fit to beat a retreat. This they now did with celerity, but they dragged their chief with them. It was no part of Jenks's programme to allow them to escape. He aimed again at the man nearest the trees. There was a sharp click and nothing more. The cartridge was a mis-fire. He hastily sought to eject it, and the rifle jammed. These little accidents will happen, even in a good weapon like the Lee-Metford.

Springing to his feet with a yell he ran forward. The flying men caught a glimpse of him and accelerated their movements. Just as he reached Iris they vanished among the trees.

Slinging the rifle over his shoulder, he picked up the girl in his arms. She was conscious, but breathless.

"You are not hurt?" he gasped, his eyes blazing into her face with an intensity that she afterwards remembered as appalling.

"No," she whispered.

"Listen," he continued in labored jerks. "Try and obey me—exactly. I will carry you—to the cave. Stop there. Shoot any one you see—till I come."

She heard him wonderingly. Was he going to leave her, now that he had her safely clasped to his breast? Impossible! Ah, she understood. Those men must have landed in a boat. He intended to attack them again. He was going to fight them single-handed, and she would not know what happened to him until it was all over. Gradually her vitality returned. She almost smiled at the fantastic conceit that *she* would desert *him.*

Jenks placed her on her feet at the entrance to the cave.

"You understand," he cried, and without waiting for an answer, ran to the house for another rifle. This time, to her amazement, he darted back through Prospect Park towards the south beach. The sailor knew that the Dyaks had landed at the sandy bay Iris had christened Smugglers' Cove. They were acquainted with the passage through the reef and came from the distant islands. Now they would endeavor to escape by the same channel. They must be prevented at all costs.

He was right. As they came out into the open he saw three men, not two, pushing off a large sampan. One of them, *mirabile dictu*, was the chief. Then Jenks understood that his bullet had hit the lock of the Dyak's uplifted weapon, with the result already described. By a miracle he had escaped.

He coolly prepared to slay the three of them with the same calm purpose that distinguished the opening phase of this singularly one-sided conflict. The distance was much greater, perhaps 800 yards from the point where the boat came into view. He knelt and fired. He judged that the missile struck the craft between the trio.

"I didn't allow for the sun on the side of the foresight," he said. "Or perhaps I am a bit shaky after the run. In any event they can't go far."

A hurrying step on the coral behind him caught his ear. Instantly he sprang up and faced about—to see Iris.

"They are escaping," she said.

"No fear of that," he replied, turning away from her.

"Where are the others?"

"Dead!"

"Do you mean that you killed nearly all those men?"

"Six of them. There were nine in all."

He knelt again, lifting the rifle. Iris threw herself on her knees by his side. There was something awful to her in this chill and business-like declaration of a fixed purpose.

"Mr. Jenks," she said, clasping her hands in an agony of entreaty, "do not kill more men for my sake!"

"For my own sake, then," he growled, annoyed at the interruption, as the sampan was afloat.

"Then I ask you for God's sake not to take another life. What you have already done was unavoidable, perhaps right. This is murder!"

He lowered his weapon and looked at her.

"If those men get away they will bring back a host to avenge their comrades—and secure you," he added.

"It may be the will of Providence for such a thing to happen. Yet I implore you to spare them."

He placed the rifle on the sand and raised her tenderly, for she had yielded to a paroxysm of tears. Not another word did either of them speak in that hour. The large triangular sail of the sampan was now bellying out in the south wind. A figure stood up in the stern of the boat and shook a menacing arm at the couple on the beach.

It was the Malay chief, cursing them with the rude eloquence of his barbarous tongue. And Jenks well knew what he was saying.

CHAPTER VIII

PREPARATIONS

THEY looked long and steadfastly at the retreating boat. Soon it diminished to a mere speck on the smooth sea. The even breeze kept its canvas taut, and the sailor knew that no ruse was intended—the Dyaks were flying from the island in fear and rage. They would return with a force sufficient to insure the wreaking of their vengeance.

That he would again encounter them at no distant date Jenks had no doubt whatever. They would land in such numbers as to render any resistance difficult and a prolonged defence impossible. Would help come first? —a distracting question to which definite answer could not be given. The sailor's brow frowned in deep lines; his brain throbbed now with an anxiety singularly at variance with his cool demeanor during the fight. He was utterly unconscious that his left arm encircled the shoulder of the girl until she gently disengaged herself and said appealingly—

"Please, Mr. Jenks, do not be angry with me. I could not help it. I could not bear to see you shoot them."

Then he abruptly awoke to the realities of the moment.

"Come," he said, his drawn features relaxing into a wonderfully pleasing smile. "We will return to our castle. We are safe for the remainder of this day, at any rate."

Something must be said or done to reassure her. She was still grievously disturbed, and he naturally ascribed her agitation to the horror of her capture. He dreaded a complete collapse if any further alarms threatened at once. Yet he was almost positive—though search alone would set at rest the last misgiving—that only one sampan had visited the island. Evidently the Dyaks were unprepared as he for the events of the preceding half-hour. They were either visiting the island to procure turtle and *bêche-de-mer* or had merely called there *en route* to some other destination, and the change in the wind had unexpectedly compelled them to put ashore. Beyond all doubt they must have been surprised by the warmth of the reception they encountered.

Probably, when he went to Summit Rock that morning, the savages had lowered their sail and were steadily paddling north against wind and current. The most careful scrutiny of the sea would fail to reveal them beyond a distance of six or seven miles at the utmost.

After landing in the hidden bay on the south side, they crossed the island through the trees instead of taking the more natural open way along the beach. Why? The fact that he and Iris were then passing the grown-over tract leading to the Valley of Death instantly determined this point. The Dyaks knew of this affrighting hollow, and would not approach any nearer to it

than was unavoidable. Could he twist this circumstance
to advantage if Iris and he were still stranded there when
the superstitious sea-rovers next put in an appearance?
He would see. All depended on the girl's strength. If
she gave way now—if, instead of taking instant measures for safety, he were called upon to nurse her through
a fever—the outlook became not only desperate but
hopeless.

And, whilst he bent his brows in worrying thought,
the color was returning to Iris's cheeks, and natural
buoyancy to her step. It is the fault of all men to
underrate the marvelous courage and constancy of
woman in the face of difficulties and trials. Jenks was
no exception to the rule.

"You do not ask me for any account of my adventures," she said quietly, after watching his perplexed
expression in silence for some time.

Her tone almost startled him, its unassumed cheerfulness was so unlooked for.

"No," he answered. "I thought you were too over-
wrought to talk of them at present."

"Overwrought! Not a bit of it! I was dead beat
with the struggle and with screaming for you, but please
don't imagine that I am going to faint or treat you to
a display of hysteria now that all the excitement has
ended. I admit that I cried a little when you pushed
me aside on the beach and raised your gun to fire at those
poor wretches flying for their lives. Yet perhaps I was
wrong to hinder you."

"You were wrong," he gravely interrupted.

"Then you should not have heeded me. No, I don't

mean that. You always consider me first, don't you? No matter what I ask you to do you endeavor to please me, even when you know all the time that I am acting or speaking foolishly."

The unthinking *naïveté* of her words sent the blood coursing wildly through his veins.

"Never mind," she went on with earnest simplicity. "God has been very good to us. I cannot believe that He has preserved us from so many dangers to permit us to perish miserably a few hours, or days, before help comes. And I *do* want to tell you exactly what happened."

"Then you shall," he answered. "But first drink this." They had reached their camping-ground, and he hastened to procure a small quantity of brandy.

She swallowed the spirit with a protesting *moue*. She really needed no such adventitious support, she said.

"All right," commented Jenks. "If you don't want a drink, I do."

"I can quite believe it," she retorted. "*Your* case is very different. *I* knew the men would not hurt me—after the first shock of their appearance had passed, I mean—I also knew that you would save me. But you, Mr. Jenks, had to do the fighting. You were called upon to rescue precious me. Good gracious! No wonder you were excited."

The sailor mentally expressed his inability to grasp the complexities of feminine nature, but Iris rattled on—

"I carried my tin of water to the pitcher-plant, and was listening to the greedy roots gurgling away for dear life, when suddenly four men sprang out from among the trees and seized my arms before I could reach my revolver."

"Thank Heaven you failed."

"You think that if I had fired at them they would have retaliated. Yes, especially if I had hit the chief. But it was he who instantly gave some order, and I suppose it meant that they were not to hurt me. As a matter of fact, they seemed to be quite as much astonished as I was alarmed. But if they could hold my hands they could not stop my voice so readily. Oh! didn't I yell?"

"You did."

"I suppose you could not hear me distinctly?"

"Quite distinctly."

"Every word?"

"Yes."

She bent to pick some leaves and bits of dry grass from her dress. "Well, you know," she continued rapidly, "in such moments one cannot choose one's words. I just shouted the first thing that came into my head."

"And I," he said, "picked up the first rifle I could lay hands on. Now, Miss Deane, as the affair has ended so happily, may I venture to ask you to remain in the cave until I return?"

"Oh, please——" she began.

"Really, I must insist. I would not leave you if it were not quite imperative. You *cannot* come with me."

Then she understood one at least of the tasks he must perform, and she meekly obeyed.

He thought it best to go along Turtle Beach to the cove, and thence follow the Dyaks' trail through the wood, as this line of advance would entail practically a complete circuit of the island. He omitted no precautions in his advance. Often he stopped and listened intently. Whenever he doubled a point or passed among the trees he crept back and peered along the way he had come, to see if any lurking foes were breaking shelter behind him.

The marks on the sand proved that only one sampan had been beached. Thence he found nothing of special interest until he came upon the chief's gun, lying close to the trees on the north side. It was a very ornamental . weapon, a muzzle-loader. The stock was inlaid with gold and ivory, and the piece had evidently been looted from some mandarin's junk surprised and sacked in a former foray.

The lock was smashed by the impact of the Lee-Metford bullet, but close investigation of the trigger-guard, and the discovery of certain unmistakable evidences on the beach, showed that the Dyak leader had lost two if not three fingers of his right hand.

"So he has something more than his passion to nurse," mused Jenks. "That at any rate is fortunate. He will be in no mood for further enterprise for some time to come."

He dreaded lest any of the Dyaks should be only badly wounded and likely to live. It was an actual relief to his nerves to find that the improvised Dum-dums had done their work too well to permit anxiety on that score. On the principle that a "dead Injun is a good Injun" these Dyaks were good Dyaks.

He gathered the guns, swords and krisses of the slain,

with all their uncouth belts and ornaments. In pursuance of a vaguely defined plan of future action he also
divested some of the men of their coarse garments, and
collected six queer-looking hats, shaped like inverted
basins. These things he placed in a heap near the
pitcher-plants. Thenceforth, for half an hour, the
placid surface of the lagoon was disturbed by the black
dorsal fins of many sharks.

To one of the sailor's temperament there was nothing
revolting in the concluding portion of his task. He had
a God-given right to live. It was his paramount duty,
remitted only by death itself, to endeavor to save Iris
from the indescribable fate from which no power could
rescue her if ever she fell into the hands of these vin-
dictive savages. Therefore it was war between him and
them, war to the bitter end, war with no humane mitiga-
tion of its horrors and penalties, the last dread arbitra-
ment of man forced to adopt the methods of the tiger.

His guess at the weather conditions heralded by the
change of wind was right. As the two partook of their
evening meal the complaining surf lashed the reef, and
the tremulous branches of the taller trees voiced the
approach of a gale. A tropical storm, not a typhoon,
but a belated burst of the periodic rains, deluged the
island before midnight. Hours earlier Iris retired, utterly worn by the events of the day. Needless to say,
there was no singing that evening. The gale chanted a
wild melody in mournful chords, and the noise of the
watery downpour on the tarpaulin roof of Belle Vue
Castle was such as to render conversation impossible,
save in wearying shouts.

Luckily, Jenks's carpentry was effective, though rough. The building was water-tight, and he had calked every crevice with unraveled rope until Iris's apartment was free from the tiniest draught.

The very fury of the external turmoil acted as a lullaby to the girl. She was soon asleep, and the sailor was left to his thoughts.

Sleep he could not. He smoked steadily, with a magnificent prodigality, for his small stock of tobacco was fast diminishing. He ransacked his brains to discover some method of escape from this enchanted island, where fairies jostled with demons, and hours of utter happiness found their bane in moments of frightful peril.

Of course he ought to have killed those fellows who escaped. Their sampan might have provided a last desperate expedient if other savages effected a landing. Well, there was no use in being wise after the event, and, scheme as he might, he could devise no way to avoid disaster during the next attack.

This, he felt certain, would take place at night. The Dyaks would land in force, rush the cave and hut, and overpower him by sheer numbers. The fight, if fight there was, would be sharp, but decisive. Perhaps, if he received some warning, Iris and he might retreat in the darkness to the cover of the trees. A last stand could be made among the boulders on Summit Rock. But of what avail to purchase their freedom until daylight? And then——

If ever man wrestled with desperate problem, Jenks wrought that night. He smoked and pondered until the storm passed, and, with the changefulness of a poet's muse, a full moon flooded the island in glorious radiance.

He rose, opened the door, and stood without, listening for a little while to the roaring of the surf and the crash of the broken coral swept from reef and shore by the backwash.

The petty strife of the elements was soothing to him.

"They are snarling like whipped dogs," he said aloud. "One might almost fancy her ladyship the Moon appearing on the scene as a Uranian Venus, cowing sea and storm by the majesty of her presence."

Pleased with the conceit, he looked steadily at the brilliant luminary for some time. Then his eyes were attracted by the strong lights thrown upon the rugged face of the precipice into which the cavern burrowed. Unconsciously relieving his tired senses, he was idly wondering what trick of color Turner would have adopted to convey those sharp yet weirdly beautiful contrasts, when suddenly he uttered a startled exclamation.

"By Jove!" he murmured. "I never noticed that before."

The feature which so earnestly claimed his attention was a deep ledge, directly over the mouth of the cave, but some forty feet from the ground. Behind it the wall of rock sloped darkly inwards, suggesting a recess extending by haphazard computation at least a couple of yards. It occurred to him that perhaps the fault in the interior of the tunnel had its outcrop here, and the deodorizing influences of rain and sun had extended the weak point thus exposed in the bold panoply of stone.

He surveyed the ledge from different points of view. It was quite inaccessible, and most difficult to estimate accurately from the ground level. The sailor was a man of action. He chose the nearest tall tree and began to climb. He was not eight feet from the ground before several birds flew out from its leafy recesses, filling the air with shrill clucking.

"The devil take them!" he growled, for he feared that the commotion would awaken Iris. He was still laboriously worming his way through the inner maze of branches when a well-known voice reached him from the ground.

"Mr. Jenks, what on earth are you doing up there?"

"Oh! so those wretched fowls aroused you?" he replied.

"Yes; but why did you arouse them?"

"I had a fancy to roost by way of a change."

"Please be serious."

"I am more than serious. This tree grows a variety of small sharp thorn that induces a maximum of gravity—before one takes the next step."

"But why do you keep on climbing?"

"It is sheer lunacy, I admit. Yet on such a moonlit night there is some reasonable ground for even a mad excuse."

"Mr. Jenks, tell me at once what you are doing."

Iris strove to be severe, but there was a touch of anxiety in her tone that instantly made the sailor apologetic. He told her about the ledge, and explained his half-formed notion that here they might secure a safe retreat in case of further attack—a refuge from which they might defy assault during many days. It was, he said, absolutely impossible to wait until the morning. He must at once satisfy himself whether the project was impracticable or worthy of further investigation.

So the girl only enjoined him to be careful, and he vigorously renewed the climb. At last, some twenty-five feet from the ground, an accidental parting in the branches enabled him to get a good look at the ledge. One glance set his heart beating joyously. It was at least fifteen feet in length; it shelved back until its depth was lost in the blackness of the shadows, and the floor must be either nearly level or sloping slightly inwards to the line of the fault.

The place was a perfect eagle's nest. A chamois could not reach it from any direction; it became accessible to man only by means of a ladder or a balloon.

More excited by this discovery than he cared for Iris to know, he endeavored to appear unconcerned when he regained the ground.

"Well," she said, "tell me all about it."

He described the nature of the cavity as well as he understood it at the moment, and emphasized his previous explanation of its virtues. Here they might reasonably hope to make a successful stand against the Dyaks.

"Then you feel sure that those awful creatures will come back?" she said slowly.

"Only too sure, unfortunately."

"How remorseless poor humanity is when the veneer is stripped off! Why cannot they leave us in peace?

I suppose they now cherish a blood feud against us. Perhaps, if I had not been here, they would not have injured you. Somehow I seem to be bound up with your misfortunes."

"I would not have it otherwise were it in my power," he answered. For an instant he left unchallenged the girl's assumption that she was in any way responsible for the disasters which had broken up his career. He looked into her eyes and almost forgot himself. Then the sense of fair dealing that dominates every true gentleman rose within him and gripped his wavering emotions with ruthless force. Was this a time to play upon the high-strung sensibilities of this youthful daughter of the gods, to seek to win from her a confession of love that a few brief days or weeks might prove to be only a spasmodic, but momentarily all-powerful, gratitude for the protection he had given her?

And he spoke aloud, striving to laugh, lest his words should falter—

"You can console yourself with the thought, Miss Deane, that your presence on the island will in no way affect my fate at the hands of the Dyaks. Had they caught me unprepared today my head would now be covered with a solution of the special varnish they carry on every foreign expedition."

"Varnish?" she exclaimed.

"Yes, as a preservative, you understand."

"And yet these men are human beings!"

"For purposes of classification, yes. Keeping to strict fact, it was lucky for me that you raised the alarm, and gave me a chance to discount the odds of mere numbers. So, you see, you really did me a good turn."

"What can be done now to save our lives? Anything will be better than to await another attack."

"The first thing to do is to try to get some sleep before daylight. How did you know I was not in the Castle?"

"I cannot tell you. I awoke and knew you were not near me. If I wake in the night I can always tell whether or not you are in the next room. So I dressed and came out."

"Ah!" he said, quietly. "Evidently I snore."

This explanation killed romance.

Iris retreated and the sailor, tired out at last, managed to close his weary eyes.

Next morning he hastily constructed a pole of sufficient length and strong enough to bear his weight, by tying two sturdy young trees together with ropes. Iris helped him to raise it against the face of the precipice, and he at once climbed to the ledge.

Here he found his observations of the previous night abundantly verified. The ledge was even wider than he dared to hope, nearly ten feet deep in one part, and it sloped sharply downwards from the outer lip of the rock. By lying flat and carefully testing all points of view, he ascertained that the only possible positions from which even a glimpse of the interior floor could be obtained were the branches of a few tall trees and the extreme right of the opposing precipice, nearly ninety yards distant. There was ample room to store water and provisions, and he quickly saw that even some sort

of shelter from the fierce rays of the sun and the often
piercing cold of the night might be achieved by judi-
ciously rigging up a tarpaulin.

"This is a genuine bit of good luck," he mused.
"Here, provided neither of us is hit, we can hold out
for a week or longer, at a pinch. How can it be possible
that I should have lived on this island so many days and
yet hit upon this nook of safety by mere chance, as it
were?"

Not until he reached the level again could he solve
the puzzle. Then he perceived that the way in which
the cliff bulged out on both sides prevented the ledge
from becoming evident in profile, whilst, seen *en plein
face* in the glare of the sunlight, it suggested nothing
more than a slight indentation.

He rapidly sketched to Iris the defensive plan which
the Eagle's Nest suggested. Access must be provided
by means of a rope-ladder, securely fastened inside the
ledge, and capable of being pulled up or let down at the
will of the occupants. Then the place must be kept
constantly stocked with a judicious supply of provisions, water, and ammunition. They could be covered
with a tarpaulin, and thus kept in fairly good condition.

"We ought to sleep there every night," he went on,
and his mind was so engrossed with the tactical side of
the preparations that he did not notice how Iris blanched
at the suggestion.

"Surely not until danger actually threatens?" she
cried.

"Danger threatens us each hour after sunset. It may
come any night, though I expect at least a fortnight's

reprieve. Nevertheless, I intend to act as if tonight may witness the first shot of the siege."

"Do you mean that?" she sighed. "And my little room is becoming so very cozy!"

Belle Vue Castle, their two-roomed hut, was already a home to them.

Jenks always accepted her words literally.

"Well," he announced, after a pause, "it may not be necessary to take up our quarters there until the eleventh hour. After I have hoisted up our stores and made the ladder, I will endeavor to devise an efficient cordon of sentinels around our position. We will see."

Not another word could Iris get out of him on the topic. Indeed, he provided her with plenty of work. By this time she could splice a rope more neatly than her tutor, and her particular business was to prepare no less than sixty rungs for the rope-ladder. This was an impossible task for one day, but after dinner the sailor helped her. They toiled late, until their fingers were sore and their backbones creaked as they sat upright.

Meanwhile Jenks swarmed up the pole again, and drew up after him a crowbar, the sledge-hammer, and the pickaxe. With these implements he set to work to improve the accommodation. Of course he did not attempt seriously to remove any large quantity of rock, but there were projecting lumps here and inequalities of floor there which could be thumped or pounded out of existence.

It was surprising to see what a clearance he made in an hour. The existence of the fault helped him a good deal, as the percolation of water at this point had oxidized the stone to rottenness. To his great joy he discovered that a few prods with the pick laid bare a small cavity which could be easily enlarged. Here he contrived a niche where Iris could remain in absolute safety when barricaded by stores, whilst, with a squeeze, she was entirely sheltered from the one dangerous point on the opposite cliff, nor need she be seen from the trees.

Having hauled into position two boxes of ammunition —for which he had scooped out a special receptacle— the invaluable water-kegs from the stranded boat, several tins of biscuits and all the tinned meats, together with three bottles of wine and two of brandy, he hastily abandoned the ledge and busied himself with fitting a number of gun-locks to heavy faggots.

Iris watched his proceedings in silence for some time. At last the interval for luncheon enabled her to demand an explanation.

"If you don't tell me at once what you intend to do with those strange implements," she said, "I will form myself into an amalgamated engineer and come out on strike."

"If you do," he answered, "you will create a precedent. There is no recorded case of a laborer claiming what he calls his rights when his life is at stake. Even an American tramp has been known to work like a fiend under that condition."

"Simply because an American tramp tries, like every other mere male, to be logical. A woman is more heroic. I once read of a French lady being killed during an earthquake because she insisted on going into a falling house to rescue that portion of her hair which usually rested on the dressing-table whilst she was asleep."

"I happen to know," he said, "that you are personally unqualified to emulate her example."

She laughed merrily, so lightly did yesterday's adventure sit upon her. The allusion to her disheveled state when they were thrown ashore by the typhoon simply impressed her as amusing. Thus quickly had she become inured to the strange circumstances of a new life.

"I withdraw the threat and substitute a more genuine plea—curiosity," she cried.

"Then you will be gratified promptly. These are our sentinels. Come with me to allot his post to the most distant one."

He picked up a faggot with its queer attachment, shouldered a Lee-Metford, and smiled when he saw the business-like air with which Iris slung a revolver around her waist.

They walked rapidly to Smugglers' Cove, and the girl soon perceived the ingenuity of his automatic signal. He securely bound the block of wood to a tree where it was hidden by the undergrowth. Breaking the bullet out of a cartridge, he placed the blank charge in position in front of the striker, the case being firmly clasped by a bent nail. To the trigger, the spring of which he had eased to a slight pressure, he attached a piece of unraveled rope, and this he carefully trained among the trees at a height of six inches from the ground, using as carriers nails driven into the trunks.

The ultimate result was that a mere swish of Iris's dress against the taut cord exploded the cartridge.

"There!" he exclaimed, exultantly. "When I have driven stakes into the sand to the water's edge on both sides of the cove, I will defy them to land by night without giving us warning."

"Do you know," said Iris, in all seriousness, "I think you are the cleverest man in the world."

"My dear Miss Deane, that is not at all a Trades Unionist sentiment. Equality is the key-note of their propaganda."

Nevertheless he was manifestly pleased by the success of his ingenious contrivance, and forthwith completed the cordon. To make doubly sure, he set another snare further within the trees. He was certain the Dyaks would not pass along Turtle Beach if they could help it. By this time the light was failing.

"That will suffice for the present," he told the girl. "Tomorrow we will place other sentries in position at strategic points. Then we can sleep in the Castle with tolerable safety."

By the meager light of the tiny lamp they labored sedulously at the rope-ladder until Iris's eyes were closing with sheer weariness. Neither of them had slept much during the preceding night, and they were both completely tired.

It was with a very weak little smile that the girl bade him "good night," and they were soon wrapped in that sound slumber which comes only from health, hard work, and wholesome fare.

The first streaks of dawn were tipping the opposite

crags with roseate tints when the sailor was suddenly aroused by what he believed to be a gunshot. He could not be sure. He was still collecting his scattered senses, straining eyes and ears intensely, when there came a second report.

Then he knew what had happened. The sentries on the Smugglers' Cove post were faithful to their trust. The enemy was upon them.

At such a moment Jenks was not a man who prayed. Indeed, he was prone to invoke the nether powers, a habit long since acquired by the British army, in Flanders, it is believed.

There was not a moment to be lost. He rushed into Iris's room, and gathered in his arms both her and the weird medley of garments that covered her. He explained to the protesting girl, as he ran with her to the foot of the rock, that she must cling to his shoulders with unfaltering courage whilst he climbed to the ledge with the aid of the pole and the rope placed there the previous day. It was a magnificent feat of strength that he essayed. In calmer moments he would have shrunk from its performance, if only on the score of danger to the precious burden he carried. Now there was no time for thought. Up he went, hand over hand, clinging to the rough pole with the tenacity of a limpet, and taking a turn of the rope over his right wrist at each upward clutch. At last, breathless but triumphant, he reached the ledge, and was able to gasp his instructions to Iris to crawl over his bent back and head until she was safely lodged on the broad platform of rock.

Then, before she could expostulate, he descended, this time for the rifles. These he hastily slung to the rope, again swarmed up the pole, and drew the guns after him with infinite care.

Even in the whirl of the moment he noticed that Iris had managed to partially complete her costume.

"Now we are ready for them," he growled, lying prone on the ledge and eagerly scanning both sides of Prospect Park for a first glimpse of their assailants.

For two shivering hours they waited there, until the sun was high over the cliff and filled sea and land with his brightness. At last, despite the girl's tears and prayers, Jenks insisted on making a reconnaissance in person.

Let this portion of their adventures be passed over with merciful brevity. Both watch-guns had been fired by the troupe of tiny wou-wou monkeys! Iris did not know whether to laugh or cry, when Jenks, with much difficulty, lowered her to mother earth again, and marveled the while how he had managed to carry forty feet into the air a young woman who weighed so solidly.

They sat down to a belated breakfast, and Jenks then became conscious that the muscles of his arms, legs, and back were aching hugely. It was by that means he could judge the true extent of his achievement. Iris, too, realized it gradually, but, like the Frenchwoman in the earthquake, she was too concerned with memories of her state of deshabille to appreciate, all at once, the incidents of the dawn.

CHAPTER IX

THE SECRET OF THE CAVE

THE sailor went after those monkeys in a mood of relentless severity. Thus far, the regular denizens of Rainbow Island had dwelt together in peace and mutual goodwill, but each diminutive wou-wou must be taught not to pull any strings he found tied promiscuously to trees or stakes. As a preliminary essay, Jenks resolved to try force combined with artifice. Failing complete success, he would endeavor to kill every monkey in the place, though he had in full measure the inherent dislike of Anglo India to the slaying of the tree-people.

This, then, is what he did. After filling a biscuit tin with good-sized pebbles, he donned a Dyak hat, blouse, and belt, rubbed earth over his face and hands, and proceeded to pelt the wou-wous mercilessly. For more than an hour he made their lives miserable, until at the mere sight of him they fled, shrieking and gurgling like a thousand water-bottles. Finally he constructed several Dyak scarecrows and erected one to guard each of his alarm-guns. The device was thoroughly effective. Thenceforth, when some adventurous monkey—swinging with hands or tail among the treetops in the morning search for appetizing nut or luscious plantain—saw one of those fearsome bogies, he raised such a hubbub that all his companions scampered hastily from the confines of the wood to the inner fastnesses.

In contriving these same scarecrows—which, by the way, he had vaguely intended at first to erect on the beach in order to frighten the invaders and induce them to fire a warning volley—the sailor paid closer heed to the spoils gathered from the fallen. One, at least, of the belts was made of human hair, and some among its long strands could have come only from the flaxen-haired head of a European child. This fact, though ghastly enough, confirmed him in his theory that it was impossible to think of temporizing with these human fiends. Unhappily such savage virtues as they possess do not include clemency to the weak or hospitality to defenceless strangers. There was nothing for it but a fight to a finish, with the law of the jungle to decide the terms of conquest.

That morning, of course, he had not been able to visit Summit Rock until after his cautious survey of the island. Once there, however, he noticed that the gale two nights earlier had loosened two of the supports of his sky sign. It was not a difficult or a long job to repair the damage. With the invaluable axe he cut several wedges and soon made all secure.

Now, during each of the two daily examinations of the horizon which he never omitted, he minutely scrutinized the sea between Rainbow Island and the distant group. It was, perhaps, a needless precaution. The Dyaks would come at night. With a favorable wind they need not set sail until dusk, and their fleet sampans would easily cover the intervening forty miles in five hours.

He could not be positive that they were actual inhabitants of the islands to the south. The China Sea swarms with wandering pirates, and the tribe whose animosity he had earned might be equally noxious to some peaceable fishing community on the coast. Again and again he debated the advisability of constructing a seaworthy raft and endeavoring to make the passage. But this would be risking all on a frightful uncertainty, and the accidental discovery of the Eagle's Nest had given him new hope. Here he could make a determined and prolonged stand, and in the end help *must* come. So he dismissed the navigation project, and devoted himself wholly to the perfecting of the natural fortress in the rock.

That night they finished the rope-ladder. Indeed, Jenks was determined not to retire to rest until it was placed *in situ;* he did not care to try a second time to carry Iris to that elevated perch, and it may be remarked that thenceforth the girl, before going to sleep, simply changed one ragged dress for another.

One of the first things he contemplated was the destruction, if possible, of the point on the opposite cliff which commanded the ledge. This, however, was utterly impracticable with the appliances at his command. The top of the rock sloped slightly towards the west, and nothing short of dynamite or regular quarrying operations would render it untenable by hostile marksmen.

The Wings of the Morning

During the day his Lee-Metfords, at ninety yards'
range, might be trusted to keep the place clear of
intruders. But at night—that was the difficulty. He
partially solved it by fixing two rests on the ledge to
support a rifle in exact line with the center of the
enemy's supposed position, and as a variant, on the
outer rest he marked lines which corresponded with other
sections of the entire front available to the foe.

Even then he was not satisfied. When time permitted
he made many experiments with ropes reeved through
the pulley and attached to a rifle action. He might
have succeeded in his main object had not his thoughts
taken a new line. His aim was to achieve some method
of opening and closing the breech-block by means of
two ropes. The difficulty was to secure the preliminary
and final lateral movement of the lever bolt, but it
suddenly occurred to him that if he could manage to
convey the impression that Iris and he had left the
island, the Dyaks would go away after a fruitless search.
The existence of ropes along the face of the rock—an
essential to his mechanical scheme—would betray their
whereabouts, or at any rate excite dangerous curiosity.
So he reluctantly abandoned his original design, though
not wholly, as will be seen in due course.

In pursuance of his latest idea he sedulously removed
from the foot of the cliff all traces of the clearance
effected on the ledge, and, although he provided supports for the tarpaulin covering, he did not adjust it.
Iris and he might lie *perdu* there for days without their
retreat being found out. This development suggested
the necessity of hiding their surplus stores and ammuni-

tion, and what spot could be more suitable than the cave?

So Jenks began to dig once more in the interior, laboring manfully with pick and shovel in the locality of the fault with its vein of antimony. It was thus that he blundered upon the second great event of his life.

Rainbow Island had given him the one thing a man prizes above all else—a pure yet passionate love for a woman beautiful alike in body and mind. And now it was to endow him with riches that might stir the pulse of even a South African magnate. For the sailor, unmindful of purpose other than providing the requisite *cache*, shoveling and delving with the energy peculiar to all his actions, suddenly struck a deep vein of almost virgin gold.

To facilitate the disposal at a distance of the disturbed débris, he threw each shovelful on to a canvas sheet, which he subsequently dragged among the trees in order to dislodge its contents. After doing this four times he noticed certain metallic specks in the fifth load which recalled the presence of the antimony. But the appearance of the sixth cargo was so remarkable when brought out into the sunlight that it invited closer inspection. Though his knowledge of geology was slight—the half-forgotten gleanings of a brief course at Eton—he was forced to believe that the specimens he handled so dubiously contained neither copper nor iron pyrites but glittering yellow gold. Their weight, the distribution of the metal through quartz in a transition state between an oxide and a telluride, compelled recognition.

Somewhat excited, yet half skeptical, he returned to the excavation and scooped out yet another collection. This time there could be no mistake. Nature's own alchemy had fashioned a veritable ingot. There were small lumps in the ore which would need alloy at the mint before they could be issued as sovereigns, so free from dross were they.

Iris had gone to Venus's Bath, and would be absent for some time. Jenks sat down on a tree-stump. He held in his hand a small bit of ore worth perhaps twenty pounds sterling. Slowly the conjectures already pieced together in his mind during early days on the island came back to him.

The skeleton of an Englishman lying there among the bushes near the well; the Golgotha of the poison-filled hollow; the mining tools, both Chinese and European; the plan on the piece of tin—ah, the piece of tin! Mechanically the sailor produced it from the breast-pocket of his jersey. At last the mysterious sign "$\frac{32}{1}$" revealed its significance. Measure thirty-two feet from the mouth of the tunnel, dig one foot in depth, and you came upon the mother-lode of this gold-bearing rock. This, then, was the secret of the cave.

The Chinese knew the richness of the deposit, and exploited its treasures by quarrying from the other side of the hill. But their crass ignorance of modern science led to their undoing. The accumulation of liberated carbonic acid gas in the workings killed them in scores. They probably fought this unseen demon with the tenacity of their race, until the place became accursed and banned of all living things. Yet had they dug a little ditch, and permitted the invisible terror to flow quietly downwards until its potency was dissipated by sea and air, they might have mined the whole cliff with impunity.

The unfortunate unknown, J. S.—he of the whitened bones—might have done this thing too. But he only possessed the half-knowledge of the working miner, and whilst shunning the plague-stricken quarry, adopted the more laborious method of making an adit to strike the deposit. He succeeded, to perish miserably in the hour when he saw himself a millionaire.

Was this a portent of the fate about to overtake the latest comers? Jenks, of course, stood up. He always stood square on his feet when the volcano within him fired his blood.

"No, by God!" he almost shouted. "I will break the spell. I am sent here by Providence, not to search for gold but to save a woman's life, and if all the devils of China and Malay are in league against me I will beat them!"

The sound of his own voice startled him. He had no notion that he was so hysterical. Promptly his British phlegm throttled the demonstration. He was rather ashamed of it.

What was all the fuss about? With a barrow-load of gold he could not buy an instant's safety for Iris, not to mention himself. The language difficulty was insuperable. Were it otherwise, the Dyaks would simply humbug him until he revealed the source of his wealth, and then murder him as an effective safeguard against foreign interference.

Iris! Not once since she was hurled ashore in his arms had Jenks so long forgotten her existence. Should he tell her? They were partners in everything appertaining to the island—why keep this marvelous intelligence from her?

Yet was he tempted, not ignobly, but by reason of his love for her. Once, years ago, when his arduous professional studies were distracted by a momentary infatuation for a fair face, a woman had proved fickle when tempted by greater wealth than he possessed. For long he was a confirmed misogynist, to his great and lasting gain as a leader of men. But with more equable judgment came a fixed resolution not to marry unless his prospective bride cared only for him and not for his position. To a Staff Corps officer, even one with a small private income, this was no unattainable ideal. Then he met with his *débâcle* in the shame and agony of the court-martial. Whilst his soul still quivered under the lash of that terrible downfall, Iris came into his life. He knew not what might happen if they were rescued. The time would quickly pass until the old order was resumed, she to go back to her position in society, he to become again a disgraced ex-officer, apparently working out a mere existence before the mast or handing plates in a saloon.

Would it not be a sweet defiance of adversity were he able, even under such conditions, to win her love, and then disclose to her the potentialities of the island? Perchance he might fail. Though rich as Crœsus he would still be under the social ban meted out to a cashiered officer. She was a girl who could command the gift of coronets. With restoration to her father and home, gratitude to her preserver would assuredly remain, but, alas! love might vanish like a mirage. Then he would act honorably. Half of the stored wealth would be hers to do as she chose with it.

Yes, this was a possible alternative. In case of accident to himself, and her ultimate escape, he must immediately write full details of his discovery, and entrust the document to her, to be opened only after his death or six months after their release.

The idea possessed him so thoroughly that he could brook no delay. He searched for one of the note-books taken from the dead officers of the *Sirdar*, and scribbled the following letter:

"DEAR MISS DEANE:

"Whether I am living or dead when you read these words, you will know that I love you. Could I repeat that avowal a million times, in as many varied forms, I should find no better phrase to express the dream I have cherished since a happy fate permitted me to snatch you from death. So I simply say, 'I love you.' I will continue to love you whilst life lasts, and it is my dearest hope that in the life beyond the grave I may still be able to voice my love for you.

"But perhaps I am not destined to be loved by you. Therefore, in the event of my death before you leave the island, I wish to give you instructions how to find a gold mine of great value which is hidden in the rock containing the cave. You remember the sign on the piece of tin which we could not understand. The figure 32 denotes the utmost

depth of the excavation, and the 1 signifies that one foot
below the surface, on reaching the face of the rock, there is
a rich vein of gold. The hollow on the other side of the
cliff became filled with anhydrate gas, and this stopped the
operations of the Chinese, who evidently knew of the existence of the mine. This is all the information the experts
employed by Sir Arthur Deane will need. The facts are
unquestionable.

"Assuming that I am alive, we will, of course, be co-
partners in the mine. If I am dead, I wish one-sixth share
to be given to my uncle, William Anstruther, Crossthwaite
Manor, Northallerton, Yorkshire, as a recompense for his
kindness to me during my early life. The remainder is to
be yours absolutely.

"ROBERT ANSTRUTHER."

He read this remarkable document twice through to
make sure that it exactly recorded his sentiments. He
even smiled sarcastically at the endowment of the uncle
who disinherited him. Then, satisfied with the perusal,
he tore out the two leaves covered by the letter and
began to devise a means of protecting it securely whilst
in Iris's possession.

At that moment he looked up and saw her coming
towards him across the beach, brightly flushed after
her bath, walking like a nymph clothed in tattered
garments. Perceiving that he was watching her, she
waved her hand and instinctively quickened her pace.
Even now, when they were thrown together by the
exigencies of each hour, she disliked to be long separated
from him.

Instantly the scales fell from his mental vision.
What! Distrust Iris! Imagine for one second that

riches or poverty, good repute or ill, would affect that loyal heart when its virginal font was filled with the love that once in her life comes to every true woman! Perish the thought! What evil spirit had power to so blind his perception of all that was strong and beautiful in her character. Brave, uncomplaining Iris! Iris of the crystal soul! Iris, whose innocence and candor were mirrored in her blue eyes and breathed through her dear lips! Here was Othello acting as his own tempter, with not an Iago within a thousand miles.

Laughing at his fantastic folly, Jenks tore the letter into little pieces. It might have been wiser to throw the sheets into the embers of the fire close at hand, but for the nonce he was overpowered by the great awakening that had come to him, and he unconsciously murmured the musical lines of Tennyson's "Maud":

> "She is coming, my own, my sweet;
> Were it ever so airy a tread,
> My heart would hear her and beat
> Were it earth in an earthy bed;
> My dust would hear her and beat,
> Had I lain for a century dead:
> Would start and tremble under her feet,
> And blossom in purple and red."

"Good gracious! Don't gaze at me in that fashion. I don't look like a ghost, do I?" cried Iris, when near enough to note his rapt expression.

"You would not object if I called you a vision?" he inquired quietly, averting his eyes lest they should speak more plainly than his tongue.

"Not if you meant it nicely. But I fear that 'specter'

would be a more appropriate word. *V'la ma meilleure robe de sortie!*"

She spread out the front widths of her skirt, and certainly the prospect was lamentable. The dress was so patched and mended, yet so full of fresh rents, that a respectable housemaid would hesitate before using it to clean fire-irons.

"Is that really your best dress?" he said.

"Yes. This is my blue serge. The brown cloth did not survive the soaking it received in salt water. After a few days it simply crumbled. The others are muslin or cotton, and have been—er—adapted."

"There is plenty of men's clothing," he began.

"Unfortunately there isn't another island," she said, severely.

"No. I meant that it might be possible to—er—contrive some sort of rig that will serve all purposes."

"But all my thread is gone. I have barely a needleful left."

"In that case we must fall back on our supply of hemp."

"I suppose that might be made to serve," she said. "You are never at a loss for an expedient."

"It will be a poor one, I fear. But you can make up for it by buying some nice gowns at Doucet's or Worth's."

She laughed delightedly. "Perhaps in his joy at my reappearance my dear old dad may let me run riot in Paris on our way home. But that will not last. We are fairly well off, but I cannot afford ten thousand a year for dress alone."

"If any woman can afford such a sum for the purpose, you are at least her equal."

Iris looked puzzled. "Is that your way of telling me that fine feathers would make me a fine bird?" she asked.

"No. I intend my words to be understood in their ordinary sense. You are very, very rich, Miss Deane— an extravagantly wealthy young person."

"Of course you know you are talking nonsense. Why, only the other day my father said——"

"Excuse me. What is the average price of a walking-dress from a leading Paris house?"

"Thirty pounds."

"And an evening dress?"

"Oh, anything, from fifty upwards."

He picked up a few pieces of quartz from the canvas sheet.

"Here is your walking-dress," he said, handing her a lump weighing about a pound. "With the balance in the heap there you can stagger the best-dressed woman you meet at your first dinner in England."

"Do you mean by pelting her?" she inquired, mischievously.

"Far worse. By wearing a more expensive costume."

His manner was so earnest that he compelled seriousness. Iris took the proffered specimen and looked at it.

"From the cave, I suppose? I thought you said antimony was not very valuable?"

"That is not antimony. It is gold. By chance I have hit upon an extremely rich lode of gold. At the most modest computation it is worth hundreds of thousands of pounds. You and I are quite wealthy people, Miss Deane."

Iris opened her blue eyes very wide at this intelligence. It took her breath away. But her first words betokened her innate sense of fair dealing.

"You and I! Wealthy!" she gasped. "I am so glad for your sake, but tell me, pray, Mr. Jenks, what have *I* got to do with it?"

"You!" he repeated. "Are we not partners in this island? By squatter's right, if by no better title, we own land, minerals, wood, game, and even such weird belongings as ancient lights and fishing privileges."

"I don't see that at all. You find a gold mine, and coolly tell me that I am a half owner of it because you dragged me out of the sea, fed me, housed me, saved my life from pirates, and generally acted like a devoted nursemaid in charge of a baby. Really, Mr. Jenks——"

"Really, Miss Deane, you will annoy me seriously if you say another word. I absolutely refuse to listen to such an argument."

Her outrageously unbusiness-like utterances, treading fast on the heels of his own melodramatic and written views concerning their property, nettled him greatly. Each downright syllable was a sting to his conscience, but of this Iris was blissfully unaware, else she would not have applied caustic to the rankling wound caused by his momentary distrust of her.

For some time they stood in silence, until the sailor commenced to reproach himself for his rough protest. Perhaps he had hurt her sensitive feelings. What a brute he was, to be sure! She was only a child in ordinary affairs, and he ought to have explained things more lucidly and with greater command over his temper. And all this time Iris's face was dimpling with amusement, for she understood him so well that had he threatened to kill her she would have laughed at him.

"Would you mind getting the lamp?" he said softly, surprised to catch her expression of saucy humor.

"Oh, please may I speak?" she inquired. "I don't want to annoy you, but I am simply dying to talk."

He had forgotten his own injunction.

"Let us first examine our mine," he said. "If you bring the lamp we can have a good look at it."

Close scrutiny of the work already done merely confirmed the accuracy of his first impressions. Whilst Iris held the light he opened up the seam with a few strokes of the pick. Each few inches it broadened into a noteworthy volcanic dyke, now yellow in its absolute purity, at times a bluish black when fused with other metals. The additional labor involved caused him to follow up the line of the fault. Suddenly the flame of the lamp began to flicker in a draught. There was an air-passage between cave and ledge.

"I am sorry," cried Jenks, desisting from further efforts, "that I have not recently read one of Bret Harte's novels, or I would speak to you in the language of the mining camp. But in plain Cockney, Miss Deane, we are on to a good thing if only we can keep it."

They came back into the external glare. Iris was now so serious that she forgot to extinguish the little lamp. She stood with outstretched hand.

"There is a lot of money in there," she said.

"Tons of it."

"No need to quarrel about division. There is enough for both of us."

"Quite enough. We can even spare some for our friends."

He took so readily to this definition of their partnership that Iris suddenly became frigid. Then she saw the ridiculous gleam of the tiny wick and blew it out.

"I mean," she said, stiffly, "that if you and I do agree to go shares we will each be very rich."

"Exactly. I applied your words to the mine alone, of course."

A slight thing will shatter a daydream. This sufficed. The sailor resumed his task of burying the stores.

"Poor little lamp!" he thought. "When it came into the greater world how soon it was snuffed out."

But Iris said to herself, "What a silly slip that was of mine! Enough for both of us, indeed! Does he expect me to propose to him? I wonder what the letter was about which he destroyed as I came back after my bath. It must have been meant for me. Why did he write it? Why did he tear it up?"

The hour drew near when Jenks climbed to the Summit Rock. He shouldered axe and rifle and set forth. Iris heard him rustling upwards through the trees. She set some water to boil for tea, and, whilst bringing a fresh supply of fuel, passed the spot where the torn scraps of paper littered the sand.

She was the soul of honor, for a woman, but there was never a woman yet who could take her eyes off a written document which confronted her. She could not help seeing that one small morsel contained her own name. Though mutilated it had clearly read— "Dear Miss Deane."

"So it *was* intended for me!" she cried, throwing down her bundle and dropping to her knees. She secured that particular slip and examined it earnestly. Not for worlds would she pick up all the scraps and endeavor to sort them. Yet they had a fascination for her, and at this closer range she saw another which bore the legend—"I love you!"

Somehow the two seemed to fit together very nicely.

Yet a third carried the same words—"I love you!" They were still quite coherent. She did not want to look any further. She did not even turn over such of the torn pieces as had fluttered to earth face downwards.

Opening the front of her bodice she brought to light a small gold locket containing miniatures of her father and mother. Inside this receptacle she carefully placed the three really material portions of the sailor's letter. When Jenks walked down the hill again he heard her singing long before he caught sight of her, sedulously tending the fire.

As he came near he perceived the remains of his useless document. He stooped and gathered them up, forthwith throwing them among the glowing logs.

"By the way, what were you writing whilst I had my bath?" inquired Iris, demurely.

"Some information about the mine. On second thoughts, however, I saw it was unnecessary."

"Oh, was that all?"

"Practically all."

"Then some part was impracticable?"

He glanced sharply at her, but she was merely talking at random.

"Well, you see," he explained, "one can do so little without the requisite plant. This sort of ore requires a crushing-mill, a smelting furnace, perhaps big tanks filled with cyanide of potassium."

"And, of course, although you can do wonders, you cannot provide all those things, can you?"

Jenks deemed this query to be unanswerable.

They were busy again until night fell. Sitting down for a little while before retiring to rest, they discussed, for the hundredth time, the probabilities of speedy succor. This led them to the topic of available supplies, and the sailor told Iris the dispositions he had made.

"Did you bury the box of books?" she asked.

"Yes, but not in the cave. They are at the foot of the cinchona over there. Why? Do you want any?"

"I have a Bible in my room, but there was a Tennyson among the others which I glanced at in spare moments."

The sailor thanked the darkness that concealed the deep bronze of face and neck caused by this chance remark. He vaguely recollected the manner in which the lines from "Maud" came to his lips after the episode of the letter. Was it possible that he had unknowingly uttered them aloud and Iris was now slily poking fun at him? He glowed with embarrassment.

"It is odd that you should mention Tennyson," he managed to say calmly. "Only today I was thinking of a favorite passage."

Iris, of course, was quite innocent this time.

"Oh, do tell me. Was it from 'Enoch Arden'?"

He gave a sigh of relief. "No. Anything but that," he answered.

"What then?"

" 'Maud.' "

"Oh, 'Maud.' It is very beautiful, but I could never imagine why the poet gave such a sad ending to an idyllic love story."

"They too often end that way. Moreover, 'Enoch Arden' is not what you might call exhilarating."

"No. It is sad. I have often thought he had the 'Sonata Pathétique' in his mind when he wrote it. But the note is mournful all through. There is no promise of happiness as in 'Maud.' "

"Then it is my turn to ask questions. Why did you hit upon that poem among so many?"

"Because it contains an exact description of our position here. Don't you remember how the poor fellow

> 'Sat often in the seaward-gazing gorge,
> A shipwrecked sailor, waiting for a sail.'

"I am sure Tennyson saw our island with poetic eye, for he goes on—

> 'No sail from day to day, but every day
> The sunrise broken into scarlet shafts
> Among the palms and ferns and precipices;
> The blaze upon the waters to the east;
> The blaze upon his island overhead;
> The blaze upon the waters to the west;
> Then the great stars that globed themselves in Heaven,
> The hollower-bellowing ocean, and again
> The scarlet shafts of sunrise — but no sail.' "

She declaimed the melodious verse with a subtle skill
that amazed her hearer. Profoundly moved, Jenks
dared not trust himself to speak.

"I read the whole poem the other day," she said after
a silence of some minutes. "Sorrowful as it is, it
comforted me by comparison. How different will be our
fate to his when 'another ship stays by this isle'!"

Yet neither of them knew that one line she had recited
was more singularly applicable to their case than that
which they paid heed to. "The great stars that globed
themselves in Heaven," were shining clear and bright
in the vast arch above. Resplendent amidst the throng
rose the Pleiades, the mythological seven hailed by the
Greeks as an augury of safe navigation. And the
Dyaks—one of the few remaining savage races of the
world—share the superstition of the people who fashioned all the arts and most of the sciences.

The Pleiades form the Dyak tutelary genius. Some
among a bloodthirsty and vengeful horde were even
then pointing to the clustering stars that promised quick
voyage to the isle where their kinsmen had been struck
down by a white man who rescued a maid. Nevertheless,
Grecian romance and Dyak lore alike relegate the influence of the Pleiades to the sea. Other stars are needed
to foster enterprise ashore.

CHAPTER X

REALITY *V*. ROMANCE — THE CASE FOR THE PLAINTIFF

NIGHT after night the Pleiades swung higher in the firmament; day after day the sailor perfected his defences and anxiously scanned the ocean for sign of friendly smoke or hostile sail. This respite would not have been given to him, were it not for the lucky bullet which removed two fingers and part of a third from the right hand of the Dyak chief. Not even a healthy savage can afford to treat such a wound lightly, and ten days elapsed before the maimed robber was able to move the injured limb without a curse.

Meanwhile, each night Jenks slept less soundly; each day his face became more careworn. He began to realize why the island had not been visited already by the vessel which would certainly be deputed to search for them—she was examining the great coast-line of China and Siam.

It was his habit to mark the progress of time on the rudely made sun-dial which sufficiently served their requirements as a clock. Iris happened to watch him chipping the forty-fourth notch on the edge of the horizontal block of wood.

[181]

"Have we really been forty-four days here?" she inquired, after counting the marks with growing astonishment.

"I believe the reckoning is accurate," he said. "The *Sirdar* was lost on the 18th of March, and I make this the 1st of May."

"May Day!"

"Yes. Shall we drive to Hurlingham this afternoon?"

"Looked at in that way it seems to be a tremendous time, though indeed, in some respects, it figures in my mind like many years. That is when I am thinking. Otherwise, when busy, the days fly like hours."

"It must be convenient to have such an elastic scale."

"Most useful. I strive to apply the quick rate when you are grumpy."

Iris placed her arms akimbo, planted her feet widely apart, and surveyed Jenks with an expression that might almost be termed impudent. They were great friends, these two, now. The incipient stage of love-making had been dropped entirely, as ludicrously unsuited to their environment.

When the urgent necessity for continuous labor no longer spurred them to exertion during every moment of daylight, they tackled the box of books and read, not volumes which appealed to them in common, but quaint tomes in the use of which Jenks was tutor and Iris the scholar.

It became a fixed principle with the girl that she was very ignorant, and she insisted that the sailor should teach her. For instance, among the books he found a treatise on astronomy; it yielded a keen delight to both to identify a constellation and learn all sorts of wonderful things concerning it. But to work even the simplest problem required a knowledge of algebra, and Iris had never gone beyond decimals. So the stock of notebooks, instead of recording their experiences, became covered with symbols showing how x plus y equaled x^2 minus 3,000,000.

As a variant, Jenks introduced a study of Hindustani. His method was to write a short sentence and explain in detail its component parts. With a certain awe Iris surveyed the intricacies of the Urdu compound verb, but, about her fourth lesson, she broke out into exclamations of extravagant joy.

"What on earth is the matter now?" demanded her surprised mentor.

"Don't you see?" she exclaimed, delightedly. "Of course you don't! People who know a lot about a thing often miss its obvious points. I have discovered how to write Kiplingese. All you have to do is to tell your story in Urdu, translate it literally into English, and there you are!"

"Quite so. Just do it as Kipling does, and the secret is laid bare. By the same rule you can hit upon the Miltonic adjective."

Iris tossed her head.

"I don't know anything about the Miltonic adjective, but I am sure about Kipling."

This ended the argument. She knitted her brows in the effort to master the ridiculous complexities of a language which, instead of simply saying "Take" or

"Bring," compels one to say "Take-go" and "Take-come."

One problem defied solution—that of providing raiment for Iris. The united skill of the sailor and herself would not induce unraveled cordage to supply the need of thread. It was either too weak or too knotty, and meanwhile the girl's clothes were falling to pieces. Jenks tried the fibers of trees, the sinews of birds—every possible expedient he could hit upon—and perhaps, after experiments covering some weeks, he might have succeeded. But modern dress stuffs, weakened by aniline dyes and stiffened with Chinese clay, permit of no such exhaustive research. It must be remembered that the lady passengers on board the *Sirdar* were dressed to suit the tropics, and the hard usage given by Iris to her scanty stock was never contemplated by the Manchester or Bradford looms responsible for the durability of the material.

As the days passed the position became irksome. It even threatened complete callapse during some critical moment, and the two often silently surveyed the large number of merely male garments in their possession. Of course, in the matter of coats and waistcoats there was no difficulty whatever. Iris had long been wearing those portions of the doctor's uniform. But when it came to the rest——

At last, one memorable morning, she crossed the Rubicon. Jenks had climbed, as usual, to the Summit Rock. He came back with the exciting news that he thought—he could not be certain, but there were indications inspiring hopefulness—that towards the west of the far-off island he could discern the smoke of a steamer.

Though he had eyes for a faint cloud of vapor at least fifty miles distant he saw nothing of a remarkable change effected nearer home. Outwardly, Iris was attired in her wonted manner, but if her companion's mind were not wholly monopolized by the bluish haze detected on the horizon, he must have noticed the turned-up ends of a pair of trousers beneath the hem of her tattered skirt.

It did occur to him that Iris received his momentous announcement with an odd air of hauteur, and it was passing strange she did not offer to accompany him when, after bolting his breakfast, he returned to the observatory.

He came back in an hour, and the lines on his face were deeper than before.

"A false alarm," he said curtly in response to her questioning look.

And that was all, though she nerved herself to walk steadily past him on her way to the well. This was disconcerting, even annoying to a positive young woman like Iris. Resolving to end the ordeal, she stood rigidly before him.

"Well," she said, "I've done it!"

"Have you?" he exclaimed, blankly.

"Yes. They're a little too long, and I feel very awkward, but they're better than—than my poor old dress unsupported."

She blushed furiously, to the sailor's complete

bewilderment, but she bravely persevered and stretched out an unwilling foot.

"Oh. I see!" he growled, and he too reddened.

"I can't help it, can I?" she demanded piteously. "It is not unlike a riding-habit, is it?"

Then his ready wit helped him.

"An excellent compromise," he cried. "A process of evolution, in fact. Now, do you know, Miss Deane, that would never have occurred to me."

And during the remainder of the day he did not once look at her feet. Indeed, he had far more serious matters to distract his thoughts, for Iris, feverishly anxious to be busy, suddenly suggested that it would be a good thing were she able to use a rifle if a fight at close quarters became necessary.

The recoil of the Lee-Metford is so slight that any woman can manipulate the weapon with effect, provided she is not called upon to fire from a standing position, in which case the weight is liable to cause bad aiming. Though it came rather late in the day, Jenks caught at the idea. He accustomed her in the first instance to the use of blank cartridges. Then, when fairly proficient in holding and sighting—a child can learn how to refill the clip and eject each empty shell—she fired ten rounds of service ammunition. The target was a white circle on a rock at eighty yards, and those of the ten shots that missed the absolute mark would have made an enemy at the same distance extremely uncomfortable.

Iris was much pleased with her proficiency. "Now," she cried, "instead of being a hindrance to you I may be some help. In any case, the Dyaks will think there are two men to face, and they have good reason to fear one of us."

Then a new light dawned upon Jenks.

"Why did you not think of it before?" he demanded. "Don't you see, Miss Deane, the possibility suggested by your words? I am sorry to be compelled to speak plainly, but I feel sure that if those scoundrels do attack us in force it will be more to secure you than to avenge the loss of their fellow tribesmen. First and foremost, the sea-going Dyaks are pirates and marauders. They prowl about the coast looking not so much for a fight as for loot and women. Now, if they return, and apparently find two well-armed men awaiting them, with no prospect of plunder, there is a chance they may abandon the enterprise."

Iris did not flinch from the topic. She well knew its grave importance.

"In other words," she said, "I must be seen by them dressed only in male clothing?"

"Yes, as a last resource, that is. I have some hope that they may not discover our whereabouts owing to the precautions we have adopted. Perched up there on the ledge we will be profoundly uncomfortable, but that will be nothing if it secures our safety."

She did not reply at once. Then she said musingly—"Forty-four days! Surely there has been ample time to scour the China Sea from end to end in search of us? My father would never abandon hope until he had the most positive knowledge that the *Sirdar* was lost with all on board."

The sailor, through long schooling, was prepared

with an answer—"Each day makes the prospect of escape brighter. Though I was naturally disappointed this morning, I must state quite emphatically that our rescue may come any hour."

Iris looked at him steadily.

"You wear a solemn face for one who speaks so cheerfully," she said.

"You should not attach too great significance to appearances. The owl, a very stupid bird, is noted for its philosophical expression."

"Then we will strive to find wisdom in words. Do you remember, Mr. Jenks, that soon after the wreck you told me we might have to remain here many months?"

"That was a pardonable exaggeration."

"No, no. It was the truth. You are seeking now to buoy me up with false hope. It is sixteen hundred miles from Hong Kong to Singapore, and half as much from Siam to Borneo. The *Sirdar* might have been driven anywhere in the typhoon. Didn't you say so, Mr. Jenks?"

He wavered under this merciless cross-examination.

"I had no idea your memory was so good," he said, weakly.

"Excellent, I assure you. Moreover, during our forty-four days together, you have taught me to think. Why do you adopt subterfuge with me? We are partners in all else. Why cannot I share your despair as well as your toil?"

She blazed out in sudden wrath, and he understood that she would not be denied the full extent of his secret fear. He bowed reverently before her, as a mortal paying homage to an angry goddess.

"I can only admit that you are right," he murmured. "We must pray that God will direct our friends to this island. Otherwise we may not be found for a year, as unhappily the fishermen who once came here now avoid the place. They have been frightened by the contents of the hollow behind the cliff. I am glad you have solved the difficulty unaided, Miss Deane. I have striven at times to be coarse, even brutal, towards you, but my heart flinched from the task of telling you the possible period of your imprisonment."

Then Iris, for the first time in many days, wept bitterly, and Jenks, blind to the true cause of her emotion, picked up a rifle to which, in spare moments, he had affixed a curious device, and walked slowly across Prospect Park towards the half-obliterated road leading to the Valley of Death.

The girl watched him disappear among the trees. Through her tears shone a sorrowful little smile.

"He thinks only of me, never of himself," she communed. "If it pleases Providence to spare us from these savages, what does it matter to me how long we remain here? I have never been so happy before in my life. I fear I never will be again. If it were not for my father's terrible anxiety I would not have a care in the world. I only wish to get away, so that one brave soul at least may be rid of needless tortures. All his worry is on my account, none on his own."

That was what tearful Miss Iris thought, or tried to persuade herself to think. Perhaps her cogitations

would not bear strict analysis. Perhaps she harbored a
sweet hope that the future might yet contain bright
hours for herself and the man who was so devoted to her.
She refused to believe that Robert Anstruther, strong of
arm and clear of brain, a Knight of the Round Table in
all that was noble and chivalric, would permit his name
to bear an unwarrantable stigma when—and she blushed
like a June rose—he came to tell her that which he had
written.

The sailor returned hastily, with the manner of one
hurrying to perform a neglected task. Without any
explanation to Iris he climbed several times to the ledge,
carrying arm-loads of grass roots which he planted in
full view. Then he entered the cave, and, although he
was furnished only with the dim light that penetrated
through the distant exit, she heard him hewing manfully
at the rock for a couple of hours. At last he emerged,
grimy with dust and perspiration, just in time to pay
a last visit to Summit Rock before the sun sank to rest.
He asked the girl to delay somewhat the preparations
for their evening meal, as he wished to take a bath, so it
was quite dark when they sat down to eat.

Iris had long recovered her usual state of high spirits.

"Why were you burrowing in the cavern again?" she
inquired. "Are you in a hurry to get rich?"

"I was following an air-shaft, not a lode," he replied.
"I am occasionally troubled with after wit, and this is
an instance. Do you remember how the flame of the
lamp flickered whilst we were opening up our mine?"

"Yes."

"I was so absorbed in contemplating our prospective

wealth that I failed to pay heed to the true significance of that incident. It meant the existence of an upward current of air. Now, where the current goes there must be a passage, and whilst I was busy this afternoon among the trees over there,"—he pointed towards the Valley of Death—"it came to me like an inspiration that possibly a few hours' hewing and delving might open a shaft to the ledge. I have been well rewarded for the effort. The stuff in the vault is so eaten away by water that it is no more solid than hard mud for the most part. Already I have scooped out a chimney twelve feet high."

"What good can that be?"

"At present we have only a front door—up the face of the rock. When my work is completed, before to-morrow night I hope, we shall have a back door also. Of course I may encounter unforeseen obstacles as I advance. A twist in the fault would be nearly fatal, but I am praying that it may continue straight to the ledge."

"I still don't see the great advantage to us."

"The advantages are many, believe me. The more points of attack presented by the enemy the more effective will be our resistance. I doubt if they would ever be able to rush the cave were we to hold it, whereas I can go up and down our back staircase whenever I choose. If you don't mind being left in the dark I will resume work now, by the light of your lamp."

But Iris protested against this arrangement. She felt lonely. The long hours of silence had been distasteful to her. She wanted to talk.

"I agree," said Jenks, "provided you do not pin me down to something I told you a month ago."

"I promise. You can tell me as much or as little as you think fit. The subject for discussion is your court-martial."

He could not see the tender light in her eyes, but the quiet sympathy of her voice restrained the protest prompt on his lips. Yet he blurted out, after a slight pause—

"That is a very unsavory subject."

"Is it? I do not think so. I am a friend, Mr. Jenks, not an old one, I admit, but during the past six weeks we have bridged an ordinary acquaintanceship of as many years. Can you not trust me?"

Trust her? He laughed softly. Then, choosing his words with great deliberation, he answered—"Yes, I can trust you. I intended to tell you the story some day. Why not tonight?"

Unseen in the darkness Iris's hand sought and clasped the gold locket suspended from her neck. She already knew some portion of the story he would tell. The remainder was of minor importance.

"It is odd," he continued, "that you should have alluded to six years a moment ago. It is exactly six years, almost to a day, since the trouble began."

"With Lord Ventnor?" The name slipped out involuntarily.

"Yes. I was then a Staff Corps subaltern, and my proficiency in native languages attracted the attention of a friend in Simla, who advised me to apply for an appointment on the political side of the Government of India. I did so. He supported the application, and I was assured of the next vacancy in a native state, provided that I got married."

He drawled out the concluding words with exasperating slowness. Iris, astounded by the stipulation, dropped her locket and leaned forward into the red light of the log fire. The sailor's quick eye caught the glitter of the ornament.

"By the way," he interrupted, "what is that thing shining on your breast?"

She instantly clasped the trinket again. "It is my sole remaining adornment," she said; "a present from my father on my tenth birthday. Pray go on!"

"I was not a marrying man, Miss Deane, and the requisite qualification nearly staggered me. But I looked around the station, and came to the conclusion that the Commissioner's niece would make a suitable wife. I regarded her 'points,' so to speak, and they filled the bill. She was smart, good-looking, lively, understood the art of entertaining, was first-rate in sports and had excellent teeth. Indeed, if a man selected a wife as he does a horse, she——"

"Don't be horrid. Was she really pretty?"

"I believe so. People said she was."

"But what did *you* think?"

"At the time my opinion was biased. I have seen her since, and she wears badly. She is married now, and after thirty grew very fat."

Artful Jenks! Iris settled herself comfortably to listen.

"I have jumped that fence with a lot in hand," he thought.

"We became engaged," he said aloud.

"She threw herself at him," communed Iris.

"Her name was Elizabeth—Elizabeth Morris." The young lieutenant of those days called her "Bessie," but no matter.

"Well, you didn't marry her, anyhow," commented Iris, a trifle sharply.

And now the sailor was on level ground again.

"Thank Heaven, no," he said, earnestly. "We had barely become engaged when she went with her uncle to Simla for the hot weather. There she met Lord Ventnor, who was on the Viceroy's staff, and—if you don't mind, we will skip a portion of the narrative—I discovered then why men in India usually go to England for their wives. Whilst in Simla on ten days' leave I had a foolish row with Lord Ventnor in the United Service Club—hammered him, in fact, in defence of a worthless woman, and was only saved from a severe reprimand because I had been badly treated. Nevertheless, my hopes of a political appointment vanished, and I returned to my regiment to learn, after due reflection, what a very lucky person I was."

"Concerning Miss Morris, you mean?"

"Exactly. And now exit Elizabeth. Not being cut out for matrimonial enterprise I tried to become a good officer. A year ago, when Government asked for volunteers to form Chinese regiments, I sent in my name and was accepted. I had the good fortune to serve under an old friend, Colonel Costobell; but some malign star sent Lord Ventnor to the Far East, this time in an important civil capacity. I met him occasionally, and we found we did not like each other any better. My horse beat his for the Pagoda Hurdle Handicap—poor old Sultan! I wonder where he is now."

"Was your horse called 'Sultan'?"

"Yes. I bought him in Meerut, trained him myself, and ferried him all the way to China. I loved him next to the British Army."

This was quite satisfactory. There was genuine feeling in his voice now. Iris became even more interested.

"Colonel Costobell fell ill, and the command of the regiment devolved upon me, our only major being absent in the interior. The Colonel's wife unhappily chose that moment to flirt, as people say, with Lord Ventnor. Not having learnt the advisability of minding my own business, I remonstrated with her, thus making her my deadly enemy. Lord Ventnor contrived an official mission to a neighboring town and detailed me for the military charge. I sent a junior officer. Then Mrs. Costobell and he deliberately concocted a plot to ruin me—he, for the sake of his old animosity—you remember that I had also crossed his path in Egypt—she, because she feared I would speak to her husband. On pretence of seeking my advice, she inveigled me at night into a deserted corner of the Club grounds at Hong Kong. Lord Ventnor appeared, and as the upshot of their vile statements, which created an immediate uproar, I—well, Miss Deane, I nearly killed him."

Iris vividly recalled the anguish he betrayed when this topic was inadvertently broached one day early in their acquaintance. Now he was reciting his painful history with the air of a man far more concerned to be scrupulously accurate than aroused in his deepest passions by the memory of past wrongs. What had happened in the interim to blunt these bygone sufferings? Iris clasped her locket. She thought she knew.

"The remainder may be told in a sentence," he said. "Of what avail were my frenzied statements against the definite proofs adduced by Lord Ventnor and his unfortunate ally? Even her husband believed her and became my bitter foe. Poor woman! I have it in my heart to pity her. Well, that is all. I am here!"

"Can a man be ruined so easily?" murmured the girl, her exquisite tact leading her to avoid any direct expression of sympathy.

"It seems so. But I have had my reward. If ever I meet Mrs. Costobell again I will thank her for a great service."

Iris suddenly became confused. Her brow and neck tingled with a quick access of color.

"Why do you say that?" she asked; and Jenks, who was rising, either did not hear, or pretended not to hear, the tremor in her tone.

"Because you once told me you would never marry Lord Ventnor, and after what I have told you now I am quite sure you will not."

"Ah, then you *do* trust me?" she almost whispered.

He forced back the words trembling for utterance. He even strove weakly to assume an air of good-humored badinage.

"See how you have tempted me from work, Miss

Deane," he cried. "We have gossiped here until the fire grew tired of our company. To bed, please, at once."

Iris caught him by the arm.

"I will pray tonight, and every night," she said solemnly, "that your good name may be cleared in the eyes of all men as it is in mine. And I am sure my prayer will be answered."

She passed into her chamber, but her angelic influence remained. In his very soul the man thanked God for the tribulation which brought this woman into his life. He had traversed the wilderness to find an oasis of rare beauty. What might lie beyond he neither knew nor cared. Through the remainder of his existence, be it a day or many a year, he would be glorified by the knowledge that in one incomparable heart he reigned supreme, unchallenged, if only for the hour. Fatigue, anxiety, bitter recollection and present danger, were overwhelmed and forgotten in the nearness, the intangible presence of Iris. He looked up to the starry vault, and, yielding to the spell, he, too, prayed.

It was a beautiful night. After a baking hot day the rocks were radiating their stored-up heat, but the pleasant south-westerly breeze that generally set in at sunset tempered the atmosphere and made sleep refreshing. Jenks could not settle down to rest for a little while after Iris left him. She did not bring forth her lamp, and, unwilling to disturb her, he picked up a resinous branch, lit it in the dying fire, and went into the cave.

He wanted to survey the work already done, and to determine whether it would be better to resume operations in the morning from inside the excavation or from the ledge. Owing to the difficulty of constructing a vertical upward shaft, and the danger of a sudden fall of heavy material, he decided in favor of the latter course, although it entailed lifting all the refuse out of the hole. To save time, therefore, he carried his mining tools into the open, placed in position the *cheval de frise* long since constructed for the defence of the entrance, and poured water over the remains of the fire.

This was his final care each night before stretching his weary limbs on his couch of branches. It caused delay in the morning, but he neglected no precaution, and there was a possible chance of the Dyaks failing to discover the Eagle's Nest if they were persuaded by other indications that the island was deserted.

He entered the hut and was in the act of pulling off his boots, when a distant shot rang sharply through the air. It was magnified tenfold by the intense silence. For a few seconds that seemed to be minutes he listened, cherishing the quick thought that perhaps a turtle, wandering far beyond accustomed limits, had disturbed one of the spring-gun communications on the sands. A sputtering volley, which his trained ear recognized as the firing of muzzle-loaders, sounded the death-knell of his last hope.

The Dyaks had landed! Coming silently and mysteriously in the dead of night, they were themselves the victims of a stratagem they designed to employ. Instead of taking the occupants of Rainbow Island unawares they were startled at being greeted by a shot the moment they landed. The alarmed savages at once retaliated by firing their antiquated weapons point-blank

at the trees, thus giving warning enough to wake the
Seven Sleepers.

Iris, fully dressed, was out in a moment.

"They have come!" she whispered.

"Yes," was the cheery answer, for Jenks face to face
with danger was a very different man to Jenks wrest-
ling with the insidious attacks of Cupid. "Up the
ladder! Be lively! They will not be here for half an
hour if they kick up such a row at the first difficulty.
Still, we will take no risks. Cast down those spare lines
when you reach the top and haul away when I say
'Ready!' You will find everything to hand up there."

He held the bottom of the ladder to steady it for the
girl's climb. Soon her voice fell, like a message from a
star—

"All right! Please join me soon!"

The coiled-up ropes dropped along the face of the
rock. Clothes, pick, hatchet, hammer, crowbars, and
other useful odds and ends were swung away into the
darkness, for the moon as yet did not illumine the crag.
The sailor darted into Belle Vue Castle and kicked their
leafy beds about the floor. Then he slung all the rifles,
now five in number, over his shoulders, and mounted the
rope-ladder, which, with the spare cords, he drew up
and coiled with careful method.

"By the way," he suddenly asked, "have you your
sou'wester?"

"Yes."

"And your Bible?"

"Yes. It rests beneath my head every night. I even
brought our Tennyson."

"Ah," he growled fiercely, "this is where the reality differs from the romance. Our troubles are only beginning now."

"They will end the sooner. For my part, I have utter faith in you. If it be God's will, we will escape; and no man is more worthy than you to be His agent."

CHAPTER XI

THE FIGHT

THE sailor knew so accurately the position of his reliable sentinels that he could follow each phase of the imaginary conflict on the other side of the island. The first outbreak of desultory firing died away amidst a chorus of protest from every feathered inhabitant of the isle, so Jenks assumed that the Dyaks had gathered again on the beach after riddling the scarecrows with bullets or slashing them with their heavy razor-edged parangs, Malay swords with which experts can fell a stout sapling at a single blow.

A hasty council was probably held, and, notwithstanding their fear of the silent company in the hollow, an advance was ultimately made along the beach. Within a few yards they encountered the invisible cord of the third spring-gun. There was a report, and another fierce outbreak of musketry. This was enough. Not a man would move a step nearer that abode of the dead. The next commotion arose on the ridge near the North Cape.

"At this rate of progress," said Jenks to the girl, "they will not reach our house until daylight."

"I almost wish they were here," was the quiet reply.

[201]

"I find this waiting and listening to be trying to the nerves."

They were lying on a number of ragged garments hastily spread on the ledge, and peering intently into the moonlit area of Prospect Park. The great rock itself was shrouded in somber shadows. Even if they stood up none could see them from the ground, so dense was the darkness enveloping them.

He turned slightly and took her hand. It was cool and moist. It no more trembled than his own.

"The Dyaks are far more scared than you," he murmured with a laugh. "Cruel and courageous as they are, they dare not face a spook."

"Then what a pity it is we cannot conjure up a ghost for their benefit! All the spirits I have ever read about were ridiculous. Why cannot one be useful occasionally?"

The question set him thinking. Unknown to the girl, the materials for a dramatic apparition were hidden amidst the bushes near the well. He cudgeled his brains to remember the stage effects of juvenile days; but these needed limelight, blue flares, mirrors, phosphorus.

The absurdity of hoping to devise any such accessories whilst perched on a ledge in a remote island—a larger reef of the thousands in the China Sea—tickled him.

"What is it?" asked Iris.

He repeated his list of missing stage properties. They had nothing to do but to wait, and people in the very crux and maelstrom of existence usually discuss trivial things.

"I don't know anything about phosphorus," said the

girl, "but you can obtain queer results from sulphur, and there is an old box of Norwegian matches resting at this moment on the shelf in my room. Don't you remember? They were in your pocket, and you were going to throw them away. Why, what are you doing?"

For Jenks had cast the rope-ladder loose and was evidently about to descend.

"Have no fear," he said; "I will not be away five minutes."

"If you are going down I must come with you. I will not be left here alone."

"Please do not stop me," he whispered earnestly. "You must not come. I will take no risk whatever. If you remain here you can warn me instantly. With both of us on the ground we will incur real danger. I want you to keep a sharp lookout towards Turtle Beach in case the Dyaks come that way. Those who are crossing the island will not reach us for a long time."

She yielded, though unwillingly. She was tremulous with anxiety on his account.

He vanished without another word. She next saw him in the moonlight near the well. He was rustling among the shrubs, and he returned to the rock with something white in his arms, which he seemingly deposited at the mouth of the cave. He went back to the well and carried another similar burthen. Then he ran towards the house. The doorway was not visible from the ledge, and she passed a few horrible moments until a low hiss beneath caught her ear. She could tell by the creak of the rope-ladder that he was ascending. At last he reached her side, and she murmured, with a gasping sob—

"Don't go away again. I cannot stand it."

He thought it best to soothe her agitation by arousing interest. Still hauling in the ladder with one hand, he held out the other, on which luminous wisps were writhing like glow-worms' ghosts.

"You are responsible," he said. "You gave me an excellent idea, and I was obliged to carry it out."

"What have you done?"

"Arranged a fearsome bogey in the cave."

"But how?"

"It was not exactly a pleasant operation, but the only laws of necessity are those which must be broken."

She understood that he did not wish her to question him further. Perhaps curiosity, now that he was safe, might have vanquished her terror, and led to another demand for enlightenment, but at that instant the sound of an angry voice and the crunching of coral away to the left drove all else from her mind.

"They are coming by way of the beach, after all," whispered Jenks.

He was mistaken, in a sense. Another outburst of intermittent firing among the trees on the north of the ridge showed that some, at least, of the Dyaks were advancing by their former route. The appearance of the Dyak chief on the flat belt of shingle, with his right arm slung across his breast, accompanied by not more than half a dozen followers, showed that a few hardy spirits had dared to pass the Valley of Death with all its nameless terrors.

They advanced cautiously enough, as though dreading a surprise. The chief carried a bright parang in his left hand; the others were armed with guns, their swords being thrust through belts. Creeping forward on tiptoe, though their distant companions were making a tremendous row, they looked a murderous gang as they peered across the open space, now brilliantly illuminated by the moon.

Jenks had a sudden intuition that the right thing to do now was to shoot the whole party. He dismissed the thought at once. All his preparations were governed by the hope that the pirates might abandon their quest after hours of fruitless search. It would be most unwise, he told himself, to precipitate hostilities. Far better avoid a conflict altogether, if that were possible, than risk the immediate discovery of his inaccessible retreat.

In other words he made a grave mistake, which shows how a man may err when over-agonized by the danger of the woman he loves. The bold course was the right one. By killing the Dyak leader he would have deprived the enemy of the dominating influence in this campaign of revenge. When the main body, already much perturbed by the unseen and intangible agencies which opened fire at them in the wood, arrived in Prospect Park to find only the dead bodies of their chief and his small force, their consternation could be turned into mad panic by a vigorous bombardment from the rock.

Probably, in less than an hour after their landing, the whole tribe would have rushed pell-mell to the boats, cursing the folly which led them to this devil-haunted island. But it serves no good purpose to say what might have been. As it was the Dyaks, silent now and moving with the utmost caution, passed the well, and were about to approach the cave when one of them saw the house.

Instantly they changed their tactics. Retreating hastily to the shade of the opposite cliff they seemed to await the coming of reinforcements. The sailor fancied that a messenger was dispatched by way of the north sands to hurry up the laggards, because the distant firing slackened, and, five minutes later, a fierce outbreak of yells among the trees to the right heralded a combined rush on the Belle Vue Castle.

The noise made by the savages was so great—the screams of bewildered birds circling overhead so incessant—that Jenks was compelled to speak quite loudly when he said to Iris—

"They must think we sleep soundly not to be disturbed by the volleys they have fired already."

She would have answered, but he placed a restraining hand on her shoulder, for the Dyaks quickly discovering that the hut was empty, ran towards the cave and thus came in full view.

As well as Jenks could judge, the foremost trio of the yelping horde were impaled on the bayonets of the *cheval de frise*, learning too late its formidable nature. The wounded men shrieked in agony, but their cries were drowned in a torrent of amazed shouts from their companions. Forthwith there was a stampede towards the well, the cliff, the beaches, anywhere to get away from that awesome cavern where ghosts dwelt and men fell maimed at the very threshold. The sailor, leaning as far over the edge of the rock as the girl's expostulations would permit, heard a couple of men groaning beneath, whilst a third limped away with frantic and painful haste.

"What is it?" whispered Iris, eager herself to witness the tumult. "What has happened?"

"They have been routed by a box of matches and a few dried bones," he answered.

There was no time for further speech. He was absorbed in estimating the probable number of the Dyaks. Thus far, he had seen about fifty. Moreover, he did not wish to acquaint Iris with the actual details of the artifice that had been so potent. Her allusion to the box of water-sodden Tändstickors gave him the notion of utilizing as an active ally the bleached remains of the poor fellow who had long ago fallen a victim to this identical mob of cut-throats or their associates. He gathered the principal bones from their resting-place near the well, rubbed them with the ends of the matches after damping the sulphur again, and arranged them with ghastly effect on the pile of rubbish at the further end of the cave, creeping under the *cheval de frise* for the purpose.

Though not so vivid as he wished, the pale-glimmering headless skeleton in the intense darkness of the interior was appalling enough in all conscience. Fortunately the fumes of the sulphur fed on the bony substance. They endured a sufficient time to scare every Dyak who caught a glimpse of the monstrous object crouching in luminous horror within the dismal cavern.

Not even the stirring exhortations of the chief, whose voice was raised in furious speech, could induce his adherents to again approach that affrighting spot. At last the daring scoundrel himself, still wielding his naked sword, strode right up to the very doorway. Stricken with sudden stupor, he gazed at the fitful gleams within. He prodded the *cheval de frise* with the parang. Here was something definite and solid. Then he dragged one of the wounded men out into the moonlight.

Again Jenks experienced an itching desire to send a bullet through the Dyak's head; again he resisted the impulse. And so passed that which is vouchsafed by Fate to few men—a second opportunity.

Another vehement harangue by the chief goaded some venturesome spirits into carrying their wounded comrade out of sight, presumably to the hut. Inspired by their leader's fearless example, they even removed the third injured Dyak from the vicinity of the cave, but the celerity of their retreat caused the wretch to bawl in agony.

Their next undertaking was no sooner appreciated by the sailor than he hurriedly caused Iris to shelter herself beneath the tarpaulin, whilst he cowered close to the floor of the ledge, looking only through the screen of tall grasses. They kindled a fire near the well. Soon its ruddy glare lit up the dark rock with fantastic flickerings, and drew scintillations from the weapons and ornaments of the hideously picturesque horde gathered in its vicinity.

They spoke a language of hard vowels and nasal resonance, and ate what he judged to be dry fish, millets, and strips of tough preserved meat, which they cooked on small iron skewers stuck among the glowing embers. His heart sank as he counted sixty-one, all told, assembled within forty yards of the ledge. Probably several others were guarding the boats or prowling about the island. Indeed, events proved that more than eighty men had come ashore in three large sampans, roomy and fleet craft, well fitted for piratical excursions up river estuaries or along a coast.

They were mostly bare-legged rascals, wearing Malay hats, loose jackets reaching to the knee, and sandals. One man differed essentially from the others. He was habited in the conventional attire of an Indian Mahommedan, and his skin was brown, whilst the swarthy Dyaks were yellow beneath the dirt. Jenks thought, from the manner in which his turban was tied, that he must be a Punjabi Mussulman—very likely an escaped convict from the Andamans.

The most careful scrutiny did not reveal any arms of precision. They all carried muzzle-loaders, either antiquated flintlocks, or guns sufficiently modern to be fitted with nipples for percussion caps.

Each Dyak, of course, sported a parang and dagger-like kriss; a few bore spears, and about a dozen shouldered a long straight piece of bamboo. The nature of this implement the sailor could not determine at the moment. When the knowledge did come, it came so rapidly that he was saved from many earlier hours of abiding dread, for one of those innocuous-looking weapons was fraught with more quiet deadliness than a Gatling gun.

In the neighborhood of the fire an animated discussion took place. Though it was easy to see that the chief was all-paramount, his fellow-tribesmen exercised a democratic right of free speech and outspoken opinion.

Flashing eyes and expressive hands were turned towards cave and hut. Once, when the debate grew warm, the chief snatched up a burning branch and held it over the blackened embers of the fire extinguished by Jenks. He seemed to draw some definite conclusion from an examination of the charcoal, and the argument thenceforth proceeded with less emphasis. Whatever it was that he said evidently carried conviction.

Iris, nestling close to the sailor, whispered—

"Do you know what he has found out?"

"I can only guess that he can tell by the appearance of the burnt wood how long it is since it was extinguished. Clearly they agree with him."

"Then they know we are still here?"

"Either here or gone within a few hours. In any case they will make a thorough search of the island at daybreak."

"Will it be dawn soon?"

"Yes. Are you tired?"

"A little cramped—that is all."

"Don't think I am foolish—can you manage to sleep?"

"Sleep! With those men so near!"

"Yes. We do not know how long they will remain. We must keep up our strength. Sleep, next to food and drink, is a prime necessity."

"If it will please you, I will try," she said, with such sweet readiness to obey his slightest wish that the wonder is he did not kiss her then and there. By previous instruction she knew exactly what to do. She crept quietly back until well ensconced in the niche widened and hollowed for her accommodation. There, so secluded

was she from the outer world of horror and peril, that
the coarse voices beneath only reached her in a murmur.
Pulling one end of the tarpaulin over her, she stretched
her weary limbs on a litter of twigs and leaves, com-
mended herself and the man she loved to God's keeping,
and, wonderful though it may seem, was soon slumber-
ing peacefully.

The statement may sound passing strange to civilized
ears, accustomed only to the routine of daily life and not
inured to danger and wild surroundings. But the soldier
who has snatched a hasty doze in the trenches, the sailor
who has heard a fierce gale buffeting the walls of his
frail ark, can appreciate the reason why Iris, weary and
surfeited with excitement, would have slept were she certain that the next sunrise would mark her last hour on
earth.

Jenks, too, composed himself for a brief rest. He felt
assured that there was not the remotest chance of their
lofty perch being found out before daybreak, and the
first faint streaks of dawn would awaken him.

These two, remote, abandoned, hopelessly environed
by a savage enemy, closed their eyes contentedly and
awaited that which the coming day should bring forth.

When the morning breeze swept over the ocean and
the stars were beginning to pale before the pink glory
flung broadcast through the sky by the yet invisible sun,
the sailor was aroused by the quiet fluttering of a bird
about to settle on the rock, but startled by the sight of
him.

His faculties were at once on the alert, though he little realized the danger betokened by the bird's rapid dart

into the void. Turning first to peer at Iris, he satisfied himself that she was still asleep. Her lips were slightly parted in a smile; she might be dreaming of summer and England. He noiselessly wormed his way to the verge of the rock and looked down through the grass-roots.

The Dyaks were already stirring. Some were replenishing the fire, others were drawing water, cooking, eating, smoking long thin-stemmed pipes with absurdly small bowls, or oiling their limbs and weapons with impartial energy. The chief yet lay stretched on the sand, but, when the first beams of the sun gilded the waters, a man stooped over the prostrate form and said something that caused the sleeper to rise stiffly, supporting himself on his uninjured arm. They at once went off together towards Europa Point.

"They have found the boat," thought Jenks. "Well, they are welcome to all the information it affords."

The pair soon returned. Another Dyak advanced to exhibit one of Jenks's spring-gun attachments. The savages had a sense of humor. Several laughed heartily when the cause of their overnight alarms was revealed. The chief alone preserved a gloomy and saturnine expression.

He gave some order at which they all hung back sheepishly. Cursing them in choice Malay, the chief seized a thick faggot and strode in the direction of the cave. Goaded into activity by his truculent demeanor, some followed him, and Jenks—unable to see, but listening anxiously—knew that they were tearing the *cheval de frise* from its supports. Nevertheless none of the working party entered the excavation. They feared the parched bones that shone by night.

"Poor J. S.!" murmured the sailor. "If his spirit still lingers near the scene of his murder he will thank me for dragging him into the fray. He fought them living and he can scare them dead."

As he had not been able to complete the communicating shaft it was not now of vital importance should the Dyaks penetrate to the interior. Yet he thanked the good luck that had showered such a heap of rubbish over the spot containing his chief stores and covering the vein of gold. Wild as these fellows were, they well knew the value of the precious metal, and if by chance they lighted upon such a well-defined lode they might not quit the island for weeks.

At last, on a command from the chief, the Dyaks scattered in various directions. Some turned towards Europa Point, but the majority went to the east along Turtle Beach or by way of the lagoon. Prospect Park was deserted. They were scouring both sections of the island in full force.

The quiet watcher on the ledge took no needless risks. Though it was impossible to believe any stratagem had been planned for his special benefit an accident might betray him. With the utmost circumspection he rose on all fours and with comprehensive glance examined trees, plateau, and both strips of beach for signs of a lurking foe. He need have no fear. Of all places in the island the Dyaks least imagined that their quarry had lain all night within earshot of their encampment.

At this hour, when the day had finally conquered the

night, and the placid sea offered a turquoise path to the infinite, the scene was restful, gently bewitching. He knew that, away there to the north, P. and O. steamers, Messageries Maritimes, and North German Lloyd liners were steadily churning the blue depths *en route* to Japan or the Straits Settlements. They carried hundreds of European passengers, men and women, even little children, who were far removed from the knowledge that tragedies such as this Dyak horror lay almost in their path. People in London were just going to the theater. He recalled the familiar jingle of the hansoms scampering along Piccadilly, the more stately pace of the private carriages crossing the Park. Was it possible that in the world of today—the world of telegraphs and express trains, of the newspaper and the motor car—two inoffensive human beings could be done to death so shamefully and openly as would be the fate of Iris and himself if they fell into the hands of these savages! It was inconceivable, intolerable! But it was true!

And then, by an odd trick of memory, his mind reverted, not to the Yorkshire manor he learnt to love as a boy, but to a little French inland town where he once passed a summer holiday intent on improving his knowledge of the language. Interior France is even more remote, more secluded, more provincial, than agricultural England. There no breath of the outer world intrudes. All is laborious, circumspect, a trifle poverty-stricken, but beautified by an Arcadian simplicity. Yet one memorable day, when walking by the banks of a river, he came upon three men dragging from out a pool the water-soaked body of a young girl into whose

fair forehead the blunt knob often seen on the back of
an old-fashioned axe had been driven with cruel force.
So, even in that tiny old-world hamlet, murder and lust
could stalk hand in hand.

He shuddered. Why did such a hateful vision trouble
him? Resolutely banning the raven-winged specter, he
slid back down the ledge and gently wakened Iris. She
sat up instantly and gazed at him with wondering eyes.

Fearful lest she should forget her surroundings, he
placed a warning finger on his lips.

"Oh," she said in a whisper, "are they still here?"

He told her what had happened, and suggested that
they should have something to eat whilst the coast was
clear beneath. She needed no second bidding, for the
long vigil of the previous night had made her very hungry, and the two breakfasted right royally on biscuit,
cold fowl, ham, and good water.

In this, the inner section of their refuge, they could
be seen only by a bird or by a man standing on the distant rocky shelf that formed the southern extremity of
the opposite cliff, and the sailor kept a close lookout in
that direction.

Iris was about to throw the remains of the feast into
an empty oil-tin provided for refuse when Jenks restrained her.

"No," he said, smilingly. "Scraps should be the first
course next time. We must not waste an atom of food."

"How thoughtless of me!" she exclaimed. "Please
tell me you think they will go away today."

But the sailor flung himself flat on the ledge and
grasped a Lee-Metford.

"Be still, on your life," he said. "Squeeze into your corner. There is a Dyak on the opposite cliff."

True enough, a man had climbed to that unhappily placed rocky table, and was shouting something to a confrère high on the cliff over their heads. As yet he had not seen them, nor even noticed the place where they were concealed. The sailor imagined, from the Dyak's gestures, that he was communicating the uselessness of further search on the western part of the island.

When the conversation ceased, he hoped the loud-voiced savage would descend. But no! The scout looked into the valley, at the well, the house, the cave. Still he did not see the ledge. At that unlucky moment three birds, driven from the trees on the crest by the passage of the Dyaks, flew down the face of the cliff and began a circling quest for some safe perch on which to alight.

Jenks swore with an emphasis not the less earnest because it was mute, and took steady aim at the Dyak's left breast. The birds fluttered about in ever smaller circles. Then one of them dropped easily on to the lip of the rock. Instantly his bright eyes encountered those of the man, and he darted off with a scream that brought his mates after him.

The Dyak evidently noted the behavior of the birds —his only lore was the reading of such signs—and gazed intently at the ledge. Jenks he could not distinguish behind the screen of grass. He might perhaps see some portion of the tarpaulin covering the stores, but at the distance it must resemble a weather-beaten segment of the cliff. Yet something puzzled him. After a steady scrutiny he turned and yelled to others on the beach.

The Fight

The crucial moment had arrived. Jenks pressed the trigger, and the Dyak hurtled through the air, falling headlong out of sight.

The sound of this, the first shot of real warfare, awoke Rainbow Island into tremendous activity. The winged life of the place filled the air with raucous cries, whilst shouting Dyaks scurried in all directions. Several came into the valley. Those nearest the fallen man picked him up and carried him to the well. He was quite dead, and, although amidst his other injuries they soon found the bullet wound, they evidently did not know whence the shot came, for those to whom he shouted had no inkling of his motive, and the slight haze from the rifle was instantly swept away by the breeze.

Iris could hear the turmoil beneath, and she tremulously asked—

"Are they going to attack us?"

"Not yet," was the reassuring answer. "I killed the fellow who saw us before he could tell the others."

It was a bold risk, and he had taken it, though, now the Dyaks knew for certain their prey had not escaped, there was no prospect of their speedy departure. Nevertheless the position was not utterly hopeless. None of the enemy could tell how or by whom their companion had been shot. Many among the excited horde jabbering beneath actually looked at the cliff over and over again, yet failed to note the potentialities of the ledge, with its few tufts of grass growing where seeds had apparently been blown by the wind or dropped by passing birds.

Jenks understood, of course, that the real danger would arise when they visited the scene of their comrade's disaster. Even then the wavering balance of chance might cast the issue in his favor. He could only wait, with ready rifle, with the light of battle lowering in his eyes. Of one thing at least he was certain—before they conquered him he would levy a terrible toll.

He glanced back at Iris. Her face was pale beneath its mask of sunbrown. She was bent over her Bible, and Jenks did not know that she was reading the 91st Psalm. Her lips murmured—

"I will say unto the Lord, He is my refuge and my fortress; my God, in Him will I trust."

The chief was listening intently to the story of the Dyak who saw the dead man totter and fall. He gave some quick order. Followed by a score or more of his men he walked rapidly to the foot of the cliff where they found the lifeless body.

And Iris read—

"Thou shalt not be afraid for the terror by night; nor for the arrow that flieth by day."

Jenks stole one more hasty glance at her. The chief and the greater number of his followers were out of sight behind the rocks. Some of them must now be climbing to that fatal ledge. Was this the end?

Yet the girl, unconscious of the doom impending, kept her eyes steadfastly fixed on the book.

"For He shall give His angels charge over thee, to keep thee in all thy ways.

"They shall bear thee up in their hands, lest thou dash thy foot against a stone. . . .

The Fight

"He shall call upon me, and I will answer him: I will be with him in trouble: I will deliver him and honour him."

Iris did not apply the consoling words to herself. She closed the book and bent forward sufficiently in her sheltering niche to permit her to gaze with wistful tenderness upon the man whom she hoped to see delivered and honored. She knew he would dare all for her sake. She could only pray and hope. After reading those inspired verses she placed implicit trust in the promise made. For He was good: His was the mercy that "endureth forever." Enemies encompassed them with words of hatred—fought against them without a cause—but there was One who should "judge among the heathen" and "fill the places with dead bodies."

Suddenly a clamor of discordant yells fell upon her ears. Jenks rose to his knees. The Dyaks had discovered their refuge and were about to open fire. He offered them a target lest perchance Iris were not thoroughly screened.

"Keep close," he said. "They have found us. Lead will be flying around soon."

She flinched back into the crevice; the sailor fell prone. Four bullets spat into the ledge, of which three pierced the tarpaulin and one flattened itself against the rock.

Then Jenks took up the tale. So curiously constituted was this man, that although he ruthlessly shot the savage who first spied out their retreat, he was swayed only by the dictates of stern necessity. There was a feeble chance that further bloodshed might be averted. That chance had passed. Very well. The enemy must start the dreadful game about to be played. They had thrown the gage and he answered them. Four times did the Lee-Metford carry death, unseen, almost unfelt, across the valley.

Ere the fourth Dyak collapsed limply where he stood, others were there, firing at the little puff of smoke above the grass. They got in a few shots, most of which sprayed at various angles off the face of the cliff. But they waited for no more. When the lever of the Lee-Metford was shoved home for the fifth time the opposing crest was bare of all opponents save two, and they lay motionless.

The fate of the flanking detachment was either unperceived or unheeded by the Dyaks left in the vicinity of the house and well. Astounded by the firing that burst forth in mid-air, Jenks had cleared the dangerous rock before they realized that here, above their heads, were the white man and the maid whom they sought.

With stupid zeal they blazed away furiously, only succeeding in showering fragments of splintered stone into the Eagle's Nest. And the sailor smiled. He quietly picked up an old coat, rolled it into a ball and pushed it into sight amidst the grass. Then he squirmed round on his stomach and took up a position ten feet away. Of course those who still carried loaded guns discharged them at the bundle of rags, whereupon Jenks thrust his rifle beyond the edge of the rock and leaned over.

Three Dyaks fell before the remainder made up their minds to run. Once convinced, however, that running was good for their health, they moved with much celerity.

The Fight

The remaining cartridges in the magazine slackened the pace of two of their number. Jenks dropped the empty weapon and seized another. He stood up now and sent a quick reminder after the rearmost pirate. The others had disappeared towards the locality where their leader and his diminished troupe were gathered, not daring to again come within range of the whistling Dum-dums. The sailor, holding his rifle as though pheasant-shooting, bent forward and sought a belated opponent, but in vain. In military phrase, the *terrain* was clear of the enemy. There was no sound save the wailing of birds, the soft sough of the sea, and the yelling of the three wounded men in the house, who knew not what terrors threatened, and vainly bawled for succor.

Again Jenks could look at Iris. Her face was bleeding. The sight maddened him.

"My God!" he groaned, "are you wounded?"

She smiled bravely at him.

"It is nothing," she said. "A mere splash from the rock which cut my forehead."

He dared not go to her. He could only hope that it was no worse, so he turned to examine the valley once more for vestige of a living foe.

CHAPTER XII

A TRUCE

Though his eyes, like live coals, glowered with sullen fire at the strip of sand and the rocks in front, his troubled brain paid perfunctory heed to his task. The stern sense of duty, the ingrained force of long years of military discipline and soldierly thought, compelled him to keep watch and ward over his fortress, but he could not help asking himself what would happen if Iris were seriously wounded.

There was one enemy more potent than these skulking Dyaks, a foe more irresistible in his might, more pitiless in his strength, whose assaults would tax to the utmost their powers of resistance. In another hour the sun would be high in the heavens, pouring his ardent rays upon them and drying the blood in their veins.

Hitherto, the active life of the island, the shade of trees, hut or cave, the power of unrestricted movement and the possession of water in any desired quantity, robbed the tropical heat of the day of its chief terrors. Now all was changed. Instead of working amidst grateful foliage, they were bound to the brown rock, which soon would glow with radiated energy and give off scorching gusts like unto the opening of a furnace-door.

A Truce

This he had foreseen all along. The tarpaulin would yield them some degree of uneasy protection, and they both were in perfect physical condition. But—if Iris were wounded! If the extra strain brought fever in its wake! That way he saw nothing but blank despair, to be ended, for her, by delirium and merciful death, for him by a Berserk rush among the Dyaks, and one last mad fight against overwhelming numbers.

Then the girl's voice reached him, self-reliant, almost cheerful—

"You will be glad to hear that the cut has stopped bleeding. It is only a scratch."

So a kindly Providence had spared them yet a little while. The cloud passed from his mind, the gathering mist from his eyes. In that instant he thought he detected a slight rustling among the trees where the cliff shelved up from the house. Standing as he was on the edge of the rock, this was a point he could not guard against.

When her welcome assurance recalled his scattered senses, he stepped back to speak to her, and in the same instant a couple of bullets crashed against the rock overhead. Iris had unwittingly saved him from a serious, perhaps fatal, wound.

He sprang to the extreme right of the ledge and boldly looked into the trees beneath. Two Dyaks were there, belated wanderers cut off from the main body. They dived headlong into the undergrowth for safety, but one of them was too late. The Lee-Metford reached him, and its reverberating concussion, tossed back and forth by the echoing rocks, drowned his parting scream.

[223]

The Wings of the Morning

In the plenitude of restored vigor the sailor waited for no counter demonstration. He turned and crouchingly approached the southern end of his parapet. Through his screen of grass he could discern the long black hair and yellow face of a man who lay on the sand and twisted his head around the base of the further cliff. The distance, oft measured, was ninety yards, the target practically a six-inch bull's-eye. Jenks took careful aim, fired, and a whiff of sand flew up.

Perhaps he had used too fine a sight and ploughed a furrow beneath the Dyak's ear. He only heard a faint yell, but the enterprising head vanished and there were no more volunteers for that particular service.

He was still peering at the place when a cry of unmitigated anguish came from Iris—

"Oh, come quick! Our water! The casks have burst!"

It was not until Jenks had torn the tarpaulin from off their stores, and he was wildly striving with both hands to scoop up some precious drops collected in the small hollows of the ledge, that he realized the full magnitude of the disaster which had befallen them.

During the first rapid exchange of fire, before the enemy vacated the cliff, several bullets had pierced the tarpaulin. By a stroke of exceeding bad fortune two of them had struck each of the water-barrels and started the staves. The contents quietly ebbed away beneath the broad sheet, and flowing inwards by reason of the sharp slope of the ledge, percolated through the fault. Iris and he, notwithstanding their frenzied efforts, were not able to save more than a pint of gritty discolored fluid.

A Truce

The rest, infinitely more valuable to them than all the diamonds of De Beers, was now oozing through the natural channel cut by centuries of storm, dripping upon the headless skeleton in the cave, soaking down to the very heart of their buried treasure.

Jenks was so paralyzed by this catastrophe that Iris became alarmed. As yet she did not grasp its awful significance. That he, her hero, so brave, so confident in the face of many dangers, should betray such sense of irredeemable loss, frightened her much more than the incident itself.

Her lips whitened. Her words become incoherent.

"Tell me," she whispered. "I can bear anything but silence. Tell me, I implore you. Is it so bad?"

The sight of her distress sobered him. He ground his teeth together as a man does who submits to a painful operation and resolves not to flinch beneath the knife.

"It is very bad," he said; "not quite the end, but near it."

"The end," she bravely answered, "is death! We are living and uninjured. You must fight on. If the Lord wills it we shall not die."

He looked in her blue eyes and saw there the light of Heaven.

"God bless you, dear girl," he murmured brokenly. "You would cheer any man through the Valley of the Shadow, were he Christian or Faint-heart."

Her glance did not droop before his. In such moments heart speaks to heart without concealment.

"We still have a little water," she cried. "Fortunately

we are not thirsty. You have not forgotten our supply of champagne and brandy?"

There was a species of mad humor in the suggestion. Oh for another miracle that should change the wine into water!

He could only fall in with her unreflective mood and leave the dreadful truth to its own evil time. In their little nook the power of the sun had not yet made itself felt. By ordinary computation it was about nine o'clock. Long before noon they would be grilling. Throughout the next few hours they must suffer the torture of Dives with one meager pint of water to share between them. Of course the wine and spirit must be shunned like a pestilence. To touch either under such conditions would be courting heat, apoplexy, and death. And next day!

He tightened his jaws before he answered—

"We will console ourselves with a bottle of champagne for dinner. Meanwhile, I hear our friends shouting to those left on this side of the island. I must take an active interest in the conversation."

He grasped a rifle and lay down on the ledge, already gratefully warm. There was a good deal of sustained shouting going on. Jenks thought he recognized the chief's voice, giving instructions to those who had come from Smugglers' Cove and were now standing on the beach near the quarry.

"I wonder if he is hungry," he thought. "If so, I will interfere with the commissariat."

Iris peeped forth at him.

"Mr. Jenks!"

"Yes," without turning his head. He knew it was an ordinary question.

"May I come too?"

"What! expose yourself on the ledge!"

"Yes, even that. I am so tired of sitting here alone."

"Well, there is no danger at present. But they might chance to see you, and you remember what I——"

"Yes, I remember quite well. If that is all——" There was a rustle of garments. "I am very mannish in appearance. If you promise not to look at me I will join you."

"I promise."

Iris stepped forth. She was flushed a little, and, to cover her confusion, may be, she picked up a Lee-Metford.

"Now there are two guns," she said, as she stood near him.

He could see through the tail of his eye that a slight but elegantly proportioned young gentleman of the sea-faring profession had suddenly appeared from nowhere. He was glad she had taken this course. It might better the position were the Dyaks to see her thus.

"The moment I tell you, you must fall flat," he warned her. "No ceremony about it. Just flop!"

"I don't know anything better calculated to make one flop than a bullet," she laughed. Not yet did the tragedy of the broken kegs appeal to her.

"Yes, but it achieves its purpose in two ways. I want you to adopt the precautionary method."

"Trust me for that. Good gracious!"

The sailor's rifle went off with an unexpected bang

that froze the exclamation on her lips. Three Dyaks were attempting to run the gauntlet to their beleaguered comrades. They carried a jar and two wicker baskets. He with the jar fell and broke it. The others doubled back like hares, and the first man dragged himself after them. Jenks did not fire again.

Iris watched the wounded wretch crawling along the ground. Her eyes grew moist, and she paled somewhat. When he vanished she looked into the valley and at the opposing ledge; three men lay dead within twenty yards of her. Two others dangled from the rocks. It took her some time to control her quavering utterance sufficiently to say—

"I hope I may not have to use a gun. I know it cannot be helped, but if I were to kill a human being I do not think I would ever rest again."

"In that case I have indeed murdered sleep today," was the unfeeling reply.

"No! no! A man must be made of sterner stuff. We have a right to defend ourselves. If need be I will exercise that right. Still it is horrid, oh, so horrid!"

She could not see the sailor's grim smile. It would materially affect his rest, for the better, were he able to slay every Dyak on the island with a single shot. Yet her gentle protest pleased him. She could not at the same time be callous to human suffering and be Iris. But he declined the discussion of such sentiments.

"You were going to say something when a brief disturbance took place?" he inquired.

"Yes. I was surprised to find how hot the ledge has become."

"You notice it more because you are obliged to remain here."

After a pause—

"I think I understand now why you were so upset by the loss of our water supply. Before the day ends we will be in great straits, enduring agonies from thirst!"

"Let us not meet the devil half-way," he rejoined. He preferred the unfair retort to a confession which could only foster dismay.

"But, please, I am thirsty now."

He moved uneasily. He was only too conscious of the impish weakness, common to all mankind, which creates a desire out of sheer inability to satisfy it. Already his own throat was parched. The excitement of the early struggle was in itself enough to engender an acute thirst. He thought it best to meet their absolute needs as far as possible.

"Bring the tin cup," he said. "Let us take half our store and use the remainder when we eat. Try to avoid breathing through your mouth. The hot air quickly affects the palate and causes an artificial dryness. We cannot yet be in real need of water. It is largely imagination."

Iris needed no second bidding. She carefully measured out half a pint of the unsavory fluid—the dregs of the casks and the scourings of the ledge.

"I will drink first," she cried.

"No, no," he interrupted impatiently. "Give it to me."

She pretended to be surprised.

"As a mere matter of politeness——"

"I am sorry, but I must insist."

She gave him the cup over his shoulder. He placed it to his lips and gulped steadily.

"There," he said, gruffly. "I was in a hurry. The Dyaks may make another rush at any moment."

Iris looked into the vessel.

"You have taken none at all," she said.

"Nonsense!"

"Mr. Jenks, be reasonable! You need it more than I. I d-don't want to—live w-without—you."

His hands shook somewhat. It was well there was no call for accurate shooting just then.

"I assure you I took all I required," he declared with unnecessary vehemence.

"At least drink your share, to please me," she murmured.

"You wished to humbug me," he grumbled. "If you will take the first half I will take the second."

And they settled it that way. The few mouthfuls of tepid water gave them new life. One sense can deceive the others. A man developing all the symptoms of hydrophobia has been cured by the assurance that the dog which bit him was not mad. So these two, not yet aflame with drought, banished the arid phantom for a little while.

Nevertheless, by high noon they were suffering again. The time passed very slowly. The sun rose to the zenith and filled earth and air with his ardor. It seemed to be a miracle—now appreciated for the first time in their lives—that the sea did not dry up, and the leaves wither on the trees. The silence, the deathly inactivity of all things, became intolerable. The girl bravely tried to confine her thoughts to the task of the hour. She displayed alert watchfulness, an instant readiness to warn her companion of the slightest movement among the trees or by the rocks to the north-west, this being the arc of their periphery assigned to her.

Looking at a sunlit space from cover, and looking at the same place when sweltering in the direct rays of a tropical sun, are kindred operations strangely diverse in achievement. Iris could not reconcile the physical sensitiveness of the hour with the careless hardihood of the preceding days. Her eyes ached somewhat, for she had tilted her sou'wester to the back of her head in the effort to cool her throbbing temples. She put up her right hand to shade the too vivid reflection of the glistening sea, and was astounded to find that in a few minutes the back of her hand was scorched. A faint sound of distant shouting disturbed her painful reverie.

"How is it," she asked, "that we feel the heat so much today? I have hardly noticed it before."

"For two good reasons—forced idleness and radiation from this confounded rock. Moreover, this is the hottest day we have experienced on the island. There is not a breath of air, and the hot weather has just commenced."

"Don't you think," she said, huskily, "that our position here is quite hopeless?"

They were talking to each other sideways. The sailor never turned his gaze from the southern end of the valley.

"It is no more hopeless now than last night or this morning," he replied.

"But suppose we are kept here for several days?"

"That was always an unpleasant probability."

"We had water then. Even with an ample supply it would be difficult to hold out. As things are, such a course becomes simply impossible."

Her despondency pierced his soul. A slow agony was consuming her.

"It is hard, I admit," he said. "Nevertheless you must bear up until night falls. Then we will either obtain water or leave this place."

"Surely we can do neither."

"We may be compelled to do both."

"But how?"

In this, his hour of extremest need, the man was vouchsafed a shred of luck. To answer her satisfactorily would have baffled a Talleyrand. But before he could frame a feeble pretext for his too sanguine prediction, a sampan appeared, eight hundred yards from Turtle Beach, and strenuously paddled by three men. The vague hallooing they had heard was explained.

The Dyaks, though to the manner born, were weary of sun-scorched rocks and salt water. The boat was coming in response to their signals, and the sight inspired Jenks with fresh hope. Like a lightning flash came the reflection that if he could keep them away from the well and destroy the sampan now hastening to their assistance, perhaps conveying the bulk of their stores, they would soon tire of slaking their thirst on the few pitcher-plants growing on the north shore.

A Truce

"Come quick," he shouted, adjusting the backsight of a rifle. "Lie down and aim at the front of that boat, a little short if anything. It doesn't matter if the bullets strike the sea first."

He placed the weapon in readiness for her and commenced operations himself before Iris could reach his side. Soon both rifles were pitching twenty shots a minute at the sampan. The result of their long-range practice was not long in doubt. The Dyaks danced from seat to seat in a state of wild excitement. One man was hurled overboard. Then the craft lurched seaward in the strong current, and Jenks told Iris to leave the rest to him.

Before he could empty a second magazine a fortunate bullet ripped a plank out and the sampan filled and went down, amidst a shrill yell of execration from the back of the cliff. The two Dyaks yet living endeavored to swim ashore, half a mile through shark-invested reefs. The sailor did not even trouble about them. After a few frantic struggles each doomed wretch flung up his arms and vanished. In the clear atmosphere the onlookers could see black fins cutting the pellucid sea.

This exciting episode dispelled the gathering mists from the girl's brain. Her eyes danced and she breathed hard. Yet something worried her.

"I hope I didn't hit the man who fell out of the boat," she said.

"Oh," came the prompt assurance, "I took deliberate aim at that chap. He was a most persistent scoundrel."

Iris was satisfied. Jenks thought it better to lie than

to tell the truth, for the bald facts hardly bore out his assertion. Judging from the manner of the Dyak's involuntary plunge he had been hit by a ricochet bullet, whilst the sailor's efforts were wholly confined to sinking the sampan. However, let it pass. Bullet or shark, the end was the same.

They were quieting down—the thirst fiend was again slowly salting their veins—when something of a dirty white color fluttered into sight from behind the base of the opposite cliff. It was rapidly withdrawn, to reappear after an interval. Now it was held more steadily and a brown arm became visible. As Jenks did not fire, a turbaned head popped into sight. It was the Mahommedan.

"No shoot it," he roared. "Me English speak it."

"Don't you speak Hindustani?" shouted Jenks in Urdu of the Higher Proficiency.

"Haň, sahib!"[1] was the joyful response. "Will your honor permit his servant to come and talk with him?"

"Yes, if you come unarmed."

"And the chief, too, sahib?"

"Yes, but listen! On the first sign of treachery I will shoot both of you!"

"We will keep faith, sahib. May kites pick our bones if we fail!"

Then there stepped into full view the renegade Mussulman and his leader. They carried no guns; the chief wore his kriss.

"Tell him to leave that dagger behind!" cried the

[1] Yes, sir.

sailor imperiously. As the enemy demanded a parley he resolved to adopt the conqueror's tone from the outset. The chief obeyed with a scowl, and the two advanced to the foot of the rock.

"Stand close to me," said Jenks to Iris. "Let them see you plainly, but pull your hat well down over your eyes."

She silently followed his instructions. Now that the very crisis of their fate had arrived she was nervous, shaken, conscious only of a desire to sink on her knees and pray.

One or two curious heads were craned round the corner of the rock.

"Stop!" cried Jenks. "If those men do not instantly go away I will fire at them."

The Indian translated this order and the chief vociferated some clanging syllables which had the desired effect. The two halted some ten paces in front of the cavern, and the belligerents surveyed each other. It was a fascinating spectacle, this drama in real life. The yellow-faced Dyak, gaudily attired in a crimson jacket and sky-blue pantaloons of Chinese silk—a man with the *beauté du diable*, young, and powerfully built—and the brown-skinned white-clothed Mahommedan, bony, tall, and grey with hardship, looked up at the occupants of the ledge. Iris, slim and boyish in her male garments, was dwarfed by the six-foot sailor, but her face was blood-stained, and Jenks wore a six weeks' stubble of beard. Holding their Lee-Metfords with alert ease, with revolvers strapped to their sides, they presented a warlike and imposing tableau in their inaccessible perch.

In the path of the emissaries lay the bodies of the slain. The Dyak leader scowled again as he passed them.

"Sahib," began the Indian, "my chief, Taung S'Ali, does not wish to have any more of his men killed in a foolish quarrel about a woman. Give her up, he says, and he will either leave you here in peace, or carry you safely to some place where you can find a ship manned by white men."

"A woman!" said Jenks, scornfully. "That is idle talk! What woman is here?"

This question nonplussed the native.

"The woman whom the chief saw half a month back, sahib."

"Taung S'Ali was bewitched. I slew his men so quickly that he saw spirits."

The chief caught his name and broke in with a question. A volley of talk between the two was enlivened with expressive gestures by Taung S'Ali, who several times pointed to Iris, and Jenks now anathematized his thoughtless folly in permitting the Dyak to approach so near. The Mahommedan, of course, had never seen her, and might have persuaded the other that in truth there were two men only on the rock.

His fears were only too well founded. The Mussulman salaamed respectfully and said—

"Protector of the poor, I cannot gainsay your word, but Taung S'Ali says that the maid stands by your side, and is none the less the woman he seeks in that she wears a man's clothing."

"He has sharp eyes, but his brain is addled," retorted the sailor. "Why does he come here to seek a woman

who is not of his race? Not only has he brought death
to his people and narrowly escaped it himself, but he
must know that any violence offered to us will mean
the extermination of his whole tribe by an English
warship. Tell him to take away his boats and never
visit this isle again. Perhaps I will then forget his
treacherous attempt to murder us whilst we slept last
night."

The chief glared back defiantly, whilst the Mahommedan said—

"Sahib, it is best not to anger him too much. He
says he means to have the girl. He saw her beauty
that day and she inflamed his heart. She has cost him
many lives, but she is worth a Sultan's ransom. He
cares not for warships. They cannot reach his village
in the hills. By the tomb of Nizam-ud-din, sahib, he
will not harm you if you give her up, but if you refuse
he will kill you both. And what is one woman more or
less in the world that she should cause strife and blood-
letting?"

The sailor knew the Eastern character too well not
to understand the man's amazement that he should be
so solicitous about the fate of one of the weaker sex.
It was seemingly useless to offer terms, yet the native
was clearly so anxious for an amicable settlement that
he caught at a straw.

"You come from Delhi?" he asked.

"Honored one, you have great wisdom."

"None but a Delhi man swears by the tomb on the
road to the Kutub. You have escaped from the
Andamans?"

"Sahib, I did but slay a man in self-defence."

"Whatever the cause, you can never again see India. Nevertheless, you would give many years of your life to mix once more with the bazaar-folk in the Chandni Chowk, and sit at night on a charpoy near the Lahore Gate?"

The brown skin assumed a sallow tinge.

"That is good speaking," he gurgled.

"Then help me and my friend to escape. Compel your chief to leave the island. Kill him! Plot against him! I will promise you freedom and plenty of rupees. Do this, and I swear to you I will come in a ship and take you away. The miss-sahib's father is powerful. He has great influence with the Sirkar."[1]

Taung S'Ali was evidently bewildered and annoyed by this passionate appeal which he did not understand. He demanded an explanation, and the ready-witted native was obliged to invent some plausible excuse. Yet when he raised his face to Jenks there was the look of a hunted animal in his eyes.

"Sahib," he said, endeavoring to conceal his agitation. "I am one among many. A word from me and they would cut my throat. If I were with you there on the rock I would die with you, for I was in the Kumaon Rissala[2] when the trouble befell me. It is of no avail to bargain with a tiger, sahib. I suppose you will not give up the miss-sahib. Pretend to argue with me. I will help in any way possible."

Jenks's heart bounded when this unlooked-for offer

[1] The Government of India. [2] A native cavalry regiment.

reached his ears. The unfortunate Mahommedan was evidently eager to get away from the piratical gang into whose power he had fallen. But the chief was impatient, if not suspicious of these long speeches.

Angrily holding forth a Lee-Metford the sailor shouted—

"Tell Taung S'Ali that I will slay him and all his men ere tomorrow's sun rises. He knows something of my power, but not all. Tonight, at the twelfth hour, you will find a rope hanging from the rock. Tie thereto a vessel of water. Fail not in this. I will not forget your services. I am Anstruther Sahib, of the Belgaum Rissala."

The native translated his words into a fierce defiance of Taung S'Ali and his Dyaks. The chief glanced at Jenks and Iris with an ominous smile. He muttered something.

"Then, sahib. There is nothing more to be said. Beware of the trees on your right. They can send silent death even to the place where you stand. And I will not fail you tonight, on my life," cried the interpreter.

"I believe you. Go! But inform your chief that once you have disappeared round the rock whence you came I will talk to him only with a rifle."

Taung S'Ali seemed to comprehend the Englishman's emphatic motions. Waving his hand defiantly, the Dyak turned, and, with one parting glance of mute assurance, the Indian followed him.

And now there came to Jenks a great temptation. Iris touched his arm and whispered—

"What have you decided? I did not dare to speak lest he should hear my voice."

Poor girl! She was sure the Dyak could not penetrate her disguise, though she feared from the manner in which the conference broke up that it had not been satisfactory.

Jenks did not answer her. He knew that if he killed Taung S'Ali his men would be so dispirited that when the night came they would fly. There was so much at stake—Iris, wealth, love, happiness, life itself—all depended on his plighted word. Yet his savage enemy, a slayer of women, a human vampire soiled with every conceivable crime, was stalking back to safety with a certain dignified strut, calmly trusting to the white man's bond.

Oh, it was cruel! The ordeal of that ghastly moment was more trying than all that he had hitherto experienced. He gave a choking sob of relief when the silken-clad scoundrel passed out of sight without even deigning to give another glance at the ledge or at those who silently watched him.

Iris could not guess the nature of the mortal struggle raging in the sailor's soul.

"Tell me," she repeated, "what have you done?"

"Kept faith with that swaggering ruffian," he said, with an odd feeling of thankfulness that he spoke truly.

"Why? Have you made him any promise?"

"Unhappily I permitted him to come here, so I had to let him go. He recognized you instantly."

This surprised her greatly.

"Are you sure? I saw him pointing at me, but he seemed to be in such a bad temper that I imagined that he was angry with you for exchanging a prepossessing young lady for an ill-favored youth."

Jenks with difficulty suppressed a sigh. Her words for an instant had the old piquant flavor.

Keeping a close watch on the sheltering promontory, he told her all that had taken place. Iris became very downcast when she grasped the exact state of affairs. She was almost certain when the Dyaks proposed a parley that reasonable terms would result. It horrified her beyond measure to find that she was the rock on which negotiations were wrecked. Hope died within her. The bitterness of death was in her breast.

"What an unlucky influence I have had on your existence!" she exclaimed. "If it were not for me this trouble at least would be spared you. Because I am here you are condemned. Again, because I stopped you from shooting that wretched chief and his companions they are now demanding your life as a forfeit. It is all my fault. I cannot bear it."

She was on the verge of tears. The strain had become too great for her. After indulging in a wild dream of freedom, to be told that they must again endure the irksome confinement, the active suffering, the slow horrors of a siege in that rocky prison, almost distracted her.

Jenks was very stern and curt in his reply.

"We must make the best of a bad business," he said. "If we are in a tight place the Dyaks are not much better off, and eighteen of their number are dead or wounded. You forget, too, that Providence has sent us a most useful ally in the Mahommedan. When all is said and done, things might be far worse than they are."

Never before had his tone been so cold, his manner so abrupt, not even in the old days when he purposely endeavored to make her dislike him.

She walked along the ledge and timidly bent over him.

"Forgive me!" she whispered; "I did forget for the moment, not only the goodness of Providence, but also your self-sacrificing devotion. I am only a woman, and I don't want to die yet, but I will not live unless you too are saved."

Once already that day she had expressed this thought in other words. Was some shadowy design flitting through her brain? Suppose they were faced with the alternatives of dying from thirst or yielding to the Dyaks. Was there another way out? Jenks shivered, though the rock was grilling him. He must divert her mind from this dreadful brooding.

"The fact is," he said with a feeble attempt at cheerfulness, "we are both hungry and consequently grumpy. Now, suppose you prepare lunch. We will feel ever so much better after we have eaten."

The girl choked back her emotion, and sadly essayed the task of providing a meal which was hateful to her. In doing so she saw her Bible, lying where she had placed it that morning, the leaves still open at the 91st Psalm. She had indeed forgotten the promise it contained—

"For He shall give His angels charge over thee, to keep thee in all thy ways."

A few tears fell now and made little furrows down her soiled cheeks. But they were helpful tears, tears of resignation, not of despair. Although the "destruction that wasteth at noonday" was trying her sorely she again felt strong and sustained.

She even smiled on detecting an involuntary effort to clear her stained face. She was about to carry a biscuit and some tinned meat to the sailor when a sharp exclamation from him caused her to hasten to his side.

The Dyaks had broken cover. Running in scattered sections across the sands, they were risking such loss as the defenders might be able to inflict upon them during a brief race to the shelter and food to be obtained in the other part of the island.

Jenks did not fire at the scurrying gang. He was waiting for one man, Taung S'Ali. But that redoubtable person, having probably suggested this dash for liberty, had fully realized the enviable share of attention he would attract during the passage. He therefore discarded his vivid attire, and, by borrowing odd garments, made himself sufficiently like unto the remainder of his crew to deceive the sailor until the rush of men was over. Among them ran the Mahommedan, who did not look up the valley but waved his hand.

When all had quieted down again Jenks understood how he had been fooled. He laughed so heartily that Iris, not knowing either the cause of his merriment or the reason of his unlooked-for clemency to the flying foe, feared the sun had affected him.

He at once quitted the post occupied during so protracted a vigil.

"Now," he cried, "we can eat in peace. I have stripped the chief of his finery. His men can twit him on being forced to shed his gorgeous plumage in order to save his life. Anyhow, they will leave us in peace until night falls, so we must make the best of a hot afternoon."

But he was mistaken. A greater danger than any yet experienced now threatened them, though Iris, after perusing that wonderful psalm, might have warned him of it had she know the purpose of those long bamboos carried by some of the savages.

For Taung S'Ali, furious and unrelenting, resolved that if he could not obtain the girl he would slay the pair of them; and he had terrible weapons in his possession—weapons that could send "silent death even to the place where they stood."

CHAPTER XIII

REALITY *V*. ROMANCE — THE CASE FOR THE DEFENDANT

RESIDENTS in tropical countries know that the heat is greatest, or certainly least bearable, between two and four o'clock in the afternoon.

At the conclusion of a not very luscious repast, Jenks suggested that they should rig up the tarpaulin in such wise as to gain protection from the sun and yet enable him to cast a watchful eye over the valley. Iris helped to raise the great canvas sheet on the supports he had prepared. Once shut off from the devouring sun rays, the hot breeze then springing into fitful existence cooled their blistered but perspiring skin and made life somewhat tolerable.

Still adhering to his policy of combatting the first enervating attacks of thirst, the sailor sanctioned the consumption of the remaining water. As a last desperate expedient, to be resorted to only in case of sheer necessity, he uncorked a bottle of champagne and filled the tin cup. The sparkling wine, with its volume of creamy foam, looked so tempting that Iris would then and there have risked its potency were she not promptly withheld.

Jenks explained to her that when the wine became quite flat and insipid they might use it to moisten their parched lips. Even so, in their present super-heated state, the liquor was unquestionably dangerous, but he hoped it would not harm them if taken in minute quantities.

Accustomed now to implicitly accept his advice, she fought and steadily conquered the craving within her. Oddly enough, the "thawing" of their scorched bodies beneath the tarpaulin brought a certain degree of relief. They were supremely uncomfortable, but that was as naught compared with the relaxation from the torments previously borne.

For a long time—the best part of an hour, perhaps—they remained silent.

The sailor was reviewing the pros and cons of their precarious condition. It would, of course, be a matter of supreme importance were the Indian to be faithful to his promise. Here the prospect was decidedly hopeful. The man was an old *sowar*, and the ex-officer of native cavalry knew how enduring was the attachment of this poor convict to home and military service. Probably at that moment the Mahommedan was praying to the Prophet and his two nephews to aid him in rescuing the sahib and the woman whom the sahib held so dear, for the all-wise and all-powerful Sirkar is very merciful to offending natives who thus condone their former crimes.

But, howsoever willing he might be, what could one man do among so many? The Dyaks were hostile to him in race and creed, and assuredly infuriated against the foreign devil who had killed or wounded, in round numbers, one-fifth of their total force. Very likely, the hapless Mussulman would lose his life that night in attempting to bring water to the foot of the rock.

Well, he, Jenks, might have something to say in that regard. By midnight the moon would illumine nearly the whole of Prospect Park. If the Mahommedan were slain in front of the cavern his soul would travel to the next world attended by a Nizam's cohort of slaughtered slaves.

Even if the man succeeded in eluding the vigilance of his present associates, where was the water to come from? There was none on the island save that in the well. In all likelihood the Dyaks had a store in the remaining sampans, but the native ally of the beleaguered pair would have a task of exceeding difficulty in obtaining one of the jars or skins containing it.

Again, granting all things went well that night, what would be the final outcome of the struggle? How long could Iris withstand the exposure, the strain, the heart-breaking misery of the rock? The future was blurred, crowded with ugly and affrighting fiends passing in fantastic array before his vision, and mouthing dumb threats of madness and death.

He shook restlessly, not aware that the girl's sorrowful glance, luminous with love and pain, was fixed upon him. Summarily dismissing these grisly phantoms of the mind, he asked himself what the Mahommedan exactly meant by warning him against the trees on the right and the "silent death" that might come from them. He was about to crawl forth to the lip of the rock and investigate matters in that locality when Iris. who also was busy with her thoughts, restrained him.

"Wait a little while," she said. "None of the Dyaks will venture into the open until night falls. And I have something to say to you."

There was a quiet solemnity in her voice that Jenks had never heard before. It chilled him. His heart acknowledged a quick sense of evil omen. He raised himself slightly and turned towards her. Her face, beautiful and serene beneath its disfigurements, wore an expression of settled purpose. For the life of him he dared not question her.

"That man, the interpreter," she said, "told you that if I were given up to the chief, he and his followers would go away and molest you no more."

His forehead seamed with sudden anger.

"A mere bait," he protested. "In any event it is hardly worth discussion."

And the answer came, clear and resolute—

"I think I will agree to those terms."

At first he regarded her with undisguised and wordless amazement. Then the appalling thought darted through his brain that she contemplated this supreme sacrifice in order to save him. A clammy sweat bedewed his brow, but by sheer will power he contrived to say—

"You must be mad to even dream of such a thing. Don't you understand what it means to you—and to me? It is a ruse to trap us. They are ungoverned savages. Once they had you in their power they would laugh at a promise made to me."

"You may be mistaken. They must have some sense of fair dealing. Even assuming that such was their intention, they may depart from it. They have already lost a great many men. Their chief, having gained his main object, might not be able to persuade them to take further risks. I will make it a part of the bargain that they first supply you with plenty of water. Then you, unaided, could keep them at bay for many days. We lose nothing; we can gain a great deal by endeavoring to pacify them."

"Iris!" he gasped, "what are you saying?"

The unexpected sound of her name on his lips almost unnerved her. But no martyr ever went to the stake with more settled purpose than this pure woman, resolved to immolate herself for the sake of the man she loved. He had dared all for her, faced death in many shapes. Now it was her turn. Her eyes were lit with a seraphic fire, her sweet face resigned as that of an angel.

"I have thought it out," she murmured, gazing at him steadily, yet scarce seeing him. "It is worth trying as a last expedient. We are abandoned by all, save the Lord; and it does not appear to be His holy will to help us on earth. We can struggle on here until we die. Is that right, when one of us may live?"

Her very candor had betrayed her. She would go away with these monstrous captors, endure them, even flatter them, until she and they were far removed from the island. And then—she would kill herself. In her innocence she imagined that self-destruction, under such circumstances, was a pardonable offence. She only gave a life to save a life, and greater love than this is not known to God or man.

The sailor, in a tempest of wrath and wild emotion, had it in his mind to compel her into reason, to shake her, as one shakes a wayward child.

He rose to his knees with this half-formed notion in his fevered brain. Then he looked at her, and a mist seemed to shut her out from his sight. Was she lost to him already? Was all that had gone before an idle dream of joy and grief, a wizard's glimpse of mirrored happiness and vague perils? Was Iris, the crystal-souled—thrown to him by the storm-lashed waves—to be snatched away by some irresistible and malign influence?

In the mere physical effort to assure himself that she was still near to him he gathered her up in his strong hands. Yes, she was there, breathing, wondering, palpitating. He folded her closely to his breast, and, yielding to the passionate longings of his tired heart, whispered to her—

"My darling, do you think I can survive your loss? You are life itself to me. If we have to die, sweet one, let us die together."

Then Iris flung her arms around his neck.

"I am quite, quite happy now," she sobbed brokenly. "I didn't—imagine—it would come—this way, but—I am thankful—it has come."

For a little while they yielded to the glamour of the divine knowledge that amidst the chaos of eternity each soul had found its mate. There was no need for words. Love, tremendous in its power, unfathomable in its mys-

tery, had cast its spell over them. They were garbed in
light, throned in a palace built by fairy hands. On all
sides squatted the ghouls of privation, misery, danger,
even grim death; but they heeded not the Inferno; they
had created a Paradise in an earthly hell.

Then Iris withdrew herself from the man's embrace.
She was delightfully shy and timid now.

"So you really do love me?" she whispered, crimson-
faced, with shining eyes and parted lips.

He drew her to him again and kissed her tenderly.
For he had cast all doubt to the winds. No matter what
the future had in store she was his, his only; it was not
in man's power to part them. A glorious effulgence
dazzled his brain. Her love had given him the strength
of Goliath, the confidence of David. He would pluck
her from the perils that environed her. The Dyak was
not yet born who should rend her from him.

He fondled her hair and gently rubbed her cheek with
his rough fingers. The sudden sense of ownership of
this fair woman was entrancing. It almost bewildered
him to find Iris nestling close, clinging to him in utter
confidence and trust.

"But I knew, I knew," she murmured. "You betrayed yourself so many times. You wrote your
secret to me, and, though you did not tell me, I found
your dear words on the sands, and have treasured them
next my heart."

What girlish romance was this? He held her away
gingerly, just so far that he could look into her eyes.

"Oh, it is true, quite true," she cried, drawing the
locket from her neck. "Don't you recognize your own

handwriting, or were you not certain, just then, that you really did love me?"

Dear, dear! How often would she repeat that wondrous phrase! Together they bent over the tiny slips of paper. There it was again—"I love you"—twice blazoned in magic symbols. With blushing eagerness she told him how, by mere accident of course, she caught sight of her own name. It was not very wrong, was it, to pick up that tiny scrap, or those others, which she could not help seeing, and which unfolded their simple tale so truthfully? Wrong! It was so delightfully right that he must kiss her again to emphasize his convictions.

All this fondling and love-making had, of course, an air of grotesque absurdity because indulged in by two grimy and tattered individuals crouching beneath a tarpaulin on a rocky ledge, and surrounded by bloodthirsty savages intent on their destruction. Such incidents require the setting of convention, the conservatory, with its wealth of flowers and plants, a summer wood, a Chippendale drawing-room. And yet, God wot, men and women have loved each other in this grey old world without stopping to consider the appropriateness of place and season.

After a delicious pause Iris began again—

"Robert—I must call you Robert now—there, there, please let me get a word in even edgeways—well then, Robert dear, I do not care much what happens now. I suppose it was very wicked and foolish of me to speak as I did before—before you called me Iris. Now tell me at once. Why did you call me Iris?"

"You must propound that riddle to your god-father."

"No wriggling, please. Why did you do it?"

"Because I could not help myself. It slid out un-awares."

"How long have you thought of me only as Iris, your Iris?"

"Ever since I first understood that somewhere in the wide world was a dear woman to love me and be loved."

"But at one time you thought her name was Eliza-beth?"

"A delusion, a mirage! That is why those who christened you had the wisdom of the gods."

Another interlude. They grew calmer, more sedate. It was so undeniably true they loved one another that the fact was becoming venerable with age. Iris was perhaps the first to recognize its quiet certainty.

"As I cannot get you to talk reasonably," she pro-tested, "I must appeal to your sympathy. I am hungry, and oh, so thirsty."

The girl had hardly eaten a morsel for her midday meal. Then she was despondent, utterly broken-hearted. Now she was filled with new hope. There was a fresh motive in existence. Whether destined to live an hour or half a century, she would never, never leave him, nor, of course, could he ever, ever leave her. Some things were quite impossible—for example, that they should part.

Jenks brought her a biscuit, a tin of meat, and that most doleful cup of champagne.

"It is not exactly *frappé*," he said, handing her the

insipid beverage, "but, under other conditions, it is a wine almost worthy to toast you in."

She fancied she had never before noticed what a charming smile he had.

" 'Toast' is a peculiarly suitable word," she cried. "I am simply frizzling. In these warm clothes——"

She stopped. For the first time since that prehistoric period when she was "Miss Deane" and he "Mr. Jenks" she remembered the manner of her garments.

"It is not the warm clothing you feel so much as the want of air," explained the sailor readily. "This tarpaulin has made the place very stuffy, but we must put up with it until sundown. By the way, what is that?"

A light tap on the tarred canvas directly over his head had caught his ear. Iris, glad of the diversion, told him she had heard the noise three or four times, but fancied it was caused by the occasional rustling of the sheet on the uprights.

Jenks had not allowed his attention to wander altogether from external events. Since the Dyaks' last escapade there was no sign of them in the valley or on either beach. Not for trivial cause would they come again within range of the Lee-Metfords.

They waited and listened silently. Another tap sounded on the tarpaulin in a different place, and they both concurred in the belief that something had darted in curved flight over the ledge and fallen on top of their protecting shield.

"Let us see what the game is," exclaimed the sailor. He crept to the back of the ledge and drew himself up until he could reach over the sheet. He returned, carrying in his hand a couple of tiny arrows.

"There are no less than seven of these things sticking in the canvas," he said. "They don't look very terrible. I suppose that is what my Indian friend meant by warning me against the trees on the right."

He did not tell Iris all the Mahommedan said. There was no need to alarm her causelessly. Even whilst they examined the curious little missile another flew up from the valley and lodged on the roof of their shelter.

The shaft of the arrow, made of some extremely hard wood, was about ten inches in length. Affixed to it was a pointed fish-bone, sharp, but not barbed, and not fastened in a manner suggestive of much strength. The arrow was neither feathered nor grooved for a bowstring. Altogether it seemed to be a childish weapon to be used by men equipped with lead and steel.

Jenks could not understand the appearance of this toy. Evidently the Dyaks believed in its efficacy, or they would not keep on pertinaciously dropping an arrow on the ledge.

"How do they fire it?" asked Iris. "Do they throw it?"

"I will soon tell you," he replied, reaching for a rifle.

"Do not go out yet," she entreated him. "They cannot harm us. Perhaps we may learn more by keeping quiet. They will not continue shooting these things all day."

Again a tiny arrow traveled towards them in a graceful parabola. This one fell short. Missing the tarpaulin, it almost dropped on the girl's outstretched

The Wings of the Morning

hand. She picked it up. The fish-bone point had snapped by contact with the floor of the ledge.

She sought for and found the small tip.

"See," she said. "It seems to have been dipped in something. It is quite discolored."

Jenks frowned peculiarly. A startling explanation had suggested itself to him. Fragments of forgotten lore were taking cohesion in his mind.

"Put it down. Quick!" he cried.

Iris obeyed him, with wonder in her eyes. He spilled a teasponful of champagne into a small hollow of the rock and steeped one of the fish-bones in the liquid. Within a few seconds the champagne assumed a greenish tinge and the bone became white. Then he knew.

"Good Heavens!" he exclaimed, "these are poisoned arrows shot through a blowpipe. I have never before seen one, but I have often read about them. The bamboos the Dyaks carried were sumpitans. These fish-bones have been steeped in the juice of the upas tree. Iris, my dear girl, if one of them had so much as scratched your finger nothing on earth could save you."

She paled and drew back in sudden horror. This tiny thing had taken the semblance of a snake. A vicious cobra cast at her feet would be less alarming, for the reptile could be killed, whilst his venomous fangs would only be used in self-defence.

Another tap sounded on their thrice-welcome covering. Evidently the Dyaks would persist in their efforts to get one of those poisoned darts home.

Jenks debated silently whether it would be better to create a commotion, thus inducing the savages to believe they had succeeded in inflicting a mortal wound, or to wait until the next arrow fell, rush out, and try conclusions with Dum-dum bullets against the sumpitan blowers.

He decided in favor of the latter course. He wished to dishearten his assailants, to cram down their throats the belief that he was invulnerable, and could visit their every effort with a deadly reprisal.

Iris, of course, protested when he explained his project. But the fighting spirit prevailed. Their love idyll must yield to the needs of the hour.

He had not long to wait. The last arrow fell, and he sprang to the extreme right of the ledge. First he looked through that invaluable screen of grass. Three Dyaks were on the ground, and a fourth in the fork of a tree. They were each armed with a blowpipe. He in the tree was just fitting an arrow into the bamboo tube. The others were watching him.

Jenks raised his rifle, fired, and the warrior in the tree pitched headlong to the ground. A second shot stretched a companion on top of him. One man jumped into the bushes and got away, but the fourth tripped over his unwieldy sumpitan and a bullet tore a large section from his skull. The sailor then amused himself with breaking the bamboos by firing at them. He came back to the white-faced girl.

"I fancy that further practice with blowpipes will be at a discount on Rainbow Island," he cried cheerfully.

But Iris was anxious and distrait.

"It is very sad," she said, "that we are obliged to secure our own safety by the ceaseless slaughter of human beings. Is there no offer we can make them, no promise of future gain, to tempt them to abandon hostilities?"

"None whatever. These Borneo Dyaks are bred from infancy to prey on their fellow-creatures. To be strangers and defenceless is to court pillage and massacre at their hands. I think no more of shooting them than of smashing a clay pigeon. Killing a mad dog is perhaps a better simile."

"But, Robert dear, how long can we hold out?"

"What! Are you growing tired of me already?"

He hoped to divert her thoughts from this constantly recurring topic. Twice within the hour had it been broached and dismissed, but Iris would not permit him to shirk it again. She made no reply, simply regarding him with a wistful smile.

So Jenks sat down by her side, and rehearsed the hopes and fears which perplexed him. He determined that there should be no further concealment between them. If they failed to secure water that night, if the Dyaks maintained a strict siege of the rock throughout the whole of next day, well—they might survive—it was problematical. Best leave matters in God's hands.

With feminine persistency she clung to the subject, detecting his unwillingness to discuss a possible final stage in their sufferings.

"Robert!" she whispered fearfully, "you will never let me fall into the power of the chief, will you?"

"Not whilst I live."

"You *must* live. Don't you understand? I would go with them to save you. But I would have died—by my own hand. Robert, my love, you must do this thing before the end. I must be the first to die."

He hung his head in a paroxysm of silent despair. Her words rung like a tocsin of the bright romance conjured up by the avowal of their love. It seemed to him, in that instant, they had no separate existence as distinguished from the great stream of human life—the turbulent river that flowed unceasingly from an eternity of the past to an eternity of the future. For a day, a year, a decade, two frail bubbles danced on the surface and raced joyously together in the sunshine; then they were broken—did it matter how, by savage sword or lingering ailment? They vanished—absorbed again by the rushing waters—and other bubbles rose in precarious iridescence. It was a fatalist view of life, a dim and obscurantist groping after truth induced by the overpowering nature of present difficulties. The famous Tentmaker of Naishapur blindly sought the unending purpose when he wrote:—

> "Up from Earth's Centre through the Seventh Gate
> I rose, and on the throne of Saturn sate,
>   And many a Knot unravel'd by the Road ;
> But not the Master-Knot of Human Fate.

> "There was the Door to which I found no Key ;
> There was the Veil through which I could not see :
>   Some little talk awhile of Me and Thee
> There was — and then no more of Thee and Me."

The sailor, too, wrestled with the great problem. He may be pardoned if his heart quailed and he groaned aloud.

"Iris," he said solemnly, "whatever happens, unless

The Wings of the Morning

I am struck dead at your feet, I promise you that we shall pass the boundary hand in hand. Be mine the punishment if we have decided wrongly. And now," he cried, tossing his head in a defiant access of energy, "let us have done with the morgue. For my part I refuse to acknowledge I am inside until the gates clang behind me. As for you, you cannot help yourself. You must do as I tell you. I never knew of a case where the question of Woman's Rights was so promptly settled."

His vitality was infectious. Iris smiled again. Her sensitive highly strung nerves permitted these sharp alternations between despondency and hope.

"You must remember," he went on, "that the Dyak score is twenty-one to the bad, whilst our loss stands at love. Dear me, that cannot be right. Love is surely not a loss."

"A cynic might describe it as a negative gain."

"Oh, a cynic is no authority. He knows nothing whatever about the subject."

"My father used to say, when he was in Parliament, that people who knew least oft-times spoke best. Some men get overweighted with facts."

They chatted in lighter vein with such pendulum swing back to nonchalance that none would have deemed it possible for these two to have already determined the momentous issue of the pending struggle should it go against them. There is, glory be, in the Anglo-Saxon race the splendid faculty of meeting death with calm defiance, almost with contempt. Moments of panic, agonizing memories of bygone days, visions of dear faces never to be seen again, may temporarily dethrone this proud fortitude. But the tremors pass, the gibbering specters of fear and lamentation are thrust aside, and the sons and daughters of Great Britain answer the last roll-call with undaunted heroism. They know how to die.

And so the sun sank to rest in the sea, and the stars pierced the deepening blue of the celestial arch, whilst the man and the woman awaited patiently the verdict of the fates.

Before the light failed, Jenks gathered all the poisoned arrows and ground their vemoned points to powder beneath his heel. Gladly would Iris and he have dispensed with the friendly protection of the tarpaulin when the cool evening breeze came from the south. But such a thing might not be even considered. Several hours of darkness must elapse before the moon rose, and during that period, were their foes so minded, they would be absolutely at the mercy of the sumpitan shafts if not covered by their impenetrable buckler.

The sailor looked long and earnestly at the well. Their own bucket, improvised out of a dish-cover and a rope, lay close to the brink. A stealthy crawl across the sandy valley, half a minute of grave danger, and he would be up the ladder again with enough water to serve their imperative needs for days to come.

There was little or no risk in descending the rock. Soon after sunset it was wrapped in deepest gloom, for night succeeds day in the tropics with wondrous speed. The hazard lay in twice crossing the white sand, were any of the Dyaks hiding behind the house or among the trees.

He held no foolhardy view of his own powers. The one-sided nature of the conflict thus far was due solely to his possession of Lee-Metfords as opposed to muzzle-loaders. Let him be surrounded on the level at close quarters by a dozen determined men and he must surely succumb.

Were it not for the presence of Iris he would have given no second thought to the peril. It was just one of those undertakings which a soldier jumps at. "Here goes for the V. C. or Kingdom Come!" is the pithy philosophy of Thomas Atkins under such circumstances.

Now, there was no V. C., but there was Iris.

To act without consulting her was impossible, so they discussed the project. Naturally she scouted it.

"The Mahommedan may be able to help us," she pointed out. "In any event let us wait until the moon wanes. That is the darkest hour. We do not know what may happen meanwhile."

The words had hardly left her mouth when an irregular volley was fired at them from the right flank of the enemy's position. Every bullet struck yards above their heads, the common failing of musketry at night being to take too high an aim. But the impact of the missiles on a rock so highly impregnated with minerals caused sparks to fly, and Jenks saw that the Dyaks would obtain by this means a most dangerous index of their faulty practice. Telling Iris to at once occupy her safe corner, he rapidly adjusted a rifle on the wooden rests already prepared in anticipation of an attack from that quarter, and fired three shots at the opposing crest, whence came the majority of gun-flashes.

Reality v. Romance

One, at least, of the three found a human billet. There was a shout of surprise and pain, and the next volley spurted from the ground level. This could do no damage owing to the angle, but he endeavored to disconcert the marksmen by keeping up a steady fire in their direction. He did not dream of attaining other than a moral effect, as there is a lot of room to miss when aiming in the dark. Soon he imagined that the burst of flame from his rifle helped the Dyaks, because several bullets whizzed close to his head, and about this time firing recommenced from the crest.

Notwithstanding all his skill and manipulation of the wooden supports, he failed to dislodge the occupants. Every minute one or more ounces of lead pitched right into the ledge, damaging the stores and tearing the tarpaulin, whilst those which struck the wall of rock were dangerous to Iris by reason of the molten spray.

He could guess what had happened. By lying flat on the sloping plateau, or squeezing close to the projecting shoulder of the cliff, the Dyaks were so little exposed that idle chance alone would enable him to hit one of them. But they must be shifted, or this night bombardment would prove the most serious development yet encountered.

"Are you all right, Iris?" he called out.

"Yes, dear," she answered.

"Well, I want you to keep yourself covered by the canvas for a little while—especially your head and shoulders. I am going to stop these chaps. They have found our weak point, but I can baffle them."

She did not ask what he proposed to do. He heard

the rustling of the tarpaulin as she pulled it. Instantly he cast loose the rope-ladder, and, armed only with a revolver, dropped down the rock. He was quite invisible to the enemy. On reaching the ground he listened for a moment. There was no sound save the occasional reports ninety yards away. He hitched up the lower rungs of the ladder until they were six feet from the level, and then crept noiselessly, close to the rock, for some forty yards.

He halted beside a small poon-tree, and stooped to find something embedded near its roots. At this distance he could plainly hear the muttered conversation of the Dyaks, and could see several of them prone on the sand. The latter fact proved how fatal would be an attempt on his part to reach the well. They must discover him instantly once he quitted the somber shadows of the cliff. He waited, perhaps a few seconds longer than was necessary, endeavoring to pierce the dim atmosphere and learn something of their disposition.

A vigorous outburst of firing sent him back with haste. Iris was up there alone. He knew not what might happen. He was now feverishly anxious to be with her again, to hear her voice, and be sure that all was well.

To his horror he found the ladder swaying gently against the rock. Some one was using it. He sprang forward, careless of consequence, and seized the swinging end which had fallen free again. He had his foot on the bottom rung when Iris's voice, close at hand and shrill with terror, shrieked—

"Robert, where are you?"

"Here!" he shouted; the next instant she dropped into his arms.

A startled exclamation from the vicinity of the house, and some loud cries from the more distant Dyaks on the other side of Prospect Park, showed that they had been overheard.

"Up!" he whispered. "Hold tight, and go as quickly as you can."

"Not without you!"

"Up, for God's sake! I follow at your heels."

She began to climb. He took some article from between his teeth, a string apparently, and drew it towards him, mounting the ladder at the same time. The end tightened. He was then about ten feet from the ground. Two Dyaks, yelling fiercely, rushed from the cover of the house.

"Go on," he said to Iris. "Don't lose your nerve whatever happens. I am close behind you."

"I am quite safe," she gasped.

Turning, and clinging on with one hand, he drew his revolver and fired at the pair beneath, who could now faintly discern them, and were almost within reach of the ladder. The shooting made them halt. He did not know or care if they were hit. To frighten them was sufficient. Several others were running across the sands to the cave, attracted by the noise and the cries of the foremost pursuers.

Then he gave a steady pull to the cord. The sharp crack of a rifle came from the vicinity of the old quarry. He saw the flash among the trees. Almost simultaneously a bright light leapt from the opposite ledge, illumining the vicinity like a meteor. It lit up the rock, showed Iris just vanishing into the safety of the ledge, and revealed Jenks and the Dyaks to each other. There followed instantly a tremendous explosion that shook earth and air, dislodging every loose stone in the southwest pile of rocks, hurling from the plateau some of its occupants, and wounding the remainder with a shower of lead and débris.

The island birds, long since driven to the remote trees, clamored in raucous peal, and from the Dyaks came yells of fright or anguish.

The sailor, unmolested further, reached the ledge to find Iris prostrate where she had fallen, dead or unconscious, he knew not which. He felt his face become grey in the darkness. With a fierce tug he hauled the ladder well away from the ground and sank to his knees beside her.

He took her into his arms. There was no light. He could not see her eyes or lips. Her slight breathing seemed to indicate a fainting fit, but there was no water, nor was it possible to adopt any of the ordinary expedients suited to such a seizure. He could only wait in a dreadful silence—wait, clasping her to his breast—and dumbly wonder what other loss he could suffer ere the final release came.

At last she sighed deeply. A strong tremor of returning life stirred her frame.

"Thank God!" he murmured, and bowed his head. Were the sun shining he could not see her now, for his eyes were blurred.

"Robert!" she whispered.

Reality v. Romance

"Yes, darling."

"Are you safe?"

"Safe! my loved one! Think of yourself! What has happened to you?"

"I fainted—I think. I have no hurt. I missed you! Something told me you had gone. I went to help you, or die with you. And then that noise! And the light! What did you do?"

He silenced her questioning with a passionate kiss. He carried her to a little nook and fumbled among the stores until he found a bottle of brandy. She drank some. Under its revivifying influence she was soon able to listen to the explanation he offered—after securing the ladder.

In a tall tree near the Valley of Death he had tightly fixed a loaded rifle which pointed at a loose stone in the rock overhanging the ledge held by the Dyaks. This stone rested against a number of percussion caps extracted from cartridges, and these were in direct communication with a train of powder leading to a blasting charge placed at the end of a twenty-four inch hole drilled with a crowbar. The impact of the bullet against the stone could not fail to explode some of the caps. He had used the contents of three hundred cartridges to secure a sufficiency of powder, and the bullets were all crammed into the orifice, being tamped with clay and wet sand. The rifle was fired by means of the string, the loose coils of which were secreted at the foot of the poon. By springing this novel mine he had effectually removed every Dyak from the ledge, over which its contents would spread like a fan. Further, it would probably deter the survivors from again venturing near that fatal spot.

Iris listened, only half comprehending. Her mind was filled with one thought to the exclusion of all others. Robert had left her, had done this thing without telling her. She forgave him, knowing he acted for the best, but he must never, never deceive her again in such a manner. She could not bear it.

What better excuse could man desire for caressing her, yea, even squeezing her, until the sobs ceased and she protested with a weak little laugh—

"Robert, I haven't got much breath—after that excitement—but please—leave me—the remains!"

CHAPTER XIV

THE UNEXPECTED HAPPENS

"You are a dear unreasonable little girl," he said. "Have you breath enough to tell me why you came down the ladder?"

"When I discovered you were gone, I became wild with fright. Don't you see, I imagined you were wounded and had fallen from the ledge. What else could I do but follow, either to help you, or, if that were not possible——"

He found her hand and pressed it to his lips.

"I humbly crave your pardon," he said. "That explanation is more than ample. It was I who behaved unreasonably. Of course I should have warned you. Yet, sweetheart, I ran no risk. The real danger passed a week ago."

"How can that be?"

"I might have been blown to pieces whilst adjusting the heavy stone in front of the caps. I assure you I was glad to leave the place that day with a whole skin. If the stone had wobbled, or slipped, well—it was a case of determined *felo-de-se*."

"May I ask how many more wild adventures you undertook without my knowledge?"

"One other, of great magnitude. I fell in love with you."

"Nonsense!" she retorted. "I knew that long before you admitted it to yourself."

"Date, please?"

"Well, to begin at the very beginning, you thought I was nice on board the *Sirdar*. Now, didn't you?"

And they were safely embarked on a conversation of no interest to any other person in the wide world, but which provided them with the most delightful topic imaginable.

Thus the time sped until the rising moon silhouetted the cliff on the white carpet of coral-strewn sand. The black shadow-line traveled slowly closer to the base of the cliff, and Jenks, guided also by the stars, told Iris that midnight was at hand.

They knelt on the parapet of the ledge, alert to catch any unusual sound, and watching for any indication of human movement. But Rainbow Island was now still as the grave. The wounded Dyaks had seemingly been removed from hut and beach; the dead lay where they had fallen. The sea sang a lullaby to the reef, and the fresh breeze whispered among the palm fronds—that was all.

"Perhaps they have gone!" murmured Iris.

The sailor put his arm round her neck and gently pressed her lips together. Anything would serve as an excuse for that sort of thing, but he really did want absolute silence at that moment. If the Mussulman kept his compact, the hour was at hand.

An unlooked-for intruder disturbed the quietude of

the scene. Their old acquaintance, the singing beetle, chortled his loud way across the park. Iris was dying— as women say—to remind Jenks of their first meeting with that blatant insect, but further talk was impossible; there was too much at stake—water they must have.

Then the light hiss of a snake rose to them from the depths. That is a sound never forgotten when once heard. It is like unto no other. Indeed, the term "hiss" is a misnomer for the quick sibilant expulsion of the breath by an alarmed or angered serpent.

Iris paid no heed to it, but Jenks, who knew there was not a reptile of the snake variety on the island, leaned over the ledge and emitted a tolerably good imitation. The native was beneath. Probably the flight of the beetle had helped his noiseless approach.

"Sahib!"

The girl started at the unexpected call from the depths.

"Yes," said Jenks quietly.

"A rope, sahib."

The sailor lowered a rope. Something was tied to it beneath. The Mahommedan apparently had little fear of being detected.

"Pull, sahib."

"Usually it is the sahib who says 'pull,' but circumstances alter cases," communed Jenks. He hauled steadily at a heavy weight—a goatskin filled with cold water. He emptied the hot and sour wine out of the tin cup, and was about to hand the thrice-welcome draught to Iris when a suspicious thought caused him to withhold it.

"Let me taste first," he said.

The Indian might have betrayed them to the Dyaks. More unlikely things had happened. What if the water were poisoned or drugged?

He placed the tin to his lips. The liquid was musty, having been in the skin nearly two days. Otherwise it seemed to be all right. With a sigh of profound relief he gave Iris the cup, and smiled at the most unladylike haste with which she emptied it.

"Drink yourself, and give me some more," she said.

"No more for you at present, madam. In a few minutes, yes."

"Oh, why not now?"

"Do not fret, dear one. You can have all you want in a little while. But to drink much now would make you very ill."

Iris waited until he could speak again.

"Why did you——" she began.

But he bent over the parapet—

"*Koi hai!*"[1]

"Sahib!"

"You have not been followed?"

"I think not, sahib. Do not talk too loud; they are foxes in cunning. You have a ladder, they say, sahib. Will not your honor descend? I have much to relate."

Iris made no protest when Jenks explained the man's request. She only stipulated that he should not leave the ladder, whilst she would remain within easy earshot. The sailor, of course, carried his revolver. He also picked up a crowbar, a most useful and silent

[1] Equivalent to " Hello, there ! "

[272]

weapon. Then he went quietly downwards. Nearing the ground, he saw the native, who salaamed deeply and was unarmed. The poor fellow seemed to be very anxious to help them.

"What is your name?" demanded the sailor.

"Mir Jan, sahib, formerly *naik*[1] in the Kumaon Rissala."

"When did you leave the regiment?"

"Two years ago, sahib. I killed——"

"What was the name of your Colonel?"

"Kurnal I-shpence-sahib, a brave man, but of no account on a horse."

Jenks well remembered Colonel Spence—a fat, short-legged warrior, who rolled off his charger if the animal so much as looked sideways. Mir Jan was telling the truth.

"You are right, Mir Jan. What is Taung S'Ali doing now?"

"Cursing, sahib, for the most part. His men are frightened. He wanted them to try once more with the tubes that shoot poison, but they refused. He could not come alone, for he could not use his right hand, and he was wounded by the blowing up of the rock. You nearly killed me, too, sahib. I was there with the bazaar-born whelps. By the Prophet's beard, it was a fine stroke."

"Are they going away, then?"

"No, sahib. The dogs have been whipped so sore that they snarl for revenge. They say there is no use in firing at you, but they are resolved to kill you and the miss-sahib, or carry her off if she escapes the assault."

[1] Corporal.

"What assault?"

"Protector of the poor, they are building scaling-ladders—four in all. Soon after dawn they intend to rush your position. You may slay some, they say, but you cannot slay three score. Taung S'Ali has promised a gold *tauk*[1] to every man who survives if they succeed. They have pulled down your signal on the high rocks and are using the poles for the ladders. They think you have a *jadu*,[2] sahib, and they want to use your own work against you."

This was serious news. A combined attack might indeed be dangerous, though it had the excellent feature that if it failed the Dyaks would certainly leave the island. But his sky-sign destroyed! That was bad. Had a vessel chanced to pass, the swinging letters would surely have attracted attention. Now, even that faint hope was dispelled.

"Sahib, there is a worse thing to tell," said Mir Jan.

"Say on, then."

"Before they place the ladders against the cliff they will build a fire of green wood so that the smoke will be blown by the wind into your eyes. This will help to blind your aim. Otherwise, you never miss."

"That will assuredly be awkward, Mir Jan."

"It will, sahib. Soul of my father, if we had but half a troop with us——"

But they had not, and they were both so intent on the conversation that they were momentarily off their guard. Iris was more watchful. She fancied there was

[1] A native ornament.　　[2] A charm.

a light rustling amidst the undergrowth beneath the trees on the right. And she could hiss too, if that were the correct thing to do.

So she hissed.

Jenks swarmed half way up the ladder.

"Yes, Iris?" he said.

"I am not sure, but I imagine something moved among the bushes behind the house."

"All right, dear. I will keep a sharp look-out. Can you hear us talking?"

"Hardly. Will you be long?"

"Another minute."

He descended and told Mir Jan what the miss-sahib said. The native was about to make a search when Jenks stopped him.

"Here,"—he handed the man his revolver—"I suppose you can use this?"

Mir Jan took it without a word, and Jenks felt that the incident atoned for previous unworthy doubts of his dark friend's honesty. The Mahommedan cautiously examined the back of the house, the neighboring shrubs, and the open beach. After a brief absence he reported all safe, yet no man has ever been nearer death and escaped it than he during that reconnaissance. He, too, forgot that the Dyaks were foxes, and foxes can lie close when hounds are a trifle stale.

Mir Jan returned the revolver.

"Sahib," he said with another salaam, "I am a disgraced man, but if you will take me up there with you, I will fight by your side until both my arms are hacked off. I am weary of these thieves. Ill chance threw me into their company: I will have no more of them. If you will not have me on the rock, give me a gun. I will hide among the trees, and I promise that some of them shall die to-night before they find me. For the honor of the regiment, sahib, do not refuse this thing. All I ask is, if your honor escapes, that you will write to Kurnal I-shpence-sahib, and tell him the last act of Mir Jan, *naik* in B troop."

There was an intense pathos in the man's words. He made this self-sacrificing offer with an utter absence of any motive save the old tradition of duty to the colors. Here was Anstruther-sahib, of the Belgaum Rissala, in dire peril. Very well, then, Corporal Mir Jan, late of the 19th Bengal Lancers, must dare all to save him.

Jenks was profoundly moved. He reflected how best to utilize the services of this willing volunteer without exposing him to certain death in the manner suggested. The native misinterpreted his silence.

"I am not a *budmash*,[1] sahib," he exclaimed proudly. "I only killed a man because——"

"Listen, Mir Jan. You cannot well mend what you have said. The Dyaks, you are sure, will not come before morning?"

"They have carried the wounded to the boats and are making the ladders. Such was their talk when I left them."

"Will they not miss you?"

"They will miss the *mussak*,[2] sahib. It was the last full one."

[1] Rascal. [2] Goatskin.

The Unexpected Happens

"Mir Jan, do as I bid, and you shall see Delhi again. Have you ever used a Lee-Metford?"

"I have seen them, sahib; but I better understand the Mahtini."

"I will give you a rifle, with plenty of ammunition. Do you go inside the cave, there, and——"

Mir Jan was startled.

"Where the ghost is, sahib?" he said.

"Ghost! That is a tale for children. There is no ghost, only a few bones of a man murdered by these scoundrels long ago. Have you any food?"

"Some rice, sahib; sufficient for a day, or two at a pinch."

"Good! We will get water from the well. When the fighting begins at dawn, fire at every man you see from the back of the cave. On no account come out. Then they can never reach you if you keep a full magazine. Wait here!"

"I thought you were never coming," protested Iris when Jenks reached the ledge. "I have been quite creepy. I am sure there is some one down there. And, please, may I have another drink?"

The sailor had left the crowbar beneath. He secured a rifle, a spare clip, and a dozen packets of cartridges, meanwhile briefly explaining to Iris the turn taken by events so far as Mir Jan was concerned. She was naturally delighted, and forgot her fears in the excitement caused by the appearance of so useful an ally. She drank his health in a brimming beaker of water.

She heard her lover rejoin Mir Jan, and saw the two step out into the moonlight, whilst Jenks explained the action of the Lee-Metford. Fortunately Iris was now much recovered from the fatigue and privation of the earlier hours. Her senses were sharpened to a pitch little dreamed of by stay-at-home young ladies of her age, and she deemed it her province to act as sentry whilst the two men conferred. Hence, she was the first to detect, or rather to become conscious of, the stealthy crawl of several Dyaks along the bottom of the cliff from Turtle Beach. They advanced in Indian file, moving with the utmost care, and crouching in the murky shadows like so many wild beasts stalking their prey.

"Robert!" she screamed. "The Dyaks! On your left!"

But Iris was rapidly gaining some knowledge of strategy. Before she shrieked her warning she grasped a rifle. Holding it at the "Ready"—about the level of her waist—and depressing the muzzle sufficiently, she began firing down the side of the rock as fast as she could handle lever and trigger. Two of the nickel bullets struck a projection and splashed the leading savages with molten metal.

Unfortunately the Lee-Metford beneath was unloaded, being in Mir Jan's possession for purposes of instruction. Jenks whipped out his revolver.

"To the cave!" he roared, and Mir Jan's unwillingness to face a goblin could not withstand the combined impetus of the sahib's order and the onward rush of the enemy. He darted headlong for the entrance.

Jenks, shooting blindly as he, too, ran for the ladder, emptied the revolver just as his left hand clutched a rung. Three Dyaks were so close that it would be folly to attempt to climb. He threw the weapon into the face of the foremost man, effectually stopping his onward progress, for the darkness made it impossible to dodge the missile.

The sailor turned to dive into the cave and secure the rifle from Mir Jan, when his shin caught the heavy crow-bar resting against the rock. The pain of the blow lent emphasis to the swing with which the implement descended upon some portion of a Dyak anatomy. Jenks never knew where he hit the second assailant, but the place cracked like an eggshell.

He had not time to recover the bar for another blow, so he gave the point in the gullet of a gentleman who was about to make a vicious sweep at him with a parang. The downfall of this worthy caused his immediate successor to stumble, and Jenks saw his opportunity. With the agility of a cat he jumped up the ladder. Once started, he had to go on. He afterwards confessed to an unpleasant sensation of pins and needles along his back during that brief acrobatic display; but he reached the ledge without further injury, save an agonizing twinge when the unprotected quick of his damaged finger was smartly rapped against the rock.

These things happened with the speed of thought. Within forty seconds of Iris's shrill cry the sailor was breast high with the ledge and calling to her—

"All right, old girl. Keep it up!"

The cheerful confidence of his words had a wonderful effect on her. Iris, like every good woman, had the maternal instinct strong within her—the instinct that inspires alike the mild-eyed Sister of Charity and the tigress fighting for her cubs. When Jenks was down below there, in imminent danger of being cut to pieces, the gentle, lovable girl, who would not willingly hurt the humblest of God's creatures, became terrible, majestic in her frenzied purpose. Robert must be saved. If a Maxim were planted on the rock she would unhesitatingly have turned the lever and sprayed the Dyaks with bullets.

But here he was close to her, unhurt and calmly jubilant, as was his way when a stiff fight went well. He was by her side now, firing and aiming too, for the Dyaks broke cover recklessly in running for shelter, and one may do fair work by moonlight, as many a hunter of wild duck can testify by the rheumatism in his bones.

She had strength enough left to place the rifle out of harm's way before she broke down and sobbed, not tearfully, but in a paroxysm of reaction. Soon all was quiet beneath, save for the labored efforts of some wounded men to get far away from that accursed rock. Jenks was able to turn to Iris. He endeavored to allay her agitation, and succeeded somewhat, for tears came, and she clung to him. It was useless to reproach him. The whole incident was unforeseen: she was herself a party to it. But what an escape!

He lifted her in his arms and carried her to a seat where the tarpaulin rested on a broken water-cask.

"You have been a very good little girl and have earned your supper," he said.

"Oh, how can you talk so callously after such an awful experience?" she expostulated brokenly.

The Unexpected Happens

The Jesuits, say their opponents, teach that at times a "white lie" is permissible. Surely this was an instance.

"It is a small thing to trouble about, sweetheart," he explained. "You spotted the enemy so promptly, and blazed away with such ferocity, that they never got within yards of me."

"Are you sure?"

"I vow and declare that after we have eaten something, and sampled our remaining bottle of wine, I will tell you exactly what happened."

"Why not now?"

"Because I must first see to Mir Jan. I bundled him neck and crop into the cave. I hope I did not hurt him."

"You are not going down there again?"

"No need, I trust."

He went to the side of the ledge, recovered the ladder which he had hastily hauled out of the Dyaks' reach after his climb, and cried—

"Mir Jan."

"Ah, sahib! Praised be the name of the Most High, you are alive. I was searching among the slain with a sorrowful heart."

The Mahommedan's voice came from some little distance on the left.

"The slain, you say. How many?"

"Five, sahib."

"Impossible! I fired blindly with the revolver, and only hit one man hard with the iron bar. One other dropped near the wood after I obtained a rifle."

"Then there be six, sahib, not reckoning the wounded.

I have accounted for one, so the miss-sahib must have——"

"What is he saying about me?" inquired Iris, who had risen and joined her lover.

"He says you absolutely staggered the Dyaks by opening fire the moment they appeared."

"How did *you* come to slay one, Mir Jan?" he continued.

"A son of a black pig followed me into the cave. I waited for him in the darkness. I have just thrown his body outside."

"*Shabash!*[1] Is Taung S'Ali dead, by any lucky chance?"

"No, sahib, if he be not the sixth. I will go and see."

"You may be attacked?"

"I have found a sword, sahib. You left me no cartridges."

Jenks told him that the clip and the twelve packets were lying at the foot of the rock, where Mir Jan speedily discovered them. The Mahommedan gave satisfactory assurance that he understood the mechanism of the rifle by filling and adjusting the magazine. Then he went to examine the corpse of the man who lay in the open near the quarry path.

The sailor stood in instant readiness to make a counter demonstration were the native assailed. But there was no sign of the Dyaks. Mir Jan returned with the news that the sixth victim of the brief yet fierce encounter was a renegade Malay. He was so confident that the enemy had had enough of it for the night that, after

[1] "Well done!"

recovering Jenks's revolver, he boldly went to the well and drew himself a supply of water.

During supper, a feast graced by a quart of champagne worthy of the Carlton, Jenks told Iris so much of the story as was good for her: that is to say, he cut down the casualty list.

It was easy to see what had happened. The Dyaks, having missed the Mahommedan and their water-bag, searched for him and heard the conversation at the foot of the rock. Knowing that their presence was suspected, they went back for reinforcements, and returned by the shorter and more advantageous route along Turtle Beach.

Iris would have talked all night, but Jenks made her go to sleep, by pillowing her head against his shoulder and smoothing her tangled tresses with his hand. The wine, too, was helpful. In a few minutes her voice became dreamy: soon she was sleeping like a tired child.

He managed to lay her on a comfortable pile of ragged clothing and then resumed his vigil. Mir Jan offered to mount guard beneath, but Jenks bade him go within the cave and remain there, for the dawn would soon be upon them.

Left alone with his thoughts, he wondered what the rising sun would bring in its train. He reviewed the events of the last twenty-four hours. Iris and he—Miss Deane, Mr. Jenks, to each other—were then undiscovered in their refuge, the Dyaks were gathered around a roaring fire in the valley, and Mir Jan was keen in the hunt as the keenest among them. Now, Iris was his affianced bride, over twenty of the enemy were killed and many wounded, and Mir Jan, a devoted adherent, was seated beside the skeleton in the gloom of the cavern.

What a topsy-turvy world it was, to be sure! What alternations between despair and hope! What rebound from the gates of Death to the threshold of Eden! How untrue, after all, was the nebulous philosophy of Omar, the Tentmaker. Surely in the happenings of the bygone day there was more than the purposeless

> " Magic Shadow-show,
> Play'd in a Box whose Candle is the Sun,
> Round which we Phantom Figures come and go."

He had, indeed, cause to be humbly thankful. Was there not One who marked the fall of a sparrow, who clothed the lilies, who knew the needs of His creatures? There, in the solemn temple of the night, he gave thanks for the protection vouchsafed to Iris and himself, and prayed that it might be continued. He deplored the useless bloodshed, the horror of mangled limbs and festering bodies, that converted this fair island into a reeking slaughter-house. Were it possible, by any personal sacrifice, to divert the untutored savages from their deadly quest, he would gladly condone their misdeeds and endeavor to assuage the torments of the wounded.

But he was utterly helpless, a pawn on that tiny chessboard where the game was being played between Civilization and Barbarism. The fight must go on to the bitter end: he must either vanquish or be vanquished. There were other threads being woven into the garment of his life at that moment, but he knew not of them.

Sufficient for the day was the evil, and the good thereof. Of both he had received full measure.

A period of such reflection could hardly pass without a speculative dive into the future. If Iris and he were rescued, what would happen when they went forth once more into the busy world? Not for one instant did he doubt her faith. She was true as steel, knit to him now by bonds of triple brass. But, what would Sir Arthur Deane think of his daughter's marriage to a discredited and cashiered officer? What was it that poor Mir Jan called himself?—"a disgraced man." Yes, that was it. Could that stain be removed? Mir Jan was doing it. Why not he?—by other means, for his good name rested on the word of a perjured woman. Wealth was potent, but not all-powerful. He would ask Iris to wait until he came to her unsoiled by slander, purged of this odium cast upon him unmerited.

And all this goes to show that he, a man wise beyond his fellows, had not yet learned the unwisdom of striving to lift the veil of tomorrow, behind whose mystic curtain what is to be ever jostles out of place what is hoped for.

Iris, smiling in her dreams, was assailed by no torturing doubts. Robert loved her—that was enough. Love suffices for a woman; a man asks for honor, reputation, an unblemished record.

To awake her he kissed her; he knew not, perchance it might be their last kiss on earth. Not yet dawn, there was morning in the air, for the first faint shafts of light were not visible from their eyrie owing to its position. But there was much to be done. If the Dyaks carried out the plan described by Mir Jan, he had a good many preparations to make.

The canvas awning was rolled back and the stores built into a barricade intended to shelter Iris.

"What is that for?" she asked, when she discovered its nature. He told her. She definitely refused to avail herself of any such protection.

"Robert dear," she said, "if the attack comes to our very door, so to speak, surely I must help you. Even my slight aid may stem a rush in one place whilst you are busy in another."

He explained to her that if hand-to-hand fighting were necessary he would depend more upon a crowbar than a rifle to sweep the ledge clear. She might be in the way.

"Very well. The moment you tell me to get behind that fence I will do so. Even there I can use a revolver."

That reminded him. His own pistol was unloaded. He possessed only five more cartridges of small caliber. He placed them in the weapon and gave it to her.

"Now you have eleven men's lives in your hands," he said. "Try not to miss if you must shoot."

In the dim light he could not see the spasm of pain that clouded her face. No Dyak would reach her whilst he lived. If he fell, there was another use for one of those cartridges.

The sailor had cleared the main floor of the rock and was placing his four rifles and other implements within easy reach when a hiss came from beneath.

"Mir Jan!" exclaimed Iris.

"What now?" demanded Jenks over the side.

The Unexpected Happens

"Sahib, they come!"

"I am prepared. Let that snake get back to his hole in the rock, lest a mongoose seize him by the head."

Mir Jan, engaged in a scouting expedition on his own account, understood that the officer-sahib's orders must be obeyed. He vanished. Soon they heard a great crackling among the bushes on the right, but Jenks knew even before he looked that the Dyaks had correctly estimated the extent of his fire zone and would keep out of it.

The first physical intimation of the enemy's design they received was a pungent but pleasant smell of burning pine, borne to them by the northerly breeze and filling the air with its aroma. The Dyaks kindled a huge fire. The heat was perceptible even on the ledge, but the minutes passed, and the dawn broadened into day without any other result being achieved.

Iris, a little drawn and pale with suspense, said with a timid giggle—

"This does not seem to be so very serious. It reminds me of my efforts to cook."

"There is more to follow, I fear, dear one. But the Dyaks are fools. They should have waited until night fell again, after wearing us out by constant vigilance all day. If they intend to employ smoke it would be far worse for us at night."

Phew! A volume of murky vapor arose that nearly suffocated them by the first whiff of its noisome fumes. It curled like a black pall over the face of the rock and blotted out sea and sky. They coughed incessantly, and nearly choked, for the Dyaks had thrown wet seaweed on top of the burning pile of dry wood. Mir Jan, born in interior India, knew little about the sea or its products, and when the savages talked of seaweed he thought they meant green wood. Fortunately for him, the ascending clouds of smoke missed the cave, or infallibly he must have been stifled.

"Lie flat on the rock!" gasped Jenks. Careless of waste, he poured water over a coat and made Iris bury her mouth and nose in the wet cloth. This gave her immediate relief, and she showed her woman's wit by tying the sleeves of the garment behind her neck. Jenks nodded comprehension and followed her example, for by this means their hands were left free.

The black cloud grew more dense each few seconds. Nevertheless, owing to the slope of the ledge, and the tendency of the smoke to rise, the south side was far more tenable than the north. Quick to note this favorable circumstance, the sailor deduced a further fact from it. A barrier erected on the extreme right of the ledge would be a material gain. He sprang up, dragged the huge tarpaulin from its former location, and propped it on the handle of the pickaxe, driven by one mighty stroke deep into a crevice of the rock.

It was no mean feat of strength that he performed. He swung the heavy and cumbrous canvas into position as if it were a dust cloth. He emerged from the gloom of the driven cloud red-eyed but triumphant. Instantly the vapor on the ledge lessened, and they could breathe, even talk. Overhead and in front the smoke swept in ever-increasing density, but once again the sailor had outwitted the Dyaks' manœuvres.

The Unexpected Happens

"We have won the first rubber," he whispered to Iris.

Above, beneath, beyond, they could see nothing. The air they breathed was hot and fœtid. It was like being immured in a foul tunnel and almost as dark. Jenks looked over the parapet. He thought he could distinguish some vague figures on the sands, so he fired at them. A volley of answering bullets crashed into the rock on all sides. The Dyaks had laid their plans well this time. A firing squad stationed beyond the smoke area, and supplied with all the available guns, commenced and kept up a smart fusillade in the direction of the ledge in order to cover the operations of the scaling party.

Jenks realized that to expose himself was to court a serious wound and achieve no useful purpose. He fell back out of range, laid down his rifle and grabbed the crowbar. At brief intervals a deep hollow boom came up from the valley. At first it puzzled them until the sailor hit upon an explanation. Mir Jan was busy.

The end of a strong roughly made ladder swung through the smoke and banged against the ledge. Before Jenks could reach it those hoisting it into position hastily retreated. They were standing in front of the cave and the Mahommedan made play on them with a Lee-Metford at thirty feet.

Jenks, using his crowbar as a lever, toppled the ladder clean over. It fell outwards and disconcerted a section of the musketeers.

"Well done," cried Iris.

The sailor, astounded by her tone, gave her a fleeting glance. She was very pale now, but not with fear. Her eyes were slightly contracted, her nostrils quivering, her lips set tight and her chin dimpled. She had gone back thirty generations in as many seconds. Thus might one of the daughters of Boadicea have looked whilst guiding her mother's chariot against the Roman phalanx. Resting on one knee, with a revolver in each hand, she seemed no puling mate for the gallant man who fought for her.

She caught his look.

"We will beat them yet!" she cried again, and she smiled, not as a woman smiles, but with the joy of a warrior when the fray is toward.

There was no time for further speech. Three ladders were reared against the rock. They were so poised and held below that Jenks could not force them backwards. A fourth appeared, its coarse shafts looming into sight like the horns of some gigantic animal. The four covered practically the whole front of the ledge save where Mir Jan cleared a little space on the level.

The sailor was standing now, with the crowbar clenched in both hands. The firing in the valley slackened and died away. A Dyak face, grinning like a Japanese demon, appeared at the top of the ladder nearest to Iris.

"Don't fire!" shouted Jenks, and the iron bar crushed downwards. Two others pitched themselves half on to the ledge. Now both crowbar and revolver were needed. Three ladders were thus cumbered somewhat for those beneath, and Jenks sprang towards the fourth and most distant. Men were crowding it like ants. Close to his feet lay an empty water-cask. It was a crude weapon, but effective when well pitched, and the sailor had never made a better shot for a goal in the midst of a hard-fought scrimmage than he made with that tub for the head of the uppermost pirate.

Another volley came from the sands. A bullet ploughed through his hair, and sent his sou'wester flying. Again the besiegers swarmed to the attack. One way or the other, they must succeed. A man and a woman—even such a man and such a woman—could not keep at bay an infuriated horde of fifty savages fighting at close quarters and under these grievous conditions.

Jenks knew what would happen. He would be shot in the head or breast whilst repelling the scaling party. And Iris! Dear heart! She was thinking of him.

"Keep back! They can never gain the ledge!" she shrieked.

And then, above the din of the fusillade, the yells of the assailants and the bawling of the wounded, there came through the air a screaming, tearing, ripping sound which drowned all others. It traveled with incredible speed, and before the sailor could believe his ears—for he well knew what it meant—a shrapnel shell burst in front of the ledge and drenched the valley with flying lead.

Jenks was just able to drag Iris flat against the rock ere the time fuse operated and the bullets flew. He could form no theory, hazard no conjecture. All he knew was that a 12-pounder shell had flown towards them through space, scattering red ruin among the amazed scoundrels beneath. Instantly he rose again, lest perchance any of the Dyaks should have gained a foothold on the ledge.

The ladders were empty. He could hear a good deal of groaning, the footsteps of running men, and some distant shouting.

"Sahib!" yelled Mir Jan, drawn from his retreat by the commotion without.

"Yes," shouted Jenks.

The native, in a voice cracked with excitement, told him something. The sailor asked a few rapid questions to make quite sure that Mir Jan was not mistaken.

Then he threw his arms round Iris, drew her close and whispered—

"My darling, we are saved! A warship has anchored just beyond the south reef, and two boats filled with armed sailors are now pulling ashore."

And she answered proudly—

"The Dyaks could never have conquered us, Robert. We were manifestly under God's protection. Oh, my love, my love, I am so happy and thankful!"

CHAPTER XV

THE DIFFICULTY OF PLEASING
EVERYBODY

THE drifting smoke was still so dense that not even
the floor of the valley could be discerned. Jenks dared
not leave Iris at such a moment. He feared to bring her
down the ladder lest another shell might be fired. But
something must be done to end their suspense.

He called to Mir Jan—

"Take off your turban and hold it above your head,
if you think they can see you from the warship."

"It is all right, sahib," came the cheering answer.
"One boat is close inshore. I think, from the uniforms,
they are English sahibs, such as I have seen at Garden
Reach. The Dyaks have all gone."

Nevertheless Jenks waited. There was nothing to
gain by being too precipitate. A false step now might
undo the achievements of many weeks.

Mir Jan was dancing about beneath in a state of wild
excitement.

"They have seen the Dyaks running to their sampans,
sahib," he yelled, "and the second boat is being pulled in
that direction. Yet another has just left the ship."

A translation made Iris excited, eager to go down and
see these wonders.

"Better wait here, dearest," he said. "The enemy may be driven back in this direction, and I cannot expose you to further risk. The sailors will soon land, and you can then descend in perfect safety."

The boom of a cannon came from the sea. Instinctively the girl ducked for safety, though her companion smiled at her fears, for the shell would have long preceded the report, had it traveled their way.

"One of the remaining sampans has got under way," he explained, "and the warship is firing at her."

Two more guns were fired. The man-o'-war evidently meant business.

"Poor wretches!" murmured Iris. "Cannot the survivors be allowed to escape?"

"Well, we are unable to interfere. Those caught on the island will probably be taken to the mainland and hanged for their crimes, so the manner of their end is not of much consequence."

To the girl's manifest relief there was no more firing, and Mir Jan announced that a number of sailors were actually on shore. Then her thoughts turned to a matter of concern to the feminine mind even in the gravest moments of existence. She laved her face with water and sought her discarded skirt!

Soon the steady tramp of boot-clad feet advancing at the double was heard on the shingle, and an officer's voice, speaking the crude Hindustani of the engine-room and forecastle, shouted to Mir Jan—

"Hi, you black fellow! Are there any white people here?"

Jenks sang out—

"Yes, two of us! Perched on the rock over your heads. We are coming down."

He cast loose the rope-ladder. Iris was limp and trembling.

"Steady, sweetheart," he whispered. "Don't forget the slip between the cup and the lip. Hold tight! But have no fear! I will be just beneath."

It was well he took this precaution. She was now so unnerved that an unguarded movement might have led to an accident. But the knowledge that her lover was near, the touch of his hand guiding her feet on to the rungs of the ladder, sustained her. They had almost reached the level when a loud exclamation and the crash of a heavy blow caused Jenks to halt and look downwards.

A Dyak, lying at the foot of one of the scaling ladders, and severely wounded by a shell splinter, witnessed their descent. In his left hand he grasped a parang; his right arm was bandaged. Though unable to rise, the vengeful pirate mustered his remaining strength to crawl towards the swaying ladder. It was Taung S'Ali, inspired with the hate and venom of the dying snake. Even yet he hoped to deal a mortal stroke at the man who had defied him and all his cut-throat band. He might have succeeded, as Jenks was so taken up with Iris, were it not for the watchful eyes of Mir Jan. The Mahommedan sprang at him with an oath, and gave him such a murderous whack with the butt of a rifle that the Dyak chief collapsed and breathed out his fierce spirit in a groan.

At the first glance Jenks did not recognize Taung

S'Ali, owing to his change of costume. Through the thinner smoke he could see several sailors running up.

"Look out, there!" he cried. "There is a lady here. If any Dyake moves, knock him on the head!"

But, with the passing of the chief, their last peril had gone. The next instant they were standing on the firm ground, and a British naval lieutenant was saying eagerly—

"We seem to have turned up in the nick of time. Do you, by any chance, belong to the *Sirdar?*"

"We are the sole survivors," answered the sailor.

"You two only?"

"Yes. She struck on the north-west reef of this island during a typhoon. This lady, Miss Iris Deane, and I were flung ashore——"

"Miss Deane! Can it be possible? Let me congratulate you most heartily. Sir Arthur Deane is on board the *Orient* at this moment."

"The *Orient!*"

Iris was dazed. The uniforms, the pleasant faces of the English sailors, the strange sensation of hearing familiar words in tones other than those of the man she loved, bewildered her.

"Yes," explained the officer, with a sympathetic smile. "That's our ship, you know, in the offing there."

It was all too wonderful to be quite understood yet. She turned to Robert—

"Do you hear? They say my father is not far away. Take me to him."

"No need for that, miss," interrupted a warrant officer. "Here he is coming ashore. He wanted to come with us, but the captain would not permit it, as there seemed to be some trouble ahead."

Sure enough, even the girl's swimming eyes could distinguish the grey-bearded civilian seated beside an officer in the stern-sheets of a small gig now threading a path through the broken reef beyond Turtle Beach. In five minutes, father and daughter would meet.

Meanwhile the officer, intent on duty, addressed Jenks again.

"May I ask who you are?"

"My name is Anstruther—Robert Anstruther."

Iris, clinging to his arm, heard the reply.

So he had abandoned all pretence. He was ready to face the world at her side. She stole a loving glance at him as she cried—

"Yes, Captain Anstruther, of the Indian Staff Corps. If he will not tell you all that he has done, how he has saved my life twenty times, how he has fought single-handed against eighty men, ask me!"

The naval officer did not need to look a second time at Iris's face to lengthen the list of Captain Anstruther's achievements, by one more item. He sighed. A good sailor always does sigh when a particularly pretty girl is labeled "Engaged."

But he could be very polite.

"Captain Anstruther does not appear to have left much for us to do, Miss Deane," he said. "Indeed," turning to Robert, "is there any way in which my men will be useful?"

"I would recommend that they drag the green stuff off that fire and stop the smoke. Then, a detachment should go round the north side of the island and drive the remaining Dyaks into the hands of the party you have landed, as I understand, at the further end of the south beach. Mir Jan, the Mahommedan here, who has been a most faithful ally during part of our siege, will act as guide."

The other man cast a comprehensive glance over the rock, with its scaling ladders and dangling rope-ladder, the cave, the little groups of dead or unconscious pirates —for every wounded man who could move a limb had crawled away after the first shell burst—and drew a deep breath.

"How long were you up there?" he asked.

"Over thirty hours."

"It was a great fight!"

"Somewhat worse than it looks," said Anstruther. "This is only the end of it. Altogether, we have accounted for nearly two score of the poor devils."

"Do you think you can make them prisoners, without killing any more of them?" asked Iris.

"That depends entirely on themselves, Miss Deane. My men will not fire a shot unless they encounter resistance."

Robert looked towards the approaching boat. She would not land yet for a couple of minutes.

"By the way," he said, "will you tell me your name?"

"Playdon—Lieutenant Philip H. Playdon."

"Do you know to what nation this island belongs?"

"It is no-man's land, I think. It is marked 'uninhabited' on the chart."

"Then," said Anstruther, "I call upon you, Lieutenant Playdon, and all others here present, to witness that I, Robert Anstruther, late of the Indian Army, acting on behalf of myself and Miss Iris Deane, declare that we have taken possession of this island in the name of His Britannic Majesty the King of England, that we are the joint occupiers and owners thereof, and claim all property rights vested therein."

These formal phrases, coming at such a moment, amazed his hearers. Iris alone had an inkling of the underlying motive.

"I don't suppose any one will dispute your title," said the naval officer gravely. He unquestionably imagined that suffering and exposure had slightly disturbed the other man's senses, yet he had seldom seen any person who looked to be in more complete possession of his faculties.

"Thank you," replied Robert with equal composure, though he felt inclined to laugh at Playdon's mystification. "I only wished to secure a sufficient number of witnesses for a verbal declaration. When I have a few minutes to spare I will affix a legal notice on the wall in front of our cave."

Playdon bowed silently. There was something in the speaker's manner that puzzled him. He detailed a small guard to accompany Robert and Iris, who now walked towards the beach, and asked Mir Jan to pilot him as suggested by Anstruther.

The boat was yet many yards from shore when Iris ran forward and stretched out her arms to the man who was staring at her with wistful despair.

"Father! Father!" she cried. "Don't you know me?"

Sir Arthur Deane was looking at the two strange figures on the sands, and each moment his heart sank lower. This island held his final hope. During many weary weeks, since the day when a kindly Admiral placed the cruiser *Orient* at his disposal, he had scoured the China Sea, the coasts of Borneo and Java, for some tidings of the ill-fated *Sirdar*.

He met naught save blank nothingness, the silence of the great ocean mausoleum. Not a boat, a spar, a life-buoy, was cast up by the waves to yield faintest trace of the lost steamer. Every naval man knew what had happened. The vessel had met with some mishap to her machinery, struck a derelict, or turned turtle, during that memorable typhoon of March 17 and 18. She had gone down with all hands. Her fate was a foregone conclusion. No ship's boat could live in that sea, even if the crew were able to launch one. It was another of ocean's tragedies, with the fifth act left to the imagination.

To examine every sand patch and tree-covered shoal in the China Sea was an impossible task. All the *Orient* could do was to visit the principal islands and institute inquiries among the fishermen and small traders. At last, the previous night, a Malay, tempted by hope of reward, boarded the vessel when lying at anchor off the large island away to the south, and told the captain a wondrous tale of a devil-haunted place inhabited by two white spirits, a male and a female, whither a local pirate named Taung S'Ali had gone by chance with his men and suffered great loss. But Taung S'Ali was bewitched by the female spirit, and had returned there, with a great force, swearing to capture her or perish. The spirits, the Malay said, had dwelt upon the island for many years. His father and grandfather knew the place and feared it. Taung S'Ali would never be seen again.

This queer yarn was the first indication they received of the whereabouts of any persons who might possibly be shipwrecked Europeans, though not survivors from the *Sirdar*. Anyhow, the tiny dot lay in the vessel's northward track, so a course was set to arrive off the island soon after dawn.

Events on shore, as seen by the officer on watch, told their own tale. Wherever Dyaks are fighting there is mischief on foot, so the *Orient* took a hand in the proceedings.

But Sir Arthur Deane, after an agonized scrutiny of the weird-looking persons escorted by the sailors to the water's edge, sadly acknowledged that neither of these could be the daughter whom he sought. He bowed his head in humble resignation, and he thought he was the victim of a cruel hallucination when Iris's tremulous accents reached his ears—

"Father, father! Don't you know me?"

He stood up, amazed and trembling.

"Yes, father dear. It is I, your own little girl given back to you. Oh dear! Oh dear! I cannot see you for my tears."

They had some difficulty to keep him in the boat, and the man pulling stroke smashed a stout oar with the next wrench.

And so they met at last, and the sailors left them alone, to crowd round Anstruther and ply him with a hundred questions. Although he fell in with their humor, and gradually pieced together the stirring story which was supplemented each instant by the arrival of disconsolate Dyaks and the comments of the men who returned from cave and beach, his soul was filled with the sight of Iris and her father, and the happy, inconsequent demands with which each sought to ascertain and relieve the extent of the other's anxiety.

Then Iris called to him—

"Robert, I want you."

The use of his Christian name created something akin to a sensation. Sir Arthur Deane was startled, even in his immeasurable delight at finding his child uninjured—the picture of rude health and happiness.

Anstruther advanced.

"This is my father," she cried, shrill with joy. "And, father darling, this is Captain Robert Anstruther, to whom alone, under God's will, I owe my life, many, many times since the moment the *Sirdar* was lost."

It was no time for questioning. Sir Arthur Deane took off his hat and held out his hand—

"Captain Anstruther," he said, "as I owe you my daughter's life, I owe you that which I can never repay. And I owe you my own life, too, for I could not have survived the knowledge that she was dead."

Robert took the proffered hand—

"I think, Sir Arthur, that, of the two, I am the more deeply indebted. There are some privileges whose value cannot be measured, and among them the privilege of restoring your daughter to your arms takes the highest place."

Then, being much more self-possessed than the older man, who was naturally in a state of agitation that was almost painful, he turned to Iris.

"I think," he said, "that your father should take you on board the *Orient*, Iris. There you may, perhaps, find some suitable clothing, eat something, and recover from the exciting events of the morning. Afterwards, you must bring Sir Arthur ashore again, and we will guide him over the island. I am sure you will find much to tell him meanwhile."

The baronet could not fail to note the manner in which these two addressed each other, the fearless love which leaped from eye to eye, the calm acceptance of a relationship not be questioned or gainsaid. Robert and Iris, without spoken word on the subject, had tactily agreed to avoid the slightest semblance of subterfuge as unworthy alike of their achievements and their love. Yet what could Sir Arthur Deane do? To frame a suitable protest at such a moment was not to be dreamed of. As yet he was too shaken to collect his thoughts. Anstruther's proposal, however, helped him to blurt out what he intuitively felt to be a disagreeable fact. Yet something must be said, for his brain reeled.

"Your suggestion is admirable," he cried, striving desperately to affect a careless complaisance. "The ship's stores may provide Iris with some sort of rig-out, and an old friend of hers is on board at this moment, little expecting her presence. Lord Ventnor has accom-

panied me in my search. He will, of course, be delighted——"

Anstruther flushed a deep bronze, but Iris broke in—

"Father, why did *he* come with you?"

Sir Arthur, driven into this sudden squall of explanation, became dignified.

"Well, you see, my dear, under the circumstances, he
felt an anxiety almost commensurate with my own."

"But why, why?"

Iris was quite calm. With Robert near, she was
courageous. Even the perturbed baronet experienced a
new sensation as his troubled glance fell before her
searching eyes. His daughter had left him a joyous,
heedless girl. He found her a woman, strong, self-reliant, purposeful. Yet he kept on, choosing the most
straightforward means as the only honorable way of
clearing a course so beset with unsuspected obstacles.

"It is only reasonable, Iris, that your affianced husband should suffer an agony of apprehension on your
account, and do all that was possible to effect your
rescue."

"My—affianced—husband?"

"Well, my dear girl, perhaps that is hardly the correct phrase from your point of view. Yet you cannot
fail to remember that Lord Ventnor——"

"Father, dear," said Iris solemnly, but in a voice free
from all uncertainty, "my affianced husband stands here!
We plighted our troth at the very gate of death. It
was ratified in the presence of God, and has been blessed
by Him. I have made no compact with Lord Ventnor.
He is a base and unworthy man. Did you but know the

truth concerning him you would not mention his name in the same breath with mine. Would he, Robert?"

Never was man so perplexed as the unfortunate ship-owner. In the instant that his beloved daughter was restored to him out of the very depths of the sea, he was asked either to undertake the rôle of a disappointed and unforgiving parent, or sanction her marriage to a truculent-looking person of most forbidding if otherwise manly appearance, who had certainly saved her from death in ways not presently clear to him, but who could not be regarded as a suitable son-in-law solely on that account.

What could he do, what could he say, to make the position less intolerable?

Anstruther, quicker than Iris to appreciate Sir Arthur Deane's dilemma, gallantly helped him. He placed a loving hand on the girl's shoulder.

"Be advised by me, Sir Arthur, and you too, Iris," he said. "This is no hour for such explanations. Leave me to deal with Lord Ventnor. I am content to trust the ultimate verdict to you, Sir Arthur. You will learn in due course all that has happened. Go on board, Iris. Meet Lord Ventnor as you would meet any other friend. You will not marry him, I know. I can trust you." He said this with a smile that robbed the words of serious purport. "Believe me, you two can find plenty to occupy your minds today without troubling yourselves about Lord Ventnor."

"I am very much obliged to you," murmured the baronet, who, notwithstanding his worry, was far too experienced a man of the world not to acknowledge the good sense of this advice, no matter how ruffianly might be the guise of the strange person who gave it.

"That is settled, then," said Robert, laughing good-naturedly, for he well knew what a weird spectacle he must present to the bewildered old gentleman.

Even Sir Arthur Deane was fascinated by the ragged and hairy giant who carried himself so masterfully and helped everybody over the stile at the right moment. He tried to develop the change in the conversation.

"By the way," he said, "how came you to be on the *Sirdar?* I have a list of all the passengers and crew, and your name does not appear therein."

"Oh, that is easily accounted for. I shipped as a steward, in the name of Robert Jenks."

"Robert Jenks! A steward!"

This was worse than ever. The unhappy shipowner thought the sky must have fallen.

"Yes. That forms some part of the promised explanation."

Iris rapidly gathered the drift of her lover's wishes.

"Come, father," she cried merrily. "I am aching to see what the ship's stores, which you and Robert pin your faith to, can do for me in the shape of garments. I have the utmost belief in the British navy, and even a skeptic should be convinced of its infallibility if H.M.S. *Orient* is able to provide a lady's outfit."

Sir Arthur Deane gladly availed himself of the proffered compromise. He assisted Iris into the boat, though that active young person was far better able to support him, and a word to the officer in command sent the gig flying back to the ship. Anstruther, during a momentary delay, made a small request on his own account. Lieutenant Playdon, nearly as big a man as Robert, despatched a note to his servant, and the gig speedily returned with a complete assortment of clothing and linen. The man also brought a dressing case, with the result that a dip in the bath, and ten minutes in the hands of an expert valet, made Anstruther a new man.

Acting under his advice, the bodies of the dead were thrown into the lagoon, the wounded were collected in the hut to be attended to by the ship's surgeon, and the prisoners were paraded in front of Mir Jan, who identified every man, and found, by counting heads, that none was missing.

Robert did not forget to write out a formal notice and fasten it to the rock. This proceeding further mystified the officers of the *Orient*, who had gradually formed a connected idea of the great fight made by the shipwrecked pair, though Anstruther squirmed inwardly when he thought of the manner in which Iris would picture the scene. As it was, he had the first innings, and he did not fail to use the opportunity. In the few terse words which the militant Briton best understands, he described the girl's fortitude, her unflagging cheerfulness, her uncomplaining readiness to do and dare.

Little was said by his auditors, save to interpolate an occasional question as to why such and such a thing was necessary, or how some particular drawback had been surmounted. Standing near the well, it was not necessary to move to explain to them the chief features of the island, and point out the measures he had adopted.

When he ended, the first lieutenant, who commanded

the boats sent in pursuit of the flying Dyaks—the *Orient* sank both sampans as soon as they were launched—summed up the general verdict—

"You do not need our admiration, Captain Anstruther. Each man of us envies you from the bottom of his soul."

"I do, I know—from the very bilge," exclaimed a stout midshipman, one of those who had seen Iris.

Robert waited until the laugh died away.

"There is an error about my rank," he said. "I did once hold a commission in the Indian army, but I was court-marshaled and cashiered in Hong Kong six months ago. I was unjustly convicted on a grave charge, and I hope some day to clear myself. Meanwhile I am a mere civilian. It was only Miss Deane's generous sympathy which led her to mention my former rank, Mr. Playdon."

Had another of the *Orient's* 12-pounder shells suddenly burst in the midst of the group of officers, it would have created less dismay than this unexpected avowal. Court-martialed! Cashiered! None but a service man can grasp the awful significance of those words to the commissioned ranks of the army and navy.

Anstruther well knew what he was doing. Somehow, he found nothing hard in the performance of these penances now. Of course, the ugly truth must be revealed the moment Lord Ventnor heard his name. It was not fair to the good fellows crowding around him, and offering every attention that the frank hospitality of the British sailor could suggest, to permit them to adopt the tone of friendly equality which rigid discipline, if nothing else, would not allow them to maintain.

The first lieutenant, by reason of his rank, was compelled to say something—

"That is a devilish bad job, Mr. Anstruther," he blurted out.

"Well, you know, I had to tell you."

He smiled unaffectedly at the wondering circle. He, too, was an officer, and appreciated their sentiments. They were unfeignedly sorry for him, a man so brave and modest, such a splendid type of the soldier and gentleman, yet, by their common law, an outcast. Nor could they wholly understand his demeanor. There was a noble dignity in his candor, a conscious innocence that disdained to shield itself under a partial truth. He spoke, not as a wrong-doer, but as one who addresses those who have been and will be once more his peers.

The first lieutenant again phrased the thoughts of his juniors—

"I, and every other man in the ship, cannot help but sympathize with you. But whatever may be your record —if you were an escaped convict, Mr. Anstruther—no one could withhold from you the praise deserved for your magnificent stand against overwhelming odds. Our duty is plain. We will bring you to Singapore, where the others will no doubt wish to go immediately. I will tell the Captain what you have been good enough to acquaint us with. Meanwhile we will give you every assistance, and—er—attention in our power."

A murmur of approbation ran through the little circle. Robert's face paled somewhat. What first-rate chaps they were, to be sure!

"I can only thank you," he said unsteadily. "Your kindness is more trying than adversity."

A rustle of silk, the intrusion into the intent knot of men of a young lady in a Paris gown, a Paris hat, carrying a Trouville parasol, and most exquisitely gloved and booted, made every one gasp.

"Oh, Robert dear, how *could* you? I actually didn't know you!"

Thus Iris, bewitchingly attired, and gazing now with provoking admiration at Robert, who certainly offered almost as great a contrast to his former state as did the girl herself. He returned her look with interest.

"Would any man believe," he laughed, "that clothes would do so much for a woman?"

"What a left-handed compliment! But come, dearest, Captain Fitzroy and Lord Ventnor have come ashore with father and me. They want us to show them everything! You will excuse him, won't you?" she added, with a seraphic smile to the others.

They walked off together.

"Jimmy!" gasped the fat midshipman to a lanky youth. "She's got on your togs!"

Meaning that Iris had ransacked the *Orient's* theatrical wardrobe, and pounced on the swell outfit of the principal female impersonator in the ship's company.

Lieutenant Playdon bit the chin strap of his pith helmet, for the landing party wore the regulation uniform for service ashore in the tropics. He muttered to his chief—

The Difficulty of Pleasing Everybody

"Damme if I've got the hang of this business yet."

"Neither have I. Anstruther looks a decent sort of fellow, and the girl is a stunner. Yet, d'ye know, Playdon, right through the cruise I've always understood that she was the fiancée of that cad, Ventnor."

"Anstruther appears to have arranged matters differently. Wonder what pa will say when that Johnnie owns up about the court-martial."

"Give it up, which is more than the girl will do, or I'm much mistaken. Funny thing, you know, but I've a sort of hazy recollection of Anstruther's name being mixed up with that of a Colonel's wife at Hong Kong. Fancy Ventnor was in it too, as a witness. Stand by, and we'll see something before we unload at Singapore."

CHAPTER XVI

BARGAINS, GREAT AND SMALL

LORD VENTNOR was no fool. Whilst Iris was transforming herself from a semi-savage condition into a semblance of an ultra *chic* Parisienne—the *Orient's* dramatic costumier went in for strong stage effects in feminine attire—Sir Arthur Deane told the Earl something of the state of affairs on the island.

His lordship—a handsome, saturnine man, cool, insolently polite, and plentifully endowed with the judgmatical daring that is the necessary equipment of a society libertine—counseled patience, toleration, even silent recognition of Anstruther's undoubted claims for services rendered.

"She is an enthusiastic, high-spirited girl," he urged upon his surprised hearer, who expected a very different expression of opinion. "This fellow Anstruther is a plausible sort of rascal, a good man in a tight place too —just the sort of fire-eating blackguard who would fill the heroic bill where a fight is concerned. Damn him, he licked me twice."

Further amazement for the shipowner.

"Yes, it's quite true. I interfered with his little games, and he gave me the usual reward of the devil's

apothecary. Leave Iris alone. At present she is strung
up to an intense pitch of gratitude, having barely escaped a terrible fate. Let her come back to the normal.
Anstruther's shady record must gradually leak out.
That will disgust her. In a week she will appeal to you
to buy him off. He is hard up—cut off by his people
and that sort of thing. There you probably have the
measure of his scheming. He knows quite well that he
can never marry your daughter. It is all a matter of
price."

Sir Arthur willingly allowed himself to be persuaded.
At the back of his head there was an uneasy consciousness that it was not "all a matter of price." If it were
he would never trust a man's face again. But Ventnor's
well-balanced arguments swayed him. The course indicated was the only decent one. It was humanly impossible for a man to chide his daughter and flout her rescuer
within an hour of finding them.

Lord Ventnor played his cards with a deeper design.
He bowed to the inevitable. Iris said she loved his rival.
Very well. To attempt to dissuade her was to throw her
more closely into that rival's arms. The right course
was to appear resigned, saddened, compelled against his
will to reveal the distressing truth. Further, he counted
on Anstruther's quick temper as an active agent. Such
a man would be the first to rebel against an assumption
of pitying tolerance. He would bring bitter charges of
conspiracy, of unbelievable compact to secure his ruin.
All this must recoil on his own head when the facts were
laid bare. Not even the hero of the island could pre-
vail against the terrible indictment of the court-martial.

Finally, at Singapore, three days distant, Colonel Costobell and his wife were staying. Lord Ventnor, alone of those on board, knew this. Indeed, he accompanied Sir Arthur Deane largely in order to break off a somewhat trying entanglement. He smiled complacently as he thought of the effect on Iris of Mrs. Costobell's indignant remonstrances when the baronet asked that injured lady to tell the girl all that had happened at Hong Kong.

In a word, Lord Ventnor was most profoundly annoyed, and he cursed Anstruther from the depths of his heart. But he could see a way out. The more desperate the emergency the more need to display finesse. Above all, he must avoid an immediate rupture.

He came ashore with Iris and her father; the captain of the *Orient* also joined the party. The three men watched Robert and the girl walking towards them from the group of officers.

"Anstruther is a smart-looking fellow," commented Captain Fitzroy. "Who is he?"

Truth to tell, the gallant commander of the *Orient* was secretly amazed by the metamorphosis effected in Robert's appearance since he scrutinized him through his glasses. Iris, too, unaccustomed to the constraint of high-heeled shoes, clung to the nondescript's arm in a manner that shook the sailor's faith in Lord Ventnor's pretensions as her favored suitor.

Poor Sir Arthur said not a word, but his lordship was quite at ease—

"From his name, and from what Deane tells me, I believe he is an ex-officer of the Indian Army."

"Ah. He has left the service?"

"Yes. I met him last in Hong Kong."

"Then you know him?"

"Quite well, if he is the man I imagine."

"That is really very nice of Ventnor," thought the shipowner. "The last thing I should credit him with would be a forgiving disposition."

Meanwhile Anstruther was reading Iris a little lecture. "Sweet one," he explained to her, "do not allude to me by my former rank. I am not entitled to it. Some day, please God, it will be restored to me. At present I am a plain civilian."

"I think you very handsome."

"Don't tease, there's a good girl. It is not fair with all these people looking."

"But really, Robert, only since you scraped off the upper crust have I been able to recognize you again. I remember now that I thought you were a most distinguished looking steward."

"Well, I am helpless. I cannot even squeeze you. By the way, Iris, during the next few days say nothing about our mine."

"Oh, why not?"

"Just a personal whim. It will please me."

"If it pleases you, Robert, I am satisfied."

He pressed her arm by way of answer. They were too near to the waiting trio for other comment.

"Captain Fitzroy," cried Iris, "let me introduce Mr. Anstruther to you. Lord Ventnor, you have met Mr. Anstruther before."

The sailor shook hands. Lord Ventnor smiled affably.

"Your enforced residence on the island seems to have agreed with you," he said.

"Admirably. Life here had its drawbacks, but we fought our enemies in the open. Didn't we, Iris?"

"Yes, dear. The poor Dyaks were not sufficiently modernized to attack us with false testimony."

His lordship's sallow face wrinkled somewhat. So Iris knew of the court-martial, nor was she afraid to proclaim to all the world that this man was her lover. As for Captain Fitzroy, his bushy eyebrows disappeared into his peaked cap when he heard the manner of their speech.

Nevertheless Ventnor smiled again.

"Even the Dyaks respected Miss Deane," he said.

But Anstruther, sorry for the manifest uneasiness of the shipowner, repressed the retort on his lips, and forthwith suggested that they should walk to the north beach in the first instance, that being the scene of the wreck.

During the next hour he became auditor rather than narrator. It was Iris who told of his wild fight against wind and waves, Iris who showed them where he fought with the devil-fish, Iris who expatiated on the long days of ceaseless toil, his dauntless courage in the face of every difficulty, the way in which he rescued her from the clutch of the savages, the skill of his preparations against the anticipated attack, and the last great achievement of all, when, time after time, he foiled the Dyaks' best-laid plans, and flung them off, crippled and disheartened, during the many phases of the thirty hours' battle.

She had an attentive audience. Most of the *Orient's*

[316]

officers quietly came up and followed the girl's glowing recital with breathless interest. Robert vainly endeavored more than once to laugh away her thrilling eulogy. But she would have none of it. Her heart was in her words. He deserved this tribute of praise, unstinted, unmeasured, abundant in its simple truth, yet sounding like a legend spun by some romantic poet, were not the grim evidences of its accuracy visible on every hand.

She was so volubly clear, so precise in fact, so subtle in her clever delineations of humorous or tragic events, that her father was astounded, and even Anstruther silently admitted that a man might live until he equaled the years of a Biblical patriarch without discovering all the resources of a woman.

There were tears in her eyes when she ended; but they were tears of thankful happiness, and Lord Ventnor, a silent listener who missed neither word nor look, felt a deeper chill in his cold heart as he realized that this woman's love could never be his. The knowledge excited his passion the more. His hatred of Anstruther now became a mania, an insensate resolve to mortally stab this meddler who always stood in his path.

Robert hoped that his present ordeal was over. It had only begun. He was called on to answer questions without number. Why had the tunnel been made? What was the mystery of the Valley of Death? How did he manage to guess the dimensions of the sun-dial? How came he to acquire such an amazing stock of out-of-the-way knowledge of the edible properties of roots and trees? How? Why? Where? When? They never would be satisfied, for not even the British navy—

poking its nose into the recesses of the world—often comes across such an amazing story as the adventures of this couple on Rainbow Island.

He readily explained the creation of quarry and cave by telling them of the vein of antimony embedded in the rock near the fault. Antimony is one of the substances that covers a multitude of doubts. No one, not excepting the doctors who use it, knows much about it, and in Chinese medicine it might be a chief factor of exceeding nastiness.

Inside the cavern, the existence of the partially completed shaft to the ledge accounted for recent disturbances on the face of the rock, and new-comers could not, of course, distinguish the bones of poor "J. S." as being the remains of a European.

Anstruther was satisfied that none of them hazarded the remotest guess as to the value of the gaunt rock they were staring at, and chance helped him to baffle further inquiry.

A trumpeter on board the *Orient* was blowing his lungs out to summon them to luncheon, when Captain Fitzroy put a final query.

"I can quite understand," he said to Robert, "that you have an affection for this weird place."

"I should think so indeed," muttered the stout midshipman, glancing at Iris.

"But I am curious to know," continued the commander, "why you lay claim to the island? You can hardly intend to return here."

He pointed to Robert's placard stuck on the rock.

Anstruther paused before he answered. He felt that

Lord Ventnor's dark eyes were fixed on him. Everybody was more or less desirous to have this point cleared up. He looked the questioner squarely in the face.

"In some parts of the world," he said, "there are sunken reefs, unknown, uncharted, on which many a vessel has been lost without any contributory fault on the part of her officers?"

"Undoubtedly."

"Well, Captain Fitzroy, when I was stationed with my regiment in Hong Kong I encountered such a reef, and wrecked my life on it. At least, that is how it seemed to me then. Fortune threw me ashore here, after a long and bitter submergence. You can hardly blame me if I cling to the tiny speck of land that gave me salvation."

"No," admitted the sailor. He knew there was something more in the allegory than the text revealed, but it was no business of his.

"Moreover," continued Robert smilingly, "you see I have a partner."

"There cannot be the slightest doubt about the partner," was the prompt reply.

Then every one laughed, Iris more than any, though Sir Arthur Deane's gaiety was forced, and Lord Ventnor could taste the acidity of his own smile.

Later in the day the first lieutenant told his chief of Anstruther's voluntary statement concerning the court-martial. Captain Fitzroy was naturally pained by this unpleasant revelation, but he took exactly the same view as that expressed by the first lieutenant in Robert's presence.

Nevertheless he pondered the matter, and seized an early opportunity of mentioning it to Lord Ventnor. That distinguished nobleman was vastly surprised to learn how Anstruther had cut the ground from beneath his feet.

"Yes," he said, in reply to the sailor's request for information, "I know all about it. It could not well be otherwise, seeing that next to Mrs. Costobell I was the principal witness against him."

"That must have been d——d awkward for you," was the unexpected comment.

"Indeed! Why?"

"Because rumor linked your name with that of the lady in a somewhat outspoken way."

"You astonish me. Anstruther certainly made some stupid allegations during the trial; but I had no idea he was able to spread this malicious report subsequently."

"I am not talking of Hong Kong, my lord, but of Singapore, months later."

Captain Fitzroy's tone was exceedingly dry. Indeed, some people might deem it offensive.

His lordship permitted himself the rare luxury of an angry scowl.

"Rumor is a lying jade at the best," he said curtly. "You must remember, Captain Fitzroy, that I have uttered no word of scandal about Mr. Anstruther, and any doubts concerning his conduct can be set at rest by perusing the records of his case in the Adjutant-General's office at Hong Kong."

"Hum!" said the sailor, turning on his heel to enter

the chart-room. This was no way to treat a real live lord, a personage of some political importance, too, such as the Special Envoy to Wang Hai. Evidently, Iris was no mean advocate. She had already won for the "outcast" the suffrages of the entire ship's company.

The girl and her father went back to the island with Robert. After taking thought, the latter decided to ask Mir Jan to remain in possession until he returned. There was not much risk of another Dyak invasion. The fate of Taung S'Ali's expedition would not encourage a fresh set of marauders, and the Mahommedan would be well armed to meet unforeseen contingencies, whilst on his, Anstruther's, representations the *Orient* would land an abundance of stores. In any event, it was better for the native to live in freedom on Rainbow Island than to be handed over to the authorities as an escaped convict, which must be his immediate fate no matter what magnanimous view the Government of India might afterwards take of his services.

Mir Jan's answer was emphatic. He took off his turban and placed it on Anstruther's feet.

"Sahib," he said, "I am your dog. If, some day, I am found worthy to be your faithful servant, then shall I know that Allah has pardoned my transgressions. I only killed a man because——"

"Peace, Mir Jan. Let him rest."

"Why is he worshiping you, Robert?" demanded Iris.

He told her.

"Really," she cried, "I must keep up my studies in Hindustani. It is quite too sweet."

And then, for the benefit of her father, she rattled off into a spirited account of her struggles with the algebraic x and the Urdu compound verb.

Sir Arthur Deane managed to repress a sigh. In spite of himself he could not help liking Anstruther. The man was magnetic, a hero, an ideal gentleman. No wonder his daughter was infatuated with him. Yet the future was dark and storm-tossed, full of sinister threats and complications. Iris did not know the wretched circumstances which had come to pass since they parted, and which had changed the whole aspect of his life. How could he tell her? Why should it be his miserable lot to snatch the cup of happiness from her lips? In that moment of silent agony he wished he were dead, for death alone could remove the burthen laid on him. Well, surely he might bask in the sunshine of her laughter for another day. No need to embitter her joyous heart until he was driven to it by dire necessity.

So he resolutely brushed aside the woe-begone phantom of care, and entered into the *abandon* of the hour with a zest that delighted her. The dear girl imagined that Robert, her Robert, had made another speedy conquest, and Anstruther himself was much elated by the sudden change in Sir Arthur Deane's demeanor.

They behaved like school children on a picnic. They roared over Iris's troubles in the matter of divided skirts, too much divided to be at all pleasant. The shipowner tasted some of her sago bread, and vowed it was excellent. They unearthed two bottles of champagne, the last of the case, and promised each other a hearty toast at dinner. Nothing would content Iris but that they should draw a farewell bucketful of water from the well and drench the pitcher-plant with a torrential shower.

Robert carefully secured the pocket-books, money and other effects found on their dead companions. The baronet, of course, knew all the principal officers of the *Sirdar*. He surveyed these mournful relics with sorrowful interest.

"The *Sirdar* was the crack ship of my fleet, and Captain Ross my most trusted commander," he said. "You may well imagine, Mr. Anstruther, what a cruel blow it was to lose such a vessel, with all these people on board, and my only daughter amongst them. I wonder now that it did not kill me."

"She was a splendid sea-boat, sir. Although disabled, she fought gallantly against the typhoon. Nothing short of a reef would break her up."

"Ah, well," sighed the shipowner, "the few timbers you have shown me here are the remaining assets out of £300,000."

"Was she not insured?" inquired Robert.

"No; that is, I have recently adopted a scheme of mutual self-insurance, and the loss falls *pro rata* on my other vessels."

The baronet glanced covertly at Iris. The words conveyed little meaning to her. Indeed, she broke in with a laugh—

"I am afraid I have heard you say, father dear, that some ships in the fleet paid you best when they ran ashore."

"Yes, Iris. That often happened in the old days. It

is different now. Moreover, I have not told you the extent of my calamities. The *Sirdar* was lost on March 18, though I did not know it for certain until this morning. But on March 25 the *Bahadur* was sunk in the Mersey during a fog, and three days later the *Jemadar* turned turtle on the James and Mary shoal in the Hooghly. Happily there were no lives lost in either of these cases."

Even Iris was appalled by this list of casualties.

"My poor, dear dad!" she cried. "To think that all these troubles should occur the very moment I left you!"

Yet she gave no thought to the serious financial effect of such a string of catastrophes. Robert, of course, appreciated this side of the business, especially in view of the shipowner's remark about the insurance. But Sir Arthur Deane's stiff upper lip deceived him. He failed to realize that the father was acting a part for his daughter's sake.

Oddly enough, the baronet did not seek to discuss with them the legal-looking document affixed near the cave. It claimed all rights in the island in their joint names, and this was a topic he wished to avoid. For the time, therefore, the younger man had no opportunity of taking him into his confidence, and Iris held faithfully to her promise of silence.

The girl's ragged raiment, sou'wester, and strong boots were already packed away on board. She now rescued the Bible, the copy of Tennyson's poems, the battered tin cup, her revolver, and the Lee-Metford which "scared" the Dyaks when they nearly caught

Anstruther and Mir Jan napping. Robert also gathered for her an assortment of Dyak hats, belts, and arms, including Taung S'Ali's parang and a sumpitan. These were her trophies, the *spolia opima* of the campaign.

His concluding act was to pack two of the empty oil tins with all the valuable lumps of auriferous quartz he could find where he shot the rubbish from the cave beneath the trees. On top of these he placed some antimony ore, and Mir Jan, wondering why the sahib wanted the stuff, carried the consignment to the waiting boat. Lieutenant Playdon, in command of the last party of sailors to quit the island, evidently expected Mir Jan to accompany them, but Anstruther explained that the man would await his return, some time in June or July.

Sir Arthur Deane found himself speculating on the cause of this extraordinary resolve, but, steadfast to his policy of avoiding controversial matters, said nothing. A few words to the captain procured enough stores to keep the Mahommedan for six months at least, and whilst these were being landed, the question was raised how best to dispose of the Dyaks.

The commander wished to consult the convenience of his guests.

"If we go a little out of our way and land them in Borneo," he said, "they will be hanged without troubling you further. If I take them to Singapore they will be tried on your evidence and sent to penal servitude. Which is it to be?"

It was Iris who decided.

"I cannot bear to think of more lives being sacrificed,"

she protested. "Perhaps if these men are treated mercifully and sent to their homes after some punishment their example may serve as a deterrent to others."

So it was settled that way. The anchor rattled up to its berth and the *Orient* turned her head towards Singapore. As she steadily passed away into the deepening azure, the girl and her lover watched the familiar outlines of Rainbow Island growing dim in the evening light. For a long while they could see Mir Jan's tall, thin figure motionless on a rock at the extremity of Europa Point. Their hut, the reef, the ledge, came into view as the cruiser swung round to a more northerly course.

Iris had thrown an arm across her father's shoulders. The three were left alone just then, and they were silent for many minutes. At last, the flying miles merged the solitary palm beyond the lagoon with the foliage on the cliff. The wide cleft of Prospect Park grew less distinct. Mir Jan's white-clothed figure was lost in the dark background. The island was becoming vague, dream-like, a blurred memory.

"Robert," said the girl devoutly, "God has been very good to us."

"Yes," he replied. "I was thinking, even this instant, of the verse that is carved on the gate of the Memorial Well at Cawnpore: 'These are they which came out of great tribulation.' We, too, have come out of great tribulation, happily with our lives—and more. The decrees of fate are indeed inscrutable."

Iris turned to him a face roseate with loving comprehension.

Bargains, Great and Small

"Do you remember this hour yesterday?" she murmured—"how we suffered from thirst—how the Dyaks began their second attack from the ridge—how you climbed down the ladder and I followed you? Oh father, darling," she went on impulsively, tightening her grasp, "you will never know how brave he was, how enduring, how he risked all for me and cheered me to the end, even though the end seemed to be the grave."

"I think I am beginning to understand now," answered the shipowner, averting his eyes lest Iris should see the tears in them. Their Calvary was ended, they thought—was it for him to lead them again through the sorrowful way? It was a heartrending task that lay before him, a task from which his soul revolted. He refused even to attempt it. He sought forgetfulness in a species of mental intoxication, and countenanced his daughter's love idyll with such apparent approval that Lord Ventnor wondered whether Sir Arthur were not suffering from senile decay.

The explanation of the shipowner's position was painfully simple. Being a daring yet shrewd financier, he perceived in the troubled condition of the Far East a magnificent opportunity to consolidate the trading influence of his company. He negotiated two big loans, one, of a semi-private nature, to equip docks and railways in the chief maritime province of China, the other of a more public character, with the Government of Japan. All his own resources, together with those of his principal directors and shareholders, were devoted to these objects. Contemporaneously, he determined to stop paying heavy insurance premiums on his fleet and make it self-supporting, on the well-known mutual principle.

His vessels were well equipped, well manned, replete with every modern improvement, and managed with great commercial skill. In three or four years, given ordinary trading luck, he must have doubled his own fortune and earned a world-wide reputation for far-seeing sagacity.

No sooner were all his arrangements completed than three of his best ships went down, saddling his company with an absolute loss of nearly £600,000, and seriously undermining his financial credit. A fellow-director, wealthy and influential, resigned his seat on the board, and headed a clique of disappointed stockholders. At once the fair sky became overcast. A sound and magnificent speculation threatened to dissolve in the Bankruptcy Court.

Sir Arthur Deane's energy and financial skill might have enabled him to weather this unexpected gale were it not for the apparent loss of his beloved daughter with the crack ship of his line. Half-frenzied with grief, he bade his enemies do their worst, and allowed his affairs to get into hopeless confusion whilst he devoted himself wholly to the search for Iris and her companions. At this critical juncture Lord Ventnor again reached his side. His lordship possessed a large private fortune and extensive estates. He was prudent withal, and knew how admirably the shipowner's plans would develop if given the necessary time. He offered the use of his name and money. He more than filled the gap created by the hostile ex-director. People argued that such a clever man, just returning from the Far East after accomplishing a public mission of some importance, must be a reliable guide. The mere cabled intelligence of his intention to join the board restored confidence and credit.

But—there was a bargain. If Iris lived, she must become the Countess of Ventnor. His lordship was weary of peripatetic love-making. It was high time he settled down in life, took an interest in the legislature, and achieved a position in the world of affairs. He had a chance now. The certain success of his friend's project, the fortunate completion of his own diplomatic undertaking, marriage with a beautiful and charming woman—these items would consolidate his career. If Iris were not available, plenty of women, high-placed in society, would accept such an eligible bachelor. But his heart was set on Iris. She was honest, high-principled, pure in body and mind, and none prizes these essentials in a wife more than a worn-out *roué*.

He seized the first opportunity that presented itself to make Sir Arthur Deane acquainted with a decision already dreaded by the unfortunate shipowner. Iris must either abandon her infatuation for Anstruther or bring about the ruin of her father. There was no mean.

"If she declines to become Countess of Ventnor, she can marry whom she likes, as you will be all paupers together," was the Earl's caustic summing up.

This brutal argument rather overshot the mark. The shipowner's face flushed with anger, and Lord Ventnor hastened to retrieve a false step.

"I didn't exactly mean to put it that way, Deane, but

my temper is a little short these days. My position on board this ship is intolerable. As a matter of fair dealing to me, you should put a stop to your daughter's attitude towards Anstruther, on the ground that her engagement is neither approved of by you nor desirable under any consideration."

It may be assumed from this remark that even the Earl's sardonic temper was ruffled by the girl's outrageous behavior. Nor was it exactly pleasant to him to note how steadily Anstruther advanced in the favor of every officer on the ship. By tacit consent the court-martial was tabooed, at any rate until the *Orient* reached Singapore. Every one knew that the quarrel lay between Robert and Ventnor, and it is not to be wondered at if Iris's influence alone were sufficient to turn the scale in favor of her lover.

The shipowner refused point-blank to interfere in any way during the voyage.

"You promised your co-operation in business even if we found that the *Sirdar* had gone down with all hands," he retorted bitterly. "Do you wish me to make my daughter believe she has come back into my life only to bring me irretrievable ruin?"

"That appears to be the result, no matter how you may endeavor to disguise it."

"I thought the days were gone when a man would wish to marry a woman against her will."

"Nonsense! What does she know about it? The glamour of this island romance will soon wear off. It would be different if Anstruther were able to maintain her even decently. He is an absolute beggar, I tell you.

Didn't he ship on your own vessel as a steward? Take my tip, Deane. Tell him how matters stand with you, and he will cool off."

He believed nothing of the sort, but he was desperately anxious that Iris should learn the truth as to her father's dilemma from other lips than his own. This would be the first point gained. Others would follow.

The two men were conversing in the Earl's cabin. On the deck overhead a very different chat was taking place.

The *Orient* was due in Singapore that afternoon. Iris was invited into the chart-room on some pretext, and Lieutenant Playdon, delegated by the commander and the first lieutenant, buttonholed Robert.

With sailor-like directness he came straight to the point—

"A few of us have been talking about you, Anstruther, and we cannot be far wrong in assuming that you are hard up. The fact that you took a steward's job on the *Sirdar* shows your disinclination to appeal to your own people for funds. Now, once you are ashore, you will be landed in difficulties. To cut any further explanations, I am commissioned to offer you a loan of fifty pounds, which you can repay when you like."

Robert's mouth tightened somewhat. For the moment he could not find words. Playdon feared he was offended.

"I am sorry, old chap, if we are mistaken," he said hesitatingly; "but we really thought——"

"Please do not endeavor to explain away your generous act," exclaimed Anstruther. "I accept it thankfully, on one condition."

"Blow the condition. But what is it?"

"That you tell me the names of those to whom I am indebted besides yourself."

"Oh, that is easy enough. Fitzroy and the first luff are the others. We kept it to a small circle, don't you know. Thought you would prefer that."

Anstruther smiled and wrung his hand. There were some good fellows left in the world after all. The three officers acted in pure good nature. They were assisting a man apparently down in his luck, who would soon be called on to face other difficulties by reason of his engagement to a girl apparently so far removed from him in station. And the last thing they dreamed of was that their kindly loan was destined to yield them a better return than all the years of their naval service, for their fifty pounds had gone into the pocket of a potential millionaire, who was endowed with the faculty, rare in millionaires, of not forgetting the friends of his poverty-stricken days.

CHAPTER XVII

RAINBOW ISLAND AGAIN — AND AFTERWARD

Sir Arthur Deane was sitting alone in his cabin in a state of deep dejection, when he was aroused by a knock, and Robert entered.

"Can you give me half an hour?" he asked. "I have something to say to you before we land."

The shipowner silently motioned him to a seat.

"It concerns Iris and myself," continued Anstruther. "I gathered from your words when we met on the island that both you and Lord Ventnor regarded Iris as his lordship's promised bride. From your point of view the arrangement was perhaps natural and equitable, but since your daughter left Hong Kong it happens that she and I have fallen in love with each other. No; please listen to me. I am not here to urge my claims on you. I won her fairly and intend to keep her, were the whole House of Peers opposed to me. At this moment I want to tell you, her father, why she could never, even under other circumstances, marry Lord Ventnor."

Then he proceeded to place before the astounded baronet a detailed history of his recent career. It was a sordid story of woman's perfidy, twice told. It carried conviction in every sentence. It was possible, of course,

to explain matters more fully to the baronet than to
Iris, and Anstruther's fierce resentment of the cruel
wrong inflicted upon him blazed forth with overwhelming
force. The intensity of his wrath in no way impaired
the cogency of his arguments. Rather did it lend point
and logical brevity. Each word burned itself into his
hearer's consciousness, for Robert did not know that the
unfortunate father was being coerced to a distasteful
compact by the scoundrel who figured in the narrative as
his evil genius.

At the conclusion Sir Arthur bowed his head between
his hands.

"I cannot choose but believe you," he admitted huskily. "Yet how came you to be so unjustly convicted by
a tribunal composed of your brother officers?"

"They could not help themselves. To acquit me meant
that they discredited the sworn testimony not only of my
Colonel's wife, but of the civil head of an important
Government Mission, not to mention some bought Chinese evidence. Am I the first man to be offered up as a
sacrifice on the altar of official expediency?"

"But you are powerless now. You can hardly hope
to have your case revised. What chance is there that
your name will ever be cleared?"

"Mrs. Costobell can do it if she will. The vagaries of
such a woman are not to be depended on. If Lord Ventnor has cast her off, her hatred may prove stronger than
her passion. Anyhow, I should be the last man to despair of God's Providence. Compare the condition of
Iris and myself today with our plight during the second
night on the ledge! I refuse to believe that a bad and

fickle woman can resist the workings of destiny, and it was a happy fate which led me to ship on board the *Sirdar*, though at the time I saw it in another light."

How different the words, the aspirations, of the two suitors. Quite unconsciously, Robert could not have pleaded better. The shipowner sighed heavily.

"I hope your faith will be justified. If it be not—the more likely thing to happen—do I understand that my daughter and you intend to get married whether I give or withhold my sanction?"

Anstruther rose and opened the door.

"I have ventured to tell you," he said, "why she should not marry Lord Ventnor. When I come to you and ask you for her, which I pray may be soon, it will be time enough to answer that question, should you then decide to put it."

It must be remembered that Robert knew nothing whatever of the older man's predicament, whilst the baronet, full of his own troubles, was in no mood to take a reasonable view of Anstruther's position. Neither Iris nor Robert could make him understand the long-drawn-out duel of their early life on the island, nor was it easy to depict the tumultuous agony of that terrible hour on the ledge when the girl forced the man to confess his love by suggesting acceptance of the Dyaks' terms.

Thus, for a little while, these two were driven apart, and Anstruther disdained to urge the plea that not many weeks would elapse before he would be a richer man than his rival. The chief sufferer was Sir Arthur Deane. Had Iris guessed how her father was tormented, she would not have remained on the bridge, radiant and mirthful, whilst the grey-haired baronet gazed with stony-eyed despair at some memoranda which he extracted from his papers.

"Ten thousand pounds!" he muttered. "Not a great sum for the millionaire financier, Sir Arthur Deane, to raise on his note of hand. A few months ago men offered me one hundred times the amount on no better security. And now, to think that a set of jabbering fools in London should so destroy my credit and their own, that not a bank will discount our paper unless they are assured Lord Ventnor has joined the board! Fancy me, of all men, being willing to barter my child for a few pieces of gold!"

The thought was maddening. For a little while he yielded to utter despondency. It was quite true that a comparatively small amount of money would restore the stability of his firm. Even without it, were his credit unimpaired, he could easily tide over the period of depression until the first fruits of his enterprise were garnered. Then, all men would hail him as a genius.

Wearily turning over his papers, he suddenly came across the last letter written to him by Iris's mother. How she doted on their only child! He recalled one night, shortly before his wife died, when the little Iris was brought into her room to kiss her and lisp her infantile prayers. She had devised a formula of her own—

"God bless father! God bless mother! God bless me, their little girl!"

And what was it she cried to him from the beach?

"Your own little girl given back to you!"

Given back to him! For what—to marry that black-

hearted scoundrel whose pastime was the degradation of
women and the defaming of honest men? That settled
it. Instantly the cloud was lifted from his soul. A
great peace came upon him. The ruin of his business
he might not be able to avert, but he would save from
the wreck that which he prized more than all else—his
daughter's love.

The engines dropped to half speed—they were enter-
ing the harbor of Singapore. In a few hours the worst
would be over. If Ventnor telegraphed to London his
withdrawal from the board, nothing short of a cabled
draft for ten thousand pounds would prevent certain
creditors from filing a bankruptcy petition. In the local
banks the baronet had about a thousand to his credit.
Surely among the rich merchants of the port, men who
knew the potentialities of his scheme, he would be able
to raise the money needed. He would try hard. Already he felt braver. The old fire had returned to his
blood. The very belief that he was acting in the way
best calculated to secure his daughter's happiness stimu-
lated and encouraged him.

He went on deck, to meet Iris skipping down the
hatchway.

"Oh, there you are!" she cried. "I was just coming
to find out why you were moping in your cabin. You
are missing the most beautiful view—all greens, and
blues, and browns! Run, quick! I want you to see every
inch of it."

She held out her hand and pulled him gleefully up the
steps. Leaning against the taffrail, some distance apart

from each other, were Anstruther and Lord Ventnor. Need it be said to whom Iris drew her father?

"Here he is, Robert," she laughed. "I do believe he was sulking because Captain Fitzroy was so very attentive to me. Yet you didn't mind it a bit!"

The two men looked into each other eyes. They smiled. How could they resist the contagion of her sunny nature?

"I have been thinking over what you said to me just now, Anstruther," said the shipowner slowly.

"Oh!" cried Iris. "Have you two been talking secrets behind my back?"

"It is no secret to you—my little girl——" Her father's voice lingered on the phrase. "When we are on shore, Robert, I will explain matters to you more fully. Just now I wish only to tell you that where Iris has given her heart I will not refuse her hand."

"You darling old dad! And is that what all the mystery was about?"

She took his face between her hands and kissed him. Lord Ventnor, wondering at this effusiveness, strolled forward.

"What has happened, Miss Deane?" he inquired. "Have you just discovered what an excellent parent you possess?"

The baronet laughed, almost hysterically. " 'Pon my honor," he cried, "you could not have hit upon a happier explanation."

His lordship was not quite satisfied.

"I suppose you will take Iris to Smith's Hotel?" he said with cool impudence.

Iris answered him.

"Yes. My father has just asked Robert to come with us—by inference, that is. Where are you going?"

The adroit use of her lover's Christian name goaded his lordship to sudden heat.

"Indeed!" he snarled. "Sir Arthur Deane has evidently decided a good many things during the last hour."

"Yes," was the shipowner's quiet retort. "I have decided that my daughter's happiness should be the chief consideration of my remaining years. All else must give way to it."

The Earl's swarthy face grew sallow with fury. His eyes blazed, and there was a tense vibrato in his voice as he said—

"Then I must congratulate you, Miss Deane. You are fated to endure adventures. Having escaped from the melodramatic perils of Rainbow Island you are destined to experience another variety of shipwreck here."

He left them. Not a word had Robert spoken throughout the unexpected scene. His heart was throbbing with a tremulous joy, and his lordship's sneers were lost on him. But he could not fail to note the malignant purpose of the parting sentence.

In his quietly masterful way he placed his hand on the baronet's shoulder.

"What did Lord Ventnor mean?" he asked.

Sir Arthur Deane answered, with a calm smile—"It is difficult to talk openly at this moment. Wait until we reach the hotel."

The news flew fast through the settlement that

The Wings of the Morning

H.M.S. *Orient* had returned from her long search for the *Sirdar*. The warship occupied her usual anchorage, and a boat was lowered to take off the passengers. Lieutenant Playdon went ashore with them. A feeling of consideration for Anstruther prevented any arrangements being made for subsequent meetings. Once their courteous duty was ended, the officers of the *Orient* could not give him any further social recognition.

Lord Ventnor was aware of this fact and endeavored to turn it to advantage.

"By the way, Fitzroy," he called out to the commander as he prepared to descend the gangway, "I want you, and any others not detained by duty, to come and dine with me tonight."

Captain Fitzroy answered blandly—"It is very good of you to ask us, but I fear I cannot make any definite arrangements until I learn what orders are awaiting me here."

"Oh, certainly. Come if you can, eh?"

"Yes; suppose we leave it at that."

It was a polite but decided rebuff. It in no way tended to sweeten Lord Ventnor's temper, which was further exasperated when he hurt his shin against one of Robert's disreputable-looking tins, with its accumulation of débris.

The boat swung off into the tideway. Her progress shorewards was watched by a small knot of people, mostly loungers and coolies. Among them, however, were two persons who had driven rapidly to the landing-place when the arrival of the *Orient* was reported. One bore all the distinguishing marks of the army officer of high rank, but the other was unmistakably a globe-trotter. Only in Piccadilly could he have purchased his wondrous *sola topi*, or pith helmet—with its imitation *puggri* neatly frilled and puckered—and no tailor who ever carried his goose through the Exile's Gate would have fashioned his expensive garments. But the old gentleman made no pretence that he could "hear the East a-callin'." He swore impartially at the climate, the place, and its inhabitants. At this instant he was in a state of wild excitement. He was very tall, very stout, exceedingly red-faced. Any budding medico who understood the pre-eminence enjoyed by *aq. ad* in a prescription, would have diagnosed him as a first-rate subject for apoplexy.

Producing a tremendous telescope, he vainly endeavored to balance it on the shoulder of a native servant.

"Can't you stand still, you blithering idiot!" he shouted, after futile attempts to focus the advancing boat, "or shall I steady you by a clout over the ear?"

His companion, the army man, was looking through a pair of field-glasses.

"By Jove!" he cried, "I can see Sir Arthur Deane, and a girl who looks like his daughter. There's that infernal scamp, Ventnor, too."

The big man brushed the servant out of his way, and brandished the telescope as though it were a bludgeon.

"The dirty beggar! He drove my lad to misery and death, yet he has come back safe and sound. Wait till I meet him. I'll——"

"Now, Anstruther! Remember your promise. I will deal with Lord Ventnor. My vengeance has first claim.

What! By the jumping Moses, I do believe—— Yes.
It is. Anstruther! Your nephew is sitting next to the
girl!"

The telescope fell on the stones with a crash. The
giant's rubicund face suddenly blanched. He leaned
on his friend for support.

"You are not mistaken," he almost whimpered. "Look
again, for God's sake, man. Make sure before you
speak. Tell me! Tell me!"

"Calm yourself, Anstruther. It is Robert, as sure
as I'm alive. Don't you think I know him, my poor
disgraced friend, whom I, like all the rest, cast off in
his hour of trouble? But I had some excuse. There!
There! I didn't mean that, old fellow. Robert himself
will be the last man to blame either of us. Who could
have suspected that two-people—one of them, God help
me! my wife—would concoct such a hellish plot!"

The boat glided gracefully alongside the steps of the
quay, and Playdon sprang ashore to help Iris to alight.
What happened immediately afterwards can best be told
in his own words, as he retailed the story to an appre-
ciative audience in the ward-room.

"We had just landed," he said, "and some of the
crew were pushing the coolies out of the way, when two
men jumped down the steps, and a most fiendish row
sprang up. That is, there was no dispute or wrangling,
but one chap, who, it turned out, was Colonel Costobell,
grabbed Ventnor by the shirt front, and threatened to
smash his face in if he didn't listen then and there to
what he had to say. I really thought about interfer-
ing, until I heard Colonel Costobell's opening words.

After that I would gladly have seen the beggar chucked into the harbor. We never liked him, did we?"

"Ask no questions, Pompey, but go ahead with the yarn," growled the first lieutenant.

"Well, it seems that Mrs. Costobell is dead. She got enteric a week after the *Orient* sailed, and was a goner in four days. Before she died she owned up."

He paused, with a base eye to effect. Not a man moved a muscle.

"All right," he cried. "I will make no more false starts. Mrs. Costobell begged her husband's forgiveness for her treatment of him, and confessed that she and Lord Ventnor planned the affair for which Anstruther was tried by court-martial. It must have been a beastly business, for Costobell was sweating with rage, though his words were icy enough. And you ought to have seen Ventnor's face when he heard of the depositions, sworn to and signed by Mrs. Costobell and by several Chinese servants whom he bribed to give false evidence. He promised to marry Mrs. Costobell if her husband died, or, in any event, to bring about a divorce when the Hong Kong affair had blown over. Then she learnt that he was after Miss Iris, and there is no doubt her fury helped on the fever. Costobell said that, for his wife's sake, he would have kept the wretched thing secret, but he was compelled to clear Anstruther's name, especially as he came across the other old Johnnie——"

"Pompey, you are incoherent with excitement. Who is 'the other old Johnnie'?" asked the first luff severely.

"Didn't I tell you? Why, Anstruther's uncle, of course, a heavy old swell with just a touch of Yorkshire in his tongue. I gathered that he disinherited his nephew when the news of the court-martial reached him. Then he relented, and cabled to him. Getting no news, he came East to look for him. He met Costobell the day after the lady died, and the two swore—the stout uncle can swear a treat—anyhow, they vowed to be revenged on Ventnor, and to clear Anstruther's character, living or dead. Poor old chap! He cried like a baby when he asked the youngster to forgive him. It was quite touching. I can tell you——"

Playdon affected to search for his pocket-handkerchief.

"Do tell us, or it will be worse for you," cried his mentor.

"Give me time, air, a drink! What you fellows want is a phonograph. Let me see. Well, Costobell shook Ventnor off at last, with the final observation that Anstruther's court-martial has been quashed. The next batch of general orders will re-instate him in the regiment, and it rests with him to decide whether or not a criminal warrant shall be issued against his lordship for conspiracy. Do you fellows know what conspir——?"

"You cuckoo! What did Miss Deane do?"

"Clung to Anstruther like a weeping angel, and kissed everybody all round when Ventnor got away. Well—hands off. I mean her father, Anstruther and the stout uncle. Unfortunately I was not on in that scene. But, for some reason, they all nearly wrung my arm off, and the men were so excited that they gave the party a rousing cheer as their rickshaws went off in a bunch. Will no Christian gentleman get me a drink?"

Rainbow Island Again

The next commotion arose in the hotel when Sir Arthur Deane seized the first opportunity to explain the predicament in which his company was placed, and the blow which Lord Ventnor yet had it in his power to deal.

Mr. William Anstruther was an interested auditor. Robert would have spoken, but his uncle restrained him.

"Leave this to me, lad," he exclaimed. "When I was coming here in the *Sirdar* there was a lot of talk about Sir Arthur's scheme, and there should not be much difficulty in raising all the brass required, if half what I heard be true. Sit you down, Sir Arthur, and tell us all about it."

The shipowner required no second bidding. With the skill for which he was noted, he described his operations in detail, telling how every farthing of the first instalments of the two great loans was paid up, how the earnings of his fleet would quickly overtake the deficit in capital value caused by the loss of the three ships, and how, in six months' time, the leading financial houses of London, Paris, and Berlin would be offering him more money than he would need.

To a shrewd man of business the project could not fail to commend itself, and the Yorkshire squire, though a trifle obstinate in temper, was singularly clear-headed in other respects. He brought his great fist down on the table with a whack.

"Send a cable to your company, Sir Arthur," he cried, "and tell them that your prospective son-in-law will provide the ten thousand pounds you require. I will see that his draft is honored. You can add, if you like, that another ten will be ready if wanted when this lot is

spent. I did my lad one d——er——deuced bad turn in my
life. This time, I think, I am doing him a good one."

"You are, indeed," said Iris's father enthusiastically.
"The unallotted capital he is taking up will be worth
four times its face value in two years."

"All the more reason to make his holding twenty instead of ten," roared the Yorkshireman. "But look
here. You talk about dropping proceedings against
that precious earl whom I saw to-day. Why not tell
him not to try any funny tricks until Robert's money is
safely lodged to your account? We have him in our
power. Dash it all, let us use him a bit."

Even Iris laughed at this naïve suggestion. It was
delightful to think that their arch enemy was actually
helping the baronet's affairs at that very moment, and
would continue to do so until he was flung aside as being
of no further value. Although Ventnor himself had
carefully avoided any formal commitment, the cable-
grams awaiting the shipowner at Singapore showed that
confidence had already been restored by the uncontra-
dicted use of his lordship's name.

Robert at last obtained a hearing.

"You two are quietly assuming the attitude of the
financial magnates of this gathering," he said. "I must
admit that you have managed things very well between
you, and I do not propose for one moment to interfere
with your arrangements. Nevertheless, Iris and I are
really the chief moneyed persons present. You spoke of
financial houses in England and on the Continent back-
ing up your loans six months hence, Sir Arthur. You
need not go to them. We will be your bankers."

Rainbow Island Again

The baronet laughed with a whole-hearted gaiety that revealed whence Iris got some part, at least, of her bright disposition.

"Will you sell your island, Robert?" he cried. "I am afraid that not even Iris could wheedle any one into buying it."

"But father, dear," interrupted the girl earnestly, "what Robert says is true. We have a gold mine there. It is worth so much that you will hardly believe it until there can no longer be any doubt in your mind. I suppose that is why Robert asked me not to mention his discovery to you earlier."

"No, Iris, that was not the reason," said her lover, and the older men felt that more than idle fancy inspired the astounding intelligence that they had just heard. "Your love was more to me than all the gold in the world. I had won you. I meant to keep you, but I refused to buy you."

He turned to her father. His pent-up emotion mastered him, and he spoke as one who could no longer restrain his feelings.

"I have had no chance to thank you for the words you uttered at the moment we quitted the ship. Yet I will treasure them while life lasts. You gave Iris to me when I was poor, disgraced, an outcast from my family and my profession. And I know why you did this thing. It was because you valued her happiness more than riches or reputation. I am sorry now I did not explain matters earlier. It would have saved you much needless suffering. But the sorrow has sped like an evil dream, and you will perhaps not regret it, for your action today binds me to you with hoops of steel. And you, too, uncle. You traveled thousands of miles to help and comfort me in my anguish. Were I as bad as I was painted, your kind old heart still pitied me; you were prepared to pluck me from the depths of despair and degradation. Why should I hate Lord Ventnor? What man could have served me as he did? He has given me Iris. He gained for me at her father's hands a concession such as mortal has seldom wrested from black-browed fate. He brought my uncle to my side in the hour of my adversity. Hate him! I would have his statue carved in marble, and set on high to tell all who passed how good may spring out of evil—how God's wisdom can manifest itself by putting even the creeping and crawling things of the earth to some useful purpose."

"Dash it all, lad," vociferated the elder Anstruther, "what ails thee? I never heard you talk like this before!"

The old gentleman's amazement was so comical that further tension was out of the question.

Robert, in calmer mood, informed them of the manner in which he hit upon the mine. The story sounded like wildest romance—this finding of a volcanic dyke guarded by the bones of "J. S." and the poison-filled quarry—but the production of the ore samples changed wonder into certainty.

Next day a government metallurgist estimated the value of the contents of the two oil-tins at about £500, yet the specimens brought from the island were not by any means the richest available.

Rainbow Island Again

And now there is not much more to tell of Rainbow Island and its castaways. On the day that Captain Robert Anstruther's name appeared in the *Gazette*, reinstating him to his rank and regiment, Iris and he were married in the English Church at Hong Kong, for it was his wife's wish that the place which witnessed his ignominy should also witness his triumph.

A good-natured admiral decided that the urgent requirements of the British Navy should bring H.M.S. *Orient* to the island before the date fixed for the ceremony. Lieutenant Playdon officiated as best man, whilst the *Orient* was left so scandalously short-handed for many hours that a hostile vessel, at least twice her size, might have ventured to attack her.

Soon afterwards, Robert resigned his commission. He regretted the necessity, but the demands of his new sphere in life rendered this step imperative. Mining engineers, laborers, stores, portable houses, engines, and equipment were obtained with all haste, and the whole party sailed on one of Sir Arthur Deane's ships to convoy a small steamer specially hired to attend to the wants of the miners.

At last, one evening, early in July, the two vessels anchored outside Palm-tree Rock, and Mir Jan could be seen running frantically about the shore, for no valid reason save that he could not stand still. The sahib brought him good news. The Governor of Hong Kong felt that any reasonable request made by Anstruther should be granted if possible. He had written such a strong representation of the Mahommedan's case to the Government of India that there was little doubt the returning mail would convey an official notification that Mir Jan, formerly *naik* in the Kumaon Rissala—he who once killed a man—had been granted a free pardon.

The mining experts verified Robert's most sanguine views after a very brief examination of the deposit. Hardly any preliminary work was needed. In twenty-four hours a small concentrating plant was erected, and a ditch made to drain off the carbonic anhydride in the valley. After dusk a party of coolies cleared the quarry of its former occupants. Towards the close of the following day, when the great steamer once more slowly turned her head to the north-west, Iris could hear the steady thud of an engine at work on the first consignment of ore.

Robert had been busy up to the last moment. There was so much to be done in a short space of time. The vessel carried a large number of passengers, and he did not wish to detain them too long, though they one and all expressed their willingness to suit his convenience in this respect.

Now his share of the necessary preparations was concluded. His wife, Sir Arthur and his uncle were gathered in a corner of the promenade deck when he approached and told them that his last instruction ashore was for a light to be fixed on Summit Rock as soon as the dynamo was in working order.

"When we all come back in the cold weather," he explained gleefully, "we will not imitate the *Sirdar* by running on to the reef, should we arrive by night."

Iris answered not. Her blue eyes were fixed on the fast-receding cliffs.

Rainbow Island Again

"Sweetheart," said her husband, "why are you so silent?"

She turned to him. The light of the setting sun illumined her face with its golden radiance.

"Because I am so happy," she said. "Oh, Robert dear, so happy and thankful."

* * * * *

POSTSCRIPT

The latest news of Col. and Mrs. Anstruther is contained in a letter written by an elderly maiden lady, resident in the North Riding of Yorkshire, to a friend in London. It is dated some four years after the events already recorded.

Although its information is garbled and, to a certain extent, inaccurate, those who have followed the adventures of the young couple under discussion will be able to appreciate its opinions at their true value. When the writer states facts, of course, her veracity is unquestionable, but occasionally she flounders badly when she depends upon her own judgment.

Here is the letter:

"MY DEAR HELEN:

"I have not seen or heard of you during so long a time that I am *simply dying* to tell you all that is happening here. You will remember that some people named Anstruther bought the Fairlawn estate near our village some three years ago. They are, as you know, *enormously* rich. The doctor tells me that when they are not squeezing money out of the wretched Chinese, they dig it in *barrow-loads* out of some magic island in the Atlantic or the Pacific — I really forget which.

[351]

The Wings of the Morning

"Anyhow, they could afford to *entertain* much more than they do. Mrs. Anstruther is very nice looking, and could be a leader of society if she chose, but she *seems* to care for no one but her husband and her babies. She has a boy and a girl, very charming children, I admit, and you seldom see her without them. They have a French *bonne* apiece, and a most *murderous*-looking person — a Mahommedan native, I believe — stalks alongside and behaves as if he would *instantly decapitate* any person who as much as looked at them. Such a procession you never saw! Mrs. Anstruther's devotion to her husband is *too* absurd. He is a tall, handsome man, of distinguished appearance, but on the few occasions I have spoken to him he impressed me as somewhat *taciturn*. Yet to see the way in which his wife even *looks* at him you would imagine that he had not his equal in the world!

"I believe there is some *secret* in their lives. Colonel Anstruther used to be in the army — he is now in command of our local yeomanry — and although his name is 'Robert,' *tout court*, I have often heard Mrs. Anstruther call him 'Jenks.' Their boy, too, is christened 'Robert *Jenks* Anstruther.' Now, my dear Helen, *do* make inquiries about them in town circles. I *particularly* wish you to find out who is this person 'Jenks' — a most vulgar name. I am sure you will unearth something curious, because Mrs. Anstruther was a Miss Deane, daughter of the baronet, and Anstruther's people are well known in Yorkshire. There are absolutely no Jenkses connected with them on either side.

"I think I can help you by another *clue*, as a very *odd* incident occurred at our hunt ball last week. The Anstruthers, I must tell you, usually go away for the winter, to China, or to their fabulous island. This year they remained at home, and Colonel Anstruther became M.F.H., as he is certainly a most liberal man so far as *sport* and *charity* are concerned.

Rainbow Island Again

"Well, dear, the Dodgsons — you remember the Leeds clothier people — having *contrived* to enter county society, invited the Earl of Ventnor down for the ball. He, it seems, knew nothing about Anstruther being M.F.H., and of course Mrs. Anstruther *received*. The moment Lord Ventnor heard her name he was very angry. He said he did not care to meet her, and left for London by the next train. The Dodgsons were *awfully* annoyed with him, and Mrs. Dodgson had the bad taste to tell Mrs. Anstruther all about it. And what do you think *she* said — 'Lord Ventnor need not have been so frightened. My husband has not brought his hunting-crop with him!'

"I was not there, but young Barker told me that Mrs. Anstruther looked very *impressive* as she said this. 'Stunning!' was the word he used, but young Barker is a *fool,* and thinks Mrs. A. is the most beautiful woman in Yorkshire. Her dress, they say, was *magnificent*, which I can hardly credit, as she usually goes about in the *plainest* tailor-made clothes. By the way, I forgot to mention that the Anstruthers have restored our parish church. The vicar, of course, is enraptured with them. I dislike people who are so free with their money and yet reserved in their friendship. It is a sure sign, when they *court* popularity, that they dread something leaking out about the *past*.

"*Do* write soon. Don't forget 'Jenks' and 'Lord Ventnor'; those are the lines of *inquiry*.

"Yours,

"Matilda.

"PS. — Perhaps I am misjudging them. Mrs. Anstruther has just sent me an invitation to an 'At Home' next Thursday. — M.

"PPS. — Dear me, this letter will never get away. I have just destroyed another envelope to tell you that the

vicar came in to tea. From what he told me about Lord
Ventnor, I imagine that Mrs. Anstruther said no more than
he deserved. — M."

NOTE. — Colonel Anstruther's agents discovered, after long and
costly inquiry, that a Shields man named James Spence, a marine
engineer, having worked for a time as a miner in California, shipped
as third engineer on a vessel bound for Shanghai. There he quitted
her. He passed some time ashore in dissipation, took another job on
a Chinese river steamer, and was last heard of some eighteen months
before the *Sirdar* was wrecked. He then informed a Chinese boarding-
house keeper that he was going to make his fortune by accompanying
some deep-sea fishermen, and he bought some stores and tools from
a marine-store dealer. No one knew when or where he went, but
from that date all trace of him disappeared. The only persons who
mourned his loss were his mother and sister. The last letter they
received from him was posted in Shanghai. Though the evidence
connecting him with the recluse of Rainbow Island was slight, and
purely circumstantial, Colonel Anstruther provided for the future of
his relatives in a manner that secured their lasting gratitude.